21, 2019

MW01148748

Nothing in this narrative's conte
or implying US government, milita... authentication or endorsement of the author's views. This materia... has been reviewed by proper authorities to prevent the disclosure of classified information.

The opinions of this gothic/military thriller do not reflect those of the artists, characters, publisher, companies or products mentioned, or any writers except that of the written author's imagination.

This is mostly a fictitious novel, however, most of chapter thirteen was based upon actual events. My wife; dad; sister Tee; mijo Justice; Tío Leon and Jack Grinnage; Goodew and Meling cousins; Kathie Browne; and friends Steve Hansen, Jeff Lindaman and John Sullivan were the inspirations for Nurse Alegría; Jerry Rockford; Sister Tréson; Justo; Jack Grumblier; Chaplain Goodew and Captain Meling; Kati Shotzski; Hans; Lindy and Sully.

The character of Count Dracula in this illustrated book was inspired by the historical Prince Vlad III (Dracula) of Wallachia who fought to keep the Ottomans from invading his homeland and Europe. He later became known as Vlad *Tepes* (the Impaler) for executing rapists, thieves and enemies at the stake. Most Romanians revere him as a brave ruler who maintained law and order. Prince Vlad III was supposedly beheaded in the late 15th century. However, in the early 1930s, one of his speculated gravesites (located in Snagov monastery) was dug up and only animal bones were discovered. Though there is no definitive proof of Vlad Tepes being a vampire, the legend of Count Dracula lives on.

Any other resemblances to actual events, locales or persons living or dead in this novel is merely coincidental.

NCDOC Wardroom,

Hope you enjoy my Gothic-military thriller. The intent is to be a patriotic read & homage to classic monsters.

Happy New Year!

JP Thorson

Thor

TABLE OF CONTENTS

PROLOGUE V
1. SOUTH OF THE BORDER 1
2. BUNKER FIVE 7
3. RAGE 12
4. BRIEFING 16
5. DEPARTURE 20
6. MUSTANGS 25
7. OPERATION GEMELA 28
8. SCARE TACTICS 33
9. DENIAL 40
10. NOSFERATU 44
11. REALITY BITES 49
12. EMERGENCY 53
13. SHADOWS FROM THE PAST 59
14. OLD TIMERS 64
15. FIRST DATE 70
16. SHADED GROVE 74
17. GUARDIAN 78
18. REGRETS 82
19. HANNIBAL LETTER 87
20. SOMETHING WICKED STIRRED 91
21. VAN HELSING'S JOURNALS 95
22. TREMORS 101
23. 1960S 105
24. MONSTERS' LAB 110
25. GARLIC & WOLFSBANE 114
26. BOOTY BLUFF 118
27. NOOKS & CRANNIES 123
28. ALIVE 128
29. FALLEN PRINCE 133
30. CASTLE DRACULA 138
31. FULL MOON 143
32. LIONS' DEN 148
33. CAGED 152
34. CHAMELEONS 157
35. BIRDS 161
36. GOLFING RENDEZVOUS 165

37. SIMILAR PLIGHTS	170
38. ALLIANCE	174
39. KARMA	178
40. A DEALER HUMBLED	181
41. JAIL BREAK	186
42. LOST BOY	189
43. BAD TO THE BONE	194
44. PUBLIC MEETING	198
45. RECKONING	203
46. RETURN TO CHÂTEAU WILDER	208
47. SILLY IDOL	212
48. MURPHY'S LAW	216
49. DESPAIR	221
50. PARTY CRASHING	226
51. BULLIES	229
52. PROFESSOR DALB AL-UKHARD	233
53. SPELLBOUND	239
54. CLOUDS IN MY COFFEE	242
55. LADIES LEAGUE	248
56. REINFORCEMENTS	251
57. STALKER	255
58. PROFESSOR SIODMAK	259
59. SNOWBIRDS	264
60. OPERATION ROGUE	268
61. MONSTER MELEE	274
62. DEMISE OF THE UNDEAD	280
63. THE UGLY TRUTH	286
64. COVER-UP	290
65. REFLECTION	295
FOREIGN VOCABULARY	299
GLOSSARY	300
ACKNOWLEDGMENTS	301
AUTHOR, ARTISTS & TALENT	302

DEDICATIONS

This illustrated story is dedicated to the memory of our dad, Jerry "Pops" Thorson; two great thriller novelists - Tom Clancy and Vince Flynn; and the men and women who have defended the United States of America - a marvelous country founded on the principles of life, liberty and the pursuit of happiness.

To Lon and Creighton Chaney, Peter Cushing, Boris Karloff, Elsa Lanchester, Sir Christopher Lee, Bela Lugosi, Vincent Price, Claude Rains, Glenn Strange, Jack Pierce, Tod Browning, Terence Fisher, Rowland V. Lee, Jimmy Sangster, Curt Siodmak, George Waggner, James Whale and all the talents involved in making Universal Classic Monster and Hammer Horror films, 1970s *Kolchak the Night Stalker* TV programs, the movies *Fright Night* (1985), *From Dusk til Dawn* (1996), *Lost Boys* (1987), *The Monster Squad* (1987) and *Salem's Lot* (1979), and William Marshall (Blacula) and legendary artist Basil Gogos - thank you for the inspiration and nightmares.

AUTHOR'S NOTE

This novel is unapologetically written in the spirit and cannon of classic monster lore.

For those not familiar with Mary Shelley's *Frankenstein* and Bram Stoker's *Dracula*, you are highly encouraged to read them. The author's intent is to remain faithful to these fantastic novels.

PROLOGUE

New Orleans, mid-1960s

A tall dark-haired man walked into a small book store near the French Quarter. "Good evening, sir. Is Leilani available?"

"Why?" the sandy-haired salesman demanded.

He sighed. "To pick up a book."

"Oh, okay… I'm her husband, Donald McDavit." The skinny man with a slight belly said, "Your name please."

"Nigel Rathbone."

He read the title out loud, "Lycanthropy & Vampirism."

His eyes smiled. "A rare gem by Professor Siodmak."

McDavit raised an eyebrow. "Such literary rubbish labeled as non-fiction."

"Perhaps Shelley and Stoker elaborated on some reality."

"Please. I earned a master's degree in economics, serve as a captain in the navy reserves and visited twenty countries."

"Early Hollywood and the classic horror writers may have been closer to the truth." He shrugged. "Of course, they probably took literary licenses with dates, details and locations."

David McDavit shook his head disapprovingly before saying in a haughty, upper-class tone, "Ubiquitous reads for simpletons."

Nigel Rathbone stink-eyed the narcistic blowhard. He was certain the man with a peculiar pinkish skin tone, sporting a navy-blue polo, regularly practiced big speeches in front of mirrors.

The six-foot tall clerk said, "What, cat got your tongue?"

Bones chuckled, "I bet Leilani needs a she-shed listening to your trap." He handed the idiot savant a pair of twenty-dollar bills.

McDavit tersely said, "Take your penny dreadful muck."

"Forgetting something? Leilani and I agreed to thirty bucks."

He smirked at the taller, burly customer. "It's a rare piece. Take it or leave it!"

He grabbed the reference book, hoping to find a remedy to his malady. "You broke a promise. I'll be speaking with your wife."

"You do that!"

Nigel Rathbone felt the three-quarter lunar beams through the skylight. His brown eyes dilated to yellow orbs. Tiny hairs seemed to bristle along his cheeks and forehead. "Careful, McDavit, you wouldn't want to meet me on a full moon."

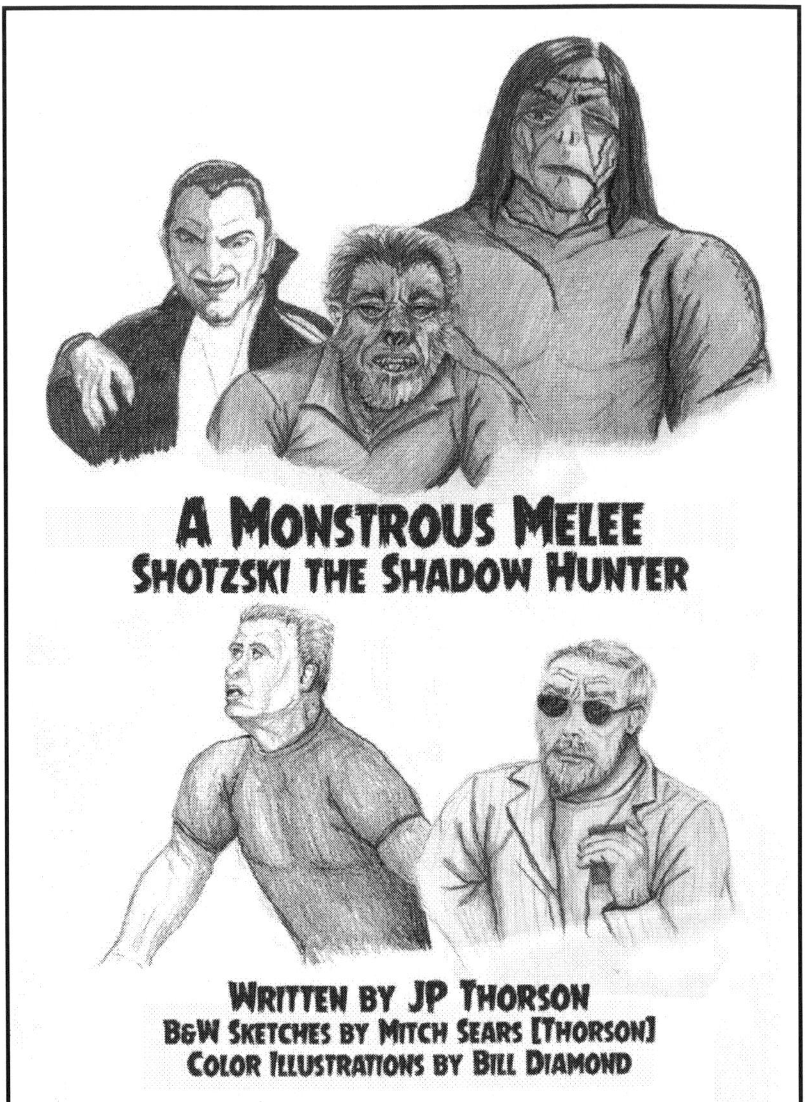
A MONSTROUS MELEE
SHOTZSKI THE SHADOW HUNTER
WRITTEN BY JP THORSON
B&W SKETCHES BY MITCH SEARS [THORSON]
COLOR ILLUSTRATIONS BY BILL DIAMOND

1 - SOUTH OF THE BORDER

Mid-December 2004

It was hotter than normal with a midnight temperature of ninety-eight degrees in the northern jungles of South America. Adolpho Ortega stopped dead in his tracks. He was within a meter of a ten-foot long Bushmaster. He trembled as he slowly reached for his AK-47 rifle. The treacherous hike, staggering humidity and lack of survival skills was getting to the urban thug. He raised the weapon and slammed the butt stock into the triangular-shaped head.

The nocturnal pit viper dodged the brunt of the force by sensing the human's thermal movements. The venomous creature then struck at the intruder's thigh, knocking him to the ground and sunk its fangs deep into his flesh.

Adolfo moaned, "Por favor, ayudeme!" His two amigos finished off the wounded reptile but left Ortega to die.

0630 Hours

The agent was conducting her daily recon, foraging for food and ensuring no predators were nearby. Her narrow, oblong face with angular cheekbones and a pointed chin appeared relaxed until she stumbled upon the dead serpent and man lying within a few paces from each other. Azúcar rolled the corpse over and sneered at Adolfo Ortega's face, "Mierda!" She immediately crouched low and scanned her surroundings. She discovered men's foot prints and some broken foliage nearby. She used her average height and smaller frame to her advantage by avoiding tree branches and stealthily following the trail through the steamy jungle.

An hour later, Azúcar smelled smoke and barely spotted two men through the canyon's foliage below. Her strait-edged nose flared as she whispered, "Jefe, I have two snakes three kilometers from your position, at nine o'clock." He clicked the toggle to his encrypted headset twice in acknowledgement.

Fidel Malvo inhaled the non-filtered cigarette.

"Oye hombre, you shouldn't be smoking!" Mahmouch suggested. The smoke and glowing red coals were an invitation to the lethal dots of a laser-sighted rifle.

Fidel shot back, "Callete Mahmouch, it is only Azúcar. Remember what we did to her last time?"

Mahmouch Khakhminejad snickered, "Sí. She is but a wounded kitten."

"This time Azúcar dies!" Fidel scanned the jungle in paranoia and wearily said, "Baboso Ortega, what I worry about is that Bushmaster's tracking us!"

She eyed both men's faces from her sniper scope and hissed, "Boss, they're definitely poisonous." She recognized both Malvo and Khakhminejad. "Bad men operating outside their country."

Mahmouch ignored his own advice and borrowed a smoke.

Azúcar crawled closer at a slow and steady pace, careful to keep her rifle's muzzle from dragging into the muddy terrain. The trim feline stopped two hundred meters away from the men's position. She reset her body alignment, took in a deep breath and talked in a low voice through the encrypted headset, "Khakhminejad murdered my husband and Malvo…"

Two shots echoed through the distance. The first bullet blew through Khakhminejad's skull. A second exploded into Malvo's groin. She ran under the triple canopy forest like a panther.

Fidel Malvo was holding his bloody mid-section. He squinted and barely recognized the catapulting figure bearing down upon him. What instantly terrified him was the savage look in Azúcar's dark eyes and that long blade clenched between her teeth. He cried out, "Mujer, please don't kill me."

She flipped on top of him and hissed, "Callete cobarde!" She danced her Bowie knife around his neck. Azúcar knew Fidel would bleed to death within hours but it was so damned hard to control her emotions. She hoped a colony of ants would come for him, slowly eating him alive. She arose and walked a few paces…

Malvo's ego got in his way, snickering, "You are like your husband, sin huevos."

Azúcar snapped back with a domineering grin, "It looks like your missing yours!"

"Bruja!" he yelled in a falsetto voice. The last thing Fidel Malvo saw was Azúcar's Bowie knife speeding toward his heart.

Killing off two of President Chavo Calles' favorite henchmen, Fidel Malvo and Mahmouch Khakhminejad, instantly, brought back bitter memories.

Both Azúcar and her husband, Pedro, were once part of the inner-circle to their esteemed leader. They acted as a crucial legal team in freeing Chavo Calles from prison and, then later, successfully managing his rise to the presidency. They really believed in Calles' cry for change, the redistribution of wealth and a united South American empire.

Unfortunately, they found out too late that Chavo was not a great man like Simón Bolívar. Azúcar used to be a die-hard socialist. That was until her husband discovered their charismatic leader was funneling oil money for personal gain.

It became clear that the president for life was only helping the poor for show and hoodwinking the masses. Calles even stole property from landowners that opposed his regime. He did so by dictating that owners had to have land titles dating back to the year of their country's independence from Spain in the early nineteenth century. However, there were no land titles granted in the country's first few years of independence.

Pedro eventually got the nerve to confront the 'presidente.' He really believed Chavo would listen to his advice and make the proper amends for the good of the state. Instead, Khakhminejad, Malvo and Ortega delivered Pedro's head to Azúcar that next day and, then, they had their way with her.

Azúcar had barely survived the beating and rape. A doctor making house calls discovered her passed out in the back alley of her upscale neighborhood. She remembered having just enough energy to warn that good Samaritan: *Avoid hospitals or suffer a worse fate under Calles' secret police.*

The sympathetic physician patched her up the best he could from his home. He contacted people opposed to the despotic regime to smuggle her out by yacht.

It had been only several years since Tío Sam recruited Azúcar. Joining the Central Intelligence Agency (CIA) was an easy choice. She used the painful memories to build herself up, both physically and mentally. During that time, she became deadly in Aikido and with various weapons. She also obtained a bachelor's degree in International Relations with a minor in History.

It became evidently clear through her recent and extensive studies that state-run enterprises stifled economic growth. Such top-down, authoritarian and heavily bureaucratic governments dominated many Latin and South American countries. The residual effects had devastating consequences for the main populace.

Looking back, Azúcar wondered how she never saw through Chavo's phony smirk. She could see it now, every time he stepped in front of a camera. After the presidente murdered her husband, she relabeled Calles' campaign as the *Audacity of Scam*.

Azúcar knew the US government would ignore his babbling but she would not. One of her main goals was to someday make amends to her beloved homeland for ushering in a 'wolf in sheep's clothing,' aka Chavo Calles.

Azúcar needed time to decompress. She dove into a deep portion of a rocky stream, stripped down, washed her clothes and purified herself from the necessary killings. The sharp features of the agent's face were merely a reflection of her entire body structure, from her slim arms and legs to her toned torso - screamed of ultra-fitness.

She was once considered a very pretty lady. Men still whistled at her curves and shiny jet-black hair but, then, they fell silent when she turned. She bore a deep scar that ran from the left side of her forehead down to the middle portion of her lower lip.

Khakhminejad, Malvo and Ortega were the ones responsible for her two broken ribs, a fractured right arm, crushed skull, marred face and feminine issues. Plastic surgery could only do so much and doctors notified her that conceiving any children would be a miracle. The agent saw her reflection, slapped at the water and wept.

Today she had not planned on removing the thugs. She just reacted. It was not revenge but a reckoning that she had long desired. The fact they'd been served up to her on a silver platter, made her wonder this chance meeting had really been coincidental, or if anything was ever by coincidence, after all. Three of her husband's murderers now lay cold, just as they were in life. Her actions did not help her feel better but this part of the world was a bit safer.

Her wet clothing quickly dried on the steaming boulders. Azúcar put on her olive-green combat fatigues over her curvaceous figure. She cleaned the Bowie knife, picked up her rifle and silently marched toward base camp at a casual pace. She met Jefe in their tent within the hour.

"Good hunting Azúcar."

"Gracias."

"As you know, we've been compromised but we're alive." He said after a long pause, "It's time to beat feet, vamos!"

Three days later, Jefe stood over a makeshift table assembled from dried jungle wood. He was configuring data files on his computer and fidgeting with a wire connected to a mini-dish pointed toward Calles' jungle retreat.

Azúcar was patrolling around the outskirts of their new hideaway. She also was fishing for fresh dinner.

A double-layer of camouflaged netting covered their small tent which housed two pieces of portable electronics, a small worn out water purifier, some meal rations, toiletries, an automatic collapsible rifle and a *Sig Sauer P-229* .40 caliber concealable pistol. All their gear could be carried off without leaving much of a trail. The double-netting kept deadly insects at bay but its main design was to prevent outsiders from noticing any interior lighting.

The female operative nicknamed her stocky coworker, 'Jefe,' but his code name was Nastea. From first look, the agents didn't look like much. She was slim and stood five-foot five inches tall, and he came off as a medium-height, balding professor, but the pair could take on eight people in hand-to-hand combat.

Nastea stared down into the deep chasm. The riverbed was beautifully scattered with various rocks that had been smoothed over by the constant flow of Andean water. A Blue Morpho butterfly flew past the tent and gracefully fluttered around the trunk of a wild banana tree a few yards away. The Morpho Rhetenor's blue metallic wings shimmered in the light and astounded the CIA operative. He was surprised to hear himself utter out loud, "Beautiful." Few people except his wife, children, and Azúcar knew that Jefe was an entomology enthusiast, butterflies being his favorite insect. The stocky field agent was entranced by the butterfly and began to walk outside. He caught himself and clenched his fists in frustration; *Come on, you got to focus on the mission and not chase butterflies.*

Jefe knew they had to depart in the near future before they ran out of supplies or were killed. An air-drop for water filters and a few other essential items were out of the question at the present moment. For some reason, he had a hunch that a few more days would provide them the time to gain some insight to key data.

Azúcar and Nastea were going to celebrate Christmas day by eating some grilled bananas and fish.

He smiled momentarily as he eyed a miniature Hawaiian style Christmas trinket. It was his only non-essential piece of gear, except for his only weakness, cigars. The plastic memento was almost two-inches high and three-inches long. His seven children had given it to him as an early present before he'd embarked on another deployment. The miniature figurine set consisted of a curvy Polynesian lady with a skimpy flowery bikini and Santa Claus, sporting hang loose, beach shorts. The festive pair wiggled aboard a miniature surf board to the repeating tunes of *Feliz Navidad, Hark the Herald Angels Sing* and *Jingle Bell Rock.*

Even Azúcar got a big kick out of the Holiday gimmick. She placed it against her ear smiling. "It is so Americano but I like."

Nastea corrected her English by saying, "American!"

"You may score well on those Spanish proficiency tests but I don't correct you when you don't roll your *r's*."

He shrugged. "Point taken!" Jefe somehow had rigged the volume so low that the Christmas music could only be heard if one placed it directly to their ear. He chuckled, "That little toy provides me a fond thought of my wife and kids."

She appeared sad, remarking, "Even hard asses need some Christmas cheer."

2 - BUNKER FIVE

December 26, 2004

Jefe's hunch paid off after deciding to remain in the area for another week. The laser DNA and brainwave mechanism had just broken out some important code. He picked up an encrypted palm device. "Secure for Sure, this is Nastea," he reported back to headquarters at a secure, underground facility known as *Bunker Five.* It was located over 50 miles north by northwest of Washington D.C. in a hilly and heavily forested area.

After 9/11, a unique cell, *Bunker Five*, had been created to protect Americans, stateside and abroad. A select group of people from other government agencies and the military were interviewed for the unit. The concept was to liquidate extremely lethal elements before they could carry out their terror plots on the citizenry.

The president envisioned a small expert force that could react quickly, working closely with law enforcement and special operations, and do their work stealthily. The Commander-in-Chief knew you could never entirely snuff out crime, but he often reminded the press corps by saying, "*If Americans work together, we can minimize bad guys' actions and give 'em hell in the process*! LARP - Look, Analyze, React and Pass it on was Bunker Five's mantra.

Bunker Five was a small organization with less than 170 employees. Their tight knit network enabled cells to work efficiently and minimize bureaucracy. Operators and technicians were capable of being deployed anywhere on the globe in a moment's notice to get done what needed getting done. Analysts covered two shifts during the day and one ad hoc staff was on standby for any ongoing ops during the graveyard shift. A small cadre of administrative and logistic specialists worked the two-day shifts.

Operational security (OPSEC) and personal security (PERSEC) was the responsibility of all hands. With the rise of high-speed communications came the risk of jeopardizing important information stored on computers and mobile computing devices. Gray hackers were a nuisance, who regularly stole personal data for financial gain. More menacing were black hats and organized cyber criminals, who could shut down electrical grids and terminals, and tap into banks, as well as thieve national secrets and copyrighted material. But the real danger were the foreign state-sponsored professionals and rogue elements who murdered anyone who opposed them. Such constant threats kept the cells sharp and on edge.

The typical Bunker Five employee shied away from social media and was savvy enough to keep a very low footprint within the cyber realm. They also regularly altered their driving routes and daily routines to remain unpredictable. Drama queens and heavily tattooed types need not apply.

Maturity and adaptability outweighed raw talent in the hiring process. Ages ranged from late twenties to mid-sixties. Personnel need only be patriotic and good at their chosen field of endeavor. The unit's operators and analysts knew the US had its warts, but it was still the best country on earth. The men and women of Bunker Five didn't think twice about spilling some blood to protect their nation's citizens, assets and vital interests. They were the sheep dogs guarding a mostly oblivious flock; patrolling the shadowy perimeters where the wolves remained mostly unseen.

By fall 2002, the Cold War installation was refurbished to serve as Bunker Five's remote operating base. No signal transmissions or cyber activity could be traced to its location. The employees also enjoyed the rural locale where outdoor activities such as fishing, hunting, hiking, kayaking and running were readily available to them. It seemed common sense and practicality prevailed the further one moved away from DC. The Beltway was still close enough to make it possible for them to attend an important meeting or take family to the Mall's monuments, parks and museums, but far enough away to avoid the hectic traffic and draining lifestyle.

After several seconds, Jefe said again, "Secure for Sure, this is Nastea."

The call from South America got the Bunker's watch team's immediate attention. “Nastea, this is Secure for Sure,” the communications sergeant replied, “I read you Lima-Charlie.”

Nastea said, “I have terrorists and a group of drug dealers coordinating plans out of Chavita-land. Their intent is to setup a secret camp southeast of New Orleans.

The high-ranking watch officer jumped out of his seat so fast that his Chai tea saturated his Air Force dress blue trousers. Colonel Sparkman ignored the searing pain and rushed over to observe the communications sergeant taking the incoming call.

Azúcar was the first to tag Presidente Chavo Calles as *Chavita*. Few knew it meant *little girl* in Spanish. The Latina CIA operative knew first hand that Calles often acted like a witch when he didn't get his way. So, she didn't mind at all when Bunker Five began to use *Chavita* as his handle over radio communications.

Jefe continued, "This narco-terrorist alliance intends to blow up US oil platforms in the Gulf of Mexico. They will also conduct a feint by first striking Guantanamo Bay."

Technical Sergeant Andrew Rice was pumped to hear the critical data he was recording. He began to rise from his chair to hand the initial notes to his colonel.

A high-ranking civilian ripped the sheet from the communications sergeant's hand. The government schedule fifteen (GS-15) stared at the notes for a moment and then forced the Air Force sergeant out of his seat.

Technical Sergeant Rice looked at Colonel Sparkman. Andrew then pointed at the prick who pushed him from his position and mouthed: *Who does this guy think he is?*

The newbie spoke into the mouth piece, "Nastea, this is Svedko."

The CIA operative thought he had heard someone mention that name before. If Jefe remembered correctly, it wasn't good.

"Are you sure this is the correct intelligence?"

Nastea didn't like the man's haughty tone and growled, "It isn't exact science but there are strong indications that Chavita is working with the Lions' Den."

"Lions' Den? Tell me what that means!"

Jefe's face flushed red. "Listen here piss-ant. I don't know who the hell you are but you should know better to keep our COMMS short!"

Before anyone privy to the conversation could get a reaction to Nastea's rebuke, the government official fired back, "My name is Svedko Lykkash."

Nastea yawned, "What's your point *Lick-ass*?"

The paunchy, peppered-hair civilian let out a wicked chuckle, "That is *Like-ash* to you."

"No. It's *Lick-ass* to me, you chatty Cathy SOB."

The workers close to the speaker tried to contain their uncalled-for grins and undignified chuckles.

Svedko hissed, "I will not be humiliated in this way. Do you hear me? I served six years in Special Operations as an officer and now am the intelligence director!"

"More like an INTEL weenie," Nastea replied, unfazed by Lykkash's admonishment. "If you knew your craft, you'd be aware what *Lions' Den* means."

"Who the hell..." but Jefe cut him off by stating, "Shut your suck ya self-righteous prick. I want to speak with the *Boss*!" meaning the colonel.

The GS-15 stood dumbfounded. "He can't talk to me like that can he? I'm a civilian equivalent to you," Svedko finished, plaintively pointing at the colonel's eagle bars."

Colonel Sparkman frowned, ignoring the director's pathetic complaint. "I apologize for that delay. Looks like your team hit a homerun. I will pass the info up to higher channels." He calmly told his technical sergeant, "Andy, please take your seat back."

The colonel immediately reported the raw data to his one-star boss back in Washington. General Stephenson shot back to the colonel, "Sparky, hell of a job your team is doing. Tell 'em to continue to keep their eyes and ears open!"

"Thank you General. We will issue an official report to the proper channels ASAP. I am sure this will stir up SOCOM." Colonel Sparkman then nodded to his communications sergeant.

The technical sergeant smiled and said, "Nastea, do you need to pass anything else?"

Jefe provided additional details before ending the conversation with, "Nastea out!" His muscular forearm revealed a US Navy Chief's tattoo as he plugged the solar adapter into the secure phone.

Colonel Sparkman coolly stated, "Mr. Lykkash, meet me in the conference room now." He then whispered to Sergeant Rice, "Alert security to have them wait at the hallway entrance."

As the colonel shut the conference room's door, Svedko shook his head and demanded, "You've got to rein in that Nastea character!"

The colonel stared silently at Lykkash before forcefully stating, "It's not in your best interest, and more importantly, the country's, to pick a fight with one of our best operatives!"

Svedko's mouth was agape, surprised to hear the colonel come off so favorably in defense of the insubordinate operative. The intelligence director had previously surmised Colonel Sparkman was just another empty uniform that would be easy to manipulate.

Sparky continued, "For your own situational awareness, *Lions' Den* is one of the most ruthless al-Qaeda cells working in South America. This terrorist cell has remained so low on the radar that the INTEL Nastea just reported is monumental."

Lykkash sighed, "Guess I'm the new kid on the block."

Colonel Sparkman flatly said, "Well that is something you ask offline. Nastea is right, you must keep COMMS brief, even on a secure line. You never know what capabilities others may have to pinpoint our people's whereabouts."

"Understood," the intelligence director graveled, "but that is no reason for Nastea to talk down to me in such a manner."

"I've been observing you for the past several months. You are one of the better briefers."

Svedko picked at his fingernails before saying, "Thank you."

"But... you are not very bright," Sparky said matter of fact.

His smile quickly disappeared. "What did you just say?"

He ignored the moron and bluntly said, "It has been reported that you've been subverting our watch team member's camaraderie by throwing around false accusations. That stunt you just pulled kicking my communications sergeant out of his seat was UNSAT! You continue this way and someone is going to knock you flat on your ass and no one will give a hoot."

Svedko begin to sweat, wondering if the high-ranking officer knew something of his past.

He scratched the back of his salt and pepper crew cut before stating, "You are one of the most mean-spirited people I've ever met." It was one of the rare moments where Lykkash didn't have a slick response. The colonel continued, "Do you have an Inferiority or a Napoleonic complex? I'd wager you're a bully because you think you can get away with it or you simply don't care."

The intelligence director's upper lip began to quiver.

He eyed Svedko and said, "That is piss poor leadership. You should know better being prior enlisted. What is worse, you're the biggest kiss-ass, I've encountered in my life."

Lykkash's entire body was tight, ready to explode.

Sparky roared, "Get the hell out of my office!"

3 - RAGE

Bunker Five, December 26, 2004

Svedko Lykkash pivoted to leave the space. His face flushed purple, full of rage. *That nice guy isn't going to tell me what to do.* He turned, storming toward the air force officer.

The colonel put up his hands. The intelligence director smirked, taking Sparkman's movements as a sign of fear. The officer-in-charge growled, "Stand down!"

The sudden dominant voice from the colonel caught Lykkash off guard.

Sparky forcefully added, "There is nothing to talk about, except you need to learn some humility."

Lykkash stammered before yelling, "How dare you! You and I are equivalents in rank, don't you ever lecture me you fu..." He caught himself and stopped.

Most of the watch floor turned around toward the loud voice booming from behind the conference room's smoky glass.

Up until that point, the colonel was going to simply reprimand Svedko, but the director crossed the boundaries of proper protocol. Sparky took in a deep breath before stating in a calm but firm voice, "I'm the watch floor's Commanding Officer."

Lykkash's hands balled up into fists.

The colonel glared at the GS-15. "I outrank you... And as smart as you sound, you sure create a lot of undue tension in our work center. Three people have written complaints about you in less than four months. And hardly anyone seems to like you."

Svedko lifted his chin in defiance. "I'd rather be feared than liked."

Colonel Sparkman shook his head. "You don't get it. We are on the same team. You on the other hand, seem to relish making enemies from within. Mark my words, Nastea, that guy you ticked off several minutes ago… He'll find where you live if you push too much. He is one of the deadliest people I have had the pleasure to work with."

The intelligence director tried to appear calm but his Adam's apple protruded as he gulped. The colonel could see fear in his eyes. He opened the door for his technical sergeant to come in and growled at Lykkash, "Now get off my watch floor you, narcissistic bastard!"

The Air Force sergeant's eyes bulged. He admired the colonel for his calm and confident demeanor, but he never remembered hearing his boss cuss before.

"I will write you up for calling me that colonel," Svedko said in an accusing voice. He pointed toward the Air Force non-commissioned officer, "The sergeant can witness what you just called me, *a narcissistic bastard.*"

The technical sergeant smiled with a grin like a Cheshire cat at the power-hungry man and coolly replied, "I didn't hear such a thing. What I recollect is Colonel Sparkman simply told you to get off his watch floor."

The Air Force officer and sergeant then escorted Svedko out to the hallway where security was standing by in the main tunnel.

Colonel Sparkman stated to the two security guards, "Mr. Lykkash is no longer permitted to be on my watch floor. Remove him from the access list. I will contact Human Resources and file a report."

Nastea was still in a good mood after passing the critical INTEL. He then thought of that schmuck, Svedko Lykkash. Three of his watch team analysts informed him before this mission that the same snake was causing quite a lot of hate and discontent back at the Bunker. *That is bad for business*, he thought before vowing to personally quash the bastard if he continued to hurt their bottom line.

Jefe took a deep breath of fresh air and gazed into the distant jungle on the other side of the bluff. It was a pristine view, minus the Minnesota-sized mosquitoes hovering outside the tent.

A high-pitched shriek descended upon the canopy floor, followed by clanging. Nastea immediately crouched low while drawing his semi-automatic pistol. A squirrel monkey's yellow arm had missed grasping the end of a branch by inches. The crash into the side of the tent broke its fall. The furry little creature had gotten too greedy by leaping more than its normal two-meter span from one tree to another. The impact sent a small tin of instant coffee and tea bags sprawling to the earth.

Jefe let out a sigh of relief and dropped his sights from the grayish-orange body. The Saimiri Boliviensis lazily rolled to all fours and attempted to shake off the dizziness. The black-headed primate studied the netting for a moment and, then, snarled toward the human stench inside. By the time Jefe reached the net's edge, the monkey had gained sanctuary in a nearby tree. He squatted down and reached for a metal mug, mixed among the fallen caffeinated comforts. He recognized his favorite blue and white speckled tin cup with the words *Lu-Lu* engraved on it.

Nastea scratched his bald head, remembering how a Navy SEAL once borrowed *Lu-Lu* for one of his teammates to drink soda mixed with another substance. One of the Frogmen forgot it at a house of ill repute in Ecuador. Even though, Leo didn't drink or sleep around, he went with his buddy to watch his back. The battered cup may have not been worth much, but it was both sentimental and the preferred means for Chief Nastea to enjoy his ritualistic morning java. He demanded that Señor Moreno and his teammate go back to the bordello, retrieve it from Señorita Lu Lu and clean the tin cup thoroughly.

Jefe's noggin returned to the present, he stretched both arms behind his thick neck and sat down eying the computer screen. He savored his favorite contraband, *un puro hecho en Cuba*. The retired chief blew out the rich tobacco smoke, thinking of one of his favorite presidents. He then shook his head sideways, grinned and said to himself, "Only with cigars does one not inhale."

Azúcar returned from her reconnaissance fifteen minutes later. Jefe handed her his last Cubano. She eyed him quizzically. "You must have gotten what you came for, no?"

"Gracias a Dios."

She unraveled a headless Fur-de-Lance from her backpack and skinned the reptile. "Jefe, how much longer we stay here?"

The covert agent began to impale the six-foot serpent along a wooden stick and replied, "I believe we should depart within the next few hours." He then lit a fire and stated, "We need nourishment first. It will be a long and sweaty trek."

She smiled, longing to sip her daily cappuccino, soak in a perfumed bubble bath, pet her gatito, Elvis, and rest on her queen-size bed at her townhouse.

"Daydreaming again?"

Azúcar blinked and admitted, "Oh Sí! I long for womanly comforts." Nastea grinned. "Jefe, other bad men come to look for us, no?"

He paused for a moment and then replied, "Especially after you kindly took care of Malvo and Khakhminejad, not to forget that nice Bushmaster snake biting Ortega."

Azúcar folded her hands across her firm breasts and frowned. "Qué? Jefe, I did not see, hear or do a thing!"

Nastea chuckled, "Azúcar, you are good woman and learning fast."

Azúcar blushed. "Gracias, boss-man."

They finished eating their reptilian steak and began sanitizing the area. Jefe grabbed his headset and announced, "Secure for sure this is Nastea. We are ready for Disney Land. I repeat we are ready for Disney Land."

A few moments passed and headquarters gave them a green light. Azúcar and Jefe both loaded up their steel-framed backpacks which held up to sixty pounds of gear. They each carried their customized rifle, a SIG pistol and a sixty-four-ounce Camelbak water pouch.

Both agents realized they probably would not be operating in this part of the world for a while. Some nark had recently tipped the enemy of their whereabouts. Tactics needed to be altered and personnel rotated. More importantly, a mole would need to be sniffed out of its hole and hunted down.

4 - BRIEFING

February 11, 2005

An elderly man swung around a corner, aiming his pistol at a Navy SEAL. Petty Officer Ross shot him twice in the chest and once above the nose. He quickly scanned the area for movement as he ducked into the shadows of a hookah bar's archway.

A woman pointed an AK-47 at him from a window across the way. He painted her with three rounds of lead.

"All clear!" the range safety officer's voice boomed.

The stocky frogman made his weapon safe before saying, "Chief. These wider polymer grips are sweet!"

Jaws said, "Oh yeah. Easier to handle for us older guys."

"Yep... Thanks for letting me test on such a tight schedule."

"No sweat. Close-quarter drills, land navigation and, hell, even SERE school, beats those damn keyboard courses any day."

Ross sighed. "I swear all that computer-based training is meant to neuter the military; just silly check in the boxes."

Chief Jaworsk said, "Thank goodness we still get to hammer on the basics with on the job training and deck plate leadership."

"Amen! Well, I gotta clean my weapon. See ya at the brief."

A hand tapped Thor Rockford on the shoulder. The SWCC operator looked up and exclaimed, "Chief Naster?" The CIA operative aka *Jefe* or *Nastea* grinned, placing his finger to his lips for his fellow linguist to be silent. Thor nodded at his old mentor.

Azúcar and Jefe initiated their briefing inside the auditorium at a secluded base. To a select group of warriors, they knew it as *Compound X.* The attendees consisted of a mixed-bag of US Special Operators, mostly from the US Army and Navy. As a smaller team, they shared their work load and, no matter the rank, they referred to each other on a first name basis except during official ceremonies. For some higher-ranking officers, this assignment would be considered a career killer. Besides being an operational joint billet, this wasn't an officer's politically correct assignment where busy work trumped the warrior ethos. It cost some a pay grade, but no matter what rank, the guys were focused on neutralizing America's enemies.

The men weren't bureaucrats; they were musketeers. The workups for the past year kept them sharp. Their mission objectives were to safeguard Americans and the United States' Gulf coast.

Relaxed grooming standards were the norm, many bore facial hair with longer locks to blend in most environments. Compound X operators even kept their previous ratings and job codes for public records to keep a lower profile. Such measures were in place to protect the command, its workers, and family and friends.

On slide four, Jefe stated, "US Special Operations Command (USSOCOM) has directed your group to interdict a dangerous alliance that has been brewing between a minor drug ring and Islamic terrorists." That got the men's attention. This was not going to be the same ole OPSEC brief many were expecting.

Azúcar said matter of fact, "The enemy is projected to set up their terrorist camp on Gemela." She clicked her remote showing photos of the secluded locale. "The major drug cartels are clever enough not to have anything to do with the likes of Osama Bin Laden. However, some of our best analysts believe Chavo Calles' hidden agenda is to pin the narco-terrorist collaboration on the major South American drug czars, use the al-Qaeda cell to do his bidding and strike a deadly blow to the US." She raised an eyebrow and added, "Or those he calls *bloated Gringos*."

Grumbling could be heard from the audience. She continued, "If we were to publicly disclose such information it could compromise the effectiveness of gathering any future INTEL and jeopardize American lives, both civilians and operatives." She eyed the audience for a moment to get their attention. "Don't underestimate Calles, he is a very dangerous man." The tough lady winced before adding, "Take it from me. Chavo murdered my husband." Azúcar's knuckles turned white as she gripped the sides of the podium. "And I barely survived his henchman."

There was stunned silence as the fit brunette departed the podium. Jefe quickly took center stage. The stocky agent provided detailed information of Gemela's history, its terrain and waterways. Near the end, over a dozen men raised their hands for follow on questions. Azúcar and Jefe took turns providing answers except one, *Satellite and Human Intelligence could not give a logical answer to why the small patch of land within the southeastern Louisiana bayou was mostly deserted for up to six months of the year.*

Jefe brought up a separate slide and pointed to the face of a pretty looking Latina. "The CIA sent one of their best operatives to Gemela within the past year, posing as a field worker. Unfortunately, the lady never returned." The group stared blankly at the two sixty-inch screens. Since this was the exact place the men were heading, the lack of information did not sit well with them.

One guy murmured, “Typical INTEL, just the data we need and don’t have.”

Carl Broadstein stood and eyed his comrades. “Maybe it is haunted?” the fifty-year-old Green Beret said with a hint of sarcasm. Most of the men threw empty paper coffee cups at his corny joke. One scrappy looking fellow put his head down for a few seconds.

Ross patted his buddy’s shoulder. “You okay, Thordog?”

Petty Officer Juleon "Thor" Rockford jolted up. “Yeah… just in deep thought.”

The Navy SEAL chided, “Don’t think too much! Never met a linguist that isn’t too damn analytical and a tad loco.”

The commanding officer, Colonel Perry Thomas, briskly made his way to the podium. The stout Green Beret nodded at his men before saying, "One update: two CH-47 helicopters will outfit you with proper supplies at the crack of dawn, eleven hours after your insertion. Camouflaged nettings, food and other gear will provide you the equipment necessary to hide in plain sight."

Commander Lawlur said, "Sir. We'll stage a perimeter guard when the Chinooks arrive and waste no time unloading the gear."

“Very well.” Col. Thomas forcefully said, “This is a real-world operation. I don’t give a damn if you liquidate or apprehend the terrorists. Just make sure your sack the evil bastards!”

The audience roared out of respect before heading to their boats, helicopters and offices. The special operators rechecked their communications equipment, maps and weapons. This part was rarely portrayed in a Hollywood film, yet it was a vital aspect of their job, constant preparation. Simple training was dangerous enough not to include actual missions or Murphy’s Law - the unexpected. Discipline, toughness and adaptability also were crucial factors for there to be any chance of success.

US Navy Senior Chief Joe Samson and Chief Warrant Officer 5 (CWO5) Michael Raven stuck around to pick the brains of the two HUMINT operatives. The two special operators knew when they were in the presence of pros. Azúcar and Jefe were not some squeaky, clean Harvard lawyer graduates working for the CIA. These two were the real deal with soiled hands.

The four heard a strange noise in the shaded corner of the room. It sounded like snoring. It even woke up the snorer followed by a loud thud. Their laughter angered the stunned person who, then, uttered a few choice words.

Azúcar silently tip toed to the corner with amazing speed. The sleepy man rubbed his hip in agony and scanned the room. He could barely make out three people at the podium and muttered, "Crap, my detachment left me high and dry."

Samson recognized that voice. He chucked an erasable pen toward the silhouette and barked, "Hugs, I heard that you slacker. You deserted your detachment by not giving your full attention to the briefs. Get to the boats you lush."

Petty Officer Hugsby balked at his senior chief. "Huggy baby, you shouldn't mock your boss." By the time he recognized her, Azúcar was straddling him with his feet and arms pinned down.

Hugs tried to roll her over. "Great, now you are out-wrestling me," he groused. She shook her shiny jet-black hair over his face. "Stop that chica, it tickles."

She cocked her head back and eyed him seriously. "You gents may be dealing with some bad elements very soon."

"Whatever!"

"No usa esta palabra, Gatito." Her eyes narrowed. "Get your head in the game, pretty boy." Hugsby only scowled at her. He was not accustomed to continuously being on the receiving end of a joke.

Azúcar helped him get to his feet. He then winked at her and slapped her firm buttocks. She grabbed his right arm, as his palm contacted her derrière. She then flipped him over with his face to the floor. He winced in pain. She whispered into his ear, "This is not the time or place, but for the record, I'll do the love-tapping."

He gritted his teeth. "Woman, you're breaking my arm."

She twisted his wrist with a wicked grin. "Me comprendes?"

"Yesss," Hugsby groaned, "and I say uncle."

Azúcar then released the joint lock. "Suck it up buttercup!" Nastea, Rav and Samson almost rolled on the floor laughing.

Hugs stumbled into some chairs as he tried to get up another time. He grabbed his belly and moaned, pointing at her, "Hell, I don't know what is worse, a nasty hangover or you." She blew him a kiss and laughed at her toy boy.

5 - DEPARTURE

I can imagine no more rewarding career. And any man who may be asked in this century what he did to make his life worthwhile, I think can respond with a good deal of pride and satisfaction: "I served in the United States Navy."
President John F. Kennedy

February 14, 2005

Azúcar and Nastea wrapped up their final mission brief to the special operators. The tactical team departed from their small Gulf base at precisely 1400 hours. An hour later, they rendezvoused at a covert station near Clermont Harbor. They took turns fueling up the boats and helicopters. The men afforded themselves the last creaturely comforts of Gatorade and snacks before they continued.

At 1630 hours, the boats and helicopters bulleted southeast across the Mississippi Sound. They briefly entered the Gulf of Mexico and changed directions at a relative bearing of 180 degrees for approximately one hour. The vessels then navigated around the western edges of Chandeleur Sound.

The forty-four men were part of a counter-narcotics/terrorist unit assigned to set up a forward operating base on Gemela. It was a private, small piece of land over forty miles southeast of New Orleans, not even marked on any maps or computer mapping programs. The special operators were to conduct their first "hands on" reconnaissance of Gemela at dusk. The cover of darkness was vital to avoid any unwanted eyes that might be part of the drug runners' vast network. They were scheduled to begin setting up their camouflaged bunkers and caches the next day.

The two heavily armed vessels of Detachment Delta pounded over turbulent waves while the pair of MH-60 helicopters hovered above. The group consisted of a platoon of Navy SEALs (Sea, Air, Land), a Special Warfare Combatant Craft Crewmen (SWCC) detachment (DET) with their pair of thirty-six feet long rigid inflatable boats (RIBSs), a platoon of Army Green Berets, Army and Navy pilots with their Nightstalker crewmen. Both MH-60 helicopters carried the Special Forces' platoon and the two RIBs carried the SEALs. The Special Operations helos had American Flags painted on their sides while Stars and Stripes proudly waved through the salty sea air above both Navy RIBs' aft antennas.

The boat detachment's weapons expert, Gunners Mate First Class (GM1) Odin, clicked his headset and said, "The ladies aren't too happy about us being away on Valentine's Day."

The real Officer-in-Charge (OIC) of the SWCC detachment, Senior Chief Joe Samson barked in a gruff voice, "Yep but we could be deployed on longer tours of duty like our sister detachment in the Middle East."

SWCC operators were commonly referred to as *Boat Guys*, *River Rats* and *Dirty Boat Guys*. SWCC pronounced "swick" were frequently confused with Navy SEALs. Their grueling basic crewmen training molded them into being solid runners, swimmers, shooters, navigators, coxswains, communicators, and most importantly team players, but frogmen they were not. Boat Guys were known for inserting, extracting and providing cover support for various US Special Operating Forces. River Rats normally were assigned to Special Boat Teams (SBTs), and operated in salt, brackish and fresh water, as long as it was not too shallow and they could maneuver their craft. Special boat operators had a reputation for driving fast and when threatened, they'd unleash a heavy arsenal on those who wished them or their riders harm.

The unofficial SWCC lineage could be traced back to a frosty Christmas in 1776 where special boat crews ferried General George Washington and his men across the frigid Delaware River in route to their daring raid on Trenton. The general's three-pronged plan of attack turned into only one. Two of his units could not cross the icy waters to execute their southern and western flanks, but it seemed Providence was on the Patriots' side: GW and his men from the north miraculously made it across the Delaware. Numerous Americans had been tortured and raped by Hessians and Red Coats, so many able-bodied civilians joined General Washington to retaliate. Four hours behind schedule, hiking ten-miles through blizzardy conditions, the future American president's unorthodox attack still caught the enemy off guard during the Holidays.

Some argued SWWC got its roots from the Patrol (PT) Boats of World War Two. One could say its most famous member was Lieutenant Junior Grade (LTJG) John F. Kennedy who served on PT-109 during World War Two in the South Pacific and later became the 35th President of the United States of America. Just as legendary in pre-SWCC history was Motor Torpedo Boat Squadron Three's rescue of General Douglas MacArthur and later the Philippine President from the Japanese Invasion of the island during

WWII. However, the River Rats and Swift Boats of the Vietnam War were officially recognized as the gangplank owners of SWCC.

A pivotal force in the evolution of both SEAL and SWCC history was Captain Phil H. Bucklew, hailed as the father of Naval Special Warfare. He had been a professional football player before becoming a naval officer, and a Navy Scouts and Raiders member, an elite force of combat swimmers who participated in many special operations during the Second World War. Captain Bucklew was just as renown for correctly theorizing that the Vietcong would use inter-coastal waterways to wage guerrilla warfare in the Vietnam War. The naval captain's keen foresight paved the way to deploy SEAL Team direct action missions and smaller craft armed to the teeth in littoral excursions against the Vietcong. One of the modern SWCC fathers was Master Chief Kelly Webb who helped streamline the pipeline by retaining experienced operators in the community while creating a tough training regimen for future crewmen. No matter the era, small boats were often ideal for reconnaissance, blockade, raiding and sabotage missions.

One of the SWCC operators, Boatswain Mate First Class (BM1) Hugsby, gawked, "Ladies, uh Mistur Gentry." Lieutenant Junior Grade (LTJG) Gentry shot Hugs a nasty look.

The crew disliked the Gentry's condescending manner and the corrosive effect it had on unit cohesion. *Jeni* as the Det called him, wiggled into the program without graduating from the intensive SWCC course. In fact, he had not attended any type of Special Warfare (SPECWAR) indoctrination training. Thanks to a favor from his father's friend, a high-ranking officer, LTJG Gentry crept into the program as Det Delta's OIC. That rank was only on paper. Operationally, the Naval Academy officer had been tagged a "soup sandwich." Many of the operators feared Jeni would get them killed due to his "got mine" flair and piss poor shooting skills.

Most guests enjoyed the first few minutes on various SWCC boats until losing equilibrium and succumbing to seasickness. The impact of every wave averaged a G-shock that exceeded training for NASA astronauts. Many Boat Guys lasted about six years in the SWCC program. After that, they experienced bad shoulders, hips and knees. One Mark V coxswain's large intestine was jolted from his anal cavity because of the impact from the turbulent waves between Los Angeles and Catalina Island. After bracing hundreds of waves, most visitors' faces changed from grins to grimaces.

Two SEALs looked sick. You could see it in their ashen faces and glassy eyes. Petty Officer Hugsby yelled, "Come on, get it over with and hurl!"

Army Warrant Officer 4 (CW4) Doug Nubiez chuckled hearing Hug's tone and jesting. It reminded him of his basic training years back. He would never forget Drill Instructor McManus's eyes bulge out in frustration, spitting as he yelled, *Nubiez, your last name is too damn girly and is complicated as hell to pronounce. You are now Nubs!* Drill Instructor, Sergeant McManus, was the meanest to roam Fort Benning's Sand Hill and Harmony Church training grounds during the 1980s. If you were screwing up, your face was in the dirt, he'd push you in the shoulder or kick you in the ass, or the DI was calling your mom and sweetheart every name in the book as his veins in his neck and forehead bulged, spitting out saliva. Several recruits quit or failed, and those that didn't heed his Vietnam lessons faired far worse. The drill sergeant's methods were to pound you into submission. This was in an era before congress was able to put too much of their politically correct talons into military training. If you were following the DI's orders, the proud American of African-Irish descent was daydreaming out loud about his fishing retirement. The sergeant made the weak strong and the strong stronger. His BA in psychology focused on making each of his future infantrymen think and act as a team to be aggressive, strategic warriors. At the beginning of basic training, the men hated McManus, but those who graduated, later respected the DI for his tough love.

The pair of frogmen began puking their guts out from the sides of Delta-two. Hugs looked back at the pair of frogmen with a devilish smile and uttered, "Finally." The SEALs still had plenty of spunk to glower at his antagonistic humor. He grabbed a bag of saltines from his pouch and tossed it to them. He eyed his diver watch: *1730 hours*. Hugsby announced his post debarkation speech, "In fifteen mikes we will have plenty of citrus, vegetables, tobacco, and seafood. The small patch of land within the bayou has two towering hills shaped like succulent breasts." The men that were paying attention to his rambling, cheered at the last statement.

Delta-two's coxswain continued, "There is a gorgeous one-hundred-year old 'Munster' looking hacienda. It includes two hundred rooms and six entertainment halls. Don't forget the cobwebbed bars, frayed tennis courts and rusty weights from Steve Reeves' *Hercules* era. For golfers you can enjoy a dilapidated twenty-seven-hole golf course. It's all on a one square-mile piece of real estate within the Louisiana bayou. That's all folks, we know you have no choice whatsoever about who transports you to your clandestine location but, nevertheless, we hope you have enjoyed your ride aboard Delta Sea Lanes."

Chief Jaworsk whispered into his headset, "Hey Sam, I don't remember the brief saying it had a golf course?" He joked, "Heck, I would have brought my clubs."

Senior laughed, "The Hugster is full of it. It was only eighteen holes."

The chief's eyes bulged. "What do you mean was?"

"SATINTEL revealed the course's old fairways are now mostly sugarcane and vegetable fields. Fig and apple trees, various citrus, blueberries, persimmons, and pomegranates were originally planted in between holes along the roughs and still are maintained. The owner would be smart to refurbish the resort, make a killing off tourism and only cultivate the edges of Gemela.

"So, what does Gemela mean in Spanish?" Jaws asked.

Senior Chief Samson responded, "It means twin. The original owners, Spanish Cajuns, named their small sugar cane and fruit plantation Gemela back in the early nineteenth century. A Mexican mobster bought the small of piece of land in the 1920s and transformed it into a golf resort neatly lined with an assortment of fruit trees. Gemela is named after its two giant mounds that appear almost identical to the naked eye. After studying the Satellite photos, even Azúcar jokingly admitted they resemble chiches"

"Huh?"

Senior cupped his pecs, "A pair of melons."

"Oh!" Chief Jaworsk bit his lip and confessed, "Joe, my Spanish sucks even after living in Panama for years."

Samson empathized with him. "Jaws, I'm slowly learning." They were the few boat guys who didn't marry olive-skinned cuties south of the US or American Latinas. In fact, over half of the special operators stationed at Compound X had come from several bases in Panama before they were shut down in the late 1990s.

6 - MUSTANGS

The Special Operators often teased both Senior Chief Joe Samson and Chief Warrant Officer 5 (CWO5) Michael Raven about how they never watched regular television programs, but they revered them. Joe was nicknamed “Fin” because he was the fastest SPECWAR swimmer. His fellow SWCC operators joked his hands and feet were webbed. He had made the Olympic freestyle tryouts, once as a twenty-year old and later in the Navy. Unfortunately, a nagging shoulder injury kept Fin from going any further in the swimming competitions. Mike was often referred to as “Rav” because it was part of his name and a cool callsign.

Senior Chief Joe Samson was proud to be part of the Chiefs' Mess. Both Fin and Rav were old school, not glamorous but get the job done type of guys. They followed orders and pushed back when necessary. They were also scholarly nerds. Fin was an astute reader with a P.H.D. in history, his dissertation on Ancient Roman Warfare. Rav had a doctorate in economics.

The pair were also father figures to many of the men who didn't have good male role models in their lives. Fin and Rav geeked out on the *History* and *National Geographic Channels*. The younger crew really didn't mind watching the older men's shows, since it afforded them new perspectives, their busy schedules rarely had allowed them to see. One thing they all enjoyed together was a constant fill of sports. Joe and Mike occasionally enlightened the younger generation to what they considered true cinema, a John Ford western, especially, starring the Duke and Jimmy Stewart, or a Laurel and Hardy comedy.

Even though Navy CWO5 Michael Raven and Army CW4 Doug Nubiez were best friends, it was Rav and Fin who were two peas in a pod. Both shared the same birth date but born ten years apart. Michael Raven was the fastest high school cross-country runner from Tennessee in the mid-1970s and Joe Samson the fastest high school swimmer from Texas in the mid-1980s. Ironically, Rav ran for the University of Texas and Fin swam for the University of Tennessee. People often confused the colleges logos since the University of Texas' Longhorns was a burnt orange and the University of Tennessee's Volunteers a UT orange. Both Raven and Samson stood at six feet tall even, but the elder had a wiry build and the younger stockier.

CWO5 Michael Raven didn't follow the normal pilots' creed of preferring exercise over golf, like his flying counterpart, Nubs. Rav and Samson were the leads for the SpecOps' physical training regimen. Rav was a die-hard tri-athlete whereas Samson a muscle conditioning guru. Joe Samson regularly instructed the men in swimming, otherwise, Fin avoided the water after burning out from daily three-hour pool practices between the ages of five to twenty years old. Senior Chief Samson respected CWO5 Raven's even-keeled style of leadership so much that he had his heart set on submitting an officer package as a Mustang.

Chief Warrant Officers (CWOs) and Limited Duty Officers (LDOs), or commissioned officers who earned a Good Conduct Medal or served as previous enlisted for five years were known as *Mustangs* in the US Navy ranks. Senior Chief Samson liked the thought of becoming a CWO or LDO due to their experience and technical backgrounds, but still retained the enlisted heart to carry out hard tasks. The term *Mustang* arose around WWII when some US Naval Academy grads snubbed them as *lower class*, but the prior enlisted officers took the term as a badge of honor. For those that *earned their commissions the hard way* by serving in the enlisted ranks first, a Mustang equated to a wild horse and not a thoroughbred; one that can be tamed and often a smarter, mixed breed that has a wild streak to buck the system when it was necessary. Actor, Major Audie Murphy, and premiere journalist, Colonel David "Hack" Hackworth, were some notable US Army Mustang officers, also, highly decorated combat veterans.

Normally, Mustangs were well respected for their leadership and experience. However, a junior officer at Samson's previous command had scarred his memory so badly that every time he thought of Lieutenant Svedko Lykkash, the senior enlisted became sick to his stomach. Though a brilliant speaker and forceful personality, Lieutenant Lykkash was such a back-stabbing prick that Samson refused to submit his polished CWO/LDO paperwork every August for the past two years.

Samson recently confided in Rav that he was battling the decision to put in a request chit for the next CWO/LDO boards due to the poor example of a lieutenant several years back. Senior Chief Samson even let CWO5 Raven know of the time Lieutenant Lykkash didn't pass the Red Cross message to his leading chief petty officer that his father died while on a Counter Narcotics/Terrorist (CNT) mission to South America. It wasn't until the funeral was over that Senior Chief Samson's friend, Chief Carlos Roberts, found out about his dad's passing and confronted the lieutenant by saying: *Why didn't you inform me of my father's death*? The prick coldly replied; *Mission comes before family*. Chief Roberts immediately delivered a left uppercut to Svedko's chin, followed by a right haymaker punch to his left eye. The final blow knocked Lykkash flat on his ass and the chief growled: *My mother needed me you son of a bitch*. The nasty shiner the junior officer received for his uncouth ways should have been a severe enough warning to keep his mouth shut but he didn't. In Samson's eyes, the lieutenant was just as bad as LTJG Gentry but should have known better being prior enlisted. Upon finding out the entire circumstances, the Special Boat Team's Commanding Officer restricted Chief Carlos Roberts to 30 days in solitary confinement for hitting an officer, but warned the lieutenant, he was lucky the boat detachment didn't hog-time him to die in the South American jungle. The SEAL skipper fired Lykkash from the boat detachment's officer-in-charge position and mustered the Chiefs' Mess to keep a hard eye out on the heartless lieutenant while he was stashed at a petty desk job in the training department.

After getting to know Samson, Rav had to remind his co-worker and close friend a few times, *Let the grudge go and not let one "bad apple" stifle your ambitions*.

The men frequently taunted Senior Chief Samson after a Hollywood agent tried to get him to test for author Vince Flynn's *Mitch Rapp* character due to his dark features and muscular frame. Fin regretfully declined the agent's offer, citing operational commitments. The Senior Chief joked to his men: *Who'd want to hire me as an actor with my Texas slang*. But deep in Samson's heart, he simply didn't want to fail, so the crusty SWCC operator never screened for the *Mitch Rapp* part.

7 - OPERATION GEMELA

Senior Chief Samson spouted off some details about the mysterious locale, “Gemela once was an old Mafia haven. The golf resort and establishment has been abandoned since early 1965. The US government seized the resort because it profited from illegal booze, drugs and prostitution. J. Edgar Hoover busted the clown who operated Gemela. Somehow the owner kept most of the land until it was sold shortly thereafter.” Fin raised his hands in resignation. “Lawyers, go figure! Uncle Sam owns the southeastern edge which consists of a concrete pier designed to dock sea planes and a small warehouse. Sorry Hugs, the hacienda resort is off limits.”

Petty Officer Hugsby puckered his lips. “We can never have any fun.”

Senior Chief Samson gave him hell by exclaiming, “Cheer up mate, as you said, we will have a fine selection of fruit and fish.”

Delta-one’s coxswain, Boats Eliot, smiled as he took in the marvelous red skyline dipping in the west. “No more MREs, constipation and IBS.”

Staff Sergeant Kramer interjected from the helicopter’s headset, “Don’t ya reckon that there is TMI, Eliyat?”

“Well Kram, at least we’ll eat some natural food for a change, Gracias a Dios.” Eliot had a foreboding inkling that a minatory presence of darkness existed very near. It sent shivers down his spine that something may turn awry.

Senior Chief Samson plumbed through his palm pilot. “FYI, Gemela is supposedly haunted.”

Jaws roared, “Not that crap again.”

Rav shook his head inside his helicopter. He pulled the mouthpiece closer to his chin and said, “Azúcar believes evil lurks on Gemela but I don’t buy that mumbo jumbo.”

Fin didn’t believe it either but he loved messing with his men’s minds. He glared wickedly at his crew. “Remember that poor CIA lady went MIA.”

Gunners Mate Odin was listening from the other RIB’s headset. He smugly remarked, “Ha, come on this is the twenty first century. There are no such things as gods, ghosts and monsters.”

Hugs acted as the detachment’s jester. “Hey Thor, perhaps all your daily devotionals will repel any spooks.”

Samson sighed at the Det's quipster. Sometimes when Hugs' SWCC mates had enough, they simply duct-taped his mouth.

Thor grabbed an empty bottle from his backpack. He opened the container letting the strong aroma permeate into Hugsby's face. "Do you need any more Huggy diapers after your date with Señorita Azúcar and the tequila two nights ago?" he asked smugly.

The coxswain backed away from the console and slightly swerved the RIB. "Get that crap away from me! I still feel nauseous."

"Yeah, but those adult-sized diapers literally saved your hide in our mission briefs yesterday," Thor noted.

Hugs smirked. "Aye-aye you dirty rat! My favorite drink tasted so good coming down but Montezuma had his revenge."

Thor corrected him by saying, "No, I think Azúcar did."

Hugs smiled thinking of her. "Azúcar is one heck of a babe and she drank me under the table."

Fin laughed, "Speaking of babe, didn't we hear Azúcar call you Huggy-baby after yesterday's briefing?"

Petty Officer Hugsby snarled, "That's not funny senior!"

Senior Chief Samson fired back, "Well, Huggy-baby, next time don't try out-drinking a prettily lil Latina with tequila. She may only weigh a buck-fifteen but she sure can kick your ass."

Rav chuckled, "Yeah, Hugs got a bit fresh yesterday with Azúcar and she flipped him to the ground." The warrant officer was up in the helo and could not see Hugs' scowl.

The detachment's funny man became beat red and hollered, "Shut up y'all." All the men listening to the multi-platform headsets from either the boats or helicopters bellowed for a few minutes. It was very seldom that somebody got the best of Hugs and, especially, when he lacked a witty comeback.

Detachment Delta viewed the last remnants of a spectacular sunset. Horizontal orange wove through the shredded cumulus low on the still blue sky, incrementally transforming into several shades of violet until the skyline gave way to the monochrome of night.

The boats and helicopters slowed down before veering in a westerly direction. The crewmen were surprised they didn't spot any fishing vessels near the inlets leading to St. Bernard Parish's southeastern boundaries.

Minutes later, CWO5 Raven eyed his GPS. He stated, "INTEL says it is clear this time of year within a five-mile radius.

We all know what we are up against." He then barked in a laconic tone, "I'll ask for forgiveness later. Lock and Load!"

Lawlur clicked his communications device in acknowledgment, followed by Samson and Jaws.

Senior Chief Joe Samson added in a low voice, "I bet some political punks wrote those petty rules of engagement. Too many of 'em probably smoked dope, never served in the military or haven't seen a shade of combat."

Boatswain Eliot protested, "But Fin, marijuana helps with my aunt's glaucoma."

Joe spit out some juice from his tobacco pouch. "That's fine, but too many losers will use that as an excuse to get high and not for medical reasons."

Bos'n Eliot grumbled, "What about people that get drunk?"

Fin rolled his eyes. "Listen Eliot, I had to go to Alcoholics Anonymous to learn that the hard way. I lost a good marriage because of it and, now, I hardly have time to visit my precious daughter four states away. Any substance if abused is bad! Hell, you guys know I switched from snuff to pouches just to give my gums a break."

Bubba-Kram shook his head at Senior Chief Samson and muttered, "Quitter." Kram then put in a pinch of snuff between his cheek and gum. "I don't know about you girls but I just need my two basic food groups," he coughed, "d-dip and beer."

Hugs grimaced, pointing at his forward fifty-gunner. "Thor, another fine mess you got us into!"

Thor Rockford's eyes narrowed. "Quiet ya clown!"

The boats still had a way to go for infiltration and decreased their speed a few more knots. The helicopters loitered further behind to minimize their signature. "See something." The other forward fifty-gunner spotted low grasslands through his NVGs and added, "Land approaching."

"Good eyes, Fitz and Thor." Petty Officer Hugsby began to babble until Senior Chief Samson grumped in a low tone, "It's time to shut your sucks and pay attention!"

Several minutes later, the boat detachment began to drift through miles of zigzagging waterways. It seemed like a snail's pace to the helicopters above.

There was a vibe in the air besides the increased buzzing of insects, thickening layer of mist and the acrid smell of the marshland that even spooked those who regularly went into harm's way.

Enormous trees covered with moss began to envelope the pair of boats. The two helicopters could barely make out the pair of SWCC vessels below.

The boats and helicopters paused at a waypoint before entering into dense fog. Senior Chief Samson eyed his GPS, *Almost Showtime*. He stated to his detachment, "Tick Tock," which meant prep for Infill.

Many of the operators suddenly appeared edgy. From the men's vantage point, the thick vapor directly in front of them looked like a massive wall guarding the outer perimeter of Gemela.

CWO5 Raven calmly spoke into his mouthpiece, "Party Shaw," which meant the first major stage of Operation Gemela had commenced. Rav immediately heard several clicks in acknowledgement from the other leaders' toggle switches.

On cue, the boats and helicopters began to maneuver through the thick fog. Delta-two boat and Rav's helicopter took perimeter guard while Delta-one and Nub's helo began infiltration of Gemela.

Raven was able to spot a small patch of land through his night vision goggles. It was separated by at least a few hundred yards of water from adjacent parcels of swampland. He remembered from the intelligence briefings that Gemela was, in many aspects, unique. The bald cypresses around its perimeter stood at least ten feet above any of the trees on neighboring patches of land. The two towering mounds were almost camouflaged at its center by foliage. Mike surmised nobody would be able to make out the difference unless they skimmed the top of the treetops.

Even its flatter core which surrounded two giant mounds was a few yards higher than the outer rocky banks, three feet above sea level. He tipped his hat to the landscapers, since this well-designed drainage system naturally pushed water out to the bayou and minimized erosion. Gemela's clever design reminded him of the Panama Canal because both eliminated standing water and malaria.

The task unit commander was amazed how his NVGs provided such clarity at over a quarter mile away. He even pinpointed several Purple Martin bird houses on its eastern edges. Mike fondly recalled helping his grandpa every summer on the farm to maintain the proper houses for the Progne Subis species, supposedly a treasured mosquito eating bird. His granddad had instilled in him to respect the aerial insectivores because they were the type of swallows that would keep many pesky flying insects to a minimum.

Gemela

Fin grumbled into his mouthpiece, “This place is way too quiet!”

Many of the special operators’ hairs on the back of their necks stood straight up out of natural instinct. The Task Unit Commander decided to break the ice and pump his navigator for a current picture. “How is it looking like down there Poseidon?”

Jaws eyed the RIB’s Furuno radar and his handheld Garmin global positioning system. "Rav, this is Poseidon - the turtles have plenty of water below and 500 meters to shore."

CWO5 Raven clicked his encrypted communication device once in acknowledgement.

8 - SCARE TACTICS

Card Night, Valentine's 2005

Ricardo Lombardi Sr. sneered at his reporter, *Shady Shotzski* who bested him in an intense round of spades. The tall bruiser sighed, "Give me about five minutes to refill our drinks."

Jack Grumblier, Jerry Rockford and Chuck Shotzski nodded appreciatively. Lombardi filled the beverages and then began applying cream to his face. The Snowbirds' editor grinned in the mirror as he inserted a pair of caps his dentists gifted him just to get a rise out of their feisty friend. "Hey Shotz. Grab the other two drinks."

Chuck Shotzski turned the corner toward the wet bar. He jumped up in fright and screamed, "Ah, crap!" A pale-faced man entered the billiard room bearing a fang of a smile. "Dick, you, putz that wasn't funny!" Shotz grumped, "You know how I feel about all that creature feature stuff."

Lombardi rubbed his shoulder against the white make-up. "This stuff itches," he observed. "Chuck… I have your drink. Take it before I spill."

Shotzski grabbed his Scotch on the rocks. "Ricky, you almost gave me a heart attack." Jerry Rockford, Jack Grumblier and Rico Lombardi roared with laughter. Chuck's eyes narrowed. "What's so funny Grumbler?"

Jack puckered his lips. "My last name is French and pronounced *Grumbli-er*!"

Rico removed the fanged inserts before scolding his coworker, "Shotzski, chill out and, FYI, there are no such thing as vampires."

Chuck scowled at his boss, "Oh, so you've forgotten about Baroness Angelique Hemos or her sidekick Timothy Meise, huh?"

Infiltration of Gemela

Two bodacious women wearing light cotton linen suddenly appeared crouching inside Nub's MH-60 helicopter. They licked their full, ruby-colored lips and seductively whispered in unison, "Hey boys."

Master Sergeant O'Brien stuttered, "What the...?"

One of the ladies latched onto OB's thick, leathery neck. The harder he pushed the erotic nightmare, the harder she drained his life force. He hugged the dishwater blonde until he heard her lower back crack. Her head slumped down.

O'Brien let out a sigh of relief until her face arched back. He knew that was his blood smeared over her lips. He felt dizzy but was still cognizant enough to be amazed at the little woman's strength. She rivaled his 240-pound six-foot frame. He had just enough strength to take a few steps in the tight space toward the open air. The master sergeant and petite female crashed into the brackish waters three-hundred feet below.

Major Jaime Oeste smacked another of the rabid beauties in the jaw. The woman rubbed her cheek and remarked, "Nice punch." He jabbed her again. She thrust her fist through the major's chest and held up his body by grasping the walls of his heart muscle.

Captains Sears and Broadstein tried to tear her away. She wouldn't let go of Oeste's slowing heart. The soldiers tackled her and all four tumbled into the bayou waters.

Vamps gliding inside helicopter

Two more curvy looking females swooped into the helicopter. First Sergeant Sullivan and Captain Cline were inspired by their friends' courage. The Green Berets delivered a handful of heavy blows that would have knocked out the stoutest men.

To the men's amazement, the deadly pair of women kept rising off the helicopter's metal deck and scratching the special force operators' faces and necks to shreds.

Blood oozed from their wounds and the soldiers realized their strength was all but gone. Sully and Cliner looked at each other and nodded. The warriors then tightly clutched the ghostlike images' waists before jumping to their doom.

Rico Lombardi patted Chuck's left shoulder. "You just exaggerated your encounters, becoming delusional with mummies, headless riders, humanoids, and so on."

Shotzski tightly squeezed his cards and raised his voice, "Dick, they were all very real. You only prefer to suppress the news."

Lombardi's forehead furrowed. "What's that Shotzski?"

Shotz responded, "Ricky. It's the truth you ignoramus."

"What's with calling me Ricky or Dick so much?" Chuck grinned mischievously. Rico shook his head at his reporter and said, "Okay ladies - let's finish the match."

Grumblier dealt out the hand of spades and winked. "Karma Chuck, it is all returning to haunt you now."

Shotzski raised his finger to lecture Jack but Lombardi silenced him. The editor sassed, "Chuck, you should write a children's book about your nightly jaunts so kids will respect their parents and not wander outside after dark."

"Wait a minute Dick, you witnessed some of it but you always deny it publicly."

Shades of purple skin began to appear beneath Lombardi's white vampire make-up. "Give it a rest Shotzski, I have suffered from indigestion and ulcers. It probably has affected my imagination."

"Come on Ricky," stated Chuck, "you were right there with me in the St. Louis police station when that century old Mr. Hyde escaped from the holding cell, hand-cuffed to boot."

Lombardi fumbled with his cards and they went flying up in the air. "Shotzski, you really know how to damper one's evening. No spin zone tonight, okay."

Shotz's eyes narrowed, pointing at his editor and stated confidently, "Ricky, you even witnessed Hyde being shot three times in his back at close-range, never to be seen again."

Rico slammed his deck of cards on the table. "Why can't you just keep quiet for a change, Chuck? Is that too much to ask?"

Grumblier coughed up some of his Fuzzy Navel in hysteria.

Shotz wryly put his hands behind his head and leaned back whistling. Lombardi pointed his index finger at Chuck and roared, "I don't want to hear another word of it, Shotzski, not a pipe! I say humbug to boogeyman."

Three Navy SEALs exited Delta-one to conduct a beach reconnaissance. They barely began to fin toward shore when one of the guys felt a strange presence.

He thought he saw a man and two women hovering above. He did a double take.

The trio swept up the combat swimmers before they could fight back or dive into the bayou's depths. They began sucking the frogmen's blood in mid-air.

The RIB crew could barely make out the SEALs convulsing in terror only thirty meters from their position.

Each of the apparitions snapped their victim's neck as they finished feeding. There was no mistake about it. The crew from Delta-one just heard the crunching of vertebrae and bones. They immediately sighted-in on their strange targets.

The three phantoms let their prey drop to the watery graves. They looked up grinning and darted toward Delta-one's bow. The crew fulminated with .50 caliber and 240 machine guns hitting the undead with no lasting effects.

Four other Navy SEALs splashed out of Delta-one's aft. Two were snatched up from the water by a pair of curvy looking wraiths. The last thing the guys saw were predator-like canines chomping down on their tanned necks.

Commander Lawlur and Chief Barnum swam several feet under the surface using hand-held oxygen breathing devices. The pair went undetected as they neared the bank.

The bayou's undercurrent suddenly smashed Chief Barnum against a large boulder lying below the murky surface. The current pounded the SEAL one more time into the jagged edges, shredding his uniform.

It took the commander two attempts before he could grab his swim buddy from the clutches of the shifting undercurrent. He felt his chief gripping the hand held breathing device. He then quickly fed Barnum oxygen as he slowly buddy-towed his fellow SEAL toward a safer underwater location.

Chief Barnum weakly padded his teammate's shoulder, signaling his gratitude.

Whatever those damn things were that attacked us defied the laws of gravity, Lawlur thought, *and we'll bide our time until the hand-held breathing devices run out of oxygen.*

The chief winced in pain when the commander's hip nudged his leg.

The SEAL officer slowed down the tempo of his scissor kicks to lessen the nudges. He surmised Barnum had at least one broken bone, not to mention some gnarly scrapes. *Shit*, he thought, *I've got to stabilize chief pretty damn soon and that means going to the surface.*

"Chuck, will you leave that damn police scanner alone," Rico Lombardi complained.

Shotzski flinched. "Just a minute, Ricky. Let me put the volume up a tad."

Grumblier and Rockford shook their heads at the pair's squabbling. The editor and reporter could pass as cousins with olive-skin, hawk-shaped noses, dark heads of hair peppered with a few white stragglers, but Lombardi was built like a six-foot two-inch defensive lineman and Shotzski a wiry five-foot ten-inch boxer.

Rico graveled, "Stifle, we got cards to play."

"You know it's my shift," Chuck reminded his editor.

Lombardi raised his hands. "Shotz, what fire, medical or police frequencies are there to monitor here? Le Grande is a small town, mostly full of medium-income retirees."

Jack jutted his chin in the air and quickly added, "Ricardo, you forget there are several golf courses and pristine beaches around our town. This attracts a lot of tourists and maintains Le Grande around ten thousand people."

Chuck eyed his stacked hand like a kid in a candy store. "Rico, don't mess with *Miss Judy-Judy*. Not only does Jacky give good advice. He is also Snowbird's restaurant connoisseur and tourism expert."

Grumblier looked dumbfounded. "Chuck that was one of the nicest things you have ever said about me."

Shotzski grinned. "Enjoy it while it lasts Grumbles."

"Both of you need to zip it," Rico shook his head, "Why are you regurgitating all of this crap to me? I know what is going on. I own the paper."

Chuck put his right index finger up in the air. "Ah huh but my Kati owns fifty-one percent of Snowbirds!" he clarified.

"Well, don't forget that I am the editor to both of you clowns! Besides, Le Grande is in the most capable hands, my son, Sheriff Ricardo Lombardi Jr."

Shotz gasped, "We play cards and it is one of the first times you have completely forgotten about work."

Rico sat back and said, "There are benefits to semi-retirement and not fighting city traffic every day."

"Waterloo traffic was not all that bad except where the interstate turns into a highway with stoplights for several blocks."

Lombardi nodded. "What's worse, the Cedar Falls city council wants to replace lights with roundabouts on University."

"Trendy morons… cars will slide on the ice and snow."

Rico added, "With lots of accidents. At least, nothing really happens here in Le Grande except for your kooky stories."

Rock slapped his cards on the table and bemoaned, "Come on! I am not sure about your loony tales but all your bickering is slowing down the game."

Jack jested, "Somebody is in a foul mood and needs a refill."

Ricardo caught Chuck fidgeting with a frequency and growled, "Shotzski!"

Chuck twirled his chair around and smiled. "Okay Rico, I know what you were going to say. You don't know what is worse, my addiction to the scanner or my dealings with things that go bump in the night, eh?"

Ricardo Lombardi shook his finger at his opponent and paused. "Actually, that was pretty close," he admitted reluctantly.

"Ah huh, you just deny reality."

"What Shotzski? That the undead fly in the air and live off the blood of their victims for ages. Humbug!"

Chuck pointed at his boss. "Look who is dressed up as a vampire and I never mentioned that they fly in the air."

Waterloo's pilot loved the rush of combat. Chief Warrant Officer 4 (CW4) Doug Nubiez knew nobody would believe this. This was a new kind of adrenaline - surreal. Sure enough, there were ghostly visages of gorgeous women flying around his helicopter. These aberrations seemed to glide more than fly. From a pilot's perspective, Nubs surmised they maxed out at thirty miles per hour on the straightaways, but their ability to change directions in the air so quickly and stop on a dime baffled him even more.

Doug thought he wouldn't mind dating one if he was single, until she opened her mouth to reveal a pair of long, marble-looking incisors. Her evil red eyes had replaced a face of unmatched radiance. CW4 Nubiez accidentally swallowed part of his tobacco and gagged. He stuttered, "H-h-holy buckets… b-b-beauty is only skin deep." The stars shined brightly but the thick haze blanketed Gemela's perimeter. Nubs lifted Waterloo to avoid the fright mares and to obtain a clearer view.

LTJG Gentry sniffled as he wildly shot his pistol at the ancient Royal. The Carpathian picked up the man from a fetal position on Delta-one's aft deck and stared into his eyes. "The most cowardly Ottoman had more courage than you." Gentry lost control of his bowels. The dark Prince lifted the tall blond above his head. He then impaled the officer into the barrel's end of a mounted 240 machine gun. "I will not drink such pathetic blood."

One of the brides swept down on Delta-one's helmsman, Eliot. She twirled skyward, sipping his blood. She then let the boatswain's body drop to the deck and began to slaughter the other men aboard. Jaws and Odin were knocked overboard in the commotion. The pair swam mostly underwater toward their sister craft.

Petty Officer First Class Koni finished coupling two broken headset wires in the aft deck. "I finally can hear y'all again," stated the big Dane. He thought it odd no one responded with the usual wisecrack. The SWCC communicator stood up puzzled at the empty crew, just as a vamp snatched him in the air.

9 - DENIAL

If you know the enemy and know yourself, you need not fear the result of a hundred battles.
Sun Tzu

Operation Gemela had gone wrong in its first stages, not due to lack of training or preparation. It was supposed to be an infiltration of the abandoned resort to setup an ambush. Instead, many skilled fighters were KIA, and not at the hand of terrorists.

The remaining elite warriors were in denial of what they were fighting. They simply didn't know this unexpected threat. They were accustomed to being the predators, but had become prey.

CW4 Doug Nubiez unloaded 7.62 volleys from the helicopter's specially outfitted, dual Gatling mini-guns. He hit the ghost-like images dead-on.

The two women crashed into the outer metal walls and spiraled toward the water. Nubs smiled at that until the pair recovered and veered toward his helo.

He was becoming really edgy that no weapons could harm these hell cats. Even worse, most of his crew was probably dead. He knew the best thing he could do was to fly erratically to prevent the eerie women from flying inside.

The spirits darted inside Waterloo despite the pilot's skillful twisting and turning. Doug kept the helicopter flying steady so the men could fight inside.

Major Ferguson and Captain Chan were the last of the Green Berets aboard. Both men just witnessed their most seasoned comrades battle these mysterious looking women to no avail. They wasted no time treating them like enemies and not ladies.

Chan delivered a side-kick to one of the snarling women's jugular. Fergi grabbed the other's left wrist and smashed the hissing woman into the metal wall. The major then side-swiped her leg, followed by a hard boot blow to her temple.

Just like before, the females recovered in seconds. Fergi and Chan fought hard by punching and slashing the steely-nailed women with their combat knives, but exhaustion began to overtake them. After several minutes, the spectral wrestled the army combat operators outside into the foggy air.

Nubiez picked up speed but a voluptuous red head entered his helicopter. “Shit!” he said under breath. He could feel the terror well within him, much scarier than combat. He grabbed his switchblade knife and concealed it within the folds of his flight suit.

The ruby stared at the pilot from his side. “You’re such a treat, lover boy.”

Nubs knew he was dead meat. All their bullets didn’t harm these strange specters. One of the SWCC boats had been decimated, no one onboard. He had been the smallest center at his high school, but the meanest. He looked up glaring at her.

The voluptuous red head said, “Cat got your tongue?” Waterloo’s pilot swiped his small blade into her stomach. The ginger grimaced as the steel cut into the pit of her navel, blood oozing out.

He swerved his helo to the side, almost pushing the wrench out the open door. She floated next to him and pulled out the knife. She let out a wicked laugh and licked the blood from the blade. Her wound healed within seconds.

“What the hell are you?” growled Doug.

Her eyes sparkled eyeing his neck and she said. “I’m the butcher!”

The pilot from the other helicopter yelled into his mouthpiece," Waterloo, Waterloo talk to me!" Nubiez ignored Raven's urgent request.

The female honed in on Doug’s Adam’s apple. Waterloo hovered above for a moment as the ruby clamped her fangs on his neck.

Nubs felt weak but angled his aircraft down into an empty Delta-one boat. There was a thunderous blast followed by an orange fireball.

The remaining crewmen from the other helicopter and SWCC boat were numb. They realized many of their brothers were now dead.

A silhouette darted in front of CWO5 Raven's helicopter. He sat in his cockpit stunned. Her evil cackle could be heard above the humming rotors. The secondary explosions woke him from the icy terror that fogged his entire being.

Survival instincts kicked-in when a trio of fanged females sailed inside his helo. Mike yelled back, “Hang on!” He juked his bird, bucking a dark-haired woman out of the bay door.

SpecOps helo crashing into SWCC boat

The Green Berets inside the helicopter stabbed, wrestled and kicked. The vicious women healed up let out unnerving hisses.

Rav was starting to believe these feminine looking creatures could be vampires but he thought to himself, *No way*!

Sergeant First Class Jacobson felt long fingernails brush the sides of his neck. He instinctively back-elbowed the vamp's sternum and followed with a knife to her eye. He twisted the blade deeper into her eye socket as he slammed her into the metal deck. Her body convulsed before going limp.

The second nosferatu grabbed Major Majerus from behind. He could feel her moist tongue lick the back of his neck. She arched her head back, mouth agape ready to feast. The Green Beret stomped his boot into her toes. She screamed, letting go of his upper body. Maj side-swiped his bony forearm into her throat. She crashed to the deck, grabbing her collapsed windpipe.

SFC Jacobson pulled the vamp's body toward the side. Her red eye's shot open and she pulled his neck to her mouth. Her ivory incisors dug into his jugular and his eyes screamed in terror. Jake yanked her by the jaw and leaned back into the open air, letting gravity pull them to the watery depths below.

The second vampire's throat healed within seconds. She tackled Majerus, biting his ankles and wrists. Bleeding profusely, Maj pretzeled his lanky frame around her extremities and rolled their bodies out of the helicopter, plummeting to the water below.

The third vamp darted back inside. She flung Cantinflas and Sergeant Kramer out of the helicopter's port door. The men barely grasped the bottom of the helo's legs.

The petite nosferatu swiped her leg under a tall, burly man. Staff Sergeant Hansen's right knee buckled and he fell to his side. His forehead met the back of the pilot's chair with full force. She sprung upon his hips straddling his torso. She slowly licked at the blood oozing from the large gash above his eyebrows.

Hans awoke to a pretty woman that appeared to be kissing his forehead. He thought it was a pleasant dream until she arched back bearing a pair of fangs. He gave her a two-finger jab in the eyes. He was woozy and passed out again.

Cantinflas flipped his agile frame back inside. The former Lebanese Golden Gloves Boxer landed an upper cut to the vampire's chin. He followed with a roundhouse to her temple. It sent her tumbling out of control toward the depths. He then grabbed Sergeant Kramer's wrist and winked. "*Saddiqqi*," meaning *friend* in Arabic, "need some help?"

Kram cursed, "Pull me up ya moron!"

Cantinflas braced his leg and pulled the bruiser aboard. Kram went sliding into the helo, grasping whatever he could get his hands on.

The buxom brunette zoomed in, pulling the startled boxer outside before sinking her razor-like fangs into his neck. She darted back inside. Sergeant Kramer surprised her by butting his M-4 rifle stock hard into her mouth. The impact knocked out one of her fangs. She fell to the deck and scrambled for her incisor, placing it back into her gum socket. She wiggled her shapely hips and giggled, "I love a big boy who fights - *dem kathir*," meaning *lots of blood* in Arabic.

Rav tossed a small cross necklace toward Kramer and yelled over his shoulder, "Use that!"

10 - NOSFERATU

Chief Jaworsk touched the side of the SWCC boat. He had been holding his breath most of the way to avoid the banshees above. Gunners Mate Odin surfaced seconds behind him.

Senior Chief Joe Samson yanked his fellow chief by the collar. Thor grabbed Odin by the armpit and pulled his SWCC buddy aboard.

Chief's field uniform dripped from the silty salt water. He slumped into Delta-two's boat and ranted, "A tall man and two women ate all the men."

The senior enlisted slapped Jaws to stifle the nonsense. His pupils narrowed and he refrained from punching Samson. Joe shook his head. "You are the leading chief petty officer and one of our bravest." He commanded, "Get a grip!"

Chief growled, "Fin. I saw what I saw when I saw!"

Odin breathed heavily, "Chief's right senior. It defies all logic! It's as if they feasted on their blood. The guns and knives went through them like they we're ghosts."

Juleon Rockford winced hearing that and uttered a quick prayer to thwart this evil. He quickly picked up two green glow sticks and broke the plastic seals. He shook the sticks and duct-taped them together. "Anyone who can make a cross, do it!" he said forcefully.

Petty Officer Hugsby screamed, "Damn Thor, this is no time for religion!"

Rockford yelled, "Hugs, they're not phantoms but vampires!"

One of the frogmen mocked Thor by saying, "Oh, Nosferatu, we're scared."

CWO5 Raven roared into his mouthpiece, "Listen to him!"

A vamp swooped down on the bellowing SEAL seconds later. Fin kneeled as Rockford thrust the glowing cross above. The Boat Guy's rigged-up icon repelled the hissing vampire brides and their master.

Senior Chief Samson stuttered, looking at Jaws and Thor, "W-w-what the hell?"

Thor ignored Fin and glared at Hugs, barking at the rest of the team, "Just do it!"

Chief Jaworsk added, "Pull your heads out of your asses… It's the only thing that has worked." Grif hustled to tape two light sticks together, but a female vampire swooped down, slapping the SWCC operator's hand before he could make the holy symbol.

Kramer dropped the tiny cross. The dark-haired vampire smiled, exclaiming the word *excellent* in Arabic, "*Mumtaz*!" She then threw Kram's husky frame back against the metal walls.

Staff Sergeant Hansen saw that Sergeant Kramer had been knocked out. He crawled along the helo's deck, grabbed the crucifix and pressed it against her knee. The creature of the night let out an unnerving cry as she fell to the metal floor. Hans then placed it on the back of her neck. The holy symbol melted into the vampire's skin. Smoke arose and her burning flesh let out an acrid smell.

The staff sergeant got to his knees and barely had enough strength to roll the undead woman out of the helicopter. He began to fall with her.

Kram caught him by the waist and rolled to one side. The back of Hans' upper neck thumped against the starboard opening. Sergeant Kramer's face cringed. "Crap that had to hurt, sorry bud."

Hansen's lower extremities were still hanging limply outside the helo. Kram's left hand clenched tightly to an interior rail and his right arm held his pal's waist. He tugged but the weight was too much. Gravity was pulling Hans down toward the sea. Sergeant Kramer let out a scream as he pulled with all his might. He fell back with his buddy in tow. He took a few breaths before yelling, "Scheisse, let's get out of here warrant."

The pilot put the pedal to the metal. "We need to regroup."

Kram secured Hans to a stretcher and began dressing his wound.

CWO5 Raven circled at a much higher speed and altitude. He could barely make out the RIB below through the haze. "Delta-two this is Rav, RTB." No one responded to the encrypted call. The pilot crinkled his nose. "Just when we need the radio the most, no joy," he graveled. "Delta-two - RTB. Do you copy?"

Sergeant Kramer injected his pal with an IV. He saw an eyelid flutter and knelt down beside his fellow Green Beret.

Hans cracked a smile. "I'm still here, eh?"

Kram rolled his eyes. "Somebody up there must like ya."

The Transylvanian and his favorite two brides made a second pass, giving the boat crew little time to regroup.

Odin shook his head under Thor's .50 forward-gunner position. "The supernatural does not exist, never!" he told himself.

The undead Count grabbed a straggler by the throat. The iron grip caused hot air to expel from Petty Officer Ross' lunges. The Navy SEAL fumbled for his hip holster and barely fired two shots between Dracula's eyes. The Count flinched just for a second, letting go of his prey.

Little did Ross realize that the pizza laden with garlic, the one he ate the night before, is what kept him safe from the vampire lord. The frogman dropped twenty feet, splashing into the sea. He swam underwater toward the belly of the nearby boat.

The predator eyed the waves below, searching for his lost victim. Instead, Dracula and his two brides angled toward a trio hitting them perfectly with three-point shots at their gliding frames.

The SEALs reloaded their pistols with fresh magazines. The flying shadows seemed to toy with the skilled shooters. The frogmen precisely unloaded their last magazines at their targets.

One of the SEALs mouthed, *Crap*, as the strange looking wraiths with white fangs picked him and his comrades into the darkness.

Seconds later, one of the brides swooped down into the boat. Chief Jaworsk instantly stabbed the she-vamp with his Benchmade knife four inches into her right lung. She laughed at what should have been a mortal wound.

Ross burst to the surface, gasping for air. Senior Chief Samson pulled the SEAL aboard.

Chief Jaworsk grabbed an eight and a half-foot long wooden boat hook from the deck's starboard side. The SWCC operator swiped the bronzed boat hook into the side of the she-vamp's left skull.

Blood gushed out of her temple for a few seconds. Ravia wiped the blood with her left hand and licked it with her tongue. She crouched down ready to strike.

The chief jumped up in fright and yelled, "Crap, why don't you wenches die?" He kept shifting the walnut boat hook to block the she-vamp's advance. Jaws felt like the special operator's constant pugil stick training was paying off until her last punch broke the wooden pole in half. The blow sent the boat guy crashing on his butt with part of the wooden boat hook in his hand.

The beautiful looking nosferatu stretched her hands forward slowly closing in on her prey. She whisked her jet-black hair around her shoulders in a playful manner. Ravia then smiled revealing her unnaturally large canines.

Jaws heeded Thor's advice and fumbled looking for his cross necklace tucked underneath his military T-shirt. His fidgety right hand finally pulled out the cross his mother had given him for 9th grade communion.

Ravia shielded her face from the shiny, dangling symbol over Jaw's camouflaged uniform. The vamp's eerie hiss sounded like a cornered alley cat.

Chief Jaworsk thrust the broken wooden boat hook toward the deep crevice between her breasts. Blood spurted out of the vampire's left chest. She weakly tried pulling out the broken walnut boat hook. Jaws instinctively grabbed his machete handle fastened over his right shoulder. In one swipe, he cut off the she-vamp's head. The chief then hurled the vampire bride's body over the side.

The ancient prince looked down and shrieked, "No!" It was too late. His loyal bride, Ravia, who served him for over four-hundred years, sunk into the Louisiana Bayou, headless. She had submitted to his authority, even after he had been destroyed several times in the past four centuries when he no longer held any power over her. The Transylvanian seethed revenge for his demonic soul mate but the glowing icon kept him at bay.

Senior Chief Samson had enough as sweat poured down his face. "Rav, Return to base, RTB. Do you copy?" he asked urgently.

"Finally," The warrant officer sighed in relief. "Delta-two this is Rav. I copy RTB, out."

Hugs thrust the throttles forward. The moonlight shined on a vertical and horizontal line of camouflaged paint above his forehead.

The large grandfather clock clanged eight times. Jack Grumblier jolted up in shock at the first chime.

Chuck squinted. "Ah ha, you see, Jacky boy, all our talk scared you stiff."

Grumblier reeled his head around out of spite. "I am not frightened Chuck," he protested. His hands kept trembling and they just teased him more. "You are all a bunch of bullies!"

A few hands passed and Chuck flipped down a Big Joker. "Shotzski is coming back in style!" he said jubilantly.

Chuck and Jer slapped hands in celebration of their Spades victory. Rock then yawned, "I don't know about you guys, but it's about time for my senior siesta."

Grumblier looked at his wristwatch and added, "Yeah, it is late, almost nine o'clock."

Rico bellowed, "Jack, you are such a rebel without a cause."

Grumblier whipped back, "Actually, I have to get up by five to instruct my morning gymnastics class."

Shotzski chuckled, "Rock, maybe you can win back your bet tomorrow?"

Jerry Rockford rolled his eyes. "Hopefully because social security won't last long you moron."

Shotzski scolded Jer, "Quit playing the violin. You co-own a farm, are a semi-retired lawyer, and built a nice home on that links course."

Chuck's wife, Kati, returned from ladies' bridge night at the Lombardis a few blocks away. Mr. Whiskers Shotzski ran toward mama. The big kitty purred and rubbed against Kati's calves.

The Shotzskis rescued the feline in South Carolina while on a holiday a few years earlier. Mr. Whiskers quickly became Chuck and Kati's youngest "child."

Kati told her boss, "Ricardo. Susi Ann told me at bridge tonight that she will be late for work Monday."

Rico took in a deep breath. "Why didn't she tell me Friday?"

Kati shrugged. "Ricky, she just asked and…"

Lombardi graveled, "That Susi Ann has been a thorn in my side since we took over the paper."

Chuck hollered, "Amen to that!"

Ricardo Lombardi Sr. settled down and winked at Kati. "Susi Ann forgets the Changs don't own our paper no more."

The men then gave Kati a hug, shouted some boyish slurs at Chuck and departed.

11 - REALITY BITES

The SpecOps helicopter and Special Warfare Combatant Craft Crewmen (SWCC) boat arrived at their small and secluded base. Compound X was a few miles from the outskirts of Le Grande. It swept inland approximately three miles and was split into two sides by a small public road.

The sleepy little town of Le Grande almost became a ghost town due to two decades of strange phenomenon. The few newcomers lured by cheap property were more often than not discouraged by the shoddy upkeep of the houses and the town's ramshackle appearance. Much of the hysteria was due to the people mistaking experimental aircraft for UFOs from the late 1940s until most of the programs were transferred to Roswell, New Mexico. Military Public Affairs were forbidden to discuss the highly-classified aerospace experiments and conspiracy theories ran amok.

However, few knew Compound X was used during the Korean War to conduct experiments on super soldiers and cloaking devices. Base commanders still joked about talking ghosts that jumped from building to building, puffed cigars in the treetops, and broke into their predecessors highly fortified offices for some nips.

For the past forty years, there had been sightings of the Skunk Monster from the Florida Everglades to the swamps surrounding Slidell, Louisiana. Various accounts from reputable doctors, lawyers, boat enthusiasts, and hunters all confirmed the Skunk Monster fit the description of a seven-feet tall Bigfoot. Besides the kooks who contradicted their stories or those found out to be con men, the credible witnesses indicated the reclusive creature exhibited a skunk like odor. Many paleontologists believed it was a smaller variation of the Gigantopithecus – a nine to twelve-feet tall ape known to have inhabited Southeast Asia thousands of years ago.

The most suppressed story by the government was the Hombre del Agua. The GIs really knew nothing except that a giant fish-man was said to be quarantined on Compound X's shore side in 1958. The towering Fish-Man supposedly became a scientific project under the study of the Naval Research Lab on the remote base. That was until the aquatic beast broke loose, wreaked havoc and escaped to the southern Louisiana Bayou. The information was kept secret in some government files, never to be released to the public. Thanks to J. Edgar Hoover, any film clips, newspapers, and photos related to the aquatic specimen were destroyed and/or confiscated by the FBI. In 1999, three surviving witnesses posted a blog on their website detailing everything they knew about the Fish-Man. The three witnesses agreed the seven-feet tall Hombre del Agua resembled something close to the man-hunting alien from the movie, *Predator*, but with webbed-feet and hands. Their website was only up for two weeks before it was suspiciously shutdown.

During the 1960s, ridiculous stories of a wolf-like creature, blood suckers, and a giant of a man standing over eight-feet tall forced out much of the populace, except for the most hardy or crazy. The lack of details only fueled more Halloween like urban legends.

All these haunts we're kept hush. In the last thirty years, the population gradually increased. Realtors did their best to quell old rumors of mysterious deaths and the macabre. Newcomers mostly developed upscale retirement homes, set up shops in the renovated downtown and built a few pristine semi-private golf clubs nearby.

Three German Shepherds and four Giant Schnauzers were not hush at all. The top-notch guard dogs loudly greeted the SF helicopter and SWCC vessel with wagging tails. These sleek muscular canines sensed something wrong. Their snouts smelled battle, fatigue, blood and loss. The faithful pooches tried to console the returning band of brothers by brushing up on them and whimpering. The men petted their four-pawed friends for a few moments.

Colonel Perry Thomas stood outside the helicopter pad. He greeted CWO5 Raven by saying, "I got your numeric signal to meet." The short Special Forces officer quickly looked around before asking, "Mike. Where the hell is the other helo and boat?"

Rav growled, "Shit hit the fan, sir! Let's go inside where it's safe to talk."

The colonel nodded at one of the best helicopter pilots he knew.

The surviving operators secured whatever sensitive equipment they still had left. Staff Sergeant Hansen tired of watching his buddies clean and inventory the weapons and communications gear. He got to his feet to help.

Sergeant Kramer yelled, "Sit down ya stubborn oaf!"

Hans waved his pal off, muttering, "I'm okay," and stepped forward. His legs felt like rubber and they collapsed underneath him.

Kram dove for Hans before he smashed his cranium a third time. “Chill out ya big dumb-dumb.”

The haggard team finished up with their duties. They mustered inside the conference room with shoulders slumped and lost looks in their eyes.

The Task Unit Commander, CWO5 Raven’s face flushed red after briefing his Commanding Officer. He stated to the group, "We all trained hard this past year and are a top-notch group." Mike’s hands tensely clenched the back of his skull before stating, "The first night most of us we're wiped out by what I thought were old-wives’ tales. My grandmother used to keep me up at night with such ridiculous stories about the undead in southeastern Europe."

The survivors eyed the warrant intensely. They ranged from mid-ranking officers to lower enlisted ranks. It was not your typical chain of command, but very cohesive and effective.

Senior Chief Samson chimed in, "Always thought some of us might go to Valhalla fighting some Pablo Escobar want to be or a swine like Osama bin Laden but not evil spirits."

Raven advised them, “I know this will be a huge investigation. For now, no one mentions the word supernatural or any other related gibberish. All we know is we got ambushed and fought hand-to-hand.”

Staff Sergeant Hansen raised his hand. “Warrant, if the investigators ask how we got sabotaged hundreds of feet above sea level in a helicopter, what do we say?”

The men looked at him strangely. Hans’ speech sounded slurred, despite his lisp.

Rav eyed the group. “Tell them they won’t believe it. We won’t be lying. If they press you, just say the enemy appeared to fly in but we’re not sure how. Let’s stick to these simple explanations for now. Okay guys?”

The remaining operators concurred. Petty Officer Ross slammed his fist into the table. “Let’s have a moment of silence," he insisted.

Chief Jaworsk was the first to raise his coffee cup. "We salute you brothers." All the men toasted their mugs high, many mixed with coffee and other concoctions to help calm the nerves.

Petty Officer Rockford remained quiet. He took another sip after toasting his comrades. He just wanted to go to bed, wake up and realize this was just one hellacious nightmare. That would not occur and a good night’s sleep, well that was fanciful at best. All he could do was give his burdens to God. Saying was one thing and doing another. He ached for his fallen brothers. They sweat and bled together. Thor especially sympathized for those who had kids and wives.

Rav whistled, “Guys, I need three of you to drive Mr. Hansen to the emergency room.” All the men raised their hands. The warrant picked out Kram, Ross and Thor, stating, “Our green beanie’s pupils don’t look so good and he talks like he’s drunk.”

Hans grumbled under his breath, enough for his boss to hear.

“Staff Sergeant Hansen, I am not in the mood for your crap,” barked Raven.

Hans mockingly saluted the warrant. “Aye-aye skip.”

“I see you haven’t lost your jack ass sense of humor. The rest of you, go home and hug your families.” CWO5 Raven’s eyes narrowed before stating, “If not me, somebody will contact you regarding this mess.” Rav was terribly depressed losing his best friend of ten years, Doug Nubiez. Like it or not, the officer-in-charge still had to conduct his official duties.

Senior Chief Samson and Chief Jaworsk remained behind to aid their superior officer, colleague and friend.

Colonel Thomas walked in and graveled, "Rav, I know you wouldn't lie." The Commanding Officer then addressed the leaders inside the room, "Gents. No one will believe this! As you know, the executive officer left on emergency leave and the operations officer is on temporary assignment in Afghanistan."

Chief Jaworsk said matter of fact, "Our sister detachment is deployed. XO and OPSO won't be back for a while. Then, we are your top echelon."

"Exactly." The colonel pursed his lips before adding, "Let's be careful how we report and stay on the same page."

The four discussed how this would be a long ordeal. So far, only one helo pilot, two Green Berets, one SEAL and a handful of Boat Guys were accounted for. It was a terrible feeling, each time a loved one heard their spouse, son or boyfriend would never be coming home.

12 - EMERGENCY

Ross, Kram and Thor escorted Hans to Le Grande's emergency room. Dr. Maria Wilder arrived seconds later. The hospital didn't call her in except with a serious head trauma. She methodically examined the patient for several minutes and reviewed the results. "Mr. Hansen, I see you're in the Special Forces. Green Berets, right?"

Staff Sergeant Hansen nodded.

"Steve, don't they have a more official name?" she asked with a pleasant smile.

"Yes, mizz, but technically we awr called ODA."

Maria raised her right eyebrow. "That acronym escapes me."

"ODA standz for Operational Detachment Alpha or A-Team." He was too stubborn to admit he was hurting. Hans jumped off the table and almost fell to the floor. "Well, thankz for your time Doc, I'll be seeing ya."

Maria put up her right palm, as if to stop him. "I don't think so. For one, I have noticed your speech was off." Hansen scowled, realizing the physician had tricked him. She continued, "Steve, you also have a serious concussion and a hairline fracture in the base of your skull." Doc placed her hands on her slender hips. "Sergeant, how did you incur these injuries?"

"You wouldn't believe it." Hans attempted to wink at her. His inability to perform such a simple reflex made him nervous. He crossed his sinewy elbows in front of his chest before saying, "Let's just zay I had a couple of bad fallz, Doc."

"Okay, let me just say you're going to be a guest here for a few days, under constant medical observation, Sergeant Hansen," the doctor ordered stone-faced.

Hans insisted in a steadier tone, "It's not that bad!"

Dr. Wilder shot back with a domineering grin, "Young man, your neck needs time to heal. You also may have a brain hemorrhage. We will run another CAT-Scan in the morning."

Kram lectured his buddy, "Now Steve, don't argue with the Doc!"

Ross teased him by saying, "Make sure you eat your peas and carrots."

Hans slightly grinned. "Get out of here ya pestering ball-bags!"

Thor gave his friend a thumbs-up. "We'll come around as much as we can."

A shapely lady in a white outfit walked up to the doorway. She gave Rockford a big smile and said, "Hello, could you move please?"

"Huh?"

She winked at the Sailor. "Sir, I need to sign the patient's chart."

Thor's eyes got as big as saucers as he admired the brown-eyed mamacita. "Oh?" He nervously sidestepped out of the way and his foot, accidentally, tripped over a blood pressure machine. "Shit!"

She giggled and helped him get back on his feet. "Are you okay?"

JT Rockford laughed at his clumsiness, "Yes and please excuse my French."

The nurse was attracted to the young man's bright blue eyes, smile, and muscular torso, but more importantly, she was impressed by his manners. She grinned and extended her hand. "Hello, my name is Lise Alegría."

The SWCC operator took her hand and almost smiled, "Juleon Rockford." Then, he remembered the ambush hours before and became despondent.

Petty Officer Ross said matter of fact, "Just call him *Thor*!"

Thor mumbled to the nurse, "Sorry. It's been a tough day."

Lise asked, "You'll be back soon..." she gestured with her eyes toward Hans, "to see your friend?"

Rockford nodded. Nurse Alegría's eyes lit up. The guys all chuckled at their love dance. Thor's mind kept spinning around the attack. He froze, staring at the floor, thinking of Sully.

First Sergeant Sullivan hailed from Petty Officer Rockford's hometown of Cedar Falls, Iowa, as did Staff Sergeant Hansen. He vividly remembered playing on the Tigers' golf team with them under coach Pat Mitchell. Besides hitting the links, Thor bowled, fished, played cards and skied with Hans and Sully.

The SWCC operator thought he missed his Cedar Falls High School pals until he stepped into Compound X. Hansen and Sullivan enjoyed the fringe bennies of being part of the training cadre and all the gloves came off during the three-month Combat Entry Course. The pair often taunted Rockford on long runs over their bullhorn with the line: *It a small world after all that one of our worst golfers had to show up to Compound X's grueling combat course just to fail!*

After being stationed together in the southern Gulf - Sully, Hans and Thor forged just as strong ties with their fellow warriors. It stung like hell losing so many patriotic and quiet professionals in what seemed like a literal nightmare, but especially a close one from his hometown.

Thor had a flashback of all the card nights when Sully would have temper tantrums, fighting to play poker over spades or hearts. But First Sergeant John "Spaulding" Sullivan was gone, because of *THOSE BASTARDS - THE UNDEAD!* Rockford thought he might have screamed the four words out loud. Unsure of himself, he glanced up at the pretty nurse and asked, "Did I just say something?"

"No." Lise softly smiled and told him in a reassuring voice, "I will pray for you and your friends."

"Thanks... we can use it." Thor thought, *A Godly woman, that's nice.*

Nurse Alegría departed the room to finish her rounds. She knew something was up. Lise had conducted the initial tests on Staff Sergeant Hansen before Dr. Wilder got to the hospital. The patient didn't divulge much information but he cussed a few times under his breath about half of his unit being killed.

Kram jabbed Thor in the chest. "It's about time that choir boy finds a girlfriend."

Ross bellowed at his pal, "Dude, get off the tip."

Hans weekly smiled at their jesting.

Thor faked a grin. He felt sick to his stomach that he had just been flirting with the olive-skinned beauty rather than remembering his slain team mates. A tear fell from his eye.

Staff Sergeant Hansen nodded at Petty Officer Rockford and stated, "Hang in their bra." Hans was to cool to show any emotions. And he sure as hell was not going to break down in front of the lads, even if he felt like it. Ross and Kram gave Steve one more roast before departing. It was their way to cope with the despair.

Nurse Alegría returned to Staff Sergeant Hansen 's room to dim the lights. He raged inside and was still in denial of the terror that massacred much of his friends. Steve politely asked, "Miss, could you please grab me the remote over there on that dresser?"

"Here you go," the nurse replied. "Do you need the covers from the foot of your bed to get some sleep... Mr. Hansen?"

Steve's neck snapped up after hearing his last name rendered so politely and in a soothing tone. He felt a spasm in his neck from the sudden movement and let out a low groan, "Oh no, but thank you," he insisted, "I'll be up for hours watching a game or two." After surfing the sports channels with no hockey or football in sight, the Green Beret began to nod off.

Rav dialed out from the office's secure phone. "Nastea, I have some terrible news. I must warn you; I wouldn't have believed what I am about to tell you, except I was there."

Nastea patiently listened. He questioned what CWO5 Raven really saw but knew the helo pilot was a straight-shooter. He then gave Rav some advice before they hung up.

Senior Chief Samson put his palms together and said, "At least we can trust Azúcar and Nastea. They both know we are on the level."

Colonel Thomas shook his head. "We are going to need them. Either way, this investigation will never make any sense." Compound X's Commanding Officer then contacted the proper authorities to start an official probe and get the ball rolling for a recovery effort ASAP.

Chief Jaworsk curled his lips and insisted, "Colonel, the recovery operation must be during the hours of sunlight. Hopefully some of the men survived!"

Thirty minutes later, one of the authorities called back. General Todd ordered, "Colonel, your men are now on lock-down. They are to go nowhere."

"Copy that," replied Colonel Thomas.

The general added, "You will not talk with your men without our consent."

Rav said, "With all due respect sir, isn't that a bit severe?"

The general shot back, "Chief Warrant Officer Raven. You informed us that 32 of your 44 men are either KIA or MIA. I believe First Sergeant Sullivan was on your roster."

"He was."

General Todd continued, "If you weren't aware, the first sergeant was a grandson to a World War II hero, one of the *Fighting Sullivan Brothers* who perished during the sinking of the USS Juneau at the Naval Battle of Guadalcanal in November 1942. Is Sullivan still alive?"

CWO5 Raven paused before responding, "Most likely not. Sully was on the helicopter that went down."

General Todd shouted, "My God man, this is an emergency. The press will have a field day with this."

He let out a heavy sigh. "Sir. I know First Sergeant Sullivan was proud to serve his country and was one of our best. Hopefully, he survived..."

The general cut the warrant off and growled, "Hopefully is all you can say? To make matters worse, you can't even tell me what exactly ambushed your elite group or where the hell your officer-in-charge is."

Michael Raven took in a deep breath, "Commander Lawlur may have survived, along with a few of our men. It is imperative that we conduct a reconnaissance!"

The superior officer replied, "I have never taken your operation as a clown show, but don't push it. Lock-down commences now. No more objections!"

Rav's knuckles turned white as he gripped the phone. "Yes sir!" conceded the warrant reluctantly.

The general flatly said, "Colonel Thomas."

"Yes sir."

"E-mail us the roster of your men's personal information so we can make appropriate arrangements. We will need Chief Warrant Officer Raven and, at least, two more survivors to accompany the recovery crew tomorrow morning."

Colonel Thomas glared at the scar on his wrist before he forcefully said, "General, we wouldn't want it any other way!"

"Make sure your team is ready to fly in the rescue helo tomorrow at 0700 hours from your compound."

Rav chimed-in, "Roger that sir! It will be done only during the day, correct?"

"For now, that is standard operating procedures." The general's interests were piqued and inquired, "Why do you ask?"

Mike paused thinking what might sound a bit logical before saying, "Well, general, the former resort and fruit plantation, known as Gemela, mists up quite a bit after the sun goes down. There will be poor visibility and the recovery helos could crash into the two peaks or trees. My recommendation would be to conduct a reconnaissance during the day."

"Muster at 0700 sharp!" General Todd stated crisply before the line went dead.

Colonel Thomas eyed his three warriors knowingly. "You got your orders." Perry winced before adding, "Sometimes in NAM, we had to improvise and NOT get approval for every move."

The trio stood and Rav replied, "Roger that, sir."

"You might want to be open to this spooky shit." The Commanding Officer of Compound X reluctantly admitted, "I once ran into a shape-shifter in Vietnam. A sassy-assed US Army Ranger and, of all people - a damn Gook saved my life."

The men looked at their no non-sense commanding officer with disbelief.

"It's true… See this scar on my wrist?" The trio nodded. He growled, "I got it while fighting off that damn soul sucker thing."

Jaws, Rav and Fin gazed around the room uncomfortably, not making eye contact with their commanding officer.

Colonel Thomas pointed at his men. "If what you told me is accurate, then don't be giving me those looks." Perry pounded his fist on top of the desk. "I want solutions. Crush whatever the hell this is... Sometimes that means not informing the brass with all the details!"

Raven whispered to Jaworsk and Samson after they left the office, "The colonel just told us to keep him out of the loop." He added, "This makes it easier for him to cover down while we take care of business."

13 - SHADOWS FROM THE PAST

Nurse Alegría was making her rounds when she heard snoring from the sergeant's hospital room. She brought Han's blanket up to his chest, turned down the television's volume and shut his door before patrolling the rest of her wing. Lise whispered, "Rest well."

As the nurse departed, she discovered a black cell phone lying on the floor inside of Han's door. She checked the profile and it read *Thor*. She decided not to disturb the patient. Instead, she placed the cellular device in her left breast pocket. She knew Thor would eventually call to see if anyone had it or try tracing its last location. Lise Alegría had a good feeling about Juleon Thor Rockford and hummed out loud as she continued her duties.

The metallic blue Ford Mustang sped off from the military compound. Petty Officer Rockford was at the wheel, deep in thought - *You live by the sword, you die by the sword.* He recalled Sun Tzu emphasizing the importance to know one's enemy. Thor had been confident in all the men's wrestling, shooting and mixed batch of street fighting skills. But earlier, just after sunset, some of the toughest and ablest grapplers were dead. None of them had a clue to what they had been up against.

Rockford looked into his rearview mirror talking to himself, "We all die." His lips pursed together, recalling the times he got pushed around as a small kid. He didn't like it and learned how to fight back before giving up his lunch money, Brussels sprouts or a Hostess Ding Dong in the elementary. After that he was convinced kind words helped but giving bullies nose bleeds made them think twice before pushing around the runt.

The "bullies" his buddies had battled with earlier and lost their lives to had been immune to their bullets and indifferent to their punches. He didn't even want to think those things could exist.

Thor contemplated about forces beyond the scope of nature. At least, the natural world he was aware of and had lived in his whole life. He believed in prayer and spiritual warfare, essentially, the invisible fight between good and evil spirits. For the first time in his life, he wondered if his mother, Betty, might have told him the truth years back about the undead.

The supernatural battle just hours before, also made Thor ponder over his four-month stay in Monterrey, Mexico, as a college exchange student:

***

In 1997, the kind-hearted Luna family opened up their wonderful hacienda to him. He especially enjoyed the flirtatious Spanish tutorials from their gorgeous, college-aged daughters, except that one night.

It was in the Luna's guest quarters, above their main kitchen that Thor had encountered a shadow bearing the exterior silhouette of a man. The dark figure was jet black and devoid of any facial features.

Rockford awoke from a heavy slumber to discover a phantom floating over his bed as if it was staring at him. He was a heavy sleeper and only woke up if his bladder was full or an alarm was beeping. That shadow hovered inches from his mouth and it felt like the thing was sucking the life force out of him.

He remembered pinching himself and looking around to make sure he was not imagining the thing for a shadow from a tree or piece of furniture. The dark specter was very real indeed as Thor's heart pounded and his lungs seemed to cave-in.

Rockford barely had enough strength to rebuke the shade *en el nombre de Cristo Jesús*. The pitch-black image quickly darted over to the open kitchenette in under a second.

They both had a staring duel, though the shade exhibited no eyes. This was more than a game for Thor who was not relying on his own power. He steadily prayed for protection even after the floating shadow vanished. He never knew when he passed out from sheer exhaustion that dreadful night.

Rockford recalled another instance in Monterrey. *La casa* had a strange history or resident. And every event occurred after dark.

One of the Luna's sons, Choi, reported that his childhood friend once saw an evil looking man suddenly appear. Both young lads were passing by the dining room in the outer court. His friend stopped in total terror. His eyes were frozen, staring inside toward the large, antique oak table.

Choi didn't see the spectral clenching a knife and fork with a creepy grin but his childhood amigo did. His buddy tried to scream but stood there in abject fear, unable to move.

Choi looked around, seeing nothing. He laughed, thinking his chum was playing a trick on him. When his pal passed out on the tile floor, he knew something wasn't right and shouted for his mom's help.

Señorita Luna calmed the boy down, caressing him in her arms with a cool wet towel. The kid eventually was able to speak, but still visibly shaken. He told Choi and his mother that he saw a gaunt looking man with long, white-disheveled hair sitting at their dining table.

The thing's face was so full of hatred. It stood and inched closer to the child. The apparition motioned with the utensils as if he wanted to slash and tear the boy apart. The kid immediately stopped visiting the Luna's hacienda for several years. And when he did visit, he was an adult and only during the day.

A servant once informed Thor that someone close to the Luna household dabbled with Tarot Cards and *brujería blanca - white witchcraft.* The individual was known to be very superstitious and wanted to protect the family. Who wouldn't? Especially, after so many haunting ordeals occurred inside the expansive grounds. The occult was that person's business, but Rockford believed such practices gave dominion to the dark side or attracted them.

The next college exchange student to reside at the hacienda told Thor he saw a similar dark figure, as well. But he saw the strange image at least six times.

They ran into each other during the summer semester at the University of Northern Iowa's weight room. Their conversation awkwardly veered toward both of their chilling ordeals in Monterrey. The other exchange student told Thor that he spoke with the Mexican father about the shadow. The generous family put up one of their faithful workers to help him overcome an illness. Unfortunately, the man passed away in the guest quarters.

Whether it was a ghost or some type of evil force, Thor wasn't sure. He knew firsthand that the jet-black specter didn't like the name of *Jesus Cristo.* The matter confirmed that a handful of people definitely experienced some strange phenomenon at the Mexican estate.

Rockford had several other dealings with the supernatural growing up. He felt like he was a magnet to the bizarre. Many of his experiences dealt with dark or evil forces. However, one was a positive, but frightening one. Possibly a brush with death or severe beating.

Thor and a Christian brother were on liberty in Greece between Operations Desert Shield and Storm. They spent the morning and early afternoon visiting the spectacular sites of the Acropolis, Parthenon, rebuilt Olympic stadium and Temple of Hephaestus. No matter how fascinating the history, their young feet were tired and wanted to chill for a few hours.

The men decided to catch a movie they never heard of, *Home Alone*. From beginning to end of the classic film, they especially enjoyed the Athenian's laughter and roars after reading the sub-titles. As the Sailors exited the theater, they remarked to each other how they hadn't laughed like that in years.

Comedy quickly took a turn toward tragedy. A crowd was burning a hanging effigy of the American president in a park. Rockford snapped his head around, hearing a famous reporter, Amina Kaburi, exclaim, "Mout Amrika." He knew that meant *death to America* in Arabic. She nodded and a bearded man lifted up a sign, motioning for the crowd to read the Greek lettering. Her cameraman began to record as the protestors loudly chanted, "Thánato stin Amerikí." A triumphant grin changed to a surprised look before she said, "It appears many Greeks don't like America. Amina Kaburi reporting from Athens for Sahte News."

A protestor spotted the pair and yelled, "Amerikanó."

Thor said, "Cálmate ya gente. Todo está bien." Hearing Spanish, threw off the agitators. The Americans calmly exited the area before the swarming began. The duo dodged most of the enraged mob with some bruises and torn threads. They quickly rounded a corner, ducking inside a small shop.

The pair gasped, seeing a figure tower over them. The six-feet eight-inch tall man said matter of fact, "You must leave. Follow me!" He then guided them a few blocks to safety. It was as if the rioters were terrified of the gigantic outsider or simply didn't see them sheltered in the shadow of his influence. Thor was fairly certain they were in the presence of an angel.

Thor then recollected the time he and Lindy may have met a fallen angel. A middle-aged fellow sat down beside him and his high school chum at a downtown Cedar Fall's pub. He and Lindy had never met the olive-skinned intruder with a slightly paunchy build and pointy nose, but he knew the name, *Juleon Thor Rockford*.

This stranger then recounted some highlights of Thor's life. At first, he didn't give the man much credit. What the peculiar fellow said was nothing outlandish, but he knew way too many details about JT Rockford.

Thor began to think this guy might have a dossier on him. He quickly reminded himself, *Get real! You're just a college student from Iowa who served in the military as an average linguist.*

Then the outsider mockingly said, "I know what you believe... You believe in Jesus."

That got Rockford's attention. For several seconds, Thor remained quiet, but did acknowledge his faith in God.

Lindy said under his breath, "This shadowy bastard is giving me the willies."

Thor ignored his ole pal, eyeing the stranger stone-cold. The man let out an eerie chuckle, staring down Rockford.

Lindy was so spooked that he picked up Thor by the collar to his towering six-foot five-inch frame and demanded, "Let's get the hell out of here!"

His friend's actions were enough of a distraction that the enigmatic man's last words were a blur to them both. But it was that sinister grin that was so unnerving.

As Lindy and Rockford walked out, the mysterious figure instantly vanished before their very eyes. And to this day, Thor's pal refuses to talk about it.

Thor still couldn't shake off what he and his comrades had encountered shortly after dusk - VAMPIRES! Something, he always considered as pulp-fiction nonsense.

Rockford needed to talk with someone about this. His missionary friend was the only person he could confide in about such matters, but the Godly man had recently passed away. Then, Thor remembered his dad's best friend, Chuck Shotzski. The retired cop probably saved his hide at least once.

14 - OLD TIMERS

February 15, 2005

Jerry Rockford took in the majestic links overlooking the US gulf shores. After Shotzski missed his ten-foot par putt, Rock downed his five-footer.

"Damn Norwegian!" Jer grinned. Chuck Shotzski grudgingly handed over a dollar to his pal on the eighteenth green.

"Your bogey golf was pretty good."

The retired cop frowned. "Rock, you only beat me by one-stroke." He quickly raised his index finger and added, "Don't get too cocky - I usually beat you."

"Sometimes Shotz. Besides, you're younger."

"Blah, blah. Get inside. We have a long drive before you pack. Within minutes, he pulled his Hawkeyes' cart in the garage.

An hour later, Jer hauled his luggage outside. He whisked tears from his olive-skinned cheeks. "I sure miss my Betty Boop."

Shotzski gave Rockford a bear hug before handing him his golf bag. "Losing a good woman is hard."

"Beatriz was my Castilian beauty queen, a faithful wife, a damn good kisser and companion, and a great cook."

"That's right. Didn't you meet her in Spain when you did your stint in the Navy?"

"Yep. Rota, Spain was a great duty station for a Sailor." Rock seemed to peer in the past before saying, "I met Beatriz one month into my two-year tour. We danced for almost four decades."

"You're a blessed man."

"Until that damn breast cancer got her." He sighed. "We would have been married thirty-eight years last week."

"Thanks for reminding me. It's our anniversary tomorrow."

Jerry swatted at Shotz. "Shame on you, ya putz. You pester me all the time for being forgetful."

He smirked. "Didn't Betty call it part-timers?"

He pointed at his old chum. "You don't have to rub it in."

"Kati would have strung me up if I forgot our big date."

Jerry chuckled before shaking his head at the trademark shades resting on the tip of Shotzski's nose. "I think your boss is right. The only fashion you know is the fancy sunglasses perched on your beak and that bird feeder on top of your fat skull." He shrugged. "Plus, the nice set of golf clubs you own."

"Rock, what's wrong with my straw golf hat?"

He shot Chuck a dead-serious look and stated, “Nothing, it is quite fashionable. The problem is what’s underneath!”

His eyes narrowed. “That’s right. I just bought three pairs of top name shades for the price of one at the nearby outlet. As for nabbing new clubs,” Shotzski said with a wink, “a golfer normally gets the best bargains from last year’s models.”

He eyed Shotz’s clothing. “When will you ever stop sporting that silly old suit and brown sneakers? They definitely don't match your trendy golf hat or shades.”

He looked at Rock as if he didn’t understand. “I like my duds - retro! Besides, they are cheap and comfortable.”

He lectured, “Chuck. W.C. Fields had more fashion than you. Well, at least Kati makes you dry clean now.”

“Wives have that affect,” he said, “and it’s a good thing.”

“You got that right, but it’s so lonely without Betty.”

“I hear you, Jer.” He added, “Cheer up, you’re tall and handsome. Even with your small gut, some fine lady will nab you.”

“Maybe we’ll come visit you and Kati?”

He grinned deviously. “Now Mr. Rockford, when you visit us, there will be no horrific base booming from your car.”

“No rap crap, eh Shotz?”

“The association comes down hard on loud DJs like you.”

“Oh yeah Chuck, I am crapping with the likes of Iced-Coffee, Snoop Kitty, and that M&M candy screwball.” Rock then snapped his fingers. “I forgot to mention. You should look up my son, Thor. He’s stationed not far from here.”

“I haven’t seen little Thor in years."

Jerry let out a hearty laugh, "My kid isn’t so little these days. He's quite the gym nerd."

Shotz slowly stroked his goatee before inquiring, "Hey, didn’t Betty normally call him, Juleon?”

“Yes. Betty honored her Castilian father by giving his first grandchild his first name. However, the elementary kids often teased our son, calling him Jules or Julie.” Jer chuckled, “He got in a lot of scraps. I told him to not get so upset when his classmates taunted him or they’d keep egging him on. But if the pestering turned ugly, I encouraged my tiger to hit the biggest bullies square on the puss. The taunts simmered down and that’s when Betty decided he would go by his given name, Thor.”

He appeared puzzled. “Don’t you mean middle?”

He said after a pause, "Betty and I probably never told you this because he will always be our son, but Thor showed up on our door step in a little basket on Thanksgiving, 1971."

Chuck cocked his head. "He was left out in the cold?"

"No… we found little JT in our three-season front porch." He added, "Couldn't make out the car. It sped off too fast."

"Anything else?"

"Just a note. His biological mother wrote that she had watched us for a few months and knew we had good hearts. A few years ago, we found out JT's real birthdate was October 31, 1970."

Shotz cackled, "An All Hallows' Eve."

"Enough with your spooky non-sense. The woman mentioned she gave birth to him naturally which made it impossible for us to trace any babies born that day. Fortunately, my associates helped us adopt him. The lady didn't sign the card but said her baby boy waved his arms like a little Viking, so she named him *Thor*. She just pleaded we would take him in and love him as our own."

"I always wondered since you and Betty were both olive-skinned brunettes."

"Genes are funny. My brother and I look alike, but he has lighter hair and skin. Chuck nodded. Jerry proudly stated, "I can say one thing, our little rascal has never given us a dull moment."

Shotz chuckled, "I remember when he got stuck in that culvert and you dragged him out."

Rock grinned. "Yep and, after that I never had to pull him out of another. We golfed twice last week before he got alerted for some kind of mission. His command won't let me know when he is supposed to return." He sighed. "And that little shit hasn't answered my calls."

He shrugged. "Typical military, it holds a tight fist with operational security."

"Yeah, al-Qaeda and similar terrorists gauge our will to fight. Thor is hard to get a hold of but, at least, my little tiger still calls me when he can and sends me cards. He has become very private, especially, after those devils hijacked those planes on 9/11."

"Jerry, a better word in Arabic to describe people associated with al-Qaeda is *Mufsidoon* which means evil doers condemned by the Koran."

"You reporter types have all the answers."

"Not really, however, the war of words is often more effective than just physical war."

"Is that some Psychological Warfare jargon?"

"Nah, I had an interview with a Muslim cleric in 2002. He informed me of a few more choice words to describe the perverse actions committed by al-Qaeda and its fellow haters."

"Well, I think we all could learn to be more united and learn from World War Two's generation." Jerry clenched his fists. "Terrorists don't respect pushovers and if we don't hunt 'em down those bastards will only keep attacking us."

Chuck's face flushed red. "I lost a reporter colleague at the World Trade Center and a Master Chief buddy at the Pentagon."

He got sick thinking of the bloody pigs and said, "My poor nephew's fiancé was on one of those flights."

"Jer, another Arabic word to describe the terrorists' actions is *Hirabah* which means an Allah-prohibited war against society."

"Too many Americans and Europeans have their heads up their asses." He fumed, "These *irhabists* mean what they say!"

"I wished more people saw it that way."

Rock changed gears to change the damper mood. "Well… my Thor is not a babbler like you."

"Seriously. Your kids are like you, social butterflies."

"You got that right. Anyhow, he'd make a great extra for golf or cards when you, duffers are short a player."

"JT wouldn't mind hanging out with some ole farts?"

"Nope. Thor's pretty mellow now." Jer laughed, "I remember the time many years ago when his jittery pals called me for some assistance. Randy and Steve woke me while I was dozing off to a Johnny Carson rerun. So, I drove down to Washington Park. My little monkey was passed out on top of a batting cage, about twenty-five feet in the air. At least those teeny boppers didn't drink and drive. For that, I took it easy on them."

Chuck grinned. "What did you do?"

"His chums got him down and I drove them to the house. Betty buttered the lads up with brownies while I got parental approval for some remedial training." He snickered, "I hosed the drunkards down with cold water. My kid got the bonus package with a thirty second bath in a large trough full of ice."

Chuck tried to one-up him by saying, "Oh yeah, my Grandma Shotzski showered me down and made me sleep in the garage the one time I came home liquored up." His eyes widened a little. "It was thirty-three degrees that night."

"You didn't hear the last of it. Betty promptly provided three sleeping bags, worn out pink t-shirts and girly short-shorts. The drunks got to camp out in our garage before I woke them up at 0500 for calisthenics and a long public run. That was the price for waking me up. Oh how, my sweetie loved hearing that story."

He sighed. "You didn't make the boys publicly PT in pink?"

"Oh yeah! Betty even took photos to keep them in check. Blackmail is not always a bad thing. Nobody could say I took it easy on my son when he was out of line." Jer grinned crookedly. "And the lads never pulled any drunken stunts like that again."

Shotzski bellowed as he shut his car's trunk, "Rock you have another nickname - the Disciplinator!" He then looked at his watch and said, "Hey, we better get you to the airport."

Ricardo Lombardi Sr. mashed in a number and barked, "Shotzski, even for a part-time reporter, you are still a half-hour late. Why have you been ignoring my messages?"

"Didn't notice."

"That's a bunch of baloney. A unit from the nearby base was supposedly ambushed last night, somewhere in the southeast section of St. Bernard Parrish."

"You don't say? That's in the heap of the Louisiana Bayou."

Lombardi sighed. "Why Chuck, it's refreshing to see you know your geography. Go sniff around the hospital's morgue!"

"I'm kind of busy."

Rico Lombardi blasted back, "Shotzski, stop stalling."

He protested, "I really am on my way to drop off Rock at the airport. What about Jacky boy? He could pay a visit to the cooler."

He eyed Grumblier. Jack gave his boss a nervous smile. The editor walked inside his glassed cubicle and said, "Chuck, you've known Grumblier ever since he was a reporter up in Iowa when we were on the force. He can't stomach blood and bodies."

"Yes sir!"

"And, Shotz, don't read too much into their deaths."

"Why Rico, whatever do you mean?"

Chuck slapped his pal's back inside the airport. "Hey Jer, what does IOWA stand for?" Jerry looked at him wearily. Shotz then waved his fingers in the air as if spelling out the acronym and said, "Idiots-Out-Wandering-Around."

"Hey, if you ain't a Hawkeye, you ain't shit."

He mockingly bowed as Rock headed for his gate. "I thought you were going to use that overused cliché: *Is this Heaven? No, it is Iowa.*"

"Traitor," Jer said with a grin, "you of all people come from such a heavenly place."

"Indeed. Well, all hail to the people from the great corn, soybean, and pork state."

Jer yelled over his shoulder, "Ya forgot Iowa beef!"

Shotz loved giving his pal shit. He would miss Jer Bear but it was time to get some work done.

Ricardo Lombardi Sr. buzzed the number. "What did you find out Chuck?" he asked in a rather urgent tone.

"Well, I ran into your son at the hospital. The good sheriff informed me the military shipped the bodies to DC. Their deaths occurred in a deserted resort over forty miles southeast of New Orleans. Needless to say, that's outside Junior's jurisdiction. The survivors cannot be interviewed."

"Shotz, git 'er done!"

He looked at his cell phone as if he were in the Twilight Zone. "Rico Suave, retirement or NASCAR is making you batty. What did you just say?"

"Write the story."

"Ricky, do you want me to fly to DC and get the scoop?"

Lombardi growled like a bear, "Not on our budget."

Chuck pleaded, "Come on, our Judy-Judy column and sports section brings in plenty of income."

He lectured, "Our little paper stays in business because we follow a basic law of economics: *Never spend on what you don't need.* You should know that being the biggest tight-ass, Shotzski. Besides, we are not solving the crime of the century, so stifle!"

He laughed, "Now that is more like my grumpy editor. Dick, you were scaring me for a sec. Ciao!"

15 - FIRST DATE

An e-mail transcript was handed to Presidente Chavo Calles after his February 18th morning brief. The note read:

Querida,

No puedo ir a vacacion. Estoy muy enferma. Otoño mejor.

Besos - Rubia

The gist of the note translated: I can't go on vacation. I'm very sick. Fall's better. It was code for: *Cancel the ambush and try again in the fall.*

President Calles immediately pulled the plug on the mission to attack the Americans. Though disappointed with the news, Chavo could always rely on his seductive, red-headed spymaster.

February 21, 2005

Nurse Alegria had been carrying someone's misplaced cell phone for a week. She was surprised the owner had not called back. Feeling like a snoop but not knowing what else to do, Lise searched the names in the contact list. One stood out and she pressed the name *Kram.*

After several rings a husky voice answered, "Hello."

"Hi… Mr. Kram?"

He asked suspiciously, "Whose speaking?"

"My name's Lise Alegria."

The staff sergeant thought he recognized her voice. "What do you need miss?"

"You know a Thor Rockford."

"Maybe."

"Well," the RN explained, "Thor left his phone at the hospital and I have it."

"Hey," Kram sassed, "you're that pretty nurse he liked."

"Oh, did he? … I mean yes, that must be me."

Kramer chuckled, "You know you are… Would you be available to meet Thor tonight?"

"Is this too much of a problem?"

"Not at all," the staff sergeant said with a laugh. "Thor should have the decency to meet you."

Lise cautiously said, “This is about a phone.”

“Is it?” Kram asked in a jovial manner. “I saw how he looked at you and you him.” The nurse remained silent. “Do you want to meet him?”

“Yes… I mean to drop off his phone.”

“Tell you what,” Kramer said in an easy-going manner, “How about meeting Choir Boy at Ma & Pa’s Café?”

“What time?”

“Six p.m. sound okay?”

Lise paused before saying, “Yes, I’ll be there and thank you, Mr. Kram.”

He replied with a gentle laugh, “No worries.”

The special forces commando found his pal reading a Tom Clancy novel under his porch. “Hey Thordog!”

The SWCC operator looked up and smiled. "Nice to see you, Kram." The staff sergeant clasped hands with Rockford that transitioned into a strong bear hug. "Hey... I thought we weren't supposed to meet?"

Kramer spit out some of his dip, "Don't really give a shit! You want your damn cell phone back?"

"Of course!” He looked at his buddy perplexed. “Do you know who has it?"

Kram’s eyes sparkled. "That nurse."

"Who?"

"Lise."

Thor tried to not sound interested. "Oh … maybe I’ll just buy another phone."

Kramer thumped Rockford in the chest. "Bullshit!" He ripped a sheet of paper from his notebook and crammed it in his pal's breast pocket. “Here's the coordinates.”

"You can't tell me what to do."

"You can ignore me," replied Kram, “but I’ve got a case of beer and a black eye says you won’t regret it.

Thor folded his arms across his forty-four-inch chest and squinted. “Whose black eye are we talking about here?”

"Look dumbass," the staff sergeant spat, “I’ll throw in a split lip and a loose tooth if you don’t go meet the señorita.”

Put at ease by the commando's exaggerated bravado, Thor dropped his hands to his sides and laughed. “You and who’s Green Beenie?”

"Alls I'm saying," Kram growled, "is pull your head out of your ass and get moving."

The cafe was busy when the young man walked in. Thor immediately locked eyes on the gorgeous brunette. She was dressed in a summer dress with tropical colored flower designs, complementing her dark brown skin and shiny black hair. Everything about her was stunning and, as he moved in her direction, his foot hooked the leg of a barstool.

She looked up at the commotion.

"Crap," the SWCC operator said in low voice. Luckily, the barstool had been unoccupied and he caught it before it had been spun to the ground. Recovering as best he could, he pivoted back to face her with what he thought was a suave grin on his blushing face. "My apologies, Ms. Alegria."

"I've heard worse but that was a nice catch," she replied casually, putting down her copy of Our Daily Bread.

"Thanks. I'm usually not this clumsy."

She raised an eyebrow. "This is like the first time we met."

"Touché!" he replied extending his hand.

"No handshakes here," she stated rising to her feet, "I'm Latina, we give hugs."

The embrace felt good. *What a lady!*

She thought, *He's so handsome and a gentleman.*

"Those are some nice devotionals."

"They help keep me grounded. I get them at church."

"I'm looking for a place to worship."

"Come with me sometime. It's non-denominational and I think you'd like it." He nodded. She added, "I really like our weekly Bible studies. We meet up with Catholics, Lutherans and Baptists to name a few."

"Sounds pretty cool."

"God is good."

"All the time."

Her smile put him at ease. He wasted no time asking, "Can I treat you to a coffee?"

"This girl can't turn down a soy latte." She added with a grin, "Decaf por favor."

He chuckled, "De nada."

She asked surprised, "Hablas español?"

"Claro!"

"Qué bueno!" Lise glanced outside noticing it was a cool night and the stars were out. "How about we meet at the fire pit."

Rockford returned with two lattes and sat across from her. The pair chatted for several hours. They quickly discovered they shared so many interests that it was spooky. They loved old classic movies, walks on the beach, sports, and most importantly, the Lord. She was structured and he spur of the moment, were their only big differences.

"I'm having such a good time," Lise said suddenly noticing the hour, "but my shift is early."

"Understand." He wanted to say more but the shy bug bit him.

She sat back down and, after staring dreamily into his eyes said, "Now, I've got something you want … don't I?"

The Boat Guy nodded hypnotically with razor edged intensity.

The nurse reached into her purse. He held his breath. She pulled out his cell phone and placed it on the table.

Thor laughed at the release of tension this simple act inspired. "Oh yeah," he said, "I'd completely forgotten the reason I'd come here."

"Me too," she chuckled. "We should do this again when the stakes aren't a misplaced cell phone."

He nodded. "Thank you, Lise."

She liked hearing him say her name. "Not a problem but please don't lose it this time."

He liked hearing her soothing voice.

The shift nurse came out in her and advised, "Do me a favor and lock your phone with a security code."

Rockford gave her a warm hug as they got up to leave. "Nice tip."

"By the way," Lise giggled, "I hope you don't mind, but I put my name and number in your contact list. Don't be a stranger!"

16 - SHADED GROVE

Late March 2005

A worn-down sign in the front of the circular driveway bore the title *SHADED GROVE.* The limbs from several oak trees bent so low that smaller tractors and trucks could barely pass through the estate's dirt road.

A stocky figure took a sip of water. It had been a long day after surveying the plantation's vast orchards and grounds. He noticed birds settling down as the sun set below the tree lines. The man got into his truck and drove to the front entrance.

A deer skirted along the road, gingerly feeding on the lush terrain. He pulled out his laptop and typed in estimates for the project. Forty-five minutes later, he caught lights bobbing up and down on the road ahead of him. The landscaper flashed his truck's headlights at the vehicle approaching the plantation's gate.

The broad SUV flicked its lights in return before coming to a halt.

"Finally!" he muttered. A hunter and landscaper, the dark didn't bother him, but it was supper time and he didn't like to Heisman his wife if she'd cooked a nice warm meal.

A very athletic woman exited the Jeep, followed by two stout looking men. They appeared to be of Slavic, Indo-European origin.

Their strong cheek bones, darker hair, above average height and intense eyes reminded him of the years he spent in southeastern Europe. The landscaper then hollered, "Was about to leave. It's so late."

The trio said nothing. He assumed the woman was the person who called him a week ago for the job. A fourth person suddenly appeared from behind a tree.

The tall, muscular landscaper nearly jumped out of his skin. He caught his breath and then said, "You scared the hell out of me!"

"Ah. My apologies. Didn't mean to startle you." The well-dressed man extended his hand. "Please call me Professor Dalb. I'm the proprietor."

"Name's Jason Lory," he said by way of introduction, trying to hide his surprise at how cold the professor's hand was.

Dalb paused perhaps a count too long before releasing the landscaper's hand. "I would like to restore my orchard and grounds to their former glory."

"Well, sir. I surveyed your land this afternoon. The plantation's soil is in very good condition, but the trees and bushes need lots of work."

“This is to be expected."

"Also, recommend putting in some tile in a few spots for proper drainage and an irrigation system."

"How soon can this project be done?"

"I reckon two to three months." It pleased and excited him that the owner didn't even ask how much the work would cost. This seeming sophisticate may well turn out to be something of a rube.

Dalb pulled out a wad of cash from his blazer. "This should take care of your supplies, gas and six weeks of pay."

“Uh, yeah, yes.” The landscaper did his best to conceal his elation. “That appears sufficient … for now.”

The prof added, "At the end of this project, replace any trees you assess are bad, but I cherish old things, so save as many as you can.”

Lory replied, "Sir, my business has many clients covering three counties."

Dalb knowingly smiled. "You need more time?"

"If many of the fruit trees are beyond saving, it may take another month or two."

"Understood. If you have any issues," the professor pointed his head to the side, "contact my assistant, Daciana."

"Yes, sir."

Daciana handed him her card and said matter of fact, "I know your address, just in case you ever lose my contact information."

Jason wondered if this was her subtle way of issuing him a warning. It didn’t worry him, though. He was, for the most part, an honest fellow. "Great. I will start first thing at dawn." He then asked, "Any issues making noise near the estate?"

Daciana replied, "No."

“Very well,” said Jason nodding his head and giving them a cursory salute. "I'll be off then."

Dalb bowed to the landscaper. His nine-hundred-acre plantation, Shaded Grove, as well as a profitable farm, would be another of Count Dracula's safe havens. A necessity of which he needed more. The recent military excursion on Gemela reinforced his certainty on that score. He hadn't used this locale lately, so it was off the radar. Strategically, the estate was remote and a hopping point to larger cities in nearby states. It would also serve as another spot for Daciana and her fellow gypsies to live.

Dalb aka Count Dracula had purchased Shaded Grove over forty years ago. Back then, Vlad had been directing the affairs of the nearby Château Wilder until Nigel Rathbone had a change of heart, his mighty servant disappeared and the hurricane almost destroyed his mansion. Suddenly, there was no brain transplant for the creature and no secure hideaway for him.

The estate should have been a perfect resting place. His main issue with Shaded Grove at the time, had been a limited nearby rural population and not enough criminal elements to hide his dietary idiosyncrasy, a thirst for blood. There were also too many fresh water streams that impeded him from using his special powers.

That's when he discovered Gemela. With a constant flow of tourists in New Orleans and resorts along the Gulf coast, and native water of the brackish or salt variety that wouldn't quash his abilities to glide for shorter distances or shape-shift into a bat or foul vapor.

He laughed inside, now Shaded Grove had nearby retirement communities to nibble on a flirting cougar. In reality, he was the saber tooth. This would provide the vampire lord with an endless supply of lonely women, where he'd never have to kill them. When he got restless, Vlad would target hardcore thugs in seedy areas.

Unless forced, Count Dracula would never give up Gemela as his preferred abode. He also liked its easy access to islands in the Gulf of Mexico and Caribbean without dealing with over-officious authorities who were not so easily bribed.

Another problem with Shaded Grove was its roof was mostly gone and the wooden structure had rotted away. It was also quite the distance north of Gemela. Travel time by boat and auto was approximately six hours. However, it would be a nice place for his gypsies to oversee the land and get a break from Gemela's monotonous routine. His loyal servants were mortal and needed an occasional distraction from the drudgery of their existence.

First, that landscaper had to finish the grounds. Dracula's gypsies would quickly demolish the wooden structures. Then, they would rebuild a small, elevated stone mansion to include a matching garage and shed to withstand hurricanes and tropical storms. Of course, he'd ensure hidden rooms would be built throughout the structures for him and his brides to rest.

The entire project would take over a year to complete. Some trees would require a few seasons to be productive. Vlad was in no hurry and wanted no red flags raised.

On the surface, the professor owned a simple orchard. Over half of the grounds were mostly citrus trees and some nut varieties, surrounding the centrally located mansion. A third of the land was open fields to the north for cattle to graze and grow crops. A wide creek kept his kind from venturing across where farmers had always rented that piece of property. Forest and swamp surrounded most of the outer edges.

The vampire lord then thought of his former servant, the giant. He was literally superhuman, stronger than twenty werewolves. Bullets and knives had no effect on him. Though lonely, the brute didn't trust most humans and the undead.

The dark prince was cold, things he touched seemed to die. He enjoyed little except power and vengeance. The creature loved the smell of plants and staring at the stars. The nosferatu envied his large friend in that sense and missed him. But both were cursed in many respects.

Daciana gawked at Lory as he walked toward his pickup. He was built like a real man, stocky with facial and body hair, not a pretty boy seen on the cover of a magazine.

17 - GUARDIAN

Daciana stared at the landscaper as he got in the truck and turned over his ignition. "That man doesn't scare easily."

"What are you suggesting?" asked Vlad.

The brunette replied, "Lory knows this area and could be a valuable guardian."

The Count sneered, "He's too independent and ethical."

Daciana shrugged. "Everyone has a price."

The word *guardian*, made Dracula think of the creature. The vampire lord never worried when the juggernaut was near his resting place during the day. *What happened to you?* he thought. It had been near this plantation where he'd encountered Frankenstein's Monster four decades before:

***

Southeastern Bayou, 1963

Around nightfall, the giant killed a ten-foot alligator near the banks of the deserted estate known as Shaded Grove.

The plantation had gone fallow since the turn of the century. Knee-high-grass and yellow Carolina jasmine ran wild along the dwelling's rusted fence. Shaded Grove was one of the Frankenstein Monster's favorite hunting grounds for deer, gator, and cottonmouth. He stayed well clear of the large structure.

On the outskirts, he tended a vegetable garden, pruned fruit trees, collected acorns, and enjoyed a wild raspberry patch. After overseeing the grounds, the goliath slung the gator over his shoulder. He hiked several miles through the swamp to his remote little islet.

The creature gathered dried tinder, leaves and logs from his covered porch and ignited a flame. He butchered part of the carcass and wrapped part of the meat underground in his rigged cooler for future meals. He impaled the gator's tail with a piece of wood hung parallel between two vertical poles over the fire pit. He poured himself some raspberry wine and took a seat. He roasted the bayou chicken, slowly rotating it a couple of feet over the fire.

Frankenstein's Creation was eating his supper when he looked up. His mouth dropped open in utter amazement. A gorgeous woman with lustrous red hair suddenly appeared yards away.

She smiled in a friendly and inviting manner, playfully twirling her wavy long locks with her fingers. It seemed strange to him the voluptuous lady, clad in linen didn't run from his glut ugliness.

Her lovely form swayed before him. He felt dizzy and dropped to his knees, mesmerized by her beauty and rhythmic motions. She began to kiss him, stroking her hands around his black matt of hair. He had never felt such exhilaration. It was the first time a female dared to even come close to him after seeing his scarred visage.

He smiled and kissed her in return. Minutes later, he felt her trying to bite his neck. The titan pulled away, horrified to see such an evil countenance. She honed in on his jugular but he pushed out his arms.

The woman went rolling along the ground. She bore long fangs and let out an evil hiss. She crouched down and charged, running at him, as if she were floating above the soil.

He grabbed her as she came at him. She thrashed about, trying to scratch out his eyes and savagely snap at him. He held her in his enormous hands like a play doll and forcefully said, "I do not know what kind of thing you are, but leave me be." He tossed her several yards away and commanded, "Go now!"

Suddenly her evil eyes and sharp teeth were replaced by an innocent face. Her sudden change was not natural and all the humans he encountered never had such strength, especially, a petite female. She turned her head toward the hulking figure with a puzzled look and, then, disappeared into the darkness.

The giant barely remembered encountering a man years ago, similar to the woman-thing that just attacked him. He appeared handsome and slim, bore a goatee, and went by the name of *Radu*.

Several nights later, Frankenstein's Creation heard a rustling sound in the branches of the trees. He could not tell if it was the wings of an eagle or another large bird. He returned to roasting his fish, thinking nothing of it.

A slim man in a black suit suddenly stood next to the behemoth. The hulk's eyes opened wide in amazement. He stood up in a defensive manner. The mysterious man gracefully bowed and said, "Excuse me, my name is Vlad."

The creature didn't know what to call himself. He couldn't help wonder how the man got here.

The newcomer noticed the high netting above the center of the hut and small campground. He smirked, wondering what he almost flew into. He thought to himself: *This giant is a clever one to conceal his resting place.*

An awkward moment of silence passed. The visitor said with a smile to break the ice. "I am new to these parts. Would I be able to sit with you by your fire?" He knew very well this goliath was the one that had easily bested one of his brides.

Frankenstein's Monster was wary of a person suddenly showing up in the remote swamp. He instantly thought of that hissing woman. He noticed the outsider had a high aquiline nose and his accent was foreign. It definitely was not the southern twang, common within this region. He occasionally saw men fishing in boats, often eavesdropping on their conversations, as he hid in the banks along the mangroves. After a long pause, he said in a deep voice, "Please sit down."

The stranger listened and talked with the creature for a few hours. He deduced the behemoth was torn between guilt from the past and feelings of loneliness. The man in the black cape knew he would need time to play on the hulking figure's bitter emotions of being cast out from society. Shortly before sunrise, Vlad stood and said, "Pardon me but I need to tend to personal affairs at my dwelling. Would you mind if I returned at the same time, the coming evening?"

The titan hesitated for a moment. He thought it was odd he didn't notice the man with slicked-back hair arrive on a boat. Yet, he enjoyed the gentleman's eloquent conversation and finally said, "Please do."

For several nights, the stranger who was slightly tall for a human, returned and they talked well into the night. He casually reinforced to the creature that it is better to have a few companions than none at all.

The giant observed there was something unnatural about this dark-haired man, but he knew he was quite uncanny himself.

The man dressed in fancy attire gave the titan directions to a plantation a few miles away. "We just moved here. And, I would like you to join us at our humble abode." Vlad knew he would have to send away his brides for a while to make the titan feel comfortable. The towering specimen would eventually discover the Count's dark ways but he needed to befriend him first.

The creature was very tired of being alone. "I know that place, *Shaded Grove*. I will be there late in the afternoon."

"Excellent. If you come early, you will meet my friend, Nigel. We three are a strange lot and will become good friends."

The horn startled the professor. "Sorry if I scared you," Jason Lory said pulling his truck alongside the owner.

"You didn't. Just thinking of this place years ago."

"*Right*... Well, I noticed these are great hunting grounds. Once I'm done landscaping, do you mind if I nab some game?"

"Not an issue Mr. Lory," he replied cordially. "My one condition is that you refrain from your *nabbing* during the planting and harvest, as there will be many workers on the property."

"Understood, sir. I appreciate your hospitality very much."

"Just check with Daciana first." Professor Dalb then said mischievously, "From one gentleman to another, I must tell you it would be best, if you refrained from camping overnight."

Jason started to ask why, but some instinct based at the very stump of his brain stopped him and he said, "Thank you for the tip. I'll be sure to clear out of here before the sun hits the treetops."

"It is for the best, my friend." The old prof winked and said with a canine-heavy smile, "One night, I might have you for dinner." Lory smiled back uneasily. Both men then burst laughing like teapots screaming to release their steam.

18 - REGRETS

A short, slim man dressed in a blue buttoned-down shirt rang the doorbell. A tall male answered the door to his Hannibal residence. The mailman looked up and exclaimed, "Oh, my goodness!"

"Oh, my, what?" asked Van Helsing somewhat tersely.

"Ah, well, y-y-you do look like Christopher Lee." Pietro Van Helsing shook his head. The postman regained his composure and sincerely said, "Sir, here's an urgent letter from Great Britain."

That got the dark-haired man's attention. Van Helsing grabbed the letter. "Thank you."

"Sorry about calling you, Christopher Lee."

Pietro sighed, "It's really a compliment. I just hear that quite often." He casually eyed the front yard before shutting the door. He smiled recognizing the handwriting on the envelope. Van Helsing poured himself some tea and opened the letter:

Dear brother:

Hope all is well. Unfortunately, my health is failing and afraid that this foggy London weather is too much for my lungs. Would it be alright, if I came to live with you and Ava in Missouri? The flat could be sold for a handsome price and I would be willing to share the proceeds with you.

As you know all too well, we are no longer in our prime. It would be very nice if I was close to family. Please contact me at the soonest.

More importantly, I recently discovered a hidden compartment with some very important documents. Enclosed is one copy written in third person by a Mina Harker. Most of dad's journals were transcribed by mom. I have the originals, but don't want to discuss the details until you get to London.

Lovingly,

Marie

Pietro opened up the copy and was amazed to skim over the journal annotated by Mina Harker. He wondered how many letters Marie had back home. He would regret it if he didn't leave for his homeland at once to assist his dear sister. He already regretted not ever having the opportunity to study any of these precious notes, especially from his papa's analysis. Most people knew his famous father as Professor Abraham Van Helsing, but he was a brilliant doctor as well. He began to read the narrative with great anticipation.

Passing of Quincey P. Morris after the destruction of Dracula

The Dutchmen and his team had already formed a circle around their ailing friend. Jonathan Harker shed a tear as he said, "You'll be alright, ole boy."

Quincey Morris coughed. He then eyed his associates and slowly nodded his head out of respect. "I will miss y'all and, especially you, Miss Mina," he said finally, and the brave Texan swaggered into the grasping clutches of history.

The group suddenly heard a thunderous explosion and fell to their knees as the earth rumbled beneath them. It looked as if fragments of the castle flew in the air and smoke rose toward the heavens. Their ears still rang from the initial crackling sound and legs felt wobbly even after the earthquake subsided.

The five survivors thought the entire structure had collapsed after the earth shook for several moments. It wasn't until the dust settled that they noticed parts of the cliff's edges collapsed hundreds of feet to the valley below and the castle suffered three cracks along its outer walls. Otherwise, the evil Boyar's fortress near Borgo Pass remained solidly intact. It took several moments for the Dutchman and his team to compose themselves. They huddled around their dear Quincey and after a moment of silence, covered his body with a blanket.

A fire was lit for both warmth and light, along with a few lanterns. Not much was said as the group prepped their gear and supplies. It was a bittersweet time, and though an evil had been vanquished, none felt at ease.

"Hurry, let's get this box sealed as soon as possible," the Dutchman exclaimed.

Professor Abraham Van Helsing, Dr. Seward, Jonathan and Mina Harker, and Lord Godalming gazed into the wooden box filled with the ashes of Count Dracula and his native soil. It seemed like a dream that Vlad had just been the living dead, one of the most lethal vampires of all time.

Lord Godalming held Quincey P. Morris's silver-edged Bowie knife high above his head. In a lofty tone, he spoke as if the evil boyar could hear him, "With our friend's blade it will be a sign to you, Count Dracula that turned you into dust for eternity!" He quickly stabbed the unique gypsy weapon into the top layer of soil mixed with the vampire lord's ashes.

"Bah, I do not like this." Van Helsing spat at the ground and continued. "You taunt and with such pride! One knows not what tomorrow brings except the good Lord."

The survivors didn't notice that the Count's ring lay hidden inside one of the corners of the box as they secured the wooden lid.

Jonathan Harker, his wife, Mina Harker, and Dr. Seward departed immediately after sunset for the town of Bistriz with their beloved Quincey P. Morris' body lying in the back of the cart.

The next morning, Dr. Seward was to follow Van Helsing's implicit instructions of him returning with a construction crew, stone, mortar, fresh food, and warm beverages.

Professor Van Helsing and Lord Godalming stood watch over the box through the night. Arthur and Abraham were armed with pistols and rifles, garlic, and a crucifix. They wrapped themselves in blankets and huddled around the fire in front of the draw bridge to Castle Dracula.

Before dawn, Dr. Seward addressed the curious villagers inside the main tavern. Except for the Count's servants, it was one of the few times anyone had come back alive from Dracula's Castle. Even so, Jack had a difficult time convincing the people of Bistriz that the evil boyar was no more.

Mina Harker suddenly stood up on a wooden chair. She swept her gaze across the crowd and loudly exclaimed, "Good people of Bistriz… we have killed Count Dracula so completely that his body turned to ash."

A thickly mustachioed man shook his hand in disgust. "Bah, you cannot kill a wampyre. They are undead. Knives cannot hurt nosferatu," he stated.

Mina Harker answered, "The slit across the Count's throat temporarily harmed him. However, the second blade we plunged into his heart was a specially crafted Bowie knife, forged of silver. So, destroy him we did!"

"We want to believe," the town's constable put up his arms despondently, "but this Drăculea has lived in these parts for centuries. This wampyre and his unholy brides have fed on our young, old, and also those foolish bold ones who have dared to wander too close to his dark fortress without the protection of the sun."

Mina smiled. "Constable, we should be proof that he is destroyed. Three of us returned with the body of our dearly departed friend. Two of our comrades wait now for your strong hands at the castle. All we need is an experienced mortar crew."

None of the villagers raised a hand. Mrs. Harker threw a small pouch on the table. "This gold is more than five years' worth of six people's wages here in Bistriz."

Jonathan whispered under his breath to his wife, "Where did you get the gold coins?"

Mina responded in a low tone, "Arthur gave them to me before we rode off shortly after sunset last evening. Van Helsing told him we would need quite the handsome fee to hire even the most non-superstitious crew."

After a few moments, a hand finally raised amongst the group. "My men will go." A bearded man in a large brimmed hat rose. He then emphatically stated, "But we come back well before nightfall!"

A few hours later, Dr. Seward and the mortar crew approached the jagged road leading up to Castle Dracula. The draught horses pulling the wooden cart came to an abrupt halt.

Van Helsing joyfully waved his hat. "Ah, it is so good to see you friend, Jack."

Dr. Seward smiled as he saw Professor Van Helsing and Lord Godalming stand to greet him. "I am grateful my comrades are still with me."

Lord Godalming grasped Dr. Seward's hand. "Did you bring food?"

Dr. Seward nodded.

"Good show, chap, good show," Godalming exclaimed.

Professor Van Helsing grinned. "Ho, ho! First, we eat, then we do the Lord's work."

After a hearty breakfast, the men all worked together moving the wooden box into a secret labyrinth below Castle Dracula's chapel. They passed large pillars that supported the castle above. The crew spotted heaps of soil and several boxes until they reached a natural stone alcove in the bowels of the great rock.

The professor noticed a line of rusty chains attached to the walls. "How fitting," exclaimed Van Helsing. "A dungeon is where will stow this unholy box."

The local masons wasted no time sealing up the archway with stone and mortar. The professor surveyed their work, ensuring the wall was solidly intact with no air gaps. He nodded to the leader in the large brimmed hat. The bearded man graveled to his crew, "Leave the picks and axes! Let's get out of this accursed place."

Van Helsing forcefully said, "Nein! You take all the tools. None will be left behind for someone to break through." The locals grasped the professor's logic and eagerly picked up their heavy equipment.

As they began to depart, Abraham said a prayer and made the sign of the cross over the sealed tomb.

Recorded by,

Mina Harker

Ava Van Helsing unlocked the deadbolt to the plain looking exterior of their home. She walked inside and found her husband sipping tea at their kitchen table. She kissed him on the cheek and asked, “What do you have there, my love?”

He handed her the copy. “It’s an important letter you must read.”

“That’s funny. I just delivered an important letter at the post office.” She then read the entire document. Her eyes grew bigger in many portions of the narrative. She looked up at her hubby when she had finished.

Pietro smiled somewhat uncomfortably.

“What is it?”

“Um, well… we need to talk about my sister coming to live with us.”

Ava said matter of fact, “Marie should have done that years before.”

“She’s not in the best health and…”

Mrs. Van Helsing demanded, “Let’s go get her!”

19 – HANNIBAL LETTER

April 14th 2005

Kati Shotzski returned from her yoga class and noticed the red flag was down. *The Postman must have passed through.* She pulled a letter from their Iowa Hawkeyes mailbox addressed to her husband. She said walking into their den, "Honey, you got mail."

"Who's it from?"

"*A. Meyer* from Hannibal, Missouri."

He clucked his tongue. "That name doesn't ring a bell."

She kissed him on the lips. "Well… someone knows you."

The Snowbirds' reporter opened the letter and read:

Mr. Shotzski:

I am writing you because I had a similar experience with a deadly vampire over sixty years ago. Since then, I have worked with a handful of people to hunt down the undead. I am in my eighties now and wanted to pass this information to you for your benefit.

I read the book by Archer Pike about your exploits with a vampiress in Dubuque. Most took it as a hoax but it was the truth.

Unfortunately, I lost my husband, Rudy to a vampire when we were newlyweds. I should have perished with him. The only reason I survived was eating garlic and rubbing it around my body. This was my routine to naturally repel insects on the days our team sabotaged Nazi troops in forested areas.

I am also writing you because we believe this very same nosferatu has been operating in the southern US for a half century. We could never track him but destroyed several of his kind.

Less than a handful of our team is still alive. My operational days are winding down. I hope a wise, like-minded persons such as yourself will join us. Please contact me at your convenience. You can find my number listed under 'AM Boutique' in Hannibal, Missouri. My work address is on the enclosed return envelope.

Sincerely,

Ava Meyer

PS - You can read my testimony below. I originally wrote this, days after it occurred. This was a very painful endeavor, but wanted to capture it fresh from memory. Parts of the German dialogue may be translated badly, but I hope the overall sense has come across and that the spirit of what happened is accurate.

Early at the onset of World War II resistance cells arose to combat the Nazi push into southeastern Europe. The groups consisted of men and women of all ages, many Jews and others with a conscience and the will to stomp out the evil spawned from the Third Reich.

The resistance often attacked truck and train routes in order to weaken supply lines to German outposts and battle fronts. The best served as small lethal teams ambushing combat-hardened Nazi troops or picking off the Gestapo.

They used speed and stealth to their advantage. Though, outnumbered and outgunned much of the time, these resistance fighters preferred to die on their own terms, instead of the Nazi's unholy death camps.

Many brave souls paid the ultimate price to fight the tyrannical dictator and his forces. A couple of Hungarians stumbled onto something much more, unwittingly unleashing another ancient evil upon this world. I was one of them and this is my story:

***

Friday, June 13th 1941

A pair of Hungarians aimed bazookas at the tracks of a Nazi Panzer tank as it approached open terrain. Two more rebels simultaneously threw grenades at the German platoon on patrol.

The Panzer's tracks were severely damaged and half of the platoon lay dead from the explosions. The tank's MG 24 machine gun immediately opened fire on the rebels to its right side. A pair of thick trees were all that stood between the Hungarian rebels and certain death as the rounds ate away at the trunks.

The other two Hungarians picked off the remaining platoon on the tank's left side. They quickly grabbed the fallen German's Mauser Karabiners before the 7.92 mm machine gun turned on them.

The German captain opened the lid of his tank and ordered, "Raus, raus! We've spent all of the machine gun's ammunition. You three," he handed them the crew's remaining rifle rounds, "go after them."

The four Hungarians split off in two different directions. Three Germans soldiers pursued the two groups. A pair of rebels fled south through the maze of trees.

The other two Hungarians headed north through the valley. They threw all of the rifles but two in a deep stream on the edge of the forest and grabbed the remaining rounds. Moments later, the rebels exchanged gunfire with the two pursuing Germans. The Hungarian woman shot one of the Nazis between the eyes with the Mauzer Karabiner 98K she had just taken off a dead German.

The officer-in-charge waited, sporadic gunfire his only company. One of the soldiers returned from the south with a flesh wound and meekly said, "Herr Kapitän, I pinned them down but then I ran out of ammo."

The Nazi captain snarled, "Dress your wound."

The other German soldier ran back several minutes later and reported, "Sir, the rebels are scaling the cliff."

"Where is Private Werner?" Captain Streicher asked.

"The woman shot him."

The German officer rolled his eyes. "Why didn't you kill both of them?"

Private Krueger stammered before responding. "I-I spent my rifle rounds shooting at the pair. They must have run out of ammunition… I found two of our rifles at the base of the escarpment."

Captain Streicher slapped the soldier. "You are Aryan. You shouldn't miss! Why didn't you fire at them with your pistol?"

"By the time, I reached the bottom of the cliff, they were out of range, at least, two hundred feet up." The private nervously added, "I shot at them but they kept climbing."

The Captain scowled and reached for his leather pouch. He gazed through his binoculars. "Schnell, schnell, I see them." The Nazi infantry officer spotted the pair scaling the cliff and commanded, "Aim the cannon toward three O'clock." He looked along the valley. It was dense with beautiful green vegetation and towering trees. He hated the thought of staying in this dark region another night. "Finish them off and let's get out of this accursed place."

The medium-tractor's turret turned and adjusted its sights. The rebels had climbed over 600 feet of the 1,000 feet cliff.

The Hungarian man saw the lower foundations of an old and mighty fortress hundreds of feet above them to the east. Rudy pointed toward the structure and suggested to his wife, "Ava, zigzag up toward the castle." Years before, the cliff to the west of the castle was unreachable, but an earthquake shook the rocky ledge. There were now clefts and edges that made it barely scalable.

The Nazi officer yelled, “Make your shot count.” He angrily shook his head at two of his soldiers. “We all are out of rifle rounds.” He waved his hand down, “Fire!”

The short-barreled 75 mm-round hit the cliff’s wall several meters below the renegades. The woman lost her footing from the impact of the mortar-round. The husband barely grabbed his wife’s wrist as she began to slip several feet. Ava coughed from the dust and looked up at her spouse. “Rudy, I cannot go on. It is too difficult.”

The man gazed at the love of his life dangling below him. “Woman, look at me,” he said gritting his teeth, “you must not give up.” His forearm muscles began to burn even after holding her petite form for only a minute. A tear trickled down Rudy’s cheek as he commanded, “Ava, pull with all your, might!”

Private Krueger snapped to attention. “Kapitän, did we hit them?”

The Captain looked through his binoculars. “I cannot tell. There is still too much dust hovering around the impact zone.”

The rebels gained another 150 feet before they heard the tank’s main gun fire off another round. The round was short, but its impact shook the thick wall all around them, yet they kept their purchase and managed to climb another 200 feet. The pair shifted along a ledge toward the western foundation of an impregnable castle built over a giant rock.

Streicher screamed, “Hurry up! I see them. Those damn Jews are almost to the top of the ledge. Shoot for the corner of the castle and the cliff.”

20 - SOMETHING WICKED STIRRED

Chuck Shotzski heated up some green tea and continued to read the letter from Ava Meyer:

***

The tank's crew shot off another high-explosive shell. It impacted the lower portion of the castle's western foundation, creating a large hole. The Hungarians disappeared into the opening.

"Scheisse!" Captain Streicher ordered, "Grab rope, we must go after them. We have pistols. There are only two of them."

One of the German soldiers hesitated before muttering, "Sir, only four rebels ambushed our platoon and disabled the tank. Why don't we go back for reinforcements?"

"Nein! It will take hours to return and the commander will shoot us on the spot if we don't return with proof of their demise."

The Hungarians drooped inside the dark chamber, exhausted from the climb. Rudy said, "We're safe. Hitler brags about his superior Aryan race but they will never scale that wall."

Ava hugged her husband and stared affectionately at him with her oval-shaped brown eyes. "My love, thank you for not letting me give up." He smiled and kissed her.

The young man collected pieces of wood he discovered inside the chamber and lit a small fire. The couple hovered around the flames, ate what little scraps they had left and then dozed off for a while to catch up on some, much needed rest.

The husband awoke, peering into the darkness and curiosity got to him. He crept around the edges, noticing an arch that probably led up to the castle. He cursed under his breath, realizing it had been sealed with mortar. He barely could make out several rusty chains attached to the walls and said, "An open dungeon."

His wife stirred. "Did you say something honey?"

He curtly replied, "No." Daylight was fading from the opening in the wall. He walked toward his wife and groaned bumping his knee on a wooden box in the middle of the large room.

"What are you doing?"

"Just scoping out the place." Rudy noticed the top was slightly loose and he pulled it back with all his strength. He peered inside. The fire provided enough light that he spotted something silvery, partially buried on top of the soil. He reached for it and cut himself on the blade. "Shit that stings!"

"You okay?"

"Sure." There was just enough light that he could see the knife had cut into flesh from his wrist down to the right palm. Blood spurted into the soil. He cursed before saying, "Grab my bandana in the bag." He then rested his hand over the wooden box as more blood flowed into the soil. "Kind of feeling faint," he said with a sigh. "Lost more blood than I thought."

Ava inched cautiously through the dimly lit chamber. She then examined the gash. Her husband needed a tourniquet. "Kneel down and rest your arm on the box, above your heart."

"Why?"

Ava growled, "To staunch the bleeding and save your skin." He quickly knelt down. She tore off a piece of cloth and then tightened up the homemade tourniquet with a small stick.

"Damn that hurts."

The resistance fighter bandaged her husband's wound. "That should do the trick but remember what I told you!"

He sassed, "Yes doctor."

She chuckled, "Honey, all the times you avoided bullets and you cut yourself with an old blade. You can be so clumsy."

"For being so old, it is sharp as your tongue."

Ava shrugged. "It was you I heard cursing moments ago."

Rudy grinned and studied the knife. "The lower half appears to be a silver blade. What a waste!" he exclaimed.

She rolled her eyes. "You're beyond frugal!" She tore off pieces of loose wood from the box and carefully stacked them on top of the bluish flames. She winked and seductively said, "Come over here and make me warm around our cozy little fire."

He carefully sat down. "Hopefully, we can depart by dawn."

She patted her husband's chest. "Rest your arm against my side to keep your hand above your heart. If all goes well, I can begin to loosen the tourniquet." The couple huddled together for a quarter of an hour when they heard several strange popping sounds. She said nervously, "What was that?"

He got up and peered outside. "Damn, those Nazis are over half-way up the cliff." He gave her a concerned look. "I don't know if I can climb the last fifty feet to the top with my cut hand. How many bullets do you have left in your pistol?"

"Five."

Rudy said, "Your aim better be pretty good because four Krauts will be here in less than thirty minutes."

Ava yawned, "I can snipe them off as they near the opening."

Several minutes later, the couple heard a scream. He looked outside through the hole and smiled. "One of the Krauts is dangling by a rope." Commands in German could be heard. Rudy peered down the cliff again and sneered, "Crap, they are pulling him up."

They both sat, occasionally looking to see how much farther the infantrymen had climbed. Another strange pop erupted. Ava said with concern, "That sounds like it came from inside."

"No, it is probably the wind. I have to go the bathroom. Wait here and keep a look out." Rudy walked ten paces past the wooden crate toward the far corner of the chamber.

"Honey, I don't like this. It's so dark that I can't see you."

Her husband said, "Talking about dark, it is dusk."

A faint moan followed by a momentary *slurping* sound travelled across the hard floor. She thought nothing of it since her husband often made odd sounds while relieving himself.

Several moments past before she called out, "You okay over there?" All she got in response was the slow, scraping sound from the blackness she peered into in vain, as if someone were intermittently pulling a rake across the dungeon's floor.

As the noise drew nearer, Ava could not contain the terror that had been welling up, ever since Rudy had disappeared into the chamber's impenetrable wall of night. "Stop joking around."

She looked outside and said, "Those Nazis will be within range in a few minutes." Her husband didn't respond as the harsh crawling noise crept closer. Ava grabbed the pistol. The steel grip was a comfort to her. She surveyed her targets. They were still out of scope for perfect shots. She pivoted toward the center of the room and nervously pleaded, "My love, talk to me." No response. The silence was more unnerving than any gunfights. The Krauts grunted as they climbed closer, grabbed her attention.

The battle-hardened woman shut her eyes to gather herself. *Rudy must have fallen*, she thought, *and he needs your help. Stop being scared of the dark. Go get him! You still have time before you have to pick off those Krauts.* Ava took a deep breath and exhaled. She opened her eyes and surveyed the middle of the dungeon. The wife thought she saw her husband's form collapsed on the floor about four paces away. She took a few steps into the darkness when her feet were pulled out from under her.

Seconds later, the Nazi infantrymen reached the opening. The captain whispered, "They must have escaped inside the bowels of the castle. Otherwise, they'd have fired on us by now."

The men smiled at him nervously.

The officer looked at his sergeant. “Crawl inside!”

“Jawohl Herr Kapitän!” The soldier pulled himself into the chamber. Two more followed. One grabbed a piece of the wood from the fire and used it as a torch to peer in the blackness. The men jumped. They discovered the Hungarian male with a broken neck sprawled along the floor. The woman was on her side, motionless.

A shadow appeared from the darkness. It snatched one of the men; his body convulsed. As the figure came closer, the others witnessed a skeleton with organs intact but no outer flesh.

Captain Streicher heard screams and pulled his body inside the vault. He stumbled into his men lying lifeless along the floor. Their faces were frozen in expressions of utter terror. A white-haired man about six feet tall in a tattered black suit grabbed him by the throat. The last thing the Nazi officer saw was a pair of burning red eyes and brilliant white fangs.

The death dealer’s hair was now black and his skin ivory white. His dark suit now appeared new. He peered back at the female lying on the floor. She appeared to be in shock and her blood was foul with that damn plant. *She is no good to you.*

The dark figure sensed something. He took a few steps toward the box from which he had only recently been liberated. Vlad peered inside and reclaimed his treasured golden ring. His face twisted into a horrific smile. Something wicked was stirred to roam the earth once again.

Chuck Shotzski finished reading the letter and grumped, "When will jokers leave me be?" He then threw it in the garbage.

He took another sip of his green tea and said to himself, "That woman or *whomever* sounded convincing." *She mentioned Vlad*, Shotz thought and then mockingly uttered, "Whatever!"

Shotz picked up the crumpled letter and read it again. He then unlocked his fire safe and placed a new folder in the "questionable" section, labeled *Hannibal Anti-Vampire.*

21 - VAN HELSING'S JOURNALS

Early May 2005

Pietro Van Helsing carefully searched his parent's study. His youngest sister, Marie, had lived in the flat her entire life. He was sad their residence had been sold, but happy his sister was to join them in America. He was more delighted she was on the mend.

His wife, Ava, walked in and gently said, "Peter. We must depart for the airport in two hours." He nodded thankfully. "I'm going back to the hotel to help your sister pack."

He raised a brow. It was essential he capture any additional details on the undead before the flat was officially sold. It had been a dozen years since his mother had passed away at 121 years old. His mum didn't advertise it, but she was the Contessa Cassandra Coretti before marrying the famous Dutchman, Dr. Van Helsing. The family was proud of the fact that the Coretti's noble bloodline could be traced back to the first century A.D.

Many people mistook Pietro Van Helsing for the acclaimed British actor, Sir Christopher Lee. Both men were approximately six-feet, five inches tall with dark features and a slim build. However, Van Helsing was sixteen years older than Lee. And like his parents, Pietro regularly used an identical air-chamber for a thirty-minute nap to boost his health and extend his lifespan.

Besides selling off antiques and the flat itself, he hadn't discovered anything of importance. His sister already set aside what she wanted and Marie insisted she had held nothing back. Pietro knew his sister was a stickler for details but she was recovering from a serious illness. It was one of the rare times, she didn't leave any coherent clues to locate their father's hidden compartment. She mumbled something about the dining room or study. He was about to exit the den when he recalled one of his first memories of his parents. *Yes, there*, he thought, *in the corner wooden panel.*

His dad had been bantering with his mom about his first name, *Pietro*. Both agreed their son's name was a fine homage to the grainy apostle of Christ known as the *Rock*. However, the two Italian vowels in a row annoyed the professor to no end, so Abe preferred to call his boy, *Petro* or *Peter*. Much to his delight and his wife's scorn, Abraham Van Helsing never called his son, Pietro.

He recalled peeping his head around while his parents squabbled over his name. That's when he first saw the tiny secret door ajar. "Mein Gott!" He sighed. "How could I have forgotten."

He began to search the grain. No crevices or buttons were visible. He then ran his fingertips along the left side of the wooden beam. “Bloody hell!” He looked to the right, no joy again.

Van Helsing snorted before whisking his hands along the starboard beam and, bingo, halfway down he felt a knot. Clever, it didn't standout to the human eye. He pressed it and a fourteen-inch wide door cracked open. What he discovered in the small enclosure astounded him. There was a sealed leather notebook, revolver, oak ammo case and two large vinyl discs. His sister didn’t mention the outdated audio devices. He joyfully said aloud, "Ah ha! Once again to hear papa's voice. I am almost certain."

Pietro grabbed the wooden ammunition box. He slid open the lid and studied the rounds. The tips were slightly oxidized. He raised an eyebrow and exclaimed, "Silver!" He was excited to read the journal. He quickly skimmed through the contents, mostly about wampyres. He looked up and exclaimed, "Papa… we could have used this earlier but thank you."

He chuckled recalling the first memories of his parents. To appease or aggravate them; he used Pietro, Petro or Peter depending on his mood. How he missed them both. He discovered the loose papers were in his dad's handwriting, but the notebook was in his mother's. *Thank God.* The discs looked to be in pristine condition. *She must have listened to the audios and transcribed them in the third person after Papa passed.* "Thanks mum," he said aloud. He sat down and began to read:

***

December 1910, Dr. Van Helsing's Journal

Abraham relished the sweet smoke from his Cubano. The pleasant tobacco aroma made him smile. An olive-skinned beauty half the age of the professor popped her head into his den. "Ah, I like this smell." He rose and gave his tall, dark-haired wife a kiss. Cassandra Van Helsing puckered her lips and wrapped her arms around his neck. "Mi dolce. Try a cigar every other day, sí?" He looked at his adorable wife like she was a tyrant about to snatch away his favorite toy.

"Daddy,” a toddler screamed running into the den, tackling the Dutchman’s leg. Abe bent down and patted Pietro’s back.

She pointed her big brown eyes at their son and said, "Dolce, you're not sixty anymore.”

The doctor conceded her point and replied, "Ja. Okay, my Italian countess." She batted her shiny dark eyes at her love out of gratitude." He raised one finger and countered by saying, "Just let me finish this one today and in peace." Cassandra smiled and gave Abe a deep kiss on the lips.

Dr. Van Helsing studied his notes for a while and took in a deep breath. He became grim as he scribbled in his journal, *Gott im Himmel! I realize just now I forgot to have Dr. Seward return with Holy Wafers on the day we sealed the chamber containing Count Dracula's ashes. It is only a minor error and not worth the trouble of breaking through reinforced stone and mortar. Every seven years, Lord Godalming and I have returned to Castle Dracula to ensure it has not been disturbed. Arthur has even brought his miniature schnauzers to sniff out any unholy rats. Fortunately, no such vermin have we encountered.*

I am now 79 years old and we have destroyed six more vampires throughout Europe. Thank God, none of them were as diabolical and powerful as the undead prince, Count Vlad Dracula. I invented what I call an air chamber. Lying in my crude contraption for an hour a day, it has revitalized my health. I am energized and feel like a strapping forty-year old. By the Lord's grace it will lengthen my life for many years to come.

Much research must be completed and compiled on the undead. Many in the scientific realm baulk at what they cannot touch or see. For instance, one does not see air but its affects, such as the swaying of a branch or blowing of grass. Yet air is still real. And, as silly as the supernatural may seem, one should always keep an open mind. Vampires are no jest but very real. The knowledge to combat them is life and death.
– Professor Abraham Van Helsing

Shortly after the Second Great War, Professor Van Helsing and his team prepared to hunt down the wampyre once more. Trained, organized and well-versed in the ways of the undead, the vampire hunters destroyed many throughout the continent. One was a deathly surprise to most of them:

***

Summer 1945. Dr. Van Helsing's Journal

The Second World War kept us from returning to Castle Dracula for far too many years. Lord Godalming, both of our sons. my great nephew and I arrived, and to our relief, the archway was still sealed up.

We have bred various breeds of terriers to aid in our endeavors to combat the nosferatu. And as in years past, these brave little ratters didn't detect any unholy vermin.

However, as we were departing the castle, my dear nephew noticed an opening, probably caused by a high explosive round, below the western foundation's outer wall. We immediately tore through the closed-up chamber with picks and discovered six skeletons inside.

The soil within the wooden box appears to have been disturbed and we discovered dear Quincey P. Morris' Bowie knife stained with what appears to be small traces of dried blood. I cannot help but wonder that blade acted as the tool for the return of Dracula. If it were not for the skeletal remains and that hole, this would not worry me. But no such corpses were inside when we sealed the chamber decades earlier. We know that as fact!

Mein Gott! For my recklessness, the fiend has been freed to prowl the night again. Perhaps, the Holy wafers would have worked. Then again, they would probably have perished over time.

Bah, I wished we would have dumped his unholy ashes and soil over the cliff, so the wind would have swept them apart forever! As the dear Brits say, 'The milk that is spilt cries out afterwards.'

God have mercy on my soul and may we find the son of the devil. I am 114 years old and in great health for my age. Lord willing, we can gather a larger team to hunt the vampire lord down. – Professor Abraham Van Helsing

Late 1945. Dr. Van Helsing's Journal

We almost got to Count Dracula at an abandoned château in northern France. Unfortunately, he escaped. But the fiend is on the run. Lord willing, we shall destroy this bloated tick.

Warning: Don't be mesmerized by the nosferatus' powers and longevity. It is all a facade. They are cursed to live an unholy existence to feed off the blood of the living. Love and joy are only a faint memory to them. Beware of their charm.

The vampire is pure evil. They may appear to be like a shiny apple on the outside, but in truth are rotten to the core. I fear there may come a day when a lost generation will revere such wickedness as the undead possess.

I cannot reiterate how deadly these demonic forces are. They are like prostitutes who rob their partners of their youth with foul diseases and drag their souls to the depths of Hell. DO NOT be fooled by their rhythmic voices, enticing bodies and empty promises. Trust in God! – Professor Abraham Van Helsing

1946, Dr. Van Helsing's Journal

A woman with thick dark hair and a few streaks of silver served her husband a cup of tea. The Dutchman grasped her hand over his shoulder. Cassandra kissed him on his cheek. "Thank you, my dear," he said with a weak smile. The aging doctor gazed out at the sea in a blank stare for what seemed like an eternity.

She cupped her hand over her mouth. A tear ran down one cheek. They had been married over fifty years and he was forty years her senior. She was lucky to have had him this long. He was in very good health until recently. Mrs. Van Helsing departed the room. It was hard to see her dear Abe decline so quickly.

Fatigue was apparent as the professor slowly began to write down his thoughts. *Some good news first: One of my men discovered a diary while on an investigation near a coastal town in Portugal. He retrieved the diary of a Dr. Jonah Waggner. The notes were slightly burned but survived the mansion's fire. This brilliant surgeon indicated that one of his patients, the Duke Radu Romaine, was in fact Dracula. After Dr. Waggner discovered Radu betrayed him and was a wampyre, he made a bonfire during daylight, and burned the coffin with the undead corpse. And, thus he destroyed this abomination.*

Though not superstitious, Waggner was perplexed how the vampire got into his dwelling without being invited, based on his understanding of said vampire lore. However, the physician discovered his wife had previously invited the Duke to visit their mansion if he ever came to Portugal. This journal noted that the coffin contained the Dracula family crest on top of its outer lid with the name "Radu" inscribed. Interestingly, the only things left after destroying the fiend was a ring, also bearing the Dracula family crest, and a golden pennant. The two pieces of jewelry had the initials of R.D. inscribed on the back. Because of these initials and his first name, we believe he was Radu Dracula, the brother of Vlad Dracula.

The doctor's writings also noted the Duke of Romaine carelessly chased after pretty women, rather than safeguarding his coffin. This annotation doesn't fit the profile of Vlad Dracula's personality, who longed for power and ensured he had backups for his resting places, before taking brides. Furthermore, the Duke was described as a skinny fashionable man and eloquent in speech with a deep voice, roundish nose, peppery colored hair and a goatee. Neither did Waggner detect a foreign accent, nor did he annotate that this Count Dracula have an aquiline-shaped nose as Prince Vlad Drakhol was oft described. As such, this largely DOES NOT fit my nemesis, previously known as Vlad the Impaler. Therefore, we conclude that Dr. Waggner destroyed the Count's brother, Radu, but not Vlad Dracula.

Dr. Van Helsing struggled to take in deep breaths. He then pursed his lips and continued writing, *Unfortunately, some of my men have been murdered recently. At first, we thought it was a thief who knifed our dear teammate but more lives were taken. We then were certain it was Count Dracula. This is one of Vlad's Achilles heels - pride and vengeance. Yet, the Count would have normally taken credit for his deeds and rubbed it in our faces. None of that have we seen. Instead, their jugulars were severed like those from a large canine. We now theorize that a werewolf is on the loose in London. The only question is that some of the men have been killed on the nights with no full moons. However, their wounds have been consistent with that of the lycanthropic mutilations.*

My health is on the decline. What can this old windbag say being over 115 years old? I'm a fossil. And, moderate exercise, my air machine and clean living can only prolong life for so long. Work, a hearty dish, an occasional cigar and one drink a day has given me small joys, but faith and family are the true blessings.

Our team is switching locations in case we are being watched. We move and sleep mostly during the day, and use various decoys as precautions. My concern is for the men and all of our families. I feel my days are numbered. We just pray to the good Lord that this evil may be vanquished. Hopefully, sooner than later. – Professor Abraham Van Helsing

22 - TREMORS

England, May 2005

An attractive woman stood at the office doorway. She was tall with dark hair and a smaller, roman-shaped nose like her father. She took a few steps and asked in a soft voice, "Dad. Are you okay?"

He spun the solid oak chair around. He smiled looking up at his daughter, Cassandra Ava Van Helsing. "Quite my love!"

She noticed some items were on the desk. "What did you find, papa?"

"Five items. Two are phonographic recordings." Peter got a bit misty-eyed before continuing, "I hope to be from my parents."

"Great. I finally will be able to hear Grandpa Abe's thick Dutch accent that you so often imitate."

"Ja," chuckled Van Helsing. He held up a leather binder. "I presume the two audios will match these notes made by your grandfather and grandmother," he beamed, "whom we named you after."

She stared at him with that same knowing look his wife would often skewer him with. "And my middle-name after mom."

He gasped, "On that note, Ava is a stickler for time. Your mother will be here in forty minutes to catch the flight back to Hannibal."

"Anything else?"

He sighed, "A revolver."

She got excited. Cassandra ensured the weapon wasn't loaded before examining it. "Needs some cleaning and lubrication."

"Never understood your fascination with guns..."

She gave him a *hello* look, "Mom's a sniper."

"What about fencing?"

"I like it just as well, but I learned something from mum."

"What's that?"

"Bullets move faster."

Pietro shook his head disappointedly.

"Dad… You should be grateful. Mother's skills ensured a lot of evil elements aren't roaming around anymore." Cass added, "She taught me to shoot just as well as you instructed me to fence and golf."

"True. Ava did kill many Nazis. She was also one of the best at hunting down nosferatu." The patriarch shrugged. "Still. I'd much rather golf."

Cassandra patted her father's shoulder. "Links I prefer the most." She opened the ammo case and exclaimed, "Silver bullets!"

Van Helsing grudgingly nodded.

"Gramps was ahead of his time."

"Quite so!"

“Sound like you’re stuck in the past.”

He bit his lip.

The tall brunette smiled. "Nothing beats slugging the undead with heart-exploding silver."

Pietro said in a lofty tone, "Wooden and silver-tipped arrows are much more refined."

Cass retorted, "Not at close-quarters."

"A silver blade," quipped her dad.

"Too close for comfort."

Van Helsing admitted to his daughter, "I'm NOT going to win this?"

"Nope," stated Cass with a grin.

"Well then. Will have to leave this revolver with our neighbors. I will call one of my friends to get the weapon shipped to the states."

"That's right. The Brits aren't much for one's right to bear arms. Power to the government, not the people." She looked at her dad and asked, "You have anything to add?"

Pietro said nothing. He didn't want to lose another debate to his daughter. Statistically, places where people could legally carry a gun had lower crime rates. Simply put, bad guys didn't like to push their luck with citizens packing heat.

Cass looked at her watch. "Do you need anything else?"

"Yes. First to the neighbors. Then, let's head to the package store and wrap these recordings." Pietro sealed the notebook and handed it to his daughter. "And Cass."

She nodded.

"Guard this leather journal with your life. When we get home, I want you to type the notes into the computer.”

“It will take less than a day.”

“Pietro grabbed his daughter’s hand. “I need you to transfer the phonographic audio recordings into digital."

“Not a problem.”

Van Helsing added, "And make several backups!"

Her father's urgent last request got her attention. "It's starting again."

"Your mother is on to something."

"We need to recruit more people." Cass eyed her dad. "You and mom are getting old."

"Ava has already begun the process."

She sighed, "I thought you, mom and that guy you served with in the Royal Air Force destroyed the last of the undead."

Pietro took in a deep breath before replying, "I wished it were so." He continued, "Ava recently got a message from a reliable source."

Cass shook her head.

"The good news it's been a while."

"Vampires sound like a virus that keep popping up."

"Nosferatu are like tremors. They often start small, but if one is not aware, they can mushroom," Pietro said with a shudder.

"Am I ready?"

"You've got the best training."

"That doesn't sound reassuring."

Van Helsing eyed his daughter. "As an assassin, you're one of the best."

"Why do I get the feeling I am lacking in something?"

"You're so good at hand-to-hand fighting and shooting, sometimes it can be too easy for you."

"Are you saying I'm impatient?"

Pietro sighed, "Not so much, but when you meet your match..."

"I could lose focus."

"Exactly!" Van Helsing nodded; happy his daughter was catching on. "Think more strategically."

Cass stated, "Locating their hiding places and attacking them when they're at their weakest."

"Similar to tracking criminals and terrorists."

"Then it shouldn't be that hard."

He put up a hand. "Remember, vampires are much deadlier than the nastiest of scum you've dealt with."

She shrugged. "The right weapon will take them down."

"They're stronger and faster." Van Helsing cautioned, "The first time you go up against one, it will be overwhelming."

"Are you telling me to be overcautious?"

“No.” Pietro recalled the times his team battled the undead. “I cannot emphasize the element of surprise enough, and if you move too fast, it might be your last.”

Cassandra looked at her watch. "Well. Let's get cracking ole chap."

"You need to work on that English accent." He grinned, "Too long in America, my love."

She scowled.

"Ah," he bellowed, "the ole man got you for once." Van Helsing rose and studied the room one last time. "Lots of fond memories."

Cassandra hugged her dad.

“I already miss this place.”

She grabbed her ole man’s hand. "On the flight home, please tell me about your time in the British Intelligence Corps."

"I am proud of my service in World War Two."

"Special Operations?"

Peter paused before adding, "Let's just say I was part of the Special Forces and leave it at that."

23 - 1960s

August 23, 2005

The eighty-year old Rosa Wilder looked into Maria's eyes. "My dear child, I have two things I should have addressed with you, years ago. First, something occurred at our château that was so terrible you will not believe it."

Maria humored her and asked, "What was it?"

Rosa sighed. "Please be patient with me. My memory is not what is used to be."

"Relax mama, we all have our moments."

"Well, I believe it was shortly after Thanksgiving in 1964. This skinny little fellow, Stan Keaton was running from the law. I ran into him at a bus station near Biloxi, Mississippi. I tried to calm him down but when I introduced myself as Dr. Rosa Wilder, he grew even more hysterical. Stan was so terrified that he couldn't stop babbling some nonsense." She laughed, "It was pretty funny until he referenced Le Grande, the undead, this château, and my sister, your moth…"

Maria didn't hear Rosa's last two words.

She continued, "Well, it was then that I took that frantic man's words quite seriously. I calmed him down and reassured him I wasn't going to try and take him back to the château. Stan then told me he had been the assistant to my sister for a number of years and recounted that dreadful night." Rosa tensed-up before stating, "I obtained the details from three sources on separate occasions. I quickly noted there were no major discrepancies between the stories of Mr. Keaton, your Auntie Gwen, and Mr. Rathbone. The real nightmare I am about to tell you are their testimonies, not the police's watered-down version:"

***

Dr. Elsa Wilder shook her head. "Just got word that Tony Valentine was killed in a car accident."

Dr. Vlasko shook his head. "That's terrible." After a pause, he said, "Where did it happen?"

"Nebraska…" She could read his eyes and added, "His brain is of no use now."

Dr. Vlasko pursed his lips. "Tony even volunteered for the operation."

Elsa sighed. "Can't blame him. He had a bent spine, half of an arm and a burned face… Valentine always said it wouldn't make any difference having the giant's scarred face, but he'd finally be healthy and super strong."

"Tony was the perfect candidate… affable and a gifted scientist." He looked at Elsa. "What can we do?"

"Cancel the operation… for now."

The lab technician, Stan Keaton, squatted down to double-check the wires connecting the machines to the heavily sedated patient he nicknamed the *Giant*, lying on a ten-foot steel table.

Dr. Vlasko whispered, "Elsa, I think Keaton would be the next best choice for our large patient's brain."

He was wary of Vlasko eyeing him. When Stan heard the physician whisper his name tied to *Patient's brain*, he got a real uneasy feeling in his stomach.

"What's Keaton's blood type?"

Her eyes grew wide. "Same as the creature."

Stan's peripheral vision barely caught the European man pointing at him. He held his gut, moaning, "Ohhh, I-I gotta go."

Dr. Vlasko eyed Keaton suspiciously as the skinny little man exited the spacious laboratory. Stan held his belly and exited the laboratory. He walked into the bathroom, waited a moment, and then darted toward the guest quarters. His hands nervously unlocked two deadbolt locks secured to a thick oak door from the outside and rapidly knocked.

Nigel Rathbone growled, "Come in."

Keaton breathed in and out, trying to speak.

"Make it quick!" Bones said dropping the chains on his bed.

Stan's limbs began to quake as he pointed to his brain, making a scissors motion around his skull. He immediately pointed his hands way over his head and clenched his fist, trying to puff out his back, chest, and shoulders.

The Scott shook his head and asked, "Mr. Keaton, I don't understand? Are you not able to talk? The lab tech nodded his head up and down. Nigel coolly stated, "Calm down!" Keaton repeated his pantomime. Rathbone looked at him quizzically. "Are you saying Dr. Vlasko plans on using your brain for the Giant?"

He was finally able to utter one word, "Y-yyyes."

Bones graveled, "I was afraid of that. The man you know as Dr. Vlasko has been distancing himself from me. It is essential you compose yourself and leave without telling anyone."

Stan left the guest quarters and ran to Elsa's bedroom. He frantically called Gwen Adams' home number.

Dr. Vlasko looked over at Dr. Wilder and asked, “Elsa, did you check to see if Nigel chained himself to the bed?”

She shook her head. “I thought you were going to do that.”

“Excuse me for a moment. I hope it is not too late.”

Elsa peered out through one of the lab’s windows. It was moments from a full moon.

Dr. Vlasko noticed a door open as he made his way to Rathbone’s room. He tucked himself in the corner, spying on Stan.

Keaton frantically said out loud, "Come on. Pick up the phone."

After five rings, a woman answered, "Hello."

Stan nervously exclaimed, “Hello Gwen..."

"Who is calling?"

"Stan Keaton. You introduced yourself to me at the coffeehouse yesterday morning."

"Oh yes."

"Do you remember that European you were inquiring about?”

“I certainly do. Dr. Rosa Wilder hired me last week to find her sister and a man from southeast Europe who goes by the alias of Dr. Vlasko.”

“Well, I have been working for Dr. Elsa Wilder here for many years since the château was completed. The European man you described showed up to the château last week. He brought with him a giant of a man, terribly scarred from head to foot. We were doing diagnostics on the large man minutes ago when Dr. Vlasko mentioned the big guy’s brain and pointed at me. That terrified me. You may want to get the law over here. I’m getting the hell out.”

As Keaton knocked on Nigel’s door, he began to ponder why Dr. Wilder had maximum strength deadbolts installed to the two-inch thick door’s exterior a week ago. “Mr. Rathbone?” Nobody answered, so he entered and said, “We must leave!”

Bones released the chains he was grasping and collapsed to the ground, yelling in a hoarse voice, “Stan, get out now!”

Keaton was horrified to see Rathbone’s body begin to transform. He slammed the door shut and ran toward the staircase.

Dr. Vlasko blocked the stairs and then herded Stan into Elsa’s bedroom. He pointed stating, “I heard you conversing with a woman on the telephone seconds ago. You were supposed to be Dr. Wilder’s confidant and not a traitor. The giant only needed some minor calibrations. I could see the terror in your eyes as we tended to my large friend."

Stan Keaton's Adam's apple dipped like a bat at dusk, before he could get the nerve to speak or make a sound, "I-I don't know who you really are, but I saw you pointing at me when you talked about the large man's brain. Dr. Wilder and I have been conducting experiments on cellular regeneration and advanced metals, but I didn't sign on to be a lab rat. I'm just her assistant."

Vlasko enjoyed taunting him. He slowly made his way toward Keaton with little space between them. "Wouldn't you like to be a lot taller?"

He backed up into a small wooden table. He grasped the edges. "Not as that poor titan!"

The undead prince snickered, "And live forever."

The lab tech pretended to cough to his side. He grabbed the base of the table and swung it hard into the physician.

He grinned mischievously as the table bounced off his torso. Fangs emerged as he declared, "I had other plans for you, but for such treachery, one way or another, your soul will be mine!" He charged the tiny mortal. Stan fainted and collapsed back into a large sliding chair. Dr. Vlasko aka Count Dracula suddenly felt that familiar bestial heartbeat pounding very near before he could hypnotize Keaton. He snarled, knowing that tenacious Rathbone had transformed.

The wolfman slammed the door open and rushed the vampire. Dracula grabbed the chair and pushed it in front of the lycan. The two creatures of the night pushed and tugged at the large wooden chair with Stan sitting in the middle.

Keaton awoke screaming for his life. The werewolf lunged for the nosferatu. The vampire rushed out of the room with the beast clawing at him. Stan gulped, relieved the terrifying creatures had vanished.

Monsters' Lab

24 - MONSTERS' LAB

Château Wilder, 1960s

The drugged patient stirred within the lab. The enormous figure began to unhook various tubes and wires from his body.

Dr. Elsa Wilder patted the giant's shoulder to calm him down and unhook the remaining wires. "Get up slowly. Go out to the hall. The master wants you to get your tiny friend, Stan."

Stan Keaton fled the room and accidentally ran away from the stairs. He made a U-turn and bumped his forehead into the muscular abdomen of Frankenstein's Monster. The terrified lab tech bounced back against the wall. A display sword crashed to the floor. Stan immediately grabbed the weapon. The tip accidentally brushed up against the brute's lower stomach.

The goliath thought the lab tech was trying to harm him with the sword and he charged the twerp.

Dr. Wilder heard the commotion from the laboratory. She saw the creature chasing Keaton and yelled, "Be gentle with Stan!" She stepped in between the titan and her terrified assistant.

He growled at her. He was still feeling the after effects of the sedation and slowly reached his hands for the doctor.

She kept backing away in the hallway until her body touched the northern balcony. Elsa was corned and slapped the towering figure. Her fingertips barely reached his chin.

Dr. Wilder's blow was not even a sting but then the creature saw her produce a titanium needle from her surgical gown. He was tired of being poked and prodded.

She nervously smiled. "This is only a mild sedative to calm you down." The closer the needle inched toward the monster of Frankenstein, the more enraged he became. He backhanded her arm to knock out the syringe. He forgot his own strength and the blow accidentally flipped the physician over the balcony. She plummeted into the ravine.

Count Dracula evaded the Wolfman by crawling up the wall, behind a tapestry that had been saturated with centuries of tobacco smoke, musty rooms and human odor.

The lycanthrope was distracted by heavy feet from behind. It twirled around and crouched down, ready to strike. Its leathery, dark nose crinkled up, eyeing the Frankenstein Monster.

The eight-feet two-inch tall figure sneered. The werewolf jumped thirty feet across the hallway, pouncing on his back. He tried to shake it loose, but the lycan dug its claws into his tough skin. He elbowed it in the gut. The blow sent it spinning backward in the air. It recovered, landing on all fours.

Those claws only felt like scratches to the creature. It was the beast's amazing speed that irked him. It kept circling him and he grew dizzy. It continued to lash at him with quick swipes. The gargantuan finally seized a furry wrist and flung it out of the lab. The wolfman's body spun through the air. The side of its skull was the first to hit the oak. The door's core shattered inside the bedroom with its outer edges still intact against the frame. Its limp body crashed hard onto the wooden floor, knocked out cold.

Keaton ran toward the stairs. The brute swiped at him. He barely evaded the massive hands, tripping on a rug. He screamed hysterically, sliding forward between the giant's legs.

Frankenstein's Monster angrily tried to scoop him off the floor. Stan rolled toward the staircase. The hulk's upper lip curled in anger. He stretched out his arms to squash the tiny man's skull.

Stan wiggled backward on his butt, reaching to feel for the stairs. "No siree, you ain't going to get me." He overreached and tumbled down the staircase into the foyer.

The wolfman's eyes shot open, not recalling its recent battle with the giant. Instead, its nostrils flared, smelling a putrid stench, something unnatural and deathlike. Then, the odor of that clumsy skinny man began to tantalize the beast's hunger. At the same time, back in the recesses of its untamed mind, a menacing memory irked its simple and savage brain. However, the natural impulse to taste a mortal's flesh during a full moon wouldn't subside. It became agitated and grunted madly. Its curse to feed warred with the notion of hunting down a much more sinister being.

Count Dracula smiled as his super sensitive ears heard the skinny man continue to ungracefully escape the creature. The vampire's body, hair and clothing defied gravity as he silently made his way along the ceiling toward the upper floor.

The yellowish-green creature was determined to crush the irritating dolt. Keaton slowly got to his feet. He saw the hulk appear at the top of the stairway. He grabbed a jade green dragon ornament from the foyer's table and chucked it. The brute deflected it but lost his footing in the process. He grunted as his enormous frame crashed through the side of the wooden railing. He flipped over, landing on his back one story below in the living room.

Keaton grabbed his wallet from a hidden compartment in the foyer and bolted out of the château.

The Frankenstein Monster angrily awoke from his daze, tired of his master's experiments on him. His eyes widened, realizing the main doorway was open and hearing that twerp's engine kick over. He spotted Stan cross the bridge on a Harley Davidson motorcycle and began to chase him with superhuman speed.

The Count heard the beast's pads lightly touch the floor. He was confident the werewolf would have succumbed to preying upon a mortal and leave him be, but it was too late.

The wolfman sensed a sanguinary force from the past. The hackles on its neck stood straight up. This insidious presence was something very familiar. It hopped from wall to floor combing steadily toward the upper château. Its ultra-acute senses drew it closer to this stygian prey, wanting to it, no matter what the cost.

Dracula reached the entryway to the upper terrace. He was seconds from his escape, trying to quietly close the metal hatch. The lycan was one story below, silently crouched in the staircase. It heard the metal hatch click as it shut, growling in frustration.

Vlad heard a commotion just in time to see a silhouette come crashing through the metal hatch. He jumped back to the pinnacle of the roof, camouflaging himself against the chimney. His keen eyes followed the lycanthrope's every move prowling the unlit terrace below. He was amazed the werewolf had curbed his desire for tasting raw flesh. It upset the Count that Rathbone's strong psyche still had such a powerful effect on the beast.

The lycan was irritated finding nothing in the uppermost terrace. It instinctively knew the stench of Hades, similar to its bane, was here. It scented the sickly oppressive smell of the undead. It wasn't a sweet aroma like the living. Little black puffs of the vampire's blood permeated the air, a deadly vapor from Hell. Its supernatural and animalistic senses allowed it to see, smell and hear what normal mortals could not. The beast arched its back, peered upward, and, then, let out a long growl. It vaguely recalled just fighting this creature of the night.

The vampire knew he had been detected. The werewolf let out a low gurgle. It instinctively sensed the bloodsucker didn't die like the humans it slaked for. The Transylvanian knew the wolfman was almost twice his might and the sun would soon shine. The lycan was too fast for Dracula to vault or glide away. He would have to use his fighting skills to escape.

The lycan snarled at its nemesis. The vampire lord hissed and jumped below toward the beast. All the wolfman saw were four large white fangs baring down upon him. Sharp claws reflexively extended further from leathery paws ready to fight the nosferatu.

Dracula flipped over in mid-air and kicked the werewolf's chest. The beast crashed back against the terrace's stone rail. The Count stood, grinning at his handiwork. He jumped a story below to the middle terrace. The wolfman spun around and eyed the wampyre below.

Vlad cursed, realizing the entire grounds were surrounded by running water. He began to glide toward the front bridge, his only escape. The lycan vaulted upward into the blackness of the night, desperately grasping after the nosferatu. Its claws dug into undead flesh. Both night creatures crashed hard into the lower terrace.

Dracula's lower ankle twitched. A pop could be heard as he reset his bone. He limped to his feet. The wolfman stirred and swiped at his nemesis' weak leg. They wrestled and clawed each other along the stone decking. The lycanthrope was shredding the vampire lord. The Count knew those supernatural canines and claws could destroy him. He finally had a chance to scratch at the lycan's eyes and kick it several stories below into the ravine. The beast crashed its head and upper torso into a boulder. Its body lay crushed and lifeless for several minutes.

Extremities twitched, joints popped back into place and bones rapidly healed. The werewolf slowly arose sniffing. The strength of the moon's rays began to fade as the first glimpses of sunshine began to rise in the eastern horizon. It looked up whimpering. The predator's appetite for a kill would not be satisfied now. Fur fell to the ground and it vanished into thin air. Dense muscle tissue diminished, large paws transformed into feet, and four canines receded. Nigel Rathbone collapsed from sheer exhaustion.

25 - GARLIC & WOLFSBANE

"Mom. Thank God there are no monsters."

The eighty-year old grinned. "It's nice to hear you acknowledge the Lord."

The young doctor sneered, "You know what I mean… no such thing as vampires and lycanthropes."

"Why do you think I always grow aconitum and allium sativum outside the windows and doors?"

Maria sassed folding her arms across her chest, "I just thought you liked cooking garlic and other herbs."

"That too." Rosa was about to broach the second subject. Something she had meant to reveal years ago, but never did. She took in a deep breath. "I gave birth to you on January 15th 1967."

"Mama, I know I was born on the day the Green Bay Packers won their first Super Bowl but that was some kind of story."

"As I said before, that was very real Maria." She mulled over her words before saying, "The second thing I should have told is your real mother, Dr. Elsa Wilder, was my sister."

Maria laughed, "It is not April 1st yet!"

Rosa put up her finger and firmly stated, "This is no joke. I was only nineteen years old in 1944, when your mother and I collaborated on the fusion of your parents' frozen egg and sperm. This occurred at the same time our entire family was forced to work for the Nazis' genetics program. You never knew your father, Dr. Carlos Tovar. He was a fine young scientist and could have safely returned to Spain. He loved your mother and remained with our family. Carlos continually objected to the presence of the Sturmabteilung (SS) and those damned, unethical experiments. Despite being a Spaniard, the SS tired of his insubordination and they dismembered him."

Maria almost fainted, hearing for the first time the true identity of her father. She winced knowing he was murdered at the cold and systematic hands of Himmler's evil Stormtroopers. She pointed at Rosa and objected nervously, "But you're my mother."

"I am sorry I never told you the truth my child. Oh, your mother was a card, quite shrewd and so liberal for her time. Elsa insisted in retaining the Wilder name, even, after their marriage." She giggled, "That even irritated your open-minded father. I guess Carlos couldn't entirely shake off his macho Spanish upbringing."

Maria smiled and drew in closer. She enjoyed such outlandish tales. She wasn't sure when Rosa's dry humor would weave fiction and non-fiction.

"Your mama feared your father's conservative Spanish family would try taking you away from me. This is one of the reasons I waited until my early forties to implant you in my womb. Nobody would have questioned that you were not mine."

Maria put her hand to her lips. She couldn't speak and began nervously wringing her hands.

She warmly hugged her before saying, "You are like a daughter to me"

The younger Wilder insisted, "No! I am your daughter."

"Yes, you are my daughter!" She frowned and added, "Just not physically."

She shook her head.

She smiled tenderly. "I love you Maria and am very proud of you. You are one of the top neurosurgeons in the world. Your paternal grandparents, the Tovars, were decent people and very proper.

"Tovars?"

Rosa raised an eyebrow. "Yes. Your biological father's parents. Unfortunately, they died several years after you were born. And I knew in my heart that I'd be able to raise you much better than a distant relative. You would have lived a life of luxury but they would have objected to your profession and independence."

The last statement hit home, even though she seriously doubted her mom's reminiscence was simply a concocted story."

She continued, "Your biological parents loved each other very much. Both sensed they would not make it out alive. Your mother wanted to know a child would continue from their wonderful union. That is how you came into this world. After your father's demise, your mother became entranced by Vlad who had liaisons with Hitler's sadistic Gestapo." The elderly Wilder shook her head disgusted. "After that, my sister was lost and shunned her professional ethics."

Maria's mouth gaped open. She finally grasped Rosa's rhetoric. "You really bore me but are not my mother?"

Rosa nodded.

"Why are you telling me now? Wait, frozen embryos didn't exist at that time. Your jesting is not funny mama."

"As I have told you it is all true." Rosa caressed Maria's hand and continued, "Your mother and I accomplished such a feat." She looked at the massive granite walls. "Papa was leery of Hitler and had most of our château transported, stone by stone, and built on top of Booty Bluff. We should have left Europe at the same time but waited too long. After America entered the war, it took longer to rebuild this château, there were fewer able-bodied men. Even the actors back then enlisted to fight the Axis Powers." Rosa frowned, stating, "How times have changed!"

Maria's hand shook as she poured both of them tea.

Her eyes seemed to peer into the past. "My father tried to help his daughter. Instead, Elsa fled the European police sometime in 1949. The Count later followed her." She sneered, "Elsa must have tricked our father to grant her legal rights to this estate before the Count murdered him. It took me years to track Elsa and that vermin down. I got here too late. I will never forget your mother's last request before she grew terribly sick - *Make sure you continue with our research to bring my child into this world.*"

Maria buried her hands in her face, sobbing in confusion.

She softly put a hand on Maria's shoulder and admitted, "I am sorry my dear child. I never felt the need to tell you that your mother was gone and I gave birth to you, twenty- three years after the war. A local physician, Dr. Pierce, helped me bring you into this world. We knew society would not accept such extreme practices at that time."

She stared at Rosa, still unsure of what was true.

Rosa was surprised to see her wolfs bane blooming near the window sill. She clenched a fist in front of her heart.

"Are you okay mama?"

"Yes, my sweet child." She slowly sipped at her tea and added, "Then there was Nige Rathbone. He preferred his proper name Nigel. He insisted it was more of a grown-up name or something like that. I loved to josh him when he wasn't in one of those somber moods. I discovered this wonderful Scotsman lying along the riverbed the next morning after that terrible ordeal."

"Oh sure! And I bet you are going to tell me that this Rathbone was tall, dark and handsome?"

Rosa flashed a quick grin. "Quite right!" She then thought of her sister and frowned. "I also found your mother along the bank. The stream must have broken her fall from the balcony. She barely had any life left in her and..."

"What?" Maria asked anxiously.

"Never mind child." The retired doctor began to feel weak and said, "For some reason, I feel what I am about to tell you is more important."

"Yes?"

"Well, I grew to love Nigel very much in such a short time." Her brow furrowed. "He kept his distance since he had killed his previous love."

"You fell in love with a killer?"

"It's not what you think." A bittersweet smile emerged. "Nigel and I had such a wonderful time together. Oh, how he was a tormented soul. I would make him wolfs bane tea, but that didn't always subdue the beast."

Maria looked up at her quizzically.

Rosa continued, "Even with all of the Wilder's unorthodox and extensive medical experience, I still could not help Rathbone's malady. We would drive to remote bayous on the nights of the full moons and his werewolf trans..."

"Werewolf? Oh, you're pulling my leg."

"Oh no, my sweetie," she said solemnly, "Nige was the ideal man... tough, caring and helped out with the housework but he was no pushover." Rosa sipped some herbal tea. She waved her index finger and added, "I almost forgot. He was a listener, such a fine and rare quality in a man."

"For goodness sake, one minute you're making this Nigel to be a saint and the next, a beast with your silly stories."

"You would be wise to believe me!"

"Please."

"One day… I surprised Nige." Rosa pointed her bony fingers toward Maria's heart. "I shot him with a silver bullet. Nigel's last words to me were - *Thank you for releasing me.* Then, I tucked him away for some peace."

Maria began to shake nervously.

"Whatever you do," Rosa's eyes grew stern, stating, "permit no one to enter the secret tomb!"

She frantically yelled, "What tomb?"

Rosa Wilder felt a sharp pain down her left arm and collapsed. Maria broke the fall and began to administer CPR.

26 - BOOTY BLUFF

South of Château Wilder, 1960s

The Frankenstein Monster ran after the annoying human on the two-wheeled machine. Stan Keaton looked back, gulping at the eight-foot two-inch tall juggernaut who was only a few feet from the olive-drab motorcycle' rear tire. The freak was running as fast as he could risk it over the gravel surface.

The lab technician skidded to the right, keeping the machine inches from the ground. The creature flew past the WWII bike and crashed into a tree. Keaton smiled, a scenic drive to Le Grande. His hands tightly gripped the handle bars after the Harley Davidson's back wheel skipped to the right. *He hadn't hit any potholes, had he?* Concerned, he looked back at the WLA motorcycle to see if there was any structural damage. A huge hand missed his shoulder by inches. Stan's eyes narrowed. He throttled back and gravel spit into the brute's face.

The titan yelled, "Master needs you!"

"No way Jose!" he said revving the engine.

The goliath's nostrils flared, losing ground on the puny human who had stuck him with high-tech needles and cut him with laser-like scalpels that could even penetrate his skin. He wanted to squash the skinny lab technician.

Keaton knew the next turn. He gunned the motor as he went between two large oaks. The monster of Frankenstein followed. The rider flew over a creek, taking three hard bounces on the other side as the road straightened out past the covered red bridge.

The giant plummeted twenty-five feet, not prepared to make a jump. The rushing water pushed him head first into a boulder. He later opened his eyes, smiling at the scenic panorama. He found himself deposited on the rocky shore of a small lake. As he scanned the surface, several fish jumped out in the open water. The lake's glassy stillness was attested to by the concentric circles growing even wider in the wake of the jumping fish. There were countless magnolia, bald cypress, oak, spruce pine and fruit trees. He felt content, no master and no lab tests. He would build a new cabin. *Alone wasn't so bad*, he thought. He definitely had his fill of humans, vampires and werewolves, and no longer hungered their company.

Château Wilder lay on top of what was previously known as Booty Bluff. The cavernous cliff served as a sanctuary for the native Indians whenever they needed to escape from the warring southeastern tribes throughout the 18th century. In the early 19th century, the elusive *Ghost Pirates*, helmed by Captain Calico Jacques O'Rourke, nicknamed the limestone hill as *Booty Bluff*, since it looked like a buccaneer boot from two vantage points. The pirates boasted they stored two types of booty inside the bowels of the giant rock, treasure and wenches.

Later, Calico was betrayed by his Irish cousin, Byran Numb Nuts O'Rourke, during a drunken quarrel over ballad selections. Numb Nuts quickly staged a mutiny and made Captain Jacques walk the plank on an early foggy morning, just south of the Pearl River's opening to the Gulf of Mexico. Unknown to his mutinous crew, a floating log saved the chained captain from drowning. Calico quickly embraced his new lease on life and returned to Booty Bluff to free the enslaved women. He shared the treasure with the ladies and they escaped to New Orleans under the protection of Jacque's French cousin, Jean Lafitte.

In the mid-1960s, Booty Bluff was ravaged by monstrous events. Dr. Rosa Wilder did her utmost to quell the damage done by her sister and stories too insane to believe. Within twenty years, the doctor's neurosurgical practice at Château Wilder earned the reputation as being the finest in the south.

August 26th 2005, a rising PGA contender known to frequent courses near Le Grande, eyed Leprechaun Link's narrow second fairway. Johnny Dulce snapped the Aldila golf shaft around his spine and his Titleist Pro V1 ball exploded off the tee.

The caddy walked up to Dulce's monstrous drive in the fairway. He noted his boss only had 255-yards to reach the 605-yard, par five in two shots. "You can do it!" Johnny then overdrew his long approaches to the green. He cursed at the bounce off the collar and, then, the splash. "It's going to be one of those days," the caddy said under his breath.

Dulce missed his usual Latte and his girlfriend dumped him the night before. He shook the two-iron at his caddy and yelled, "You suck!"

The caddy rolled his eyes and murmured, "Frou-frou golfer."

"Caddies are supposed to gauge distances well. I should have used a five wood. I hit it straighter." Dulce shouted.

“Then why didn’t you?”

Johnny kicked his caddy in the butt and roared, “That’s your job bonehead!”

The caddy put his hands up in the air and said, “You insisted that I golf with you on my day off." The drama queen stared blankly at him. "Sí o no, boss man?"

"Yes," Dulce admitted reluctantly.

"And that's when I normally spend time with my wife and kids, But I know you've had a tough week, amigo." The PGA golfer bit his lip. The caddy said, "So, today we golf as friends, no?"

Johnny's eyes opened wide. "Hello. I still need your assistance. This is your paycheck too."

The caddy defiantly crossed his arms. "Again, this is my day off and, besides, you didn’t ask!”

Johnny raised his voice, "I shouldn't have to."

He tired of his boss' moodiness. "You're worse than my wife. Did you have your latte?"

"No!"

The caddy shook his head. "I'll be back."

The angry golf pro had enough. Dulce yelled unintelligibly, bent his iron and hurled it toward the bay. It fell short of the water and landed on the bank’s edge.

August 29th 2005, Hurricane Katrina pounded the central Gulf Coast with one-hundred and forty-five mph winds. The undercurrent and massive waves caused by the horrendous gusts shifted old timber that had been preserved beneath the western bank of St. Louis Bay since Hurricane Camille. The outer edges of Katrina ransacked many of Le Grande's cheaply constructed homes and businesses. Windows shattered, roofs were peeled open by the wind and water steadily progressed inland. Most of the seasoned Gulf residents had blocked windows and doors with plywood and sandbags hours before the storm hit. Many learned from the past and built their buildings slightly higher off the ground to minimize flood damage. But even the best countermeasures could only do so much as Mother Nature unleashed her fury.

The Frankenstein Monster sat back against the tree on his deer hunting stand in a remote area of southern Mississippi as Hurricane Camille drew close in 1969. He slowly raised his homemade spear as the animal approached. The storm startled the approaching stag and it fled northward. He looked above, not accustomed to such weather when ferocious winds from Hurricane Camille blew him into the bay.

Almost four decades later, bubbles suddenly shot to the surface and a long thick carcass was released from its brackish den a hundred yards from the bank. The current pushed the blob in a westerly direction toward the swampy shore. The thing lay next to a small shrub on the golf course's bank and a bent two-iron. Later, lightning struck the iron's metal shaft. It shot electricity into the water-logged carcass and its extremities trembled.

Hurricane Katrina, 2005

Many miles to the northwest, various debris and shrubbery crashed into the southern and eastern cliffs of Château Wilder as stone griffins guarded the larger windows above. The blast from Hurricane Katrina uprooted massive trees surrounding the estate's thirty-five-foot high limestone basin.

Three decades earlier, Dr. Rosa Wilder tried to freshen up Booty Bluff by installing new windows and landscaping the perimeter with lush gardens. People normally did not notice its base blooming with colorful flowers and manicured hedges, or the swaying palms along the southern terrace, and fruit trees neatly arranged around the estate. Instead, onlookers were instantly awestruck by the harrowing gothic towers. Its grayish granite walls were quite the contrast to the nearby magnolia trees and the Pearl River below the western ramparts. The château's pinnacle jutted over a hundred and twenty feet above the surrounding flatter terrain.

At the moment, vegetation was just struggling to survive. The hurricane gales uprooted a magnolia tree from Booty's western bank. A few moments later, a huge oak tree began to tilt from the heavy winds near the estate's driveway in the southeast corner. The great oak then plummeted on top of the garage attached to the château's front foundation. Fragmented pieces of mortar and brick revealed a small black hole in the garage's back wall.

Château Wilder

27 - NOOKS & CRANNIES

September 1, 2005

Semper Construction arrived at Château Wilder to assess the damages inflicted by the hurricane. Three men dispersed to check the foundation, roof and interior. The owner, Ernie Semper, had replaced many windows, remodeled rooms and refurbished the elevator for Rosa during the past two decades. He was mostly proud of gutting the library's back rotting frame, cutting through the massive granite blocks to enlarge the opening and replacing it with an eight-foot wide French door. It provided the library with a nice view to the château's cavernous dock and about 600 square-feet of Pearl River backwater. He smiled at his craftsmanship as he shuffled down the two-tiered ramp. He probed crevices, walls and the dock's two-story high ceiling with his powerful Surefire flashlight. He hollered up toward the open door, "Hey Doc, no foundation damage down here but ya gotta follow me."

Maria exited the library and remarked, "I barely remember my moth... Rosa putting in this concrete ramp and pier."

He nodded. "Whoever the crew was they did some fine workmanship." The forty-by-forty-foot stone alcove provided shade and protection for small craft during inclement weather. The marine enclosure could tightly fit in a pair of twenty-five feet long boats. It also had a center levy to pull up a kayak or a jet ski.

They walked outside overlooking the southern ravine for an eighth of a mile which led up to the château's front southeast corner. He pointed. "Besides a few loosened stones on the southwest terrace, the garage here is what got the brunt it."

They avoided the damage from the fallen oak. "Doc, it appears there is a small cave beyond the garage's fractured wall." He pointed his flashlight inside and said, "Well, lookie there!"

"What is it Ern?"

"It appears to be some kind of rectangular wooden chest?" He whistled, "Chainsaw and a metal pike." The crew cut off a large branch and, then, tore open a few bricks. He squeezed his wiry frame through the tight opening. The foreman's boots lifted up dust that had been left undisturbed for forty years. Maria crawled in behind him.

He grasped a crusty, pale yellow flower from the floor. "Hmm… I remember studying about Aconitum Vulparia in my college botany class. Most folks call it wolfs bane." He looked at

Doc and asked, "Do you suppose your ma put this crate inside here?"

"All I know is my mother replaced the shed with this three-car garage when the development was built." Maria didn't correct Ernie that Rosa was technically her aunt. *To hell with it*, she thought, *Rosa brought me into this world and raised me. I always called her mom and I always will.* "This was the back wall to our shed as far as I can remember."

"Either way, I reckon this small nook was blocked up for no one to get in or out." He pried the lid open and jumped back in fright, gasping, "They didn't embalm this one. He looks more like a fresh mummy with wolfs bane scattered all over him." He looked at her suspiciously. "This was more like a prison than a tomb."

Maria whispered reading a tarnished bronze inscription: *"My wonderful Scotty Nige: Woe to those noble souls who are bitten by a lycan and lives, for they will become a beast at the full moon's first light."* It was too much and she fainted. The retired Marine caught Doc in his arms before her head dashed into the wooden crate.

Later that afternoon, Sheriff Rico Lombardi Jr. arrived. He placed his hand on Doc's shoulder. "Maria, my condolences about your mother," he said tenderly.

She gave him a fierce hug. "Thank you."

Rico then tilted his hat in respect as the man's remains were carried off in a gurney. The sheriff sighed. "Rosa indicated that this man wanted to die in her last Will and Testament. There is no record of an autopsy. All you know is his name was Nige?"

"That's what the inscription says. I just read my mother's Will and Testament a few minutes ago. This is all new to me."

Ernie came running in, almost out of breath, "Doc… You probably won't like it."

"Spit it out!" she grumped.

"I found a secret door underneath the fallen magnolia."

Maria frowned. "It is below the tree?"

"Not really, it looks like someone built up dirt and planted the tree to obstruct the opening." His knees quaked. "Crap, for a second, I swore I saw a woman chained inside, crying out for help. That damn passage even winds all the way up to your gym."

"That is impossible! I was a snoopy kid and have found it."

The foreman escorted the physician and sheriff up the spiraling ramp until they reached the wall that opened into the solarium and exercise room.

"Amazing, this was ma's laboratory and medical practice until she upgraded it to another part of the château. I can't believe she never told me about the winding tunnel?"

"Doc, no offense but your entire château always gives me the creeps. Your garage's open staircase leading up to the library's bookshelf was no secret. Rosa asked me to install that so she would avoid being drenched during heavy rains." Ern gulped, "I'm afraid what else my crew may encounter behind these walls after finding that eerie crate and tunnels. If you don't mind, we would prefer working here during the day."

"That is fine, sissy."

"Maria, now that is a cheap shot." The lawman snickered. The former Marine frowned. "Where's the respect? Sheriff, I reckon ya still need that leaky roof patched up. Now, I figure Mrs. Lombardi wouldn't be too happy if my construction crew were too busy. Is that so?

"That is so, Ernie."

"That's more like it." He stink-eyed the physician. "I'd be careful with your sassing, Doc. You have a lot of chores around here… don't ya?"

She blushed. "Sorry for calling you a sissy, Ern."

His eyes bulged out. "Another thing, don't be surprised to discover more hidden nooks and crannies. Your mother was savvy to hire a lot of high falutin' out of town contractors." Semper added with piss and vinegar in his voice, "And I sure as hell don't want to be the one to find out!"

Doc still wrestled with the notion that she was probably the first frozen embryo to be born in the world. She did her best to hide any body language contrary to what she really knew. Ernie Semper and Sheriff Lombardi had been friends for years. She had to find out more facts before sharing information. She didn't want explain to them the confusing parental relationship at the present time, nor things that sounded so ludicrous, like monsters. The hidden passages explained how Rosa was always able to disappear from a room. She was beginning to understand her mother's superstitious ways. It also became very clear why many of the original locals gave Rosa and herself the cold shoulder. She murmured, "Mama, why didn't you tell me all this earlier?"

Ernie and Rico looked at her quizzically. Sheriff Lombardi's cell phone rang. He recognized the Palm Springs number. "Hey Gwen. How's it hanging?"

The spry senior laughed at his macho sarcasm, "Very funny sheriff. Your deputy informed me that you would be at Château Wilder. Maria has not been answering her phone…"

"Hey Doc. It's your mother's lawyer, Gwen Adams."

"Is this my Auntie Gwen? We haven't spoken in ages."

"It's been ten years as a matter of fact. Honey, I am sorry to hear about your Aunt Rosa," she goofed, "I mean mother."

Maria whispered, "You always knew she was my aunt?"

Gwendolyn replied, "Only Dr. Pierce and I knew the truth. Rosa didn't want to confuse you."

"That's what this is to me now, a big headache!"

"She meant it for the best. I just wanted to inform you that Mrs. Millicent, Mr. Mueller and Judge Kevan cleared the floorplans years ago. I just e-mailed the county our copies. The clerk informed me all their older paperwork was destroyed in the hurricane." Gwen paused. "Did Rosa ever tell you what really happened?"

"A little bit but it is some crazy stuff." Maria distanced herself from the Rico and Ern before saying, "Mom mentioned a vampire, giant, and werewolf just moments before she died."

"Believe me, it is all true," Gwen Adams reassured her. "The authorities couldn't make any sense of it. The only truth to come out of it was some fine people died of unnatural causes."

Maria pursed her lips. "Mom didn't go too far into details."

"Rosa hired me to investigate. Dr. Austin from Le Grande's hospital helped me piece together the terrible details. We knew better to not tell the authorities the truth. After solving the case, Dr. Austin and I left. We got tired of the cold stares from the locals. Rosa was tough as nails; she could take anything."

"That's mom alright!"

Gwen sighed. "My dear Austin broke his neck in a skiing accident on a late honeymoon." Her voice sounded bittersweet, "We were married just over a year but they were good times... I was then blessed to marry dear Thomas."

"Wasn't Uncle Tom a general?"

"Yes, General Turnage. However, I kept my last name for business purposes and worked for Millicent and Mueller. We helped Rosa retain the château after the whole debacle. I am now semi-retired in Palm Springs but happy to provide any legal services."

Dr. Wilder said, "If my mom trusted you then so will I."

"Great!"

"Aunt Gwen, thank you for straightening out all the legalities. Our stationary has your phone numbers and e-mail address. Is all your contact information still the same?"

"Yes. Please feel free to contact me." Gwen took in a deep breath, "Make sure Rathbone's remains get buried as soon as the autopsy is completed."

"Oh, I almost forgot about him," Doc said despondently. "I probably will have some more questions later. It is just so hard to gather my thoughts."

"Maria, don't wait too long!" her attorney insisted. Auntie Gwen's urgent tone haunted the physician. Her scientific mind struggled with things she counted as pure rubbish. She wanted to scream. Instead, she handed the lawman his cell phone and excused herself for the evening.

Sheriff Lombardi knew better to press her under the circumstances.

Doc's first order of business was to heed Rosa's age-old advice: *After a tough day when you've done all you can do, then, pour yourself one, cold stiff drink and soak your body in a hot bath, because tomorrow will still come.*

28 - ALIVE

September 2, 2005

Shortly before dawn, something resembling Victor Frankenstein's Creation stumbled up from a muddy bank. The thing fell to the ground on all fours and hurled out murky water. His skin appeared clammy and ashen. His body twitched and convulsed for several moments, before he clumsily got to his feet.

A bird screeched in the sky above. The giant turned his scarred face toward the hawk. Water drained from one of his ears as he gazed up at the magnificent looking specimen. He slowly studied his surroundings, not sure where he was. He wasn't accustomed to the sick and bloated feeling. He had feint recollections of being entombed in ice, sand and mud. It seemed like this had been the fourth time he had been revived from hibernation, but different than that first:

***

Arctic Region, summer 1840s

Sections of ice cracked and melted due to extremely warm Arctic temperatures in mid-July. One large piece eventually drifted south. It settled along the outer banks of an inlet late in the autumn season. A very large figure lying on the shore was the only object left from the melted ice.

The sun was shining and large green trees began to sway. The fragrant smell of evergreen pines drifted through the increasing gusts of wind. Late in the afternoon, dismal gray skies signaled a drastic change of weather was on the horizon for the next few days.

Days later, an unnatural electrical field with one-hundred mile an hour winds swept past the huge carcass. The howling wind transformed to a chilling stillness.

Birds chirped as the skies cleared. Several deer stirred from their shelter to face the calm. A hare emerged from the tall grass and began to feed close to the lush shoreline.

A gull inched closer to the inanimate thing along the shore. It sensed micro-tremors coming from the body, flapped its wings and flew away. On the Day of the Dead, the Frankenstein Monster's lungs expanded and his eyes shot open.

The creature's focus steadily improved as he walked along the link's bank. He seemed to have a distant memory of a bride accepting him after his first hibernation. He wasn't sure if it was a dream or reality, so he forced himself from revisiting that subject. Instead, the waterlogged carcass dragged himself toward the remote side of the golf course. Though his mind still felt pickled and dull, he instinctively knew to avoid humans. Not many were kind to him, but through the fog, he began to recall a handful of people that showed him kindness:

The last time the Frankenstein Monster roamed the earth in the early twentieth century, he defended his boat's captain from a mutinous crew. It was another painful reminder to him of man's depraved state:

The century-old fishing vessel was overdue for a port call, but the skipper needed one more large catch in the Chukshi Sea before heading south through the Bering Strait.

Fruit and supplies were sparse, and scurvy on the rise, the crewmen rebelled. They stabbed and shot the brute to no avail.

Captain Peck lay bleeding from a pistol wound in his lower left rib.

The mutineers shot a cannon ball at the monster but missed, instead splitting the wooden mast in half.

Frankenstein's Creature yelled out, "Traitorous devils," batting them overboard with part of the broken mast.

The cannon ball did its damage, plunging though the ship's deck and port hull. Frigid salt water quickly rose through the holes. The mutinous crew's bounty was death.

The ship went down in the icy waters and the behemoth tried to swim toward the southeast, pushing his leader on a piece of broken timber. Terrified to lose another friend, he tried to keep the captain above the icy waters. Peck was a tough skipper who had always treated the giant with dignity, not horrified by his enormous stature or gruesome features.

Seventy-two hours later, the frigid water even got to the superhuman freak of nature. The goliath began to lose consciousness and sunk into the depths. His body was pushed in a northerly undercurrent. Wedged and eventually entwined under the crevice of a small iceberg, he lay frozen in a suspended hibernated state once again.

The Arctic went through some of the hottest weather in recorded history from the mid to late 1930s. Summer temperatures of four degrees higher than normal caused mammoth slabs of ice to crack loose along the Arctic Ocean, north of the Bering Strait.

Early September 1938, an iceberg, the size of fast-frigate drifted south toward the Bering Strait. Weeks later it slowly passed by the Aleutian Islands. By the time the ice reached the territorial seas of British Columbia it had melted down to the exterior dimensions of a small house.

Mid-November 1938, the ice had shrunk to the size of a large pick-up truck. It eventually drifted toward the shoreline, wedging itself under a dilapidated wooden pier which supported an old lookout post that had been used to signal ships at sea.

Several days later, the slab of ice cracked into several pieces. A large apparition plunged into the Pacific waters and floated toward shore. Hellish windstorms began to blow through the coastline of Canada's Pacific Southwest. The strong winds tugged at a power line that was connected from land to the pier's lookout post. The line finally snapped and whipped toward a very long body lying on the beach. The electrical current surged through its gigantic form.

On November 23rd 1938, extremities trembled. The Frankenstein Monster took its first breath in years. The creature was freed from his arctic burial yet again. He slowly crawled away from the Pacific shoreline and disappeared into the dense forest.

Days later, the behemoth discovered an elderly gentleman crying and talking to the remains of a woman wrapped in a blanket near a partially dug grave.

"Oh, my dear wife, I will surely miss you. For fifty-seven years, you were like a fragrant and lovely flower." The elderly Canadian then fell to his knees sobbing.

The giant cleared the forest line just yards from the white-haired man. He lightly grabbed the shovel from the grieving soul and softly spoke in his deep voice, "Sir, I will finish digging your wife's grave."

The elderly man was in such a state of shock, he wasn't even startled by the sudden appearance of a stranger in the Canadian wilds. To the creature's immediate relief, he soon discovered the old man had very poor vision. It was one of the few times, no one fled in terror from his hideous form.

Ten years later, Frankenstein's creation was now mourning over his dear, old friend. The blind man had lived a long life for a mortal, at eighty-seven years old. Besides, his greatly diminished eyesight, he was sharp in mind and had a relatively healthy body for his age until he caught pneumonia.

He gently placed the remains of one who had only showed him kindness. For the past decade, it was the first time the Creature of Frankenstein enjoyed the love of a father figure. He immediately called the kind Canadian, *Pa*, and the childless man called him, *son*. From the first day they met, the ravages of glaucoma had already taken its toll on his adopted dad to where he could barely see.

The giant gladly took over the elder's chores of chopping wood, cultivating their small plot of land, and hunting for food. The retired Latin professor was delighted to have company. They spent much time fishing, speaking multiple languages, making raspberry and blueberry wine, repairing the log cabin, and playing chess.

The creature remained in the cabin for several months after the blind man's death. He often talked to his Pa as if he were still with him, even though, he knew the Canadian was deceased. He was just grateful there was no family to kick him out this time.

The titan bitterly recalled the moment he almost befriended the blind Frenchman, De Lacey, over a century ago. He was almost at the point of explaining to De Lacey that he was the protector of his family, that he gathered their firewood and tended their garden. That was until Felix, Safie, and Agatha returned to their cottage. They were horrified at the site of the monstrous Image. The son, Felix, beat him down. Instead of retaliating that dreadful day, Frankenstein's Daemon fled with a broken heart.

Months passed and the giant enjoyed his afternoon routine of tea time under the cabin's expansive porch. He smiled thinking of how Pa showed him how to brew various berry and herbal teas. He missed the old man. The monster dozed off in the large chair he had made years before.

A voice came from below the steps, "We are lost, sir. Can you help us?" Frankenstein's creation stirred from his nap; his massive body hidden from the stranger's view. The Canadian hunters' faces reflected relief that they had found the cabin in their time of distress.

The hulking figure stood up to greet the pair, forgetting they could see him, unlike his adopted Pa. The men's eyes expressed terror at the grotesque and huge form before them. The goliath put up his hands. "Please, stay calm."

One of the men fired his rifle and the round hit the brute's lower left shoulder. The hulk winced from the bullet. It barely pierced through his skin and fell to the wooden porch with a thud.

The Monster of Frankenstein looked up and snarled, "Put your weapons down now, if you want to live." The hunters' teeth chattered as they slowly placed their weapons on the ground. The pair then walked backward into the forest line and fled in terror.

The giant was amazed that his wound healed almost instantly. It made him think of Victor Frankenstein. He began to wonder if his creator even had a clue of how powerful his unnatural creation would become.

As much as the creature loved Pa's cabin, he knew it was time to move on again. People would return in numbers to confront him. He had learned humans feared strange things, and knew it was futile to think otherwise. He grabbed his essential items and headed south.

The thing groggily walked alongside an electrical substation. He thought of a Scottish couple who were very loving to him, but he blocked out another painful memory of death and loss. The hulk then thought of a dark figure who treated him with respect, but the man was cold like a corpse. He seemed to remember his name: *D-r-a c…*

Small bursts of energy shot through the air. His body seemed to perk up, as if he had absorbed stray volts from the substation. His eyes smiled with delight. He suddenly felt much stronger and alert. The monster of Frankenstein was alive.

29 - FALLEN PRINCE

Witch of Endor, I Samuel 28: 8-18

So, Saul disguised himself, putting on other clothes, and at night he and two men went to the woman. "Consult a spirit for me," he said, "and bring up for me the one I name."

But the woman said to him, "Surely you know what Saul has done. He has cut off the mediums and spiritists from the land. Why have you set a trap for my life to bring about my death?"

Saul swore to her by the Lord, "As surely as the Lord lives, you will not be punished for this."

Then the woman asked, "Whom shall I bring up for you?"

"Bring up Samuel," he said.

When the woman saw Samuel, she cried out at the top of her voice and said to Saul, "Why have you deceived me? You are Saul!"

The king said to her, "Don't be afraid. What do you see?"

The woman said, "I see a ghostly figure coming up out of the earth."

"What does he look like?" he asked.

"An old man wearing a robe is coming up," she said.

Then Saul knew it was Samuel, and he bowed down and prostrated himself with his face to the ground.

Samuel said to Saul, "Why have you disturbed me by bringing me up?"

"I am in great distress," Saul said. "The Philistines are fighting against me, and God has departed from me. He no longer answers me, either by prophets or by dreams. So, I have called on you to tell me what to do."

Samuel said, "Why do you consult me, now that the Lord has departed from you and become your enemy? The Lord has done what he predicted through me. The Lord has torn the kingdom out of your hands and given it to one of your neighbors—to David. Because you did not obey the Lord or carry out his fierce wrath against the Amalekites, the Lord has done this to you today."

September 2, 2005

Dracula had just returned snacking from a rundown section in southern New Orleans. He had acquired Gemela from an infamous Mexican mobster, Pablo Villa, who had strong ties to the Sicilian Mafia, La Cosa Nostra.

Gemela provided a luxurious and loose lifestyle from the roaring twenties until the mid-1960s. Pablo's resort was infamous as the southern US hotspot that provided the best decadence money could buy.

A staunch prohibitionist tagged the locale as the ultimate highway to hell. The Big Easy judges ensured the law looked the other way during the prohibition era thanks to bribes and threats similar to the greasy politicos from Chicago. It was one of the few places that guaranteed jobs during America's Great Depression.

Gemela had been filled with bare-breasted ladies in the pool and elsewhere. The resort spa provided the best cigars, cuisine, golf, liquor and tennis money could buy. It also had the best of the bad to include cocaine, heroin, pills, and prostitution.

The golden days on Gemela weren't so innocent. It once had an infirmary with a full-time doctor and staff who tried to relieve the infamous from sexual transmitted diseases, drug addictions and hangovers. In the early years, such guests included Al Capone, Lucky Luciano, Bugsy Siegel and other members of the mob. Curvaceous women desperate to work for Pablo were a dime a dozen and didn't last long. Many became drug-addicts, alcoholics or worse.

Señor Villa's thriving business ceased after much of his staff mysteriously began dying. Some of them were found decapitated and others simply vanished. This terror began late in 1964. Gemela's Christmas wasn't such a banner season that year for Villa's business or the vacationing Mafiosos.

Even the toughest of the mob began to get shaky. Their bodyguards who were lucky enough to survive claimed gorgeous little ladies with fangs bruised them up. Being Latino, Pablo Villa did the sensible thing concerning the supernatural – he fled before becoming the undead.

Less than a year passed before a lawyer approached Pablo in Mexico. He represented a Middle Eastern gentleman by the name of Professor Dalb Al-Ukhard who wanted to purchase Pablo's share of the fertile patch of land. The sixty-five-year old Señor Villa gladly obliged. The resort ceased bringing in cash flow and property tax was killing him. The prior presidency wasn't taking it easy on the mobs' properties and bribes weren't as effective. The Latino couldn't complain. He had made millions from the resort haven, even if he lost a substantial amount from its true estate's value.

The Count had his furtive ways. Few knew Professor Dalb Al-Ukhard and Count Dracula were one in the same. Gemela even brought in hefty profits for various produce each year. He made it abundantly clear to his brides not to feast on migrants who tended Gemela's crops. At times, Dracula had to make a spectacle of a defying or runaway bride. He normally impaled them or tied the she-vampire's feet and hands to the ground, cursing them under a spell so they were unable to escape with their special powers. Vlad's harsh examples, maintained order when other vampires saw the rebelling bride's bones dried up by the sun the following night. As back up, vombies protected the migrant workers at night during the busy harvest season. The hired hands feared the superstitious rumors. They only came to the plantation as a last resort to support their families back home. Otherwise, any living soul stayed clear of Gemela.

From March to September, Dracula sporadically traveled with his favorite brides to other large urban settings like Atlanta, Baltimore, Birmingham, Buffalo, the nation's Capital, Chicago, Cleveland, Detroit, Houston, Kansas City, Los Angeles, Memphis, Miami, Minneapolis, Newark, Oakland, Orlando, Philadelphia, St. Louis and Stockton. The lively cities attracted a vibrant supply of tourists or crime was often high in the metropolitan areas they frequented to blend in and cover their tracks. As sport, Vlad enjoyed hunting down murderous gang members, major drug dealers, rapists and child molesters. He chuckled, thinking, *Habits die hard.* He enjoyed seeing the look of terror in the "tough" guys' faces and hearing them squeal like pigs.

The Count only bit men for nourishment and, if he did, he usually destroyed them. He enjoyed being the sole male. He normally didn't suck all of a victim's blood in one bite. Three bites guaranteed that he would be master over them as long as he was the undead. Otherwise, draining all of a victim's blood at one time made for an unruly and unmanageable blood sucker. Such vampires rarely were careful to select their prey or destroy them after feeding. An increased number of rogue nosferatu was a bad thing. It only raised awareness to a few open-minded and competent public figures that vampires may exist. Professor Abraham Van Helsing had been one such as that. The professor was his greatest arch-enemy but that crafty man had been dead for years.

The last time Count Dracula saw Dr. Van Helsing was late 1945 on the northern coast of France:

***

The vampire lord was awakened at dusk to a familiar sound from long ago, the ramming of a wooden gate. He stood within the shadows of the château's upper terrace; eyeing who dared enter his temporary abode. "Professor, you are wise as a serpent in finding me." Dracula stared at the center court below, amazed at how stout the Dutchmen appeared. He noticed Van Helsing's head of hair was no longer red, but all white. *How could the mortal still be alive?* The Count thought, *His nemesis had to be at around 115 years old.*

Professor Abraham Van Helsing scanned the terrace above. "Ah, I see you dance for the devil once again. Similar to King Saul, you consulted witches and trusted in black magic, rather than the Lord God Almighty. You, Vlad Drakhol of Wallachia, have forsaken the faith of your forefathers. As it is written: *Give no regard to mediums and familiar spirits; do not seek after them, to be defiled by them: I am the Lord your God.*"

The fallen prince was enraged at the reproof but replied in a crisp tone, "You forgot to mention Professor I am Székely, not just Wallachian."

Dr. Van Helsing added, "Count Drakhol, you once had Székely and Wallachian blood flowing through your veins. Now your unholy body is like a bloated tick, merely a polyglot of your victims' blood."

He shouted, "How dare you denounce my royal lineage – you swine!"

Abe chuckled, "The Székely were indeed the finest warriors of medieval Transylvania and Wallachia."

The Count's right eyebrow rose in curiosity from the flattery. "Rightly so you are Professor Van Helsing!"

The doctor bellowed, "However, Vlad, you have wrongly recounted history about part of your bloodline. Contemporary historians are now contemplating that the Székely race is probably a mix of Maygar, Scythian, and Turkic."

The vampire lord's nostrils flared. "Turkic – that is blasphemy!" He was about to jump three stories below to battle his nemesis, until he spotted fourteen men hidden deep within the château's shadows.

The men were armed with bows and wooden arrows, Holy Water, and blessed wafers. They even wore leather neck collars and wrist bands.

Dracula's high aquiline-shaped nose crinkled. "You will not outlive me Professor Van Helsing."

The professor leaned on his wooden cane with a concealable silver sword tucked inside. His demeanor suddenly became very serious and he stated, "Whether I live another day or not is up to the good Lord. The important matter is my men continue to gird themselves up in the full armor of God in order to confront your kind, the prince of darkness' unholy children. For against the wampyre it is both a spiritual and physical battle."

The Count's green eyes now narrowed to red slits as he leaned over the terrace's railing. "You are wise in your old age, but the nerve of you to rebuke one who has lived through seven centuries and commanded armies to defend Europe's southeastern flank."

Dr. Abraham Van Helsing snickered, knowing he stalled Vlad long enough through their loud verbal exchange.

The vampire lord heard heart beats approaching the upper terrace. "Too cunning for your own good professor," the Count warned Van Helsing. He jumped to the roof, escaping a dozen of wooden arrows whizzing by his undead body.

Professor Abraham Van Helsing spread gasoline throughout the dilapidated structure's main floor. He bent down at the front door and ignited a spark with the cherry of his lit cigar. The professor grinned as he saw the fire spread rapidly. "Ah, good, just one less nest for this unholy, vermin to rest," he said to himself.

Count Dracula scowled as flames began to spread to the upper floors of the abandoned château. He swung the side of his right fist against the chimney and chunks of mortar exploded into the air. Van Helsing's band of vampire hunters were adapting too well for the undead prince's own comfort. He had never encountered such a deadly combination of brashness, strategy, and tactics. He concentrated for a moment and seconds later, leathery wings flapped past the château's roof.

30 - CASTLE DRACULA

Vlad paused, reflecting under the main building's massive porch. He was a keen historian, learning from mistakes and triumphs. He had always been careful to reveal his adept transfigurations into a bat, mist, rats, or wolf to only a select number of his brides. Too many had rebelled in the past. Now, only his trusted brides held such special transformational powers. He reserved a special corps resting in nearby graves. He would only awaken them as a last resort.

Gemela's two towering mounds were named Las Chiches Madre by Pablo Villa over seventy-five years ago. The 120 feet tall summits provided extra shade for the resort mansion nestled within the northern ridge during sunrise and sunset. The former resort measured just over one mile east to west and three-quarters of a mile north to south.

Prince Vlad Tepes III had done well investing in many enterprises. Besides power, he relished times like these where he could rest outside before the sun rose above the eastern mound. This was that moment. He sat under the portico on his wicker throne. The sun was barely out but not hitting the northern ridgeline between the two high mounds.

Deep in thought, the Count peered northward. He groaned for his dark rest. He focused more. Some force that he previously mastered was nigh. He was not a mind reader but Dracula had been given the dark gift to sense things. He could also pass messages to those under his power and slightly control the weather around him. Sometimes, it felt as if an invisible being was whispering over his shoulder.

The Count's long bony fingers grasped a silver-tipped scepter by its wooden shaft. The memento was made from an extinct gopher wood. The silver head was shaped in the form of a dragon with piercing red eyes made from rubies. His father and he earned their family reputation as being fearless fighters of their homeland with the title of *Drakhol*, meaning *dragon.*

Dracula was also referred to as *son of the devil* and Vlad *Tepes* - the *Impaler*. The Ottomans titled him *Kazikli Bey* - the *Impaler Prince*. Few things did the cold and calculating vampire lord cherish beside his golden crescent ring and scepter. Oddly, the antique cane was a personal gift from a Godly man, the Holy Roman

Emperor. It was a reward from Emperor Sigismund for guarding southeastern Europe against the onslaught of Islamic expansionism.

Count Dracula had once been a man, an autocratic ruler. Even as the undead, Prince Vlad Drakhol had looked out for the good of his people those first hundred years but never afterward.

Five centuries ago, his countrymen of Wallachia began to question his mortality. He never aged beyond a youthful looking forty and only revealed himself at night. It was then his beloved people began to shun him despite his orderly rule.

He even had look-alikes pose as him, especially, during the day, until he was supposedly killed in battle. He quickly changed tactics when his double's head was displayed in Turkey. Even in hiding, rumors began to spread that Vlad was the same Voivode, sovereign ruler, governing behind the scenes and under different names for over a century.

From his ungodly genesis and being the region's supreme authority, Dracula had a bountiful selection of blood victims who were mostly captured enemies, traitors or criminals. That was until he had to go underground.

The vampire lord later relocated to his favorite castle in Transylvania, several miles southeast of Borgo Pass. No one knew him as Vlad there, only a boyar and much later by the name of Count Dracula. It was almost a medium-sized castle, not small like Poienari or large like Bran.

The Count preferred the Borgo Pass fortress because it extended out on the corner of a great rock, quite impregnable on three sides. The massive front walls were backed-up by a thirty-foot deep by thirty-foot wide moat that steadily angled down to the cliff on each side. A sufficient amount of oil or water poured down upon any mortal trapped in the moat ensured a slide to their doom, nearly a thousand-foot drop to the valley below.

Small slits in the upper floor of the keep and main forward towers were the only openings, strategically placed to defend the castle's front. The drawbridge's entrance angled up into a courtyard with a fountain at its center. Stables and barracks faced a winged dragon defiantly posed in the middle of the fountain.

Several thick wooden doors fortified with iron gave access to various parts of the castle. The center archway was the largest, the only one ornate with scenes of battle along its sides. Besides the stone dragon and main doorway, the rest of the courtyard appeared very Spartan.

Castle Drakhol

Even though, the structure remained mostly unkempt for centuries, its quality craftsmanship weathered well against the elements. Great windows were only located along the fortress' exterior three sides where sling, bow or culverin could not reach. The drawbridge was the only access point for mortals to intrude upon the vampire's haven.

Vlad Drakhol hired out of area Szganzy Gypsies to seal up four secret entrances shortly after he became the undead.

How Count Dracula longed for his native fortress near Borgo Pass, but the blood supply in the nearby villages weren't sufficient to sustain him and a few brides.

As a vampire, Dracula was unable to jump or fly across fresh running waterways utilizing his supernatural powers. He had to rely on fallen logs or bridges to cross streams and rivers in his human form. This hindered the Count from travelling to inhabited areas like Bistriz in an hour solely as a bat. And to make matters more difficult, the locals had keenly defended themselves against his kind since the mid-nineteenth century. Even the best of predators could only wait so long in an area before it became too dry. He doubted if the Great War had changed the villagers' superstitious ways even today.

Count Dracula thought to himself, *Gemela is not fortified like my mountaintop lair in Transylvania. However, my hidden abode is remote and Gemela has easy access to prey that doesn't believe in the undead. Then, there is Shaded Grove, only a hopping point and not an ideal, secure resting place, but more fools to feed upon.* The vampire lord smiled with a red light of triumph in his eyes that even Judas in Hell might be proud of. *It is almost too easy in America.*

Over the years, the vampire virus and the pact Dracula unknowingly made with his sinister lord in the fifteenth century had hardened his soul. The Count still vividly remembered the elderly looking Scholomance instructor pitch the deal:

***

"Prince Vlad Tepes Drakhol of Wallachia, within six nights, you will become immortal after three nightly visits from the most beautiful looking woman." The enigmatic man then hissed like a serpent and bore the most devilish grin, "It is a mere formality your highness, you need only to bow if you concur."

Prince Vlad dipped to one knee without question. Why wouldn't he? The Scholomance wizard patiently taught Dracula everything from alchemy to the highest secrets of the dark arts.

In deep reflection, the Count regretted succumbing to that deal and the fangs of the lovely looking Lilith but it was too late. After feasting on Dracula's blood, the second time, the female vampire advised Vlad Tepes to spread his native soil inside a coffin in a dark and secluded area. After being bitten the third time by Lilith, Vlad grew incredibly weak and was presumed dead by his closest adviser. However, Dracula rose again.

Professor Van Helsing's initial findings were incorrect, Prince Vlad Drakhol did not overcome the grave by a slow transformation instead the process was tortuously expeditious. Nor was the professor's analysis correct in that the undead royal began with the thought process of a child's brain, slowly developing over centuries.

Dr. Van Helsing reassessed his findings years later: *Boyar, prince, soldier, statesmen, and one who knew no fear or remorse, such faculties Count Dracula retained from the start of his unholy transformation. Indeed, the fiend is so powerful he can lift coffins like they are mere toys. Ah ha, but finding subjects to protect the undead prince and move his boxes filled with native soil is a major weakness for my men to exploit, if he ever ventures out of his homeland again.*

The further Prince Vlad delved into the occult, the more he had lost love for his fellow man, even relatives and friends. During the past five centuries, his only consolation was the lust for power.

The dark prince had already felt the first sting of death from the oldest female vampire, Lilith, and he could never turn back. Because of that Vlad would do whatever was necessary for his alliance to prevail.

Count Dracula could feel the morning air and knew he had little time before having to return to his arcane lair. The sun was about to peak over the eastern mound and its pure radiance was death to his kind. His undead body grew tired. He craved his native soil as the solar rays enveloped the atmosphere.

He still perceived of something important. He concentrated more. He envisioned electricity. The lord of the vampires sensed that familiar unspoken whisper over his shoulder. *Something big and born of lightning.* His muscular frame convulsed with delight. "The creature roams the earth once again!"

31 - FULL MOON

September 17, 2005 - 0655 Hours

The morgue technician read the report and shook his head. "Stashed in a cavern for about forty years and in such a humid climate," Marty sighed, "afraid not much will be left of you, pal"

Over the years, the technician got in the habit of talking to stiffs. It helped him deal with the long nights, as well as the inherent morbidity of the job. The tech put on his gloves and pulled the file open. "What's the story here, I wonder?"

The cadaver outlined through the body bag spoke of flesh as well as bone; Marty was intrigued. He looked at his watch, 0700 hours. "Only thirty minutes to go. Hey bra," he winked at the as-yet unrevealed corpse, "it wouldn't be right to rush you. We'll let the dayshift know, I'd like to be the first to look at you on my next shift." He then slid the tray back into the cooler.

The sun began to shine through the office windows. The skinny technician chuckled, "Enough time to get some sleep and nine rounds of golf before my next shift."

September 18, 2005 - Early morning

After his dog-watch lunch, Marty headed to his boss' desk. He sifted through the preliminary findings on the body known as *Nigel Rathbone.*

When he checked his cubby, he was pleased to receive an endorsement from his supervisor for the delayed examination of the Rathbone case. The technician knew he was well-thought of when it came to forensic science, and figured his request would not be met with too much resistance. He was right, and skipped into the next room to the cooler where the stiffs lived.

Marty opened the freezer drawer and pulled open the tray. As he unzipped the bag, the technician stood back, aghast at what lay before him. "You sure you weren't stashed in some Egyptian pyramid?" The expression on his face went from disbelief to one of cool professionalism as he went about the task of setting up all his forensic instruments.

The morgue technician noted in his journal that it was 0140 hours when he began the autopsy of this unique, partially mummified specimen. Marty examined the entire body from head to toe before attempting to crack inside the carapace. He noticed a small hole in the upper left chest and chuckled, "I bet this is what killed ya." He made an incision.

Several minutes later, the tech pulled out a metal ball from Nigel Rathbone's heart. He placed it under the strong light. "Silver!" He raised his eyebrows as he glared down at the corpse with added scrutiny. "You some kind of monster, pal?" He laughed at his own joke, then was overcome by an acute pang of terror that rolled through him like a tidal wave.

Marty's hands began to tremble, as he slowly backed away, then turned and ran toward the cabinet. After a few minutes of staring at the bottle of whiskey, he walked back toward the stainless-steel table. "Oh well, sorry chap that we kept you waiting in the freezer for the past two weeks." He winked at the corpse before saying, "Not that you need it but I'll hook you up with an embalming special."

0201 hours, the moon's luminous rays began to pour through the large double-insulated windows. The technician had not yet discarded Rathbone's worn but well-preserved pants. He scribbled down some additional details in his note pad. He turned toward the body that now appeared almost alive. "Whoa I need a quick nip. I'm seeing things or those Keystone Cops are playing tricks on me again."

Marty ran to his cabinet and took a swig from a bottle of whiskey. "Ohhh, did I need that." His nerves numbed for the moment, he reeled around toward the stainless-steel table to continue his task.

A hairy arm yanked at the morgue technician's neck and the entire fifth spilled all over a salivating wolfman.

September 18, 2005 - Noon

Sheriff Ricardo Lombardi was looking forward to picking up Tommy's two for one fish taco special after patrolling the limits of his jurisdiction. He spotted a large bird circling above through his squad car's windshield. "Some poor animal is about to be din-din," he said out loud. The vulture landed near the side of the road.

The sheriff took a sip of his iced-coffee as he drove closer to the scavenger and its meal. The bird suddenly took flight. "Must not be dead yet?" chuckled Rico.

The lawman was a half-mile away from Tommy's Taco Shack when he skidded his squad car to an abrupt halt. Sheriff

Lombardi nearly ran over the body on the side of the road. "That is no dead animal," he graveled.

Ricardo pulled over to a safer location and informed dispatch of the situation. He sighed, "Oh well. The fish tacos will have to wait."

The sheriff ensured his video camera was pointing toward the downed suspect before exiting the vehicle. Wary of a ruse, he scanned the immediate area for a possible ambush. He un-holstered his weapon. *Watering hole* techniques were often used when a person appeared maimed and, then bam, the good Samaritan gets attacked by a bushwhacking band of brigands. *Looks clear*, he thought. It was not wise to attack the law and get caught on video, but to him, *most criminals were dumbasses.*

Rico approached the body with his pistol at the ready. He called out, "You okay?" The person did not respond. The man's arms were clear and no weapons visible. The lawman gently pressed his boot into the individual's back a couple of times. He then tried to trick the suspect and ordered, "Get up!" Again, no response.

Sheriff Lombardi circled the man to see if his eyes or body might react. After detecting no movement, he holstered his weapon. He then felt his carotid artery. He shrugged. "Well, you have a pulse."

The man moaned but didn't open his eyes.

"Lucky you're alive," said the lawman, "not smart sleeping along the road." He then made a beeline for his vehicle.

Rico Jr. threw a blanket over the middle-aged man wearing only shredded trousers. The sheriff tried to wake up the haggard looking individual. "Great, another vagabond." Eyes fluttered and Lombardi said, "Come on big guy it’s time to visit the bird cage."

Nigel Rathbone stirred, rolling over and then sitting up. He stretched and yawned. The sheriff handed him a plastic bottle of water. Rathbone felt the clear container with fascination. "Never seen water in such a contraption." He could peer through it like glass, but the strange looking bottle crumpled in his hands.

Lombardi shook his head. "Drink some. Looks like you need it."

"Do you have an opener?"

"Are you pulling my leg?"

"No, sir." Nigel then attempted to pull off the top to no avail. He politely asked, "How do I open it?"

Sheriff Lombardi looked at the man strangely, "Are you serious?" Rathbone nodded. Rico made a left screwing motion with one hand, "You twist it open."

"Ah, quite so. Just like my old canteen."

"Are you British?"

Bones sighed, "I'm American and Scottish."

Rico looked at the down and out man. "Are you on drugs?"

"Heavens NO! I've mostly drank coffee, lots of water and some ale." Nigel took a sip, "Thank you."

The sheriff stated, "For some reason, you look familiar. Have we met before?"

Nigel cracked a small smile. "Not that I can remember."

"What's your name?"

"Nigel Rathbone." He rubbed his brow and eyed the sheriff quizzically. "Sir, where am I?"

Lombardi cocked his head and laughed, "What did your wife leave ya?"

Rathbone swept his fingers through the crop of thick brown hair. Two cars slowly passed them, gawking at the lawman and suspect. Nigel squinted as he looked around. "No and those aren't 1960s automobiles."

The Sheriff rolled his eyes. "Time to get up."

"Can you help me up?"

"Dude… are you serious?

"It's been a while since I stood."

Lombardi shook his head as he helped the stranger get to his feet. Nigel Rathbone slowly rose and almost doubled-over. "Easy there, big guy," advised the sheriff. The man's six-foot two inchish frame and brawny build matched his own. He thought this peculiar fellow could have passed as a Lombardi with the olive-skin and taller stature.

Rathbone politely inquired, "What year is it?"

Rico's jaw tightened. The guy was funny, but trying his patience. "Enough with the riddles Sherlock," he groused, "it is mid-September, 2005. You are loitering in Le Grande, Mississippi, and you reek of sauce."

Rathbone's hands jittered. "Sheriff, I haven't consumed alcohol in years but I am a murderer. I do not want to kill but I do whenever the moon is full."

The Sheriff bellowed, "Yeah, and the Pope is Jewish. If you haven't drunk, then why are your hands so damn shaky?" He gave the man a knowing look. "Seriously, the bourbon's strong."

"Sir, you must believe me!" demanded Rathbone.

"It's okay. The first step is to admit you have a problem."

Nigel's fists and body tightened. His eyes grew wide, frantically darting from side to side. "I'm tell..."

Lombardi shot back, "Relax with your body language there, bub. You just play along and we will take you down to the station. Clean yourself up, get some new digs and grab a nice warm meal." He winked at him. "Things will make more sense later on."

Rathbone caught himself from sticking his index finger in the peacemaker's chest and stated, "I am not lying about the moon and…"

Sheriff Lombardi cut Nigel off by saying, "Stifle with that crap." He then grinned and admitted, "But that moon is full quip made my day."

Rathbone's body language relaxed, realizing it was futile to reason with the lawman about the supernatural. "Who would believe such rubbish?" graveled Nigel.

Lombardi smiled as he handcuffed Nigel Rathbone and read him his Miranda Rights. "Chill out bud. We will verify that you have no criminal record. Then may be Reggie's homeless program can help you get back on your feet and start working."

32 - LIONS' DEN

The Mole informed Presidente Chavo Calles of the strange details concerning the Americans on Gemela earlier in the year. He wasn't sad to hear about the Valentine's Day slaughter to say the least, but because of it, the Lions' Den altered their plans to attack the infidels. No further information could be obtained from Calles' female spymaster. His buxom red-head went dark once again, but she had done her job.

The al-Qaeda cell operating in South America was still determined to blow up oil platforms in the Gulf of Mexico while simultaneously attempting to free some of their Islamic brothers from Guantanamo Bay. The half-year delay gave the Lions' Den extra time to practice their marksmanship, boat handling and bomb-making skills.

It was nearing dusk in a remote and secure South American port. Most of the dock was covered by tin roofs with open structures. The Lions' Den finished concealing explosives into one of their vessels. Kabir looked at his second in command and asked, "Hussein, do you think the men are getting too comfortable with these Latino pigs?"

Hussein casually replied, "No. They are just fitting in with the infidels' customs, so we don't stand out."

Kabir hissed, "I don't like our men whoring around and drinking so much."

Hussein casually nodded to his boss. "By the grace of Allah, we will accomplish our mission and gain his favor." The second in command was not sure what he truly believed anymore. He would never admit that to Kabir or his growing preference for non-Muslim women was becoming an obsession.

The leader departed to inspect the fiberglass panels where they hid the explosives. Kabir grumbled to one of his men, "Look, that secret door isn't flush. You must screw it in slightly more, so it is not visible."

Hussein leaned over the yacht's aft railing. He lit a cigarette and thought about home. It had been over a year since he last spoke with his uncle before departing for South America:

***

The young man walked outside to the patriarch's centrally, located garden. The old man finished watering his prune trees and smiled at Hussein. He moved slowly, using his cane and firmly shook his nephew's right hand and exchanged the customary kisses on the sides of the face before he said, "*As-salam alaykum,*" meaning *Peace be upon you* in Arabic.

Hussein responded in kind. The elder motioned for his youngest nephew to take a seat under the open pillared gallery. He offered him a hot cup of tea, "*Shai*?"

Hussein graciously replied, "*Minfadlik 'ammy,*" *Please uncle.*

Hosni poured them each a cup. "*Halib*?" *Milk* he asked.

"*La shukran,*" *No thank you.* Hussein fondly recalled his dearest relative teaching him how to play chess and watching soccer games from this veranda. This dwelling was dear to Hussein. His father had died when he was a toddler and his oldest uncle, gladly took him under his wing.

The uncle stirred the cream into his tea with a spoon. "It is a pleasure to see you, my child. I miss your Saturday visits, but you have missed four in a row as a matter of fact."

"My apologies Uncle Hosni. I may not see you for a while," he paused thinking of the right words, "but I hope to make you proud."

"Whatever you do, Hussein, remember to treat people with love and respect."

The patriarch's answer puzzled the young man. "What happened to you, uncle? You used to be so strict." His eyebrows furrowed. "I must humbly ask... are you not so strong in your beliefs?"

The head of the family frankly admitted, "I never had faith until recently." The nephew almost fell backward, surprised by his uncle's confession. Hosni rubbed his right hand through his peppery beard. "Before it was more about morality, law and order." His eyes grew stern. "However, blowing up innocent civilians and cutting off their heads," he shook his head, "that gives our great Arab culture a very bad name."

Hussein's eyes flashed with anger, but he held his tongue.

The family elder opened up his hands and asked in a gentle voice, "Did I instill such bitterness in you, my son?"

Hussein looked at the ground and said, "No!"

"Please let me see your eyes when we speak," the uncle continued. "If I have wronged you in any way, please forgive me."

"There is nothing to forgive, 'ammy. You have always been gracious to me."

"Then what have I taught you?" inquired the elder.

The nephew stared at his uncle with uncertainty. "You had taught me to be proud and strong."

"Hmm." Hosni gave his nephew a knowing look. "Do you not think I don't know what you and your *friends* are up to? My generation may sip a lot of shai," he then placed the cup of tea on the table, "but we watch and listen, my son. The people you are associating with are like the ones who attacked the Americans on 9/11."

"But the West invaded Afghanistan and Iraq," Hussein said exasperated.

"You forgot one thing. Al-Qaeda started this lunacy. And because of it, too many decent Arabs are paying the price."

Hussein protested by saying, "Are you sympathizing with those dogs?"

His uncle growled, "Not at all! But attacking women and children, only gave the Americans a license to invade our soil."

"But those infidels are ruining our youth with their foul music and film."

Hosni raised an eyebrow. "Yet, your group takes to their pornography and immorality as an excuse to fit in?"

Hussein was surprised that his uncle knew so much, but remained silent. It shouldn't have surprised him. The elder was a retired detective.

"America may appear like a healthy flower, but she is wilting within," Hosni continued. "If al-Qaeda would have struck those in Hollywood and other industries that make such filth, then that would have been one thing. That is not something I condone, but many of our people would have understood." The old man took another sip of his tea. "Murder is not the way my son. We must focus on building people up and not destruction."

The nephew appeared disappointed. "Uncle Hosni, you are not the fiery man who taught me to be militant in our ways."

"I have learned over the years that most quarrels are unnecessary and *a gentle answer turns away wrath*." Hosni then winked at his nephew. "America is quickly losing her grasp of what is good. Her people are growing very immoral and she hires foreigners to do her work."

Hussein nodded. "Evil and lazy."

The uncle raised an eyebrow. "It is only for Allah to judge. I am personally no fan of the Jihadist murderers or the West with its declining values." The nephew bit his lip. "Just leave the US alone and that nation will die in its sleep." His tone became deadly serious as he continued. "Whatever you do, don't awaken America from her slumber or she may grow great once again!"

That last conversation with his uncle haunted Hussein. The patriarch even asked him to forgive him. *What was that all about*, he thought to himself, *'ammy never used to speak to me like that. And in such a gentle manner*. The more he dwelled on the topic, the more he vehemently resented the USA for being so powerful. He wanted the Middle East to be magnificent again. It had been centuries since the Arabs ruled in their supremacy of their land, being the masters of mathematics, science and law. Hussein took the last drag of his smoke and flicked it into the gulf's water. What he wanted most was to tear out America's heart and feed it to her.

Kabir and Hussein discussed at length that their group needed a remote base camp close enough to strike the infidels in many directions. Gemela was still that perfect area; small, shrouded by two tall hills and trees for cover, and a few docks to moor their craft. Most importantly, the marshland islet was fairly secluded except for a small number of migrant workers that cultivated the land, primarily from mid-spring to early fall before the hurricane season began. The South American al-Qaeda cell reassessed that later in the year was the perfect time to mount their attack. 9/11 was out of the question, but December 7th was a better option. They didn't need much time from Gemela's solitary location to be out of sight, before they sprung their surprise. Kabir and Hussein believed a two-pronged attack on the anniversary of *Pearl Harbor* would terrify the infidels.

Since late August, the al-Qaeda cell had been loading the pair of fifty-six feet long cruising vessels to travel north. The two crews of twenty-two men had a pair of yachts, several jet skis, and multiple weapons and explosives at their disposal. The Lions' Den was preparing to leave Presidente Calles' homeland in the middle of September. The first cell planned to arrive at Gemela on September 27, 2005. If all went well, the jihadists would strike a blow to the gringos for Calles and rescue some of their own. In the end, the presidente would have plausible denial while gas prices soared to his advantage. And al-Qaeda would strike fear in their enemy's hearts once again.

33 - CAGED

September 19, 2005

Lunar beams shone through the window high upon the cell wall where three inmates lingered. The moon was going to be close to three-quarters full. Nigel Rathbone knew it without looking. He felt it in his bones. He could sense its pull on his entire being. His mental outlook turned morose as he ruminated upon the slight physical monstrosity he might soon become.

Normally, on nights of a three-quarter moon he would get moodier, otherwise remain human. But if pushed, he'd grow hairier around his forehead and hands, and get aggressive. He told himself: *Stay calm and you will be alright.* Rathbone reflected of his past, longing for a physician like Dr. Waggner. There was a time when he was free of his damned curse, thanks to that brilliant doctor from Portugal.

***

Dr. Jonah Waggner used cultured extracts from green tea, willow bark and other medicinal ingredients to treat his condition. The tricky part of the operation was to systematically apply the formula into his bloodstream. The physician purged Nigel's system with an entire blood transfusion while spiking the formula into key pressure points throughout his body.

The doctor theorized that the operation would completely clean out the abnormally high levels of testosterone that caused Rathbone's wolf-like transformations and rewire the circuitry of his entire body. And it was successful, for a while.

Nigel learned of Dr. Waggner's unorthodox procedures, known to be one of the most successful within his field. The problem was that the doctor had been hiding from the Nazis since the onset of World War Two. Because Jonah was part Portuguese and German, he feared the Third Reich would recruit him to be one of their scientists. And Dr. Waggner detested everything about Hitler and his henchmen. So, he fled to his family's retreat hidden in the Portuguese hill country. And that is where Bones had found him.

Shortly after the Great Second War and the operation, Nigel hoped to seek out his sweetheart, Shelly, and immediate family. He knew if some were still alive, they would be much older. Shelly and his relatives would be stunned to see him, not to mention their surprise at his appearing to not have aged much since the time they'd known him. But they would know why. He just wanted to tell Shelly he was fine and see his kin one more time.

Rathbone trekked for several months from Dr. Waggner's mansion in Portugal to northern France. He felt free at last and enjoyed working along the way to cover his vagabond style of living. He was good with his hands, fixing everything from electrical, mechanical or minor construction jobs. He was excited to return home and start a new life in Scotland, or, preferably, in the States with the help of his father's relatives. Nigel knew he couldn't live at his Scottish estate, since he was already declared dead. The villagers would never welcome him. He could, however, meet Shelly and some of his relatives for a short while before having to travel on.

As Bones got closer to the northern shores of the old continent, he grew agitated on the nights of a full moon. On the fourth, he suffered such a terrible headache that it knocked him unconscious. Looking back, he should have known better and tried to take his life when he may have had the chance. Yet his heart longed for home, so he took a boat north. Unfortunately, that fifth full moon, he grew hairier and became very violent, barely able to control himself from fighting a few Londoners on the street.

Nigel put his hands into his face and heard himself cry out in anguish, "Why can't I just die?"

One of the blond inmates stood up. "We can help you with that."

Rathbone warned the man in a guttural tone, "I wouldn't do that if I was you."

"You think you're tougher than us?"

"No!" He sensed the lunar rays beaming brightly. His eyebrows furrowed. Nigel stood and pleaded, "Just please let me be."

The short, stocky blond rose. "We can't do that ya see." He spread out his arms in an all-encompassing manner. "We just don't like your kind." The skinhead pushed Rathbone down on the edge of the cot. "You look like a mongrel, some type of half-breed."

Bones slowly shook his head up and down. "So, what if I am?"

The inmate thumped Nigel in the chest. "Darker hair and kind of olive-skinnish and all. What are you a Spic or something?"

Rathbone asked curtly, "In a way, aren't we all?"

"Speak for yourself, ya no good dark-skinned ass..."

Nigel delivered a fast punch to the punk's lower belly. The inmate doubled-over. The Scot was typically pleasant, even with pricks but those last five words pressed a button. He added in a sarcastic tone, "And such language for a wee LAD!"

The shorter skinhead back-handed Nigel across the face.

Rathbone didn't budge but said, "You hit like a girl." The moon was pulling him into a dark mood. He had been prodded to the point where he welcomed his anger.

The Neo-Nazi cocked his arm back, ready to deliver a round-house. Nigel crouched down and pushed the man full force up into the bars so quickly that the prick didn't know what happened to him.

The inmate felt blood in the back of his skull. "We'll get you when you're asleep."

"Typical cowards. Bloody wanna-be Nazis."

The other inmate jumped the Scot from behind and began choking him. Rathbone elbowed the skinhead in the stomach, and proceeded to thrash the two inmates.

The frantic cries from the Neo-Nazis alerted the jailers. Deputies shocked Nigel with stun guns and put him in a strait jacket.

One of the jailers stared at Rathbone's hirsute hands before locking him up in a solitary cell. "Hey Benji, lay off the Rogaine." Bones seemed to growl at him.

Sheriff Lombardi studied Rathbone's actions via a hidden camera. "This guy has no criminal record, no identification, nothing. He doesn't exist unless he's the same chap who was born over a hundred and twenty years ago.

A deputy interjected, "No way!"

The sheriff continued, "These old records reveal that Scotland Yard was on to a guy with the same name but never indicated why."

The deputy replied, "Sheriff, unfortunately there are no fingerprints for any Nigel Rathbone. And this guy looks to be a hair shy of forty."

"Look at those eyes, totally wild," noted Lombardi. Bones gnawed through most of the straight jacket. The sheriff scratched his head. "Well, whoever he is... Cujo has issues."

The deputy added, "He won't be going anywhere soon!"

Three days later, Deputy Rufino Cabrera escorted a Cuban gang member on a stretcher with part of his brains hanging out.

Dr. Maria Wilder and Nurse Lise Alegría were washing their hands as the deputy walked by.

Deputy Cabrera tugged at Maria's sleeve. "An elderly lady shot this cat and his white-trash friend. They tried raping her but ole mama's *Smith and Wesson* had a bit more to say." He then whispered, "Let this scum die. Punks like him give us Latinos a bad name."

Dr. Wilder frowned. "I took an oath to help save lives. If he lives, he will be severely handicapped or a vegetable. Besides, the oncoming shift will operate."

The muscular Latino exhaled in relief knowing the best neurosurgeon in the southeast region would not be working to save this viscous gang banger. He uttered in Spanish, "Hay justo a veces!"

Maria shook her head and mockingly said, "*There is justice at times*."

"Forgot you knew some Spanish." Rufino continued, "You know, Doc. We got this loco guy in jail. He claims to have been born in Scotland in the late 1800s." The deputy shook his head. "No way, he looks your age, fairly young."

She playfully sneered at his sarcasm, "You're not scoring any points."

The deputy winked at her. "This fella raves about murdering someone lately. There has been no one killed except for that morgue technician up north."

"Who?" inquired Maria.

"Can't remember his name."

"What shift did he work?"

"Graveyard shift."

Doc nervously asked, "Was his name Marty?"

Rufino nodded. "Believe that was him."

"That's terrible."

"A quirky little guy," he sighed, "but can you blame him working the morgue at nights."

Maria tearfully laughed, "Yes… Marty was a bit eccentric and one hell of a golfer."

"Didn't know you knew him."

She whisked a tear away before saying, "We played in several tournaments together."

"My condolences."

Doc stood there dumbfounded.

Deputy Cabrera shrugged. "Authorities discovered a broken window to the morgue with dog prints leading to the rabid stray they had earlier put down." He then said, "Guess what?"

"Huh?" Maria asked apprehensively.

"The tech's blood showed traces of rabies. The detective working the case grumbled it was way too coincidental to swallow. Hay Dios, it is what it is."

Dr. Wilder looked up puzzled. "Uh huh," was all she could say in response. Maria didn't remind Deputy Cabrera that Rathbone's remains had been brought up to the very same morgue, after Hurricane Katrina severely damaged La Grande's facility.

Deputy Cabrera put on his Latin charm and smiled. "How about going for a coffee or cocktail later?"

Normally, Maria may have taken up the deputy's offer just for some innocent male companionship. Sleek, strong, handsome and a PT nut Cabrera was. However, her life was too crazy at the present time. Besides she thought, *Rufino wasn't her type - too talkative, and he doesn't golf or watch football.* Doc meekly smiled and said, "Ah, no thanks. It's tough… I'm still in mourning."

34 - CHAMELEONS

Beware of cowards like al-Qaeda who infiltrate our country, abuse our freedoms, befriend us with the wink of an eye, and then slaughter the innocent in the streets.
Anonymous SpecOps Commander

September 26, 2005

The sports watch beeped several times at 11:45 a.m. Hussein pressed a button to turn off his alarm. He then began to compare their navigation chart to the GPS coordinates. At noon, he spoke six words into his radio, "Twelve o'clock and time to fish," which was pre-arranged code meaning their boat was at its final waypoint several miles southeast of Gemela.

Kabir, the Lions' Den leader did not respond. He kept his voice off the net as much as possible. Though fluent in Spanish and English, he struggled to pronounce the letters *g, k and h* without giving away his native tones.

The second in command's English accent was first rate, learning to master the language at Oxford for several years. Hussein also spoke French and Spanish fluently. Listening to him in the three languages, no one would guess he was of Arab descent. His straight brown hair, medium-sized facial features and light olive skin appeared to be more of a *mestizo*, a mix of Spanish and native Indian heritage. Hussein easily blended in with the Latin American and Caribbean populace. His average build and ability to come off as easy going, even put the most suspicious at ease.

Hussein's boss, Kabir, on the other hand, bore a huge hook nose with fiery black eyes and semi-curly dark hair for him to stand out as the stereotypical Middle Eastern male. He stood six-foot three inches tall and was a gifted power lifter. Kabir rarely spoke. Even after studying engineering and English at the University of Minnesota for five years, he only spoke to non-Muslims when he had to.

The fifty-six feet long cruising yacht was travelling at fifteen nautical miles per hour before navigating through the swamplands. The hybrid vessel was built for long distance sailing and comfort similar to the one Kabir was on several hundred miles to the south. Each power boat consisted of four double-berth cabins for eight, two heads, a large saloon and galley, and a forward cabin and head for three crewmen. The funds used to purchase the yachts came from money laundering and opium sales. It would be virtually impossible for anyone to trace the boats to Calles. If it appeared the cells were going to be captured, they were prepared to die rather than compromise their handlers.

Hussein estimated his crew would hover at a safe distance from the shoreline the first day. Their cover was to appear like ordinary men on a fishing junket, drink some refreshments and enjoy the balmy weather.

Dressed in casual shorts and t-shirts, and only speaking English and Spanish, even the most observant wouldn't give them a second look. The plan of the narco-terrorists' alliance was to observe the islet for several days from the south, west, north and east. If no military or migrant workers were spotted, Hussein would relay to Kabir for the second vessel to move in.

The crew caught a medium-sized Redfish in the brackish water late in the afternoon. They finished eating Spanish rice, beans and their catch. The group spotted no unusual activity on the south shore during the entire day.

Hussein nodded to the coxswain and said, "Head a few miles west of Gemela in one of the inlets and set anchor there for the night."

September 27, 2005

No calls were sung at dawn. Besides one of the three rotating coxswains standing watch at the helm, the rest of the crew began to stir around eight in the morning. The Salat, the second pillar of Islam was prayer. The men were strictly prohibited from praying toward Mecca five times a day. Kabir didn't like that fact, but remaining incognito was of supreme importance while they operated throughout the American hemisphere.

The crew of eleven heated up their shai and began to prepare their fishing gear. By mid-day, they switched from drinking tea to cracking open local beers. Within two hours, two men each caught a Warfish Grouper. Like the day before, the Lions' Den spotted no people or boats on or near Gemela.

After the cell departed the South American port over a week ago, they ceased calling themselves by their Arab names. They now went by common English or Spanish first names to throw off any possible observers. After, preparing and eating their catch of the day, Hussein said to his coxswain, "Tomás, let's head to the north shore."

The man at the helm nodded. "Hasanan!" meaning *Okay*.

Hussein gave the helmsman a knowing look and said in a slow voice, " Tomás..."

The coxswain caught on that he wasn't supposed to speak Arabic and corrected himself by saying, "Okay Harry."

Hussein was feeling confident. Day two went off without a hitch. He patted the helmsman on his back and said, "Tonight, drop anchor a mile to the north and prep the jet skis in the back." He grinned. "Tomás, tomorrow we will fish and enjoy the water craft for some sightseeing."

The coxswain dropped anchor one mile north of the center of Gemela at 6:30 p.m. Minutes before sunset, the crew finished tying the jet skis to the vessel's aft end.

Five men began their nightly ritual of boozing it up and heading below to watch a soccer match or movie in the galley. Two sat at the bow lighting their smokes. Tomás and Kobe were at the helm discussing watch duty rotations.

Hussein and another were on the aft deck, admiring the radiant horizon before it was erased by darkness. He threw the butt of his cigarette into the gulf's water. The second in command looked at his watch, it read 7:12 p.m. *Time for a shower*, he thought.

At 7:25 p.m., George walked into Hussein's berthing and whispered, "Harry, two men are missing."

"Did anyone see anything?"

George answered, " Tomás seems to be in shock. He said they were some sort of genies that picked the men up and swept them into the air."

The second in command looked at him with disbelief before heading up to the helm.

Tomás and Kobe stared nervously into the darkness. Both had retrieved their pistols from their holsters.

"What's going on here?" Hussein demanded.

Tomás stuttered before saying, "G-g-genies snatched two smokers from the front deck just minutes ago."

"I know you just got off watch, Tomás. Did you just grab something to drink?" Hussein asked smiling.

"No!" Tomás nervously replied.

"I saw it also!" stated Kobe.

Screams echoed from the galley. By the time, George and Tomás got below, blood was splattered along the walls but there were no bodies to be found.

Hussein pushed on a section of fiberglass. A spring mechanism released a hidden compartment. He quickly handed George a pistol and grabbed a sawed-off shot shotgun for himself, strapping it over his shoulder on a sling. "Search all the cabins!"

Five shots were fired from above. The three ran top-side. All that was left was the smear of blood across the helm.

Tomás and George forgot all OPSEC and panicked, speaking in Arabic.

Hussein yelled, "*Uskut*!" *Shut up.* The second in command barely could make out a shadow of a woman swoop down and pick up George. He blasted the gliding apparition with one shotgun shell.

The woman fell to the deck with its prey. She looked back at Tomás and Hussein for a moment. Her red eyes glared wickedly at them before she disappeared into the night.

Hussein quickly spoke into the radio, "Kevin this is Harry. *Cease fishing and return home*," which meant *abandon the mission and return to their secure port in South America.* The second in command heard no response and repeated, "Kevin this is Harry. Cease fishing and return home."

Kabir replied by urgently asking, "Harry, are you absolutely sure?" and continued. "We were looking forward to fishing."

The second in command responded by saying, "We have run into some very nasty weather. Fishing is no good!"

Kabir slammed his radio into the console from their position several hundred miles to the south.

Tomás motioned to Hussein for them to escape on the jet skis. Both men started the engines and navigated through the inlets as fast as the small recreational craft could go.

The two darted through the brackish waterways for several miles with little separation between them. Tomás gave Hussein a thumbs-up seconds before he was snagged and carried off screaming into the dark sky.

Numb with fear, the second in command looked up into the darkness. He could barely make out a silhouette of a man sailing in the air. It was mostly a blur to Hussein, but he would have sworn that the thing chomped down on Tomás' neck as it headed back toward the direction of Gemela.

35 - BIRDS

There is only one 'retirement plan' for terrorists.
General James Mattis, USMC (Iraq, 2004)

September 28, 2005 - 0810 Hours

Colonel "Sparky" Sparkman exited Bunker Five's tunnel with a vigorous step in his giddy-yap. A burly security guard lowered his salute and smiled, "Nice workout, sir?"

The high-ranking officer nodded. "Better than nothing." Sparky had just finished his "easy" PT session with a 5K run followed by three continuous sets of 40 pushups, 40 leg lifts, 10 pull-ups, 40 air squats, 40 crunches and 12 dips. At 50 years of age, he wasn't about to let age define him.

A pretty woman of average height and a sleek build greeted her boss by saying, "Good morning, Colonel Sparkman."

The wiry, five-foot nine-inch tall colonel crisply replied, "Good morning, Miss Jefferson."

Vilma Jefferson was easy on the eyes with green eyes, high-cheek bones, and wavy hair. What really made her standout was her character of being honest, hard-working and humble.

Technical Sergeant Andrew Rice had a smirk on his face as the peppery-haired battle watch commander walked by his station. Ever since his boss had canned that prick, Lykkash, the watch flowed much more efficiently. One of the benefits Rice immediately noticed, Colonel Sparkman had become more relaxed, but still the same PT nut and a stickler for precision.

Sparky shook his head at the tall and lanky sergeant. "What's going on Rice?"

"Nothing, sir," Andy said trying to conceal his grin.

The colonel nodded to his communications Ace. He veered toward his desk to grab his coffee cup. It wasn't there. Sparky looked at the sergeant, "Aha," he uttered in an irritated tone. Rice looked away. "You better tell me now, buster, or you'll pay."

The technical sergeant tactfully replied. "You're too much of standup guy, sir,"

Colonel Sparkman growled, "You haven't seen me without my favorite coffee cup."

"Still not buying it, colonel."

"My Para Rescue days maybe dust in the wind. Keep it up," the colonel pointed at the youngster, "You and I will do some mando PT during lunch."

Andy gulped, "That's harassment, sir."

Sparky shook his head with a *you want to challenge me grin.* "Not if I PT with you." Sergeant Rice didn't say a word, but pointed his tongue inside his cheek toward the kitchenette. The colonel made a beeline toward the back.

Vilma motioned to the battle watch commander. "I cleaned your cup for you, sir." The colonel gave the relatively new employee stink-eye as he grabbed his Mickey Mouse cup. She read her boss' eyes. "Sir. I apologize if you don't like your cup being cleaned but it had some nasty green stuff growing inside."

He defiantly said, "Just enzyme buildup." He then saw the tray in the kitchenette full of assorted teas. His eyes grew wide with delight. "Nice selection, Miss Jefferson." She meekly smiled.

He poured hot water into his ceramic cup and placed an earl grey pouch inside. After toasting a raisin bagel, he headed for his desk. Vilma slid a manila envelope to the colonel. He knew the contents would be satellite images by the size of the folder.

Satellites normally rotated in several types of orbits: Low Earth (0 to 1,240 miles), Medium-Earth (1,200 to 22,236 miles), Geo-Synchronous (at 22,236 miles), and High-Earth (above 22,236 miles). The type of reconnaissance satellite used by a government, depended on the mission.

He shook his head recollecting of naive US students recently protesting American's usage of satellites. *Anyone who believed Russia and China weren't utilizing satellites to edge out allies or adversaries, was a supreme dipstick*, Sparky thought. The Russians had been spymasters for hundreds of years, way before the US was even a thought, and China eons before. Sadly, it was a growing trend that the average American student didn't have much of a clue on the militaristic philosophy of Sun Tzu or the truth about other historical figures who looked good on a T-shirt. *Close-minded professors pushing their agendas in liberal universities were the large culprits of so many of the brain-dead snowflakes.*

The colonel had been a satellite and space expert for three decades. Many in his field relied solely on the orbiting reconnaissance technology. He often bucked that trend. Satellites, often referred to as *birds*, only provided a glimpse of the entire picture.

"Everything alright, sir?"

"Yes." He tried sipping his tea, but it was too hot. He looked at her and said, "You seem open-minded, Miss Jefferson."

"I'd like to think I am."

"Here's a tip from a crusty Air Force dog. I've worked years with Joint Special Operations and spooks, not just in some air-conditioned spaces staring at images. And without a seasoned Recon team or agent's eyes, these birds don't mean squat."

"Fair enough." Vilma then grinned and said, "By the way, a satellite picked up these shots from the north side of Gemela at 0700. Thought they may be of interest."

"Is this all we have?"

"Yes, sir."

He laughed at the irony of his previous words. "Well, sometimes, we MUST make the best of it with only satellites."

Vilma winked. "But when you can, gather other data to get the panoramic view."

"Very astute." The US Air Force Intelligence Officer sipped his tea as he studied the images. "How long is the yacht?"

"Imagery calculates over fifty-five feet long. This class of cruising vessel can hold up to eleven personnel."

"Interesting." *Ideal number of trained men to do small hits*, Sparky thought. "Are those bodies floating close to the yacht?"

"Yes. So far, we count six bodies, based off the images."

He graveled, "As I said, satellites can only do so much." He thought of a SpecOps commander he previously deployed with and muttered, "Chameleons!"

She said dumbfounded, "Did you just say chameleons?"

He crinkled his nose. "Al-Qaeda cells. Wouldn't doubt those *haters* were trying to come off as friendlies, just to blow us up."

Technical Sergeant Andrew Rice nodded. "I'd wager a pretty penny that's a spot-on hunch, colonel."

Jefferson growled, "There is only one 'retirement plan' for terrorists!"

"Sad to say that is often the case."

"Don't give a damn!" A tear ran down her cheek. "Lost two friends on 9/11."

He said glumly, "So, did I." After a long pause, the colonel looked at his team. "Heck with the satellites. Where's our boots on the ground?"

The technical sergeant said, "Sir, a female HUMINTer went missing at that very same locale over a year ago."

"That's right. Thanks for reminding me, Andy." Sparky looked at his watch and asked, "Vilma, you said the satellite captured these images about an hour ago?"

The GS-14 replied, "Affirmative, sir."

He winced. "Spin up a team to go down to Gemela with NCIS." Both Rice and Jefferson nodded. Colonel Sparkman looked up at his INTEL analyst and stated, "Vilma, make sure it's Jefe and Azúcar that snoops around!" He took another sip of his tea and then grinned. "By the way, great catch Miss Jefferson!"

Her eyes lit up before responding, "Thank you, colonel."

He grumped, "Just don't mess with my coffee cup!"

"Understood." She then said matter of fact, "You know where the donation jar is, sir."

The high-ranking officer laughed at her newfound feistiness. "Don't get too brave, young lady." He then announced to the watch floor, "Let's tag some bad guys and save innocent lives!"

Jefferson wasted no time putting out a discreet tipper to Jefe and Azúcar to come in for a "conference."

Sergeant Rice knew his boss. The communications and cyber guru had just posted an update to the objectives regarding *Op Gemela* on one of the big screens. It was a nice visual reminder for the watches to remain focused.

Vilma worked very hard at this assignment for the past few months. She smiled. The tea selections and *bird* images were the first compliments she had received from the boss, and that meant a lot to her. Her predecessor must have been some piece of work. The first morning on the job, the colonel had pulled her aside and she recalled his words vividly: *Work hard, get along with others and leave the ego outside the door. DON'T BE LIKE THE GUY YOU REPLACED!*

36 - GOLFING RENDEZVOUS

Far better is it to dare mighty things, to win glorious triumphs, even though checkered by failure... than to rank with those poor spirits who neither enjoy nor suffer much, because they live in a gray twilight that knows not victory nor defeat.
President Theodore Roosevelt

September 29, 2005

Thor Rockford pumped out his last rep from the leg press machine. He just finished a morning workout by super setting back and legs while jamming to Rush's, *A Farewell to Kings*. He grabbed the CD from the gym's stereo and glanced up at the large wall clock: *Thirty-five minutes to tee time.* He headed to the men's locker room to take a quick shower. Twenty minutes later, the Special Warfare Combatant Craft Crewmen (SWCC) operator sped into the parking lot to his favorite golf haven, Leprechaun Links. Normally, working out or golfing was his means to relieve stress. Today, he was not in the best of moods. In fact, he had delayed setting up this meeting several times, but his dad kept egging his son to follow through.

A wiry man with a slightly bow-legged gait walked up to the starter accompanied by a pretty woman at his side. The elderly gent looked the same height as himself, at five-feet ten-inches tall. Thor instantly recognized the man's face except he now sported a goatee. The chap still had the same full head of dark hair but with a few silver strands. It had been years since young Rockford last saw his dad's best friend win the Waterloo-Cedar Falls Police Departments' boxing championship.

Chuck Shotzski noticed the same young man eyeing him. He tipped his stained, perforated golf hat. "Why Mr. Rockford you have grown in both height and muscles!"

"It happens!" said Thor flatly.

Chuck smiled and said, "This is my wife, Kati Shotzski."

The young man removed his Packers' cap before replying, "Pleased to meet you, Mrs. Shotzski. My name is Juleon Rockford, but most people call me Thor."

She took Thor's hand and insisted, "Please call me Kati."

Shotz made eye contact with Thor. "Rock told us you might call for a golf outing."

Young Rockford looked down at the ground and muttered, "Dad wanted us to chat."

Shotzski didn't know what to make of Thor's melancholic mood, so he simply stated, "For starters, let's golf." He hit a respectful two-hundred and fifteen-yard drive with a slight fade down the first fairway.

"Honey, you've got to follow through to hit it straight and farther." Kati then gracefully swung her King Cobra Lady Ti driver. The ball landed dead center of the fairway, settling five yards past her husband's ball.

Chuck stuck his tongue out at Kati. "Thanks for out-driving me honey. It's great for my male ego."

Thor seemed to cheer up at their banter. He then smacked his ball two-hundred and seventy yards with his Callaway X-driver.

Shotzski ducked down the best he could with his haggard knees. He saw sparks fly as the titanium head ignited with the grass containing tiny granules of fertilizer and pebbles. "Whoa where's the thunder and lightning? Just joking Thor, but that was one heck of a drive. How long have you and Jer Bear been golfing?"

Rockford grinned. "Pheasant Ridge was kitty corner to our backyard. Pops and I began hopping the fence to play three holes every other night during the summer about twenty-eight years ago."

Chuck nodded. "Jer is a good man."

"Yep," Thor agreed, "Pa's the best. My dad took the time to play catch, taught me to defend myself and earn my keep by mowing neighbors' lawns, and disciplined me when necessary. Not many kids get that kind of well-rounded upbringing these days."

Mrs. Shotzski sensed Rock's son was at unease about something. She thought, *Humor is a great way to break the ice,* so Kati asked, "Thor, have you been stuck in some culverts lately?"

Thor Rockford let out a laugh, "Pops can never keep a secret. I am afraid of what else he told you about me."

Kati smiled. "Jer just said you were a lively kid and didn't like your first name."

Young Rockford nodded. "Juleon is a great Spanish name but my elementary peers teased me with *Julie-on*. I laugh now but that didn't fly at the time. I gave and received a few bloody lips."

Shotzski could not quite put his finger on it but his gut told him there was something else that Jerry Rockford didn't divulge about his son.

"Kati, how often do you both see my dad?"

"Twice a year. It hasn't been the same since your mother passed away." Kati held Thor's hand. "Our condolences about Betty," she said tenderly.

A tear trickled down Rockford's left cheek. "I appreciate that. I know it's harder on dad, but there isn't a day I don't think about my sweet mother. At least, I enjoyed three years with my mom and dad while studying full-time back home."

"No kidding, what did you study?" Shotz asked.

"I graduated three-years ago with a major in Journalism and a minor in Spanish. Mom spoke to me in Spanish, so that was an easy grade." Thor admitted, "Hispanic poetry is the best, but it can be a bear to translate."

Chuck shook his hand. "Congratulations on your BA. I'm a reporter now."

"That's what dad said."

Shotzski raised an eyebrow. "Do you plan on becoming a journalist someday?"

"Journalism seems to run in my blood, but now is not the time. I feel the media is too biased," Thor bit his bottom lip, "Just recently our detachment was watching one of the Sahte News broadcasts. Its news clip reported that approximately seven US Marines shot and killed over a dozen Iraqis. SNN portrayed the American troops as cold-blooded murderers. Something smelled fishy, so we changed channels to Fox News. Fox revealed the Iraqis shot first, so the Marines retaliated in self-defense."

"It appears Sahte News edited out important facts," Chuck sneered, "woe that is yellow!"

Thor graveled, "That crap unnecessarily puts us in harm's way, dupes our families back home, and emboldens terrorists."

"Perhaps you are correct?" That question did not sit well with Shotzski. His long career as a cop and army national guardsman, and more recent stint as a journalist seemed to balance him out.

Chuck's bluntness, sassiness and unquenchable pursuit for facts probably cost him a few awards and bennies in his business. He couldn't help to tell the truth and nothing but the truth and, as a result, he got branded as an undesirable for it.

Snowbirds, the small newspaper he worked for was very successful because the news was straightforward. However, Shotzski was ashamed of the predominantly liberal bias in the press.

It ticked him off that his colleagues didn't put the perpetrators of 9/11 on the front burner.

Shotzski now believed a proper balance was needed between safeguarding America and divulging too much information publicly just for a scoop. He hated to admit it but al-Qaeda was manipulating the dickens out of the media, especially American networks. He massaged the sides of his temples: *Where is a Teddy Roosevelt or Harry Truman when we need them? Hell, maybe I am out of touch, wising up as Rico would hope or just losing some testosterone in middle-age.*

Thor eyed Chuck. "You okay Mr. Shotzski?"

"Yeah sure…"

Rockford continued, "As I was saying, perhaps someday I will take up reporting but nothing beats working with good friends. I also get paid to PT, travel and serve my country.

Kati's eyes lit up. "That's great. Enlisted or officer?"

"Enlisted," he said with a shrug, "I believe everybody should enlist for a four-year stint or more before going to the dark side."

She smiled. "That makes sense."

"It didn't help that I threw my coffee into an armed robber's face at a convenience store in Pensacola. I would have probably been a goner but a guy returning with an empty keg, hammered the thief's gun out of his hand. One round popped off in front of my feet. I then clobbered the punk over the head with one of the store's stainless-steel coffee pump dispensers."

Kati's eyes opened. "Oh my, that was so brave!"

"Not at all. I was scared Mrs. Shotzski," Thor admitted. "But when that creep shot that old lady in the leg at the register and, then, I saw two young girls crying behind the coffee counter, rage overcame my trepidation. That freak looked like he was on drugs, his eyes were totally bloodshot, and his body shook uncontrollably." He shook his head in disgust. "That happened the day before I reported for Officer Candidate School in Pensacola. JAG encouraged me to submit another officer package three-years after that incident."

Mrs. Shotzski put her hands to her hips. "You mean that kept you from becoming an officer?"

"Yep. The civilian judge even wanted to nail me with a felony, since the metal coffee dispenser to the armed robber's head almost killed him."

Kati seethed hearing that, "What the hell's wrong with our courts? Too many criminals are coddled and innocent citizens pay the price when they defend themselves."

Thor Rockford explained, "Fortunately, the jury cared more about the rights' of the old lady and innocent bystanders, so all I got was a $500 fine for excessive force. Both lawyers even shook my hand for doing the right thing, but told me off the record, *rules are rules*, as far as the legal system has devolved. You see, a fine over $300 revokes your right to apply for any officer program within three years. I later found out the armed robber was on crack, and he got his gun off the black market. The police psychologist indicated the thug was more intent on killing somebody than stealing cash."

Shotzski chuckled after one-putting the ball into the hole with his Scotty Cameron putter - Thor Rockford had grown up. He admired the young man's inkling toward rugged individualism.

As they walked to the eleventh green, Thor opened up a bit and asked, "Kati, have you and Chuck ever played Amana in the fall?

"No… What is so special about Iowa in autumn?"

"Besides its prestigious golf course, that region has some majestic rolling hills, rustic leaves, fresh apples and outstanding Curd cheese."

"That does sound fun and romantic," Mrs. Shotzski said, looking at Chuck.

Thor winked at Kati. "Your husband should have the decency to window shop with you at the Amana Colonies after a round of golf."

Kati eyed her hubby, daring him not to interrupt her. "Chuck would love it."

Shotzski quickly switched subjects to avoid another playful jab from his wife. "Rock is one of the few people I've kept in touch with over the last thirty years." He then added with a grin, "That putz has a wicked sense of humor."

"Yep, dad used to take me to the mall sometimes as a young boy. He'd point out the finer attributes of ladies strolling by while mom shopped inside."

Chuck's eyes sparkled. "What are such attributes?"

Thor grinned. "Personality but looks and shape help."

Chuck Shotzski let out a hearty laugh, "Jer said he'd give me your number but he's so forgetful."

37 – SIMILAR PLIGHTS

Leprechaun Links

The SWCC operator began to relax golfing with his dad's best friend and his lovely wife, Kati. He still felt trepidatious to touch on the real subject at hand.

After playing a hole in silence, Chuck Shotzski had enough and said, "Okay, give it up! What's eating you, buster?"

Juleon Thor Rockford paused for a moment before muttering, "Pops said you and I have something in common." Shotz raised an eyebrow and took a step closer. JT added, "Most of my coworkers were killed recently."

"My condolences… Was that your group that got ambushed southeast of New Orleans?"

Thor slammed his golf club into the ground and gritted his teeth. "Yesss!!! What I am about to tell you stays here, okay?"

Shotzski nodded. "Not a problem."

Rockford's brow began to sweat heavily and his limbs seemed to be in a state of paralysis for a few seconds. "Here is where it gets dicey… Dad told me you've had your run-ins with some zany stuff Mr. Shotzski."

"It depends on what your definition of zany is?" the reporter said matter of fact.

Young Rockford grinned nervously, spat at the ground and, then, looked Shotzski straight in the eyes. "What slaughtered over half of my friends were some damned vampires."

He shrugged. "We're all loons, kiddo but I'm all ears."

Chuck's nonchalance made Thor want to challenge his dad's ole pal, so he said, "Okay, when I was four years old, a demonic looking poltergeist tried pushing me out of the top floor window at Lincoln's Office Supply. Of course, nobody saw it. The authorities couldn't explain the bruises around my arms, neck, and torso that were from naked hands but no fingerprints."

"I remember that case." Shotz pointed at young Rockford. "Who do you think was at the scene?"

"You?" he asked with his mouth open in disbelief.

"Yep. You probably blocked that out."

"Maybe." JT Rockford shook his head. "My parents had some very heated discussions about my ghastly ordeals."

"The gargoyle, killer clowns in the mall and waking up in St. Ansgar after falling asleep in your bedroom in Cedar Falls."

"You do remember!"

"You don't forget stuff like that, kid."

"Of course, my dad never wanted to believe it. Mom often cited you, Chuck, saying it was a possibility."

He sighed. "Well, it shook the hell out of your parents."

"Shook," Rockford's jaw tightened, "hell, I pissed my pants. After that I have had at least eight other dealings with the bizarre. So, what strange tales to you have for me?"

He grinned warily. "We seem to share similar plights."

"Specifics please."

Shotz raised an eyebrow. "I've destroyed several vampires, had a witch coven curse me with a shadow demon and stabbed a werewolf in the heart from broken glass laced with silver." He graveled, "And I could regurgitate dozens more."

Thor said, "Any advice on how to defeat these creatures?"

Kati looked at her husband with concern. He smiled at her and said, "I can at least share what I know with your crew."

"That would be appreciated." JT uncomfortably admitted, "You helped me in the past and knew I wasn't crazy."

"Like I said, been there too many times myself, kiddo."

Kati placed her right hand on the young man's shoulder. "Not crazy at all. I've been with Chuck on a few strange encounters. Once was too much!"

Thor stepped forward. "My biological mother left a strange quote in my baby basket when she gave me away. It said, *Be on guard from the undead.* I bet my dad never told you that?"

Shotz replied, "Nope… Rock is as practical as they come. No mumbo jumbo for him."

"Well, I sure do appreciate you listening." He shook his head saying, "Our unearthly encounters are something the normal Joe can't stomach."

"Not unless you want a one-way ticket to the loony bin."

Rockford sighed relief. "You're not kidding." He then looked at the reporter and asked, "So, how did you and Kati meet?"

Chuck kind of snickered, "On the grounds of Pines Logging Corporation..."

Kati double-squeezed her husband's hand to hush him up before saying, "We dated off and on for three years until he got the gumption to ask me to marry him."

Shotz kissed his wife on her ruby lips. "It has been the best years of my life."

"You may not know this, but Chuck and I are both retired police officers," she said with a pretty smile.

Thor studied Mrs. Shotzski's face and stature for a moment. "Kati, you do look familiar. Were you on any *Six Million Dollar Man, Charlie's Angels* and *Barnaby Jones* episodes?"

"Wow, I have a fan in my ranks," she beamed.

Shotzski crinkled his nose. "Here we go again."

Kati pushed her hubby aside. "As a matter of fact, I acted in several TV shows, but playing a cop wasn't as good as being one. So, I returned home and joined the Biloxi Police Department." She proudly smiled. "My dad, Captain Black, was happy one of his kids followed in his footsteps."

Chuck looked down and whispered, "I never saw such an elegant lady, with a fine physique and mesmerizing charm rise through the ranks of Biloxi's finest so fast."

She fired back, "My radiance had no effect on you."

"Oh, it did my lovely wife but Beelzebub comes in many forms," he said sarcastically.

She ignored her husband. "Thor, a detective's salary may not be huge but, at least, it has a pension."

He groused, "Honey, you even cuffed me. Remember?"

Kati smirked. "I had to because your risky reporting at Pines Logging Corporation turned into a fiasco."

Shotz put his index finger in the air and said, "Now wait just one minute. I saved your hides from that swamp beast. Where's the gratitude?"

"Let it go honey." She then told her spouse the code word, "muskrat!" for him to be quiet. He folded his arms in rebellion. She hugged him. "Well, Chuck did save our hides but he needs to learn some tact when dealing with corporate executives and authorities."

Shotzski switched subjects. "Kati and Rico Lombardi Sr. own a small newspaper here in town." He grabbed his collar in satisfaction and stated, "I am Snowbirds' premiere reporter."

"I know," Rockford admitted, "been reading your articles for months."

Chuck smiled. "Our paper provides great golf and restaurant discounts. It reads well for our predominant senior community."

"Heck, my young co-workers rave about Snowbirds. Most people I know prefer a real paper in their hands with a cup of coffee. Too many big newspapers nowadays have mutated into liberally slanted manifestos and reduced the sports sections by half."

Kati said with a twinkle in her eye, "That's our secret. Stick with the facts and don't cheat the sports' enthusiasts."

Thor put up his hands. “And the newspaper conglomerates wonder why their sales have been at all-time lows?”

The reporter chuckled, “I second that motion!”

She added, “Snowbirds also owns the rights to the Miss Judy-Judy column which is distributed nationally."

Rockford’s eyes widened a bit and said, “Really? She gives excellent advice.”

Kati Black Shotzski cackled, “She’s a he.”

“It’s Jack’s forte,” Chuck clarified, “and much to my surprise, Mr. Grumblier does justice to the memory of the original writer, Mrs. Archilena Leach.”

Thor then hit a hundred and seventy-yard fade with his Ping Zing II six-iron. The Titleist ball landed on the upper tier of the par-three green. He asked, "Do you mind if I call you, Shotz?"

Shotzski swung his five-iron and casually said, "Not at all, most friends do." He topped the ball on his down swing and it skipped twice over the water. The ball then ricocheted on top of a rock, soared forty feet in the air and settled inches from the cup. Both men gave each other high-fives.

Kati shook her head, walked up to the women’s tee and struck her five-wood perfectly. The ball accelerated one hundred and sixty-five yards into the sky, landing in the middle of the two-tiered green. The high slope caused it to pop up and spin back. The pink golf ball lost momentum as it hit the fringe’s edge. It then trickled into some bathing flamingos.

Chuck turned away to conceal a grin.

Mrs. Shotzski shook her fist at her hubby and snarled, “You get so lucky with your sloppy shots.”

He chuckled, “C’est la vie Sherrie.”

38 - ALLIANCE

Thor said to Shotz after hitting their approaches to the eighteenth green, "We could use your skills to fight the undead."

"Are you pitching an alliance?"

"Definitely!"

Kati shot her husband another concerned look. Chuck grinned. "Whatever I can do to help, but I'm no spring chicken."

Mrs. Shotzski stated, "You need prayer and holy water to battle vampires!"

Rockford eyed both of them. "Do you believe in God?"

Kati Black Shotzski smiled. "Of course!"

Chuck Shotzski admitted, "After that two-hundred-year old vampire almost killed me, yeah, I caught on quickly and embraced the rugged old Cross." The reporter winked. "Though, I do enjoy my nip in moderation, *suum cuique*."

Thor angled his head to one side. "Shotz, what was that you muttered?"

"For Heaven's sake, you're a professional linguist who speaks Spanish, Arabic and some Italian."

"I'm a Boat Guy now; a bit rusty in Arabic and Italian."

The Snowbirds' reporter said, "Still…"

Kati interrupted her husband, "Just ignore my sawed-off Romeo."

Juleon Thor Rockford smiled at Mrs. Shotzski. "Chuck and my dad aren't happy unless they're busting somebody's chops."

The reporter's right eyebrow rose. "Spanish and Italian are Romance languages. What is your major malfunction?" he asked JT with a hint of sarcasm.

He didn't miss a beat and replied, "It helps if you could speak with a decent accent."

Shotz pointed at the youngster. "Dead languages aren't meant to be spoken there Socrates."

"Touché," Rockford reluctantly admitted.

Chuck continued, "And just for your edification, *suum cuique* is Latin meaning *each to his own*."

"What?" Thor grinned mischievously. "Are you leery of those that forbid drinking but stuff themselves silly at a Sunday brunch?"

Shotzski laughed, "Something like that. I've run into some unusual things over the years. I've survived by using all sorts of items, not just crucifixes."

"When I first became a believer most of my friends thought I joined a cult. I just knew I needed forgiveness. I think my abrupt change was too much for my buddies to stomach. I had been one of the main catalysts for enticing them into wild partying and chasing the ladies." Thor sighed relief. "I just thank the good Lord's mercy by forgiving all the wrong I have said, done or thought."

Kati smirked. "That sounds just like Jer's middle name – trouble with a big T."

"Women are beautiful creatures, just like my Kati Black." Chuck gently took the top of his wife's right hand and kissed it. "And I have been faithful to my sweet rose for all these years."

Mrs. Shotzski softly blew a kiss toward her hubby with a tender smile. Suddenly, her pupils narrowed as she stared down her husband. Kati's typical soothing voice sounded more like a rising growl as she stated, "Chuck darling, you better or you'll wake up castrated!"

Chuck Shotzski half-bowed to his wife with a grin. "That's my feisty mama, keeping me on the straight and narrow."

Young Rockford cracked a smile thinking of his Latina girlfriend. "I have a lovely lady. Her name is Lise Alegría. We've been steady for about seven months. She left yesterday for a nursing convention."

Kati held Thor's hand. "We would love to meet your girlfriend."

Thor admitted, "I know Lise would like to meet friends of the family."

Shotzski's cell phone rang as they scooted off the eighteenth green. Chuck answered, "Hey Jer! How's Iowa?"

"Fine," Jerry Rockford replied. "How are you, Shotz?"

Chuck Shotzski was onto Rock. "We just got done playing some golf with Thor."

Rock's voice sounded eager as he inquired, "How did it go?"

Shotz winked at Thor and Kati. "Strange but fine!" he stated cryptically.

Jer didn't know how to say what was on his mind, so he asked, "How's Mrs. Shotzski?"

Chuck answered slowly, "Oh, she's fine..."

Jerry Rockford added, “What’s the weather like?”

Shotzski replied, "The weather is quite balmy down here. How are your early autumn skies up there, Jer?”

“Okay Shotzski, you are toying with me,” Jerry grumbled. “What in Sam Spade are you up to?”

Shotz chuckled, “I could say the same about you, Rock. Why were you holding out on me?”

Rockford deflected by saying, “I don’t know what the hell you are talking about?”

Chuck Shotzski fired back, “Uh huh. I think you neglected to tell me about Thor’s recent supernatural encounter.”

“Not that mumbo jumbo crap again!” Rock sneered.

“Jer, I think you should talk with your son.” Chuck handed young Rockford his cell phone.

“Hey pops,” Thor said to his dad. “Thanks for pointing me to Shotz.”

He knew his son losing over half of his friends was tough and asked, “How are you holding up Tiger?”

“The loss of my teammates will always sting, but it helps talking about the other stuff with someone who understands.”

“Well, your stories are too weird for me,” Jerry grumped. “I figured Chuck could relate better. I love you son.”

“Love you too, Pops.”

“Hey, let me talk with the putz again.”

“Okay.” Thor handed Shotz his cell phone.

“Chuck, I can’t stomach your weird tales,” Jerry admitted, “but thanks for helping my kid.”

“No problem Rock.” Shotzski added, “It’s beyond belief and one heck of a coincidence.”

Jer couldn’t control throwing out the last jab to his distant pal and said, “Hey Shotz, I guess you’re not the putz I always thought you were.”

Chuck and Kati Shotzski were amazed when Thor walked over to the trunk of a 1967 *Ford Mustang* hardtop. Shotz whistled at the kid, “Like my 1949 Dodge Coronet?”

“Oh yeah, she looks sweet.”

“How come your dad doesn’t drive an ole classic?” asked Chuck.

“Not pops, he likes new cars. For some reason, I’ve always been attracted to 1960s Stangs?”

The trio shook their heads in bewilderment that both sported vintage automobiles. Chuck gently patted his wife's back before saying, "Kati had it repainted a few years back as a gift."

She put up her hands. "The rusted blue hurt my eyes."

Shotzski wasn't much for keeping up with the Jones'. "Lifted the suspension a few inches and put in a 1960s four-cylinder diesel engine. My sweet girl now tops forty mpg and it has no computer chip, so it will still run if some loons hit the US with an Electromagnetic Pulse device." He eyed his wife mischievously. "She made me do it."

Kati backhanded the base of Chuck's skull. "Your Coronet's overhaul was an expensive birthday gift you ungrateful lil twerp. If it wasn't for me, your blue boat would still be clunking out every other day and you'd be living in some cheap condo!"

Shotz winced. "Thanks for the love tap sugar."

They laughed and then exchanged cell phone numbers before they drove off in separate directions.

Chuck Shotzski wondered what else Rock's son and he had in common, besides a penchant for journalism and classic cars. He looked at Kati and asked, "How about grabbing a snack honey?"

She batted her eyes and said, "It depends where?"

Shotzski smiled and dialed Thor's cell phone. "Are you up for some *Outback Steak House*?"

"Sure, I was just about to see if you and Kati wanted to have a frosty brew with salad, steak and garlic mashed potatoes."

"No kidding? Well, garlic keeps the vampires away, eh?"

JT Rockford replied, "Shotz that's a bit fresh in my memory. I'll be there in fifteen mikes."

Chuck then prayed with Kati out loud but kept his eyes on the road, "Lord, thank you for showing me I'm not the only loon who runs into the bizarre. If it be your will, help Thor and I ward off evil in the coming days."

Kati added, "And please protect them almighty God, Amen."

39 - KARMA

September 29, 2005 - 1730 Hours

Jefe initiated radio communications by saying, "Birdman, this is Nastea."

Technical Sergeant Rice handed the head piece to his boss. "Nastea, this is Birdman," Colonel Sparkman replied.

"The yacht's gone!" he said matter of fact.

"What's going on?" Sparky exasperated. "SAT images just picked up that vessel yesterday morning."

"Not sure," Nastea admitted. "We searched the perimeter."

"What's the body count at?"

"The helicopter crew is retrieving a second body from the water. We've got one on the shore. A total of three out of six."

"Try to retrieve as many bodies as you can. Any updates let us know." The colonel recalled Azúcar saying at the pre-mission meeting, *All the fatal incidents on Gemela occurred after dark.* His instincts kicked in and he ordered, "Get out before sundown!"

Jefe replied, "Roger. Nastea out."

Azúcar, Jefe and two Naval Criminal Investigative Service (NCIS) special agents found another corpse along the northern bank.

Special Agent Peterson observed the dead body for several minutes. She stood up and admitted reluctantly, "Same as the rest - broken neck and lost lots of blood."

Azúcar studied the face. She looked at her partner and held up two fingers. Nastea nodded before he spoke into his mouthpiece, "Sir. We got a fourth body. It appears that we have two facial matches to previous Guantanamo detainees."

Colonel Sparkman ordered, "I want DNA and biometrics done on these jackasses... the whole nine yards!"

Azúcar's eyes darted up toward the fading sunlight and then pointed at her watch. He read the time, *1840 hours. Sundown's in thirty minutes*, the CIA operative thought. "Time to beat feet!"

The other NCIS special agent objected by saying, "No way. We've gotz some daylight to burn to search for the other two!"

"Are you deaf," asked the CIA operative.

Lohder replied in a slow smart aleck tone, "Nooo."

She grinned at the tiny man. "Napoleonic complex?"

"Screw you."

"No thanks."

"Who the hell do you think you are?"

She ignored him and said, “Let’s body bag the bodies.”

Special Agent Lohder jabbed his index finger into the middle of her chest and stated, "I'll make the decisions around here, sugar!"

Azúcar twisted his arm, forced his palm to point lateral and then snapped his wrist downward. "Jefe and I've got the Conn!"

He dropped to one knee to alleviate the extreme discomfort and painfully said, "Listen to me or…"

She pressed her knife against his jugular. "You wish to say something, mister?" she said, daring him to escalate the situation.

Jefe stated, "Pay for exactly what... touching her breasts?"

Special Agent Peterson exclaimed, "Cut the crap Lohder! You're out of line."

Azúcar coldly said, "Karma's a bitch, eh muchacho?"

"Come on, you’re better than this." Peterson eyed her partner and mouthed; *You're not fooling anyone.*

He grimaced looking up at Azúcar and pleaded, “Okay.”

She released her hold on the muscular little prick and sheathed her blade. "Don't you ever touch me like that again!"

Special Agent Peterson glared at her co-worker and said, "Now be a professional and apologize to the lady."

Lohder stood up, holding his sore wrist and said, "My bad."

Peterson shook her head. "That's it?"

The special agent got to his feet and grumbled, "What? Are two CIA operatives afraid of the dark?"

"Mister. We aren't afraid of squat but some unexplained spooky shit happens at this place after dark." Jefe eyed both agents and said matter of fact, "You should know better. NCIS has lost several of their own checking this place out after sunset!" He pointed to the helicopter hovering above and continued. "That is our bird and we say when it is time to go. You two bone heads want to stick around, that's your call."

Peterson saw *the screw you look* on Lohder's face. Still, she was surprised her pint-sized partner had the prudence to keep his mouth shut. Time had moved slowly for the tall NCIS agent since she began working with Lohder. Both ranked at the top among their peers, so it seemed logical to team up the junior agents after being tutored by some of the best in their field. At first, she admired his assertiveness but quickly realized he was arrogant rather than confident. She heard her aunt' words, *Quick to hear and slow to speak*, almost every time her co-worker tried her patience.

Lohder used intimidation to get his way. However, he learned not to cross Peterson's no non-sense persona or Harlem street smarts. It was comical to her when he tried to give off attitude. Gary Coleman did a better job on *Different Strokes*.

Both Lohder and Peterson were gifted agents and of African heritage but the similarities stopped there. He talked too much trash and she let her actions speak for themselves. He bragged that he grew up in the hood south of D.C. but she discovered he grew up in in a posh neighborhood. He had two loving parents who were still married whereas her parents died when she was a child. She spent many nights not eating and fighting for her life until her aunt rescued her. His pose for street cred seemed pathetic to her.

Special Agent Peterson was certain Lohder's five-feet three-and a half-inch stature was the reason for his inferiority complex. It shouldn't have been. He was a solid agent except when showboating. She normally kept her co-worker in check but tired of babysitting. She hoped Azúcar's stern schooling might sink in. She glared at her partner and said, "Jefe. We will leave with you."

The CIA operative nodded and then said, "Big Bird, this is Nastea. We're ready to depart in three mikes!"

"Nastea, this is Big Bird. Roger," replied the helicopter pilot as he made his descent to Gemela's northern shore.

A man released the line between a yacht and a small ship in the Gulf of Mexico. Daciana said, "Let me know the moment you get two miles away from that junk."

"Okay," he replied. Minutes later the helmsmen radioed back, "Just outside the rust bucket by two nautical miles."

Daciana pressed a button and the fishing vessel went up into smithereens. Chucks of metal and debris exploded skyward, crashing into the waters within a mile radius of its impetus. She was certain those explosives could have taken down something like the Eiffel Tower. She was glad they destroyed the material. She hoped not too many sea creatures were killed in the process and the mangled metal would help create some coral sanctuaries.

40 - A DEALER HUMBLED

September 30, 2005 - 6:00 p.m.

Daciana pulled the fifty-six feet long yacht into Grekio's large Caribbean dock after a day's journey from Gemela. Two of her fellow gypsies followed in their master's smaller craft.

Grekio made most of his money legitimately in the trade and repair of smaller seafaring vessels. His business also allowed him to delve into the black market without raising unwanted attention.

She walked up the stone steps to the front porch where a large guard stood. She noticed that Grekio had made several modifications to the simple looking stucco building since her last visit. The roof was pitched higher to withstand severe weather.

The guard frisked her. He snatched a knife inside her boot and smirked. "You will get this back after you talk to the boss."

She snorted, "Your boss."

A buzzer sounded and Daciana opened the metal door into the concrete reinforced edifice. She surmised several of the deco items hanging on the outside walls were covering gun slits. The interior had been updated with dark mahogany furniture and shelves, new electronics and bright coral painted walls.

The owner greeted the fit brunette by saying, "Buenas tardes señorita. What brings you here?"

She cocked her head back toward the two vessels. "I'd like to trade both yachts for one similar to the larger one."

Grekio stroked his peppery mustache for a moment. He eyed the two vessels from his office's bullet proof window.

"Check out the interior side panels. There are about fifty high-grade rifles and handguns inside, plus a lot of ammo." She didn't tell him her crew kept ten of their favorites.

"How much?"

"Fifteen-grand."

"My team will inspect the weapons."

She shrugged. "You might want to clean the interior walls and decking. Someone had a ton of explosives sealed in plastic."

"Where's the explosives?"

"Gone!" The killer smiled. "Even we have ethics. Hate to see some terrorists get that stuff."

He nodded, not sure what to say, but he liked the fifty-six feet long cruising vessel. It was sleek, efficient and brand new. "Return in a month and we'll recompense you in the trade."

"Proper paperwork and no funny business." Daciana said forcefully, "Remember my master's previous visit."

The black-market dealer grabbed his throat in fear at the thought of his last encounter with that mysterious figure:

***

Grekio didn't pay Daciana the cash they agreed upon. When she protested, he called in his guard to be more persuasive. She barely got past the thug after dealing each other major blows.

Several nights later, Grekio had his television volume on high watching a soccer match. He was caught off guard when a strange mist crept under the bolted door. The vapor enveloped his body like a large snake constricting its prey. What he saw next was even more terrifying. The fog transformed into a man with red eyes and sharp fangs. He asked in disbelief, "Who the hell are you?"

"Daciana's master."

The dealer regained his bravado, thinking this was some sort of hoax and said, "What is it to you?"

"You almost killed my servant over money."

"It was a fair deal."

The vampire lifted Grekio two feet off the ground. His left hand was like a vice grip around the human's throat. "You lie. You promised Daciana ten-thousand dollars after the trade. Even worse, you harmed her."

The dealer tried to respond, but the stranger's death grip prevented him from speaking. After several seconds, Dracula let the mortal fall to the tile. Grekio gasped for air. After a minute, he replied in a hoarse voice, "I will transfer the funds into your account tomorrow."

"You better or next time I will make this personal. The Count eyed the man intently and asked, "You wouldn't want your family to pay for your treachery, would you?"

"No!" he pleaded, trembling on his knees.

"I understand you have to make money and this type of business can be risky. Therefore, I have always treated you fairly and not asked for much."

"Sí señor."

Dracula snarled, "I demand the same." He pointed at Grekio. "NEVER SWINDLE ME!" The dealer's extremities began to shake, staring at the enigmatic figure in total terror. The vampire added, "As a parting gift, I have left you something outside the door to warn you against ever crossing me again."

Grekio looked toward the front door and when he turned around, the man in the dark suit was gone. He passed out in fear. He thought it was a dreadful dream until he awoke. He discovered his six-feet six-inch tall strongman lying motionless on the covered patio. The guard's throat was slit open and his body bloodless.

He was even more horrified when he reviewed his surveillance video system. The first image showed his muscular bodyguard fighting off an invisible figure before having his throat slashed open in a sideways motion. The dealer then clearly saw himself being lifted in the air. His head was inches from hitting the ceiling but the digital footage captured no one holding him. He knew all too well it was real. He could still see those terrifying red eyes and feel the superhuman grip around his throat.

"Grekio, are we clear?" said Daciana. He didn't respond. His eyes conveyed paralyzed fear. She slammed her palm on his desk before demanding in a loud voice, "Are we clear?"

The black-market dealer jumped from his nightmarish recollection. "Si. Perfectly clear," he gulped, "No funny business."

She stated, "Wise choice. The larger yacht is yours. We will return for a newer vessel." She exited the door and grabbed her knife from the patio table before the guard could stop her.

He reached for his gun and guard spoke into his walkie talkie, "You okay boss?"

Daciana spun around. Her elbow was already cocked back, the knife ready to strike her target as she calmly said, "I wouldn't do that if I was you."

The muscular guard held up his hands in a 'give up manner.'

Grekio swung open the door and ordered, "Never harm her!"

Mid-October 2005

Jason Lory raked freshly laid mulch around the last fruit tree. The sweet, pungent aroma was a reminder of a job well done. In the past week, he replaced fifty frost-tolerant citrus trees. Planting earlier this far south, due to extreme heat would be unwise.

He walked into the newly constructed stone exterior pump shed and turned on the sprinklers. The landscaper then surveyed five quadrants of the large orchard. After the long walk, he was content. The irrigation worked perfectly. He had also pruned and pleated the older trees, salvaging at least one-hundred of them. A truck drove up. He recognized the stunning facial features, even behind the smoky glass. Jason smiled as Daciana exited the SUV. "Good afternoon."

She dryly said, "My boss is pleased with your work."

"Much appreciated."

"He especially liked your construction of the underground cement tanks." She added, "My master..." The landscaper looked at her strangely. "I mean my boss... is all about efficiency. He was impressed how the tanks will capture rainwater from the roof for the orchard's sprinkler system."

"Save money and use less water." He added, "I also set it only to water when the soil is dry."

"Very intelligent." Daciana added, "Here's your payment."

"Thank you," he said before stashing the cash in his windbreaker's interior pocket.

"Once we're done with the walls and roof, you're welcome to hunt in the fall." She pointed her chin toward the new construction. "Just don't wander inside. You might fall into a dark hole."

He slowly grinned at her comment. Lory had noticed earlier of the larger home's foundation and thick cemented-walls. A basement was a few feet above ground-level, built to withstand flooding and severe weather. A gradual incline began a hundred feet from the front and sides of the home up to the main floor. The back opened to a walkout basement on the north side with a pool.

The shapely vixen eyed him before asking, "You don't scare easily, do you?"

Jason replied without batting an eye, "Nope!" *She's a strange one and so is the design of that basement*, he thought. He had previously noted what looked to be a tunnel going from the main home to the garage. "If I may?"

She replied a bit anxiously, "Yes."

"Your boss has been very generous. I'd be happy to put in irrigation around the perimeter of the house and garage once it's completed. At a discounted price, of course."

After a pause, Daciana asked, "How much?"

"Probably eight-hundred for piping and other supplies." He scratched his head and said, "Gas to drive way out here and labor… about twelve-hundred. Two-thousand total."

She replied with a hint of surprise, "That's reasonable!"

Besides her subtle threat earlier in the year, the landscaper sensed some pleasant emotions from her for the first time. He showed her where he'd install the irrigation as they walked toward the pump shed. He then instructed her how to use the gauges for the orchard's sprinkler system. He pointed to a shelf and said, "Here's a simple laminated instruction in case anyone needs it."

She was impressed. She liked his confident, rugged and easy-going style. The pump shed and sprinklers got her thinking about a part of her life she had neglected. She barely cracked a naughty grin before handing him a wad of cash.

He beamed. "More work?"

"Keep the change."

Jason thought: *That feline is coming onto me.* Daciana was jaw-dropping, but he was married and to a fine woman.

Her left arm drew in his waist to hers before whispering into his ear, "Otherwise, contact me if it is not enough."

Her firm figure and warm breath were exhilarating. He felt dizzy. He stepped back and faked a sneeze. "Pardon me."

She responded in a sultry voice, "To your health."

"Much obliged." She moistened her lips. He tried to it by politely saying, "Must be coming down with something."

"No. You just need something to warm you up."

Her mannerisms reminded him of a female praying mantis that often ate the male while mating with him. He slowly backed up thinking, *Lord and wife.* She stepped forward and began to undo her dark blouse. Her black lingerie barely hid her appealing curves.

He had never seen a woman with such a taut frame but supple breasts. *Get out of Dodge quick, Jase!* She eyed him like a tigress. He looked down at his watch. "Well. It's suppertime with Mrs. Lory." In truth, his wife was visiting family up north.

The brunette slowly moved forward to press her warm body against his. “I’ll give you something to nibble on.”

The landscaper stepped to the side as she missed her target. He wanted to run but had to ask, "When can I begin?"

His question caught her off guard. Daciana was fantasizing of putting her nails into his back. "Oh.... well.” Reality sank in and she disappointedly said, "Come back in March."

He nodded and headed home to take a cold shower.

41 - JAIL BREAK

October 17, 2005

Dr. Maria Wilder visited the county jail at midnight. The previous evening, she had nightmares of Nigel Rathbone's corpse coming back to life. All day, she kept telling herself the horrific dreams were only that but the suspense gnawed at her until she left work one hour early.

A tall man instantly stood up as Deputy Rufino Cabrera escorted Maria toward his solitary cell. She recognized Nigel Rathbone from the two treasured photos Rosa stored in her curie. He was a dead ringer for the mysterious man her mother would rarely talk about. She smiled at the deputy and asked, "Can I have some privacy with this man for a moment?"

Cabrera retreated to the far side of the jail, still able to eye any suspicious moves made by the man his fellow lawmen labeled *Cujo*. A tinge of jealousy sprouted from Rufino's heart, wondering why Doc would give a possible convict the time of day but not him.

Rathbone pressed against the bars. "You sure do look familiar," he said curiously.

"I am a spitting image of my mother in her youth." Both she and Rosa shared the same auburn hair, slim figure and almond shaped eyes, as did Elsa. For a moment, he thought the woman in front of him was Rosa. Maria raised an eyebrow and whispered, "You should know. Rosa, let you reside with her at Château Wilder for almost a year." Nigel nodded. Her voice saddened. "She passed away two months ago."

He sat down before responding, "My condolences. Your mother was a noble woman and a very attractive lady." Doc did something she only did with patients but not strangers. She grasped his hands through the bars.

Deputy Cabrera enviously barked, "Hey Cujo, no touching!" Maria glared at Rufino as they released hands.

Rathbone's head hung low as he admitted, "I kept my heart from Rosa for her own safety. I vowed I would never repeat the same mistake as with my previous sweetheart." After a short pause, he added, " She was a dear friend, very private, tough and loyal as they come."

"Ma was the best."

"Rosa was truly a rose." She smiled at him and his face perked up.

Deputy Cabrera looked at his clock. "Three more minutes!"

"By the way, my name is Maria Wilder." She was about to extend her hand but stopped, remembering the rules.

“Nigel Rathbone.”

She cackled, “Rosa didn’t say a lot about you but enough.”

The luminous rays beamed intensely through the night’s sky. His voice muffled, "You must leave now!" She was baffled by his mood swing. She then saw him jerk about. The inmate’s shoes began to crumple and large paws with razor sharp claws began to emerge. The half-hoary beast’s shirt burst at the buttons. Dr. Wilder barely caught a glimpse of the scar of the lycan on his upper left shoulder before fur began to cover it. She couldn’t move or breathe.

A primal howl erupted, “Awgh, awgh.” The guttural pitch echoed throughout prison. Doc and the four lawmen stared in amazement. They all felt the savage terror of the wolfman.

The beast stood six feet three-inches tall but instinctively crouched lower. Dense muscle tissue and wiry hair finished bulging out of Rathbone’s torn threads. The jailer grimaced, screeching, “I wished we would have kept the straight jacket on him.”

Doctor Wilder gasped, “This is not real,” as she lost her balance and fell back into the concrete wall.

"Okay guys… You scared us with the Jack Pierce stunt."

The jailer stammered, "Rufino. This ain't no makeup trick!"

The lupine gazed at Maria, confused. He sniffed the air and salivated. It crept closer and began to shake the cage. Being locked up normally kept the werewolf at bay, but the immediate scent and view of humans was too much of a temptation.

One of the deputies drew his sidearm and shot the lycan two times center mass. It only growled and continued to quake the metal cage. Small particles of mortar crumbled to the floor. The tiny cracks were now larger ones. The recent hurricane had damaged parts of the concrete foundation and jolted the ceiling. None of the lawmen had noticed until now.

The jailer shot two rounds between the metal bars into the beast's skull with his *Glock* pistol. The wolfman collapsed on the concrete floor. He holstered his weapon, turned around, leaned against the bars and exhaled a sigh of relief. Seconds later, large furry hands and titanium like claws grabbed the relaxed jailer.

Two deputies unloaded their pistols. Blood oozed out from the hoary chest and the beast fell on the concrete slab. Blood began to retract into its body. It was a sick repetition as the werewolf jumped back up and onto the bars. The metal creaked and began inching apart. Both lawmen switched weapons and pumped shotgun rounds at the lycan, knocking it down. The accursed beast yelped an unnerving cry.

Doc screamed and passed out. Deputy Cabrera broke her fall. He immediately threw her over his left shoulder, carrying her to his squad SUV. The lycanthrope hopped back up, growling, "Aarh."

The second jailer was enraged and shouted, "No animal that size can take as much lead and live." He reloaded his shotgun and shot the rest of his ammunition into the wolfman. The impact pushed the lycan back a few feet and it slumped against the thick concrete wall.

The deputy radioed dispatch, "Thing down."

"What thing?" The beast sprung at the bars. The deputy screamed hysterically and the dispatcher mandated, "Repeat your last." The fallen steel bars crushed the lawmen.

42 - LOST BOY

October 31, 2005

A kid began to panic searching for any swamp markings his dad had routinely schooled him. "Shucks," he said noticing daylight was fading fast. He also recognized the fact he was running scared and on the edges of the marsh, he rarely frequented.

He took in a deep breath and told himself, "Dangnabbit Justo, stop freaking out." His eyes surveyed the area and thought, "*I don't recognize a darn thing*." He yelled, "Pa, I am lost. Help me!" He then disobeyed one of the rules his father had sternly stated to him so often: *Never ever run like a mad dog in a swamp!*

Seconds later, Justo tripped over a log and crashed into the edges of the murky backwater. Blood oozed from a gash in his knee and he frantically screamed, "Daddy, I'm caught under a branch… HELP!" The Frankenstein Monster's keen ears heard the boy's yelps and ran a quarter of a mile through the bayou.

A fourteen-foot long alligator eyed the kid and slithered into the water. The titan spotted the struggling little lad and jumped thirty-five feet into the marshy waters. The crocodilian's head emerged from the surface and opened its jaws. He stopped the great gator from clamping down on its trapped prey. Within two quick movements, he ripped the alligator's jaws apart and snapped its neck, tossing the broken reptile toward the bank. He kneeled beside the boy before tearing his shirt free from the branch. The giant reached out with open palms as his mouth quivered, "F-friend?"

The kid hugged him, saying "Thank you, sir."

He smiled. A tear trickled down his cheek and he gently carried the tike out of the water. "What's your name?"

"Justo." He then inquired, "What's yours?"

"Don't know."

"Dunno?" he said, admiring the nice fellow who just saved him. The hulk was relieved the lad didn't look away in revulsion from his scarred visage. "That's silly," Justo exclaimed, "everyone should have a name."

His amalgamated body parts seemed to have their own tactile memories of places and events, before his creator brought him to life. He sighed. "Victor sometimes called me, *Deucalion*."

That reminded him of school. "No. Sounds Greek to me."

"Think that's what it is." He added in a low chuckle, "Some kids called me *Mr. Tower* long ago."

Creature saves child

"Nah but that's pretty close."
He cast his head down and said, "Frankenstein?"

“Nope… that name’s too long.” Justo put a finger on his chin before declaring, “We’ll call ya, *Franki*!”

“Okay?” said the titan astonishingly. How a child could provide him with an appropriate name so quickly amazed him.

A man suddenly ran with his 12-gauge pump shotgun aiming at the large stranger and yelled, “Get away from my son!”

He growled, “Ruh.” He carefully put the child behind him and gestured with his hands for the man to lower the gun.

Justo jumped between his new friend and his father, insisting, "Pa, don't shoot.” The little lad pointed toward the dead reptile and stated, “Franki saved me from that big gator."

The dad put his weapon on safe and set it down. He hugged his son. "Sir, I apologize,” he said looking up at the brute. “Justo is my only child. I got scared with his screams and seeing you holding him. There’s a bunch of demented folks out there.” Frankenstein’s Creation understood, nodding his head. “My wife,” the southerner said fighting back tears, “his ma just died two weeks ago.”

Franki softly said, “My condolences.”

“Appreciate that. Unfortunately, most of my family has had nothing to do with us since this redneck wed a black lady. Well, my ma and pa saw that brown and white skins are all alike. They treated us just fine.” He sadly stated, “Both have been dead for a season.”

The hulking wretch yearned for their fates and said in a dreamy tone of voice, “I want long sleep.”

The swamp man shook the creature’s hand. “Name’s Jedidiah. Most folk call me Jed.”

He couldn’t help but grin, thinking of how Justo nicknamed him just moments ago. “Please call me Franki,” he said confidently. *It was nice to have a name, some identity*, he thought.

The redneck stared over two feet up into the giant’s eyes and graciously stated, “Well, Mr. Franki, I can never thank you enough for saving my lil Justo. And I mean that with all due sincerity, sir." A genuine smile emerged, something the brute had not experienced for a long while. Jedidiah jostled him. "Why don't we take that gator and bring it back to my shack. We'll kindle it over a fire, eat some vittles and drink some fine shine."

The creature nodded appreciatively and lightly tapped the man’s chest. His gentle knock sent Jed tumbling back. He yearningly gazed at the father and son. "Family good.” He easily hefted the large carcass over his shoulders.

After supper, Justo's curly head of hair nestled under Franki's bicep. The lad rested peacefully with a smile on his face.

He handed a jug to his guest. "Try this moonshine!"

The titan gulped the clear liquid, "Um, moonshine strong."

He cackled, "It sure has a bite. Over eighty-proof distilled three times in my copper pot still." Jed's eyes grew wide. "How did you kill that gator?" The creature opened up his enormous forearms. "Bare-handed?" the bayou man noted, finally realizing his enormity. "Your shoes look like they've been mummified and busting out of the seams. My wife's family can make you some new boots."

"That would be nice." Captain Peck had been the last human to make him new boots.

He compared his size ten shoes to the giant's worn stompers. "I'd reckon you need abouts a size twenty-five shoe." Franki nodded graciously, as he gently placed Justo to his side. They shared the jug and ate some more roasted gator around the campfire. After the moonshine went dry, the host quickly returned with another large ceramic container and said with a smile, "Do you want more of my homemade white lightning?"

"Yes… Lightning is my mother." Frankenstein's Creation then chugged a fifth of the contents in one gulp.

He said wide-eyed, "Meeting you reminded me of when I saw Blarny Kranklund turn into a big wolf one full moon in 1966." The giant sneered and Jed continued, "I was just a kid, but our family is a superstitious lot. Hungarian-Gypsy runs deep in our veins. That's when I found my pa and he shot that four-legged werewolf smack dab in the middle of the heart with a silver bullet."

"Silver is the best way to destroy such beasts."

"Next thing ya know, the beast changed back into the clothing store's owner, Mr. Kranklund. I'll never forget poor ole Blarny utter those last words with his silly lisp: *Thank you for releasing me from the torment*." He burped, "That Blarn was a nice fellow but one hell of a swindler." The bayou man slowly began to nod asleep as his chin dropped to his chest and rise back up.

Franki chuckled to himself, watching the swamp resident's head bobbing routine. He enjoyed the quiet company as he slowly sipped the strong, clear liquid. It wasn't until he began to recall the savage fights, he had with another werewolf many years ago that he got a bitter taste in his mouth. *That Rathbone!* He then thought of those who treated him kindly. With the master hypnotizing him frequently, not many stood out and it was mostly a blur. Dracula did speak with him, and provided food and shelter. Then there was that couple, Mrs. Marge and Mr. James who hired him to be the caretaker of their estate, Captain Peck and the Canadian blind man whom he called *Pa.* Such rare kind souls saw past his terrifying appearance. Those were pleasant memories but didn't last. He took a swig and wailed, "Nice people die and then I'm alone again!"

He jolted up. "As I was saying… My dad and I got in the routine of patrolling from the outskirts of town to our swamp on full moons." He looked at his hands, realizing he didn't have the jug. He scowled, seeing the shine was in his guest hands. "Sir, may I?" The giant smiled handing him the home brew. Jed took a sip and continued, "That's more like it. Now, there was another werewolf we hunted down five-months after shooting Kranklund."

"I don't care for wolfmen."

"Neither do I," the host mumbled. "Well, where was I?

The giant graveled, "Werewolves."

"Oh yeah. One evening, Pa and I went fishing near Reid's Bait Shop. Hamilton Reid's store was located on a small, crooked hill that had a view of the surrounding waterways."

Franki motioned for the ceramic container. He didn't mind but his host was a talker. The redneck chugged more of the shine before he handed back to his guest for a long swig.

Jed said, "Now, my dad and I witnessed somebody fishing along the banks suddenly shape shift into a large wolf. This time we both had guns packed with silver bullets. Pa got off the first shot but only nicked its side." His finger shook as he pointed. "Mark my words, that darn thing was soaring in the air toward pa. Pops would have been a goner, but I shot that lycan center mass."

The Frankenstein Monster chuckled, "Ja!"

"No shit, that beast transformed back into the bait shop's owner." Jedidiah lazily laughed, "Pa always said Hamilton Reid was a sniveling wind-bag, besides being a dingy werewolf." He was about to take another sip but passed out. The giant gently grabbed his friend and snatched the moonshine before it spilled. *It turned out to be a nice night*, Franki thought.

43 - BAD TO THE BONE

November 1, 2005 - 5:30 p.m.

Daciana steered the yacht into the black-market dealer's pier. It had been a long boat ride. The constant pounding over the waves sapped much of her energy. Her knees and lower back ached. She wasn't looking forward to the voyage back but knew better than to make the master wait.

Two of her fellow gypsies quickly moored the lines. They appeared just as beat and tired.

The security guard reported to his boss on the radio, "Jefe. Daciana está aquí."

Grekio looked out his bullet proof window. "Frisk her but treat her with respect."

"Okay, boss."

The silhouette of a stunningly athletic female, clad in dark clothes approached the bottom of the stairs. The guard motioned for her to ascend the staircase.

She calmly made her way up the terra cotta tile steps. The assassin casually scanned the area for anything that could be a threat. Newly hidden surveillance cameras were all she noted but her game was slightly off today.

The stout guard did not try to block her. He simply stood to the side and let her gain access to the covered patio. Daciana looked up at the man in a detached cool manner and handed over her knife. He frisked her and found no other weapons than the one she'd relinquished. He spoke into his mouthpiece, "She's clear."

She thought, *Ah. They upgraded. No more walkie talkies.*

A buzzer sounded and the guard opened the heavy door.

Grekio said with a smile, "Buenas noches. Nice to see you, Daciana." She didn't reply but only yawned. He asked, "Would you like a cup of coffee?"

She saw a fancy coffee machine behind his large desk. "Can you make a cappuccino?"

"Of course."

"Uno por favor." Grekio was surprised to hear Daciana say please. She thought of her crew and inquired, "Could you make two more?"

"Definitely," he said smiling.

"All to go if you have cups."

"Claro!" He called his guard to make the coffees.

She handed him the keys to her master's older yacht. "Do you have all the proper paperwork," Daciana cocked her head back toward the dock and said, "for that forty-feet long cruiser?"

Grekio looked through his bay window and nodded. "It has been fully serviced. I even updated the yacht with a new GPS."

Daciana grinned. "This will please the master."

Every time he thought of that dark figure, his heart rate doubled. He never wanted to get on her master's bad side ever again.

The security guard brought her covered coffees. She said smiling, "Haven't had a cappuccino in a while. Ah. Nice flavor."

"Glad we could be of some service to you." *She must be tired*, he thought, *because she's normally a robotic bitch*. The dealer forced a business smile. "Just a few more documents."

She signed the papers before they walked down to the vessel. He then began to demonstrate the control functions of the new yacht to Daciana and her two crewmen. The caffeine must have taken affect. Grekio could see her changing back to her cold-blooded demeanor as he finished the hands-on training.

With a leering smile she said, "If there are no glitches, you will have gained favor with my employer." After she and her crew left, the normally ballsy racketeer let out a quivering sigh of relief.

Early morning, November 16, 2005

Nigel Rathbone was exhausted after working ten hours in the citrus groves and then walking over twenty miles.

He recollected his fellow fruit pickers this past season, many who recently came to the United States of America for a better life. Though many of them didn't speak the same language, some mild humor and chit chat made the grueling days pass by quickly.

What Rathbone truly liked about America was the opportunity one had to climb up and down the social ladder. Most US citizens weren't born into wealth as an aristocracy or stuck into one job for life, like in a socialist state. He had experienced that in many of his travels, which had already spanned three centuries.

One of the beauties of Americana depended on a person's work ethic and drive. Nigel knew many of his fellow workers were newly arrived immigrants who sacrificed on their part for their children to have a shot to become a skilled worker, medical professional, engineer, scientist or small business owner. Such liberty to improve one's position elsewhere in the world was rare.

Bones as his associates called him was grateful that his cantankerous boss, Joab Van Halen, gave him a ride several miles along I-10 before hiking the last leg on foot.

He took a long sip of water from his Camelbak and tucked his hand-held compass into his pocket. He then studied the topographical map, knowing he just reached the southeast section of the Pearl River Wildlife Management Area.

He got paid under the table for picking fruit in season in order to keep a low profile. Since there were no guaranteed days off, he worked overtime each day for the past week. The season was dwindling to a close as winter approached, so the orchard employer bid Rathbone farewell hours before. He was surprised when boss-man Joab thanked him for his hard work ethic and quiet demeanor. It was one nice thought before his mood began to grow dim.

The Scot sighed reaching into his left cargo pocket for the keys to unlock the handcuffs. He grimaced looking up at the sky. He could sense the moon about to rise and fidgeted with the keys. Finally, the cuffs sprang open. Beads of sweat poured down his forehead as he wrapped his front torso around a Cypress tree. He slid the steel one-click around both of his wrists just before the change.

0057 hours, an escaped convict, Bobby Malatosis, heard a terrible howl as he skirted through the southeastern portion of the Pearl River Wildlife Management Area. He thought nothing of the eerie sound.

Bobby was still giddy that he snagged a pair of civilian jeans and a long-sleeved t-shirt off a clothesline the day before as the sun was setting. He suddenly tripped on a root and his shin came down hard on a stone. He cursed before muttering, "Why do bad things always happen to me?"

"Argh, argh" echoed throughout the swamp.

The Jersey thug looked around in paranoia for a moment. He began to rub his aching shin. He then eyed the stone quizzically for a moment. He picked it off the ground and tied his prison clothes around it. He tossed the rock into the murky water and smiled knowing it would be harder for any canines to sniff him down.

Bobby Malatosis had always been crafty, deceiving many with fake smiles and temporary good manners. A New Orleans judge had ordered the wife beater to be moved from a high security prison to a half-way house after a pattern of good behavior. Bobby then waited to get the trust of the staff before making his escape.

A large snout sniffed the scent of its food quickly approaching. The beast instantly settled down as it heard twigs snap within its immediate proximity.

The criminal cut himself against a sharp branch. "Damn that that stings," he hissed before brushing up against what he thought was another tree until a very hairy face with canines snapped at him.

The human scent was too much. The wolfman tried to break the handcuffs, grunting madly.

Malatosis let out a high-pitched scream, "Someone, help me!" The escaped convict turned around and fled. Like a bad dream, he ran slowly and branches snagged around his body.

The lycanthrope began to gnaw frenziedly through parts of its hairy forearms. It wildly yanked multiple times at the loosening handcuffs. Finally, free, the wolfan smelled its immediate surroundings. Its body almost healed instantly from the self-inflicted wounds.

The inmate ran into a tree trunk. Disoriented, he rammed his head into it again before stumbling away.

The werewolf initially rushed its prey on all fours before leaping for the kill. Claws slightly extended and the beast's left arm swept up into the felon's lower spine. Bobby Malatosis, the misogamist was no more.

44 - PUBLIC MEETING

November 19, 2005

Several athletic looking men passed an autumn medley of Thanksgiving and leftover Halloween decor spread throughout the coffeehouse. A figure hissed, swiveling to one side. Some of the special operators held up their fists at the red-eyed dummy facing them. Its white long fangs seemed too real.

Kramer shook his head and unplugged the life-sized vampire prop from the wall.

A barista noticed and said, "What's ya doing mister?"

The Green Beret said as pleasantly as he could, "It ain't Halloween anymore, missy!" The pretty blonde was about to protest until the entire group stood, giving her mean Clint Eastwood stares. Her petite shoulders sank and she went back to her duties.

Ross nodded at Kram. "Thanks bra. I was about to punch that fanged bastard in the mouth." The ghostly decorations may have been a ritualistic comfort to them as kids but now only added to their dour mood. It was too unsettling, even for these tough guys.

Some of the special operators glared suspiciously at the people sipping java nearby their table. Most onlookers couldn't help but notice the men sporting barreled chests, large diver watches and sandals. The only time the fellows were able to officially gather together was at the base chapel during their comrades' funeral service in February. Any other meetings had been forbidden by JAG and NCIS. The boys stealthily had gotten together, despite the legalities.

The men's chats helped them all cope with loss and feelings of despair. Their perilous encounter also stimulated ongoing debates of natural science, philosophy, and theology. They always wondered if Barnum, Lawlur or Sullivan survived, since their bodies were never recovered from Gemela. They never stopped grumbling where the hell Staff Sergeant Hansen had been shipped.

Many times, the group had to individually kayak, swim or run through rough terrain to meet in remote locations. They departed from different directions to throw off anyone tailing them. It felt good that the men could finally be seen together in public. After everyone was present, Petty Officer Thor Rockford stood up and stated, "This is my dad's friend, Mr. Chuck Shotzski. He is a retired cop and now a reporter."

"How ya doing fellas," the newcomer said. The operators only responses were eyeing him suspiciously.

Rockford could tell his pals were leery of a stranger in their midst. He calmly said, "Chuck has run into some weird things like we all did this past Valentines." His comrades appeared stunned in the back corner of Le Grande's trendy Ma & Pa's Café.

"Please call me Chuck or Shotz." A few nodded but many stared at him. He whistled to get the attention of a pretty barista, "Miss, I'll treat these gents to their choice of caffeine."

The blonde barista scowled at Kram before taking the men's orders. The burly Green Beret winked at Ansley and she cracked a smile. The men all nodded in appreciation as their drinks were served. Shotzski's generosity had put them at ease.

CWO5 Michael Raven whistled, "Okay men, we've been under the eyes of NCIS for nine months. Thank you for not telling what really happened. We were in a no-win situation."

Azúcar appeared from the shadows and said, "The truth would have guaranteed you men a permanent stay in the cuckoo's nest." They chuckled at her words, but were amazed at her uncanny ability to appear or disappear. She was light on her feet and it shamed the special operators of their situation awareness, or lack thereof.

Hugs winked at her. Azúcar ignored him and announced, "We have a pleasant surprise for you." Jefe, codename *Nastea*, smiled escorting the five and a half-foot tall Commander Elsworth Lawlur toward the table.

The men smiled seeing the man they called Lawdog. His elfish appearance could be deceiving. Once, in 2003 a six and a half-foot tall green beret constantly harassed the SEAL commander by calling him *Frodo Baggins*. After a few weeks of putting up with this, he challenged the towering special forces commando to a "friendly" brawling match during Compound X's weekly hand-to-hand sessions. After delivering the strapping army officer to the medical office with a broken nose, bloody lip and a disjointed shoulder, Elsworth was rarely called *Frodo*.

Lawdog gave all his comrades firm handshakes. He looked into their eyes and said, "Barnum is in the hospital. He is recovering after doctors reset his broken bones." They sympathized knowing the pain their friend had to endure, even with medication.

The frogman recounted their escape, "I made a makeshift raft out of two logs and moved Barnum north through the bayou. We lived off the land by day and hid out at night until a Coast Guard boat saw my flashing mirror. Since we travelled several miles to the northeast, your recovery crew missed us. I wasn't going to have us settle near Gemela after what we encountered that dreadful night."

Ross choked up and muttered, "I had a feeling the two of you were still alive. The authorities recovered most of our guys. They concluded the only missing three: you, Barnum and Sullivan got swept out to sea."

"That's a shame about Sully. Hopefully, the government has him under lock and key like."

Nastea sadly said, "Unfortunately, Sullivan is MIA."

Lawdog shook his head before saying, "Some agents interdicted the Coast Guard cutter after arriving to their base. The Coasties were even read a memorandum by the G-men not to mention that they took us up to John Hopkins. The men in black even deleted their ship's log about us."

Senior Chief Samson shook his head. "Hell, Rav, Jaws and I circled that entire bayou around Gemela three times and searched the warehouse. We knew any survivors would be smart enough to stay clear of the hacienda."

The commander exclaimed, "Senior, like I said, we were so far away, we didn't hear a thing during the recovery effort. However, Chief Barnum and I did have ample time to discuss the importance of not telling the authorities what actually occurred. I am just glad we were able to flag them down with my portable mirror."

Petty Officer Ross eyed the commander. "How long have you and chief been back in the states?"

Commander Lawlur put his hand to his chin. "About six months but the investigators kept us on lock-down in DC."

Ross snickered, "Those spooks are as sneaky as we are. Did you ever run into Staff Sergeant Hansen?"

Lawlur's eyes grew wide. "No! What happened to Hans?"

Ross chuckled, "Weird as all get out, one night the staff sergeant is in the hospital, the next morning he is gone."

Nastea quickly changed subjects. He shook his head and admitted, "All your testimonies seem illogical but your unofficial version even is absurd. The autopsies never could make sense of the bite marks, large quantities of missing blood and broken spines."

The men were amazed that all their statements coincided over such a period of time, despite small discrepancies.

The commander shrugged. “We strongly advised the investigation team not to stay the night without giving specifics.”

Azúcar’s nostrils flared. “You Americans are quick to mock at what you cannot see.”

“You are right Azúcar," Elsworth continued. "The investigation team laughed at our warnings and one crew remained on Gemela. Their broken bodies were recovered floating along the bank, days after we warned them.” He shook his head. “Every corpse was missing approximately thirty percent of their blood supply and had two bite marks on the neck. NCIS is at a loss for an answer.”

Thor mouthed the word *vampires* at Jefe. The CIA operative ignored his prior teammate and continued, "If it makes any of you feel better, several men were discovered with broken necks and missing the same amount of blood near Gemela’s shore during our last reconnaissance. Experts believe they were all part of an al-Qaeda cell." He held up his index and middle finger. "Two of their DNA samples were perfect matches to freed Guantanamo detainees."

The SEAL commander growled, "So much for reform,”

Nastea appeared testy. He didn't like talking about such hot topics in an open environment. "Whatever the hell attacked your group, appears to have wiped out the terrorists as well."

CWO5 Raven sensed the CIA operative’s hesitation to speak openly and asked, "Any further details that you can provide us in a more suitable location?"

"No!" Jefe put his black coffee down on the table. “You men are fortunate we were speaking on your behalf. Some of the big honchos from NCIS and JAG wanted to burn your chaps and send you to Fort Leavenworth.”

Petty Officer Odin sneered hearing that, “That is all the thanks we get for serving our country.”

Nastea smiled at Odin’s spunk. “Now that NCIS and JAG are in the same boat as you guys, they are rambling around and do not know what to do.”

Azúcar folded her arms. “I advised the authorities to slide this under the carpet.”

Hugs smiled at her. “I think you meant slide it under the rug, there sweetie.”

Lawlur's body tensed up. "I am surprised whatever creeps by night never found Barnum and I, as we inched northward from Gemela?"

Ross patted him on the shoulder. "Perhaps it just wasn't your time Lawdog."

Nastea said, "Reliable sources indicate you will be authorized thirty-days leave."

CWO5 Raven interjected, "I want to crush this evil. I understand if anyone wants out of this one. Some of us may die. It will be under your own cognizance."

"Jefe and I did not hear of such plans," she said eyeing the men, "but we'd be planning something similar."

The retired chief stared each man down as he addressed the whole group, "Azúcar and I need to leave for headquarters up in the Beltway. We will keep in touch. You will have a pleasant surprise in a few days. We are not allowed to disclose that now."

The men knew better than to ask.

Petty Officer Hugsby gave Azúcar a hug. "I always enjoy your company."

"It was only business," she replied.

Hugs whispered into her ear, "Woman, you can be so cold." The SWCC operator didn't see it but Azúcar had one tear rolling down her scarred cheek as she left the café.

45 - RECKONING

As Azúcar and Jefe departed Ma & Pa's Café, many of the operators were opening their eyes that the monsters from Hollywood's golden-era cinema might exist.

Sergeant Kramer tightened up his fists. "Nobody wipes out our boys without payback!" Some women turned their heads at the burly man. He waved politely at them. "Sorry ladies."

Thor had told his buddies some facts about vampires. Though shocked, they knew this was not a terrible dream but very real. Their pledge was not to exact revenge but a reckoning.

Naval Investigators did their best to stop the men spin up any matching, doctored-up stories. They had been closely monitored at work. Many were separated and sent temporary duty to nearby bases. Even Azúcar and Nastea were only allowed to confer with the survivors during official interviews.

Chief Jaworsk slid his chair back. "Let's stomp those bastards back to hell."

Gunners Mate First Class Odin looked perplexed and inquired, "What works against these monsters?"

"I've had run-ins with vampires." That got their attention and Shotzski continued, "Two of the incidences occurred over a decade ago in Iowa. Believe me, you won't read any of it in any FBI or police files. Many of those spineless officials are dead or too afraid to even think about it." They eyed him wearily until they began having flashbacks of their own ghastly ordeal. "A hospital crew tagged me *Shotzski the Shadow Hunter*," he said shaking his head, "and that damn name spread like wildfire… my nom de guerre."

Rockford raised his right eyebrow. "Why?"

"It's a long story. My friend, Dr. Cory McMullen, got his revenge with my nickname. He didn't care for the title I gave him as *Kid Coroner*. So, he billed me the *Shadow Hunter* after destroying the undead, Baroness Angelique Hemos." Chuck gritted his teeth and stated, "The authorities even had the audacity to threaten me for murder or the asylum, even though, I saved their hind ends."

Thor gave him the turn down the volume motion with his fingers. Shotz grumbled a few unintelligible words before calmly saying to his dad's best friend, "It's all good."

The reporter frustratingly put his hands in the air. "I know but I just get so angry thinking about it. Damn politicians and the Law just wanted to save their careers."

"Shotz, do you think people would have believed you?" He asked him with a wake-up expression on his face.

He almost yelled, "No, but it was the truth!"

Thor's mouth dropped open and said in a low voice, "Come on Chuck. All of us here dealt with vampires and still we do not want to believe."

He took in a deep breath and exhaled to settle down, "What I know is that vampires are hard to destroy but it can be done. Silver or a real piece of wood jammed into their hearts will finish them off. Never remove them without burning their corpses or cutting off their heads. They do not cast reflections in mirrors. Crosses and garlic repel them."

Hugs said, "The vamps we encountered could glide in the air and manipulate their shadows."

Chuck scratched his head. "That is news to me."

Grif said testily, "Or they have no shadows at all."

An elderly blonde lady had her left hand cupped to her ear. She overheard parts of their conversation and exclaimed, "Oh, my." Another woman whispered something to her friends. The ladies raised their eyebrows as they glanced at the boys.

Griffin smiled at the nicely dressed women and nodded out of respect. "Hey guys, let's go somewhere a bit more secure."

The Special Operators met at Shotzski's three-season porch with a panoramic of Leprechaun's Links. The view was etched with a mixture of the course's palm, magnolia and pines trees.

Chuck pulled out a hardbound text with an engraved image of Professor Van Helsing entitled *Nosferatu and the Supernatural.* "I discovered this reference after destroying two blood suckers. Van Helsing talks about his dealings with Dracula. I had always joked the Count was just a made-up character until reading this."

Fitz perused the book, saying, "Vampires need their native soil to rest in during the day."

Chief Jaworsk read over his buddy's shoulder, "They have been known to survive without their native soil but become weaker and lose some of their powers."

Petty Officer Fitz grumbled, "This professor writes that Holy Water burns through them like acid."

Gunner Odin exclaimed, "We could use super soakers."

Fitz read the next paragraph, "Once they are invited into a person's private dwelling they can come in unimpeded."

Sergeant Kramer cocked his head and asked, "Unim what?"

Fitz replied shaking his head, "Unimpeded means once invited a vampire can come in anytime it pleases."

Kramer grabbed the book to ensure Fitz wasn't making it all up. He squinted pulling the pages closer to him. "Very few discover their power to change into a bat, mist, rats, and wolf. Actually, Van Helsing's research says vampires have been around for ages." He read a cited Biblical verse regarding the redeemed, "*The body is sown in corruption, it is raised in incorruption.* The professor goes on to surmise vampires' unholy bodies may be the opposite of resurrected Heavenly bodies. He believes the undead are a representation of the damned that will endure torment in Hell for eternity."

Petty Officer Odin gulped, "That is some heavy stuff."

Fitz gave Kramer a knuckle swipe to the head and ordered, "Give it back Bubba-Kram."

"Don't call me Bubba!"

Odin chanted, "Bubba, Bubba, Bubba – yowza, yowza."

Kramer sneered, "Enough with your satire, ya Nipsey Russell wanna be." Both Odin and Kram puffed out their chests and locked arms. Shotzski's treasured text went flying in the air. Jaws caught the book with his hands as if it were fresh eggs.

Odin tripped his buddy to the ground and moved his head from side to side, bragging, "Bubba Kram - you're not the bomb."

Kramer twisted Odin's left torso and rolled on top of him, responding, "Russell should wear a bustle."

Petty Officer Griffin put up his hands between the two and firmly said, "Guys, no wrestling in Mr. Shotzski's house. Kram, you do look like a Bubba. And, Odin, you are the spitting image of the great Nipsey Russell but you're no comedian."

Gunners Mate Odin stared down his two chums. "Uh huh, these fists will snap both your wrists."

Chief Jaworsk growled, "Chill!

They punched each other's shoulders and then laughed. They were quick to rumble but the first to defend one another among strangers. The pair's taste for music puzzled their fellow operators. Odin was black but jammed to hard rock and despised rap. Kram looked like the model redneck but loved his Motown. One thing both men enjoyed was listening to country western.

Jaws handed the book back to Fitz who read, "The most adept learn to transform into a bat which enables them to travel much faster. The professor also notes many vamps never realize their true power except for jumping higher and having immense strength. A new wampyre is three-quarters stronger than their mortal state. Mature ones, about one and a half times more powerful. Master vampires are said to be three times stronger."

Sergeant Kramer appeared agitated and graveled, "Damn dude… This does not factor in their bite, speed or nails."

Fitz continued, "Experienced non-master vampires can grow at least twice as strong as their human condition."

Odin pondered, "So, a fit little lady vamp that has feasted on lots of victims could rival a three-hundred-pound athlete?"

Hugsby's eyes widened. "Likely so."

The gunners mate shook his head. "Just imagine that mixed with any known fighting skills like Drac."

Fitz skimmed over another paragraph and said, "You are exactly right. Van Helsing identified Count Dracula as the most lethal, largely due to the fact he was a very cunning, skilled and strong warrior before he became a master vampire."

Kram thought out loud, "So this Dracula was probably twice as strong as a normal dude, and if he was a master vampire, then he would have the strength of six men."

Ross' forehead furrowed. "That sounds about right."

Odin leaned back into his chair and sighed in relief, "Thank goodness we ain't fighting *The* Count."

Hugs said, "No kidding."

Fitz read, "Interestingly, the Dutch Professor later reassessed his findings that Dracula's might of twenty men was an estimation of his superhuman strength combined with his speed, fangs, claws, vast fighting skills, and transformative abilities. He can grow larger, or tiny enough to fit through small cracks, such as a closed coffin."

Raven' eyes narrowed and stated, "This is good to know. We never know who or what we are up against."

Ross nodded. "Those vampires whooped us perty good."

Jaws grinned. "Yeah but now we know how to battle those bastards." The group of men cheered.

Shotzski raised his arms to get their attention. "Hold on fellas. I got more to add. Take heed because these are the craftiest of all the undead. Three single bites within a week normally turns a person into a vampire. However, if the victim's blood is mostly or completely drained, they may transform into the undead within minutes to hours." He placed his hand to his chin. "I almost forgot, vampires will drown if they fall into streams or rivers."

Odin said, "What about the ocean?"

"Nope. It's got to be fresh running water." Chuck sighed. "That's what saved my hide in Dubuque!"

Fitz flipped the page. "If a vampire does fall into salt water, they cannot fly or glide away until they get to a dry place."

Hugsby speculated, "I suppose they would drown if they didn't know how to swim."

Chief Warrant Officer Raven raised his right eyebrow. "That is another critical vulnerability, if the undead cannot swim fast enough and reach a resting place before sunrise."

The reporter looked at Rav and scratched his head. "I can't believe I missed that in Van Helsing's book."

Odin said, "You're getting sloppy, ole man." Chuck shot the gunners mate a playful sneer.

Fitz closed the book as if it were sacred as Samson said to their host, "Mind if we prep here, Mr. Shotzski?"

He chuckled thinking of his ornery boss, "Git 'er done!"

46 - RETURN TO CHÂTEAU WILDER

November 20, 2005

Ernie Semper's construction crew cleaned up their material from Château Wilder. It took two months for his carpenters to replace several granite blocks and overhaul the entire garage since many other homes and businesses were also in need of repair after the devastating hurricane.

Living close to the Gulf of Mexico's and southeastern Atlantic's shores had its advantages, the downside being the warm weather and tropical currents bred hurricanes. Another problem was finding a trustworthy contractor to fix the damages caused by severe flooding and wind. A complete restoration in less than three months was considered fast. There were only so many carpenters handy in a given region. The Law wasted no time coming down hard on hucksters and thieves after a natural disaster. It was bad enough when families were strapped for cash and homeless. Fortunately, most neighbors put their differences aside and came together.

For years, the best of American generosity was evident during fires in the West Coast, floods and tornadoes in the Midwest, and hurricanes in the East Coast. Several organizations such as Habitat for Humanity, the Red Cross and Salvation Army traveled to ravaged areas to help people get back on their feet.

It was later in the morning when the foreman installed a securable door to the western cliff's passage. It was virtually undetectable to the naked eye. He was happy with his work and collected his gear, making the trek around the grounds to the front. He could have walked a shorter route through the hidden labyrinth and up into the château's main floor. But the retired Marine saw *something* months earlier. He only went inside those dark chambers with Maria. *Call me crazy, I don't give a shit,* he thought.

The rest of Semper Construction had departed earlier. His team was on their way to help struggling families patch up some roofs and install windows. He dialed Maria's number. He left her a message when she didn't answer, "Hey Doc, this is Ernie Semper. We got your bird house installed on the west side." He proudly smiled. "I must say, this is one of our best jobs. Left you an invoice under your front mat. Call me if you have any concerns."

Dr. Wilder also had Semper's crew replace the ravaged magnolia tree with a new eight-footer. She wanted extra camouflage to cover the cliff's secret west entrance.

The master craftsman loaded his supplies into his pickup. He glanced back as he sat down in the driver's seat and suddenly got the chills. He tried to ignore the feeling of paralysis, fumbling to stash the paperwork into his metallic case. The towering Château seemed to stare down at him, whispering, *Ernie, look up, Ernie.* His eyes slowly rose and the aging Marine froze in terror. The structure's windows and doors looked like a wicked grin. Château Wilder gave him the heebie-jeebies with all those hidden passageways and subterranean vaults. He shuddered trying to avoid the structure's shadow. He sighed relief as his truck crossed the bridge.

Nigel Rathbone felt several cold stares in the back of his neck as he made his way to the château along Wilder's Ridge. He thought to himself, *new faces always stand out.* Fortunately, the Le Grande was filled with tourists year-round, so faces constantly changed, *but keeping a low profile in this tight-knit neighborhood was bloody hard.*

The melodies of several birds filled the peaceful street as a handful of young girls played hopscotch under a tree. Screams came in intermittent bursts as boys skinned their knees and elbows during a rowdy game of football, as mothers nervously watched from their porches, sipping their sweet teas.

He finally arrived at the bridge's tall, metal gates that marked the estate's entrance. On each side, lavender bougainvilleas with prickly thorns threaded their way along the metal fence.

A stocky fellow finished trimming the grass along the inner edges to the upper circular driveway with a self-propelled Lawn-Boy mower. He noticed a tall man approaching down at the gate.

Nigel smiled at the rosy colored camellias and neatly trimmed oleanders as he hiked up toward the château.

He pushed the rugged mower down the ramp. He met the stranger near the garage, greeting him with a firm handshake, "Good morning, I'm Jackie Alegría."

"The grounds look meticulous."

"Thanks. I like to work and help things grow when I'm not studying. It pays for my doctorate fees at the university, plus free room and board. Doc's a generous woman." Jackie noticed he was rambling and abruptly asked, "What may I help you with, sir?"

"Oh, pardon me. My name is Nigel Rathbone. I met Dr. Wilder recently. Is she available?"

"Yes, Maria said you may stop by. She took the day off for a long run and some rest." The landscaper bowed in respect and then straddled a riding mower to trim the estate's lower, grounds.

Rathbone ascended the steep and winding driveway. He clamped a huge ring from one of the thick main entrance doors. Wondering aloud, he said, "What fine knockers."

"Thanks, and they're real," Maria added as she snuck up behind him, returning from a run.

He turned around embarrassed. "I meant those brass knockers. They remind me of my family estate in Scotland."

"Gotcha," she said, pointing at him in a playful manner.

"Wasn't this a larger wooden door?"

"Yes, but the door was old and it didn't help that I ran into the entrance when my mother was teaching me how to drive," she admitted. "At least, the double-insulated metal doors save energy."

He looked and said, "The château was all by itself. When was the neighborhood along the lower ridge built?"

She pointed toward the estate's private gate that intersected with the public cul-de-sac. "Developers connected the thin strip to our estate over thirty years ago. They then lined it with mini-mansions on each side of the ridgeline for over three-quarters of a mile."

"What happened to the sturdy wooden bridge connecting the ridge to your estate?" Bones protested, "I worked many hours constructing the oaken bridge."

Dr. Wilder flashed a grin, "Nothing was wrong with it. Ma didn't mind her new neighbors footing the bill with a new granite bridge, driveway and garage, plus extra cash."

A smile slowly emerged. "Rosa was always a clever lady."

"Businessmen often cursed that she was one sly negotiator."

He was amazed at the changes. "Except for the towering main structure, I hardly recognize this place, especially, with those fancy large homes dotting along the eastern road."

"It is still our private cliff because of the bridge." She took in a deep breath and opened up her palms, "There's something about you Nige that makes me feel comfortable."

"Did Rosa tell you I prefer to be called Nigel?"

Maria put her hands on her hips and said, "But of course!"
He let his guard down at this enticing woman. "Well, I just need to

get this off my chest, only Gwen Adams knows. Rosa was technically my aunt and she gave birth to me in her early forties."

Bones grimaced. "What?"

"My biological mother, Elsa Wilder, and her sister, Rosa, developed the first frozen embryo, me," Doc said matter of fact.

He remembered Rosa's sister, Elsa, who had been hypnotized under Dracula's spell. Nigel said, "Speak to me plainly. I'm not quite understanding what you're saying!

"Rosa carried me in her womb by being artificially inseminated years later." He raised an eyebrow, not knowing what to think. "Science has improved but we can discuss that later."
Maria shrugged. "I feel better now. Mom was right, you listen."

"Most of the time."

"Women appreciate that." She laced elbows with Nige and escorted him into the antechamber, near the baroque staircase.

Rathbone recognized the library's antique furniture except for one item. "What do you call that square black mirror? It barely casts a reflection."

Doc laughed, "Oh, I forgot that you've been literally out of it for a while. This is actually a computer. One can search information on it via the internet, type up reports, save data, listen to music or watch movies."

"Films in that?" She nodded. "What's an internet?"

"Just think of it as an obscure place connected to that plastic computer where you can look up all sorts of information, store photos and e-mail friends from all over the world."

He asked testily, "What the hell is an e-mail?"

Maria chuckled, "Think of it as a phone-typewriter."

"I don't know?" Bones nervously grinned. "Technology may have advanced, but what I've seen, society seems to have taken a step back with too much access and less common sense."

"You must be a pessimist?"

"No, a realist. People can be very kind and noble. At the same time, if we're given things too easily, it's just human nature not to be satisfied with what we have."

"Hmm… Never thought of it that way."

47 - SILLY IDOL

"You've done well with the château." Nigel Rathbone briskly walked to the rear of the library and noted, "Hey, this glass door leading down to the cave wasn't here before." Dr. Wilder giggled at his detailed curiosity. He looked quizzically to the right and asked, "What happened to the private study?"

"Ma needed better access to the kitchen and space to install our elevator. Like I said, we drastically remodeled much of the château, especially, after my car accident."

Bones bowed to one knee and kindly said, "I'm glad the car crash didn't scar your pretty face, your royal highness."

Maria gently tapped his shoulders like she was knighting him with her water bottle. "You may now arise, Sir Rathbone."

He blushed. She unscrewed the pommel of her sword and took a sip of water. Doc then said, "Mom warned me about you. I won't bite and neither will you, for now." He looked down at the floor uncomfortably.

"I am usually a shy one with men I admire but ma gave you such a good report." A rare smile began to emerge from Nigel's lips. She grabbed his hand and admitted, "I didn't learn about your affliction until she died in my arms."

"Rosa gave me some peace for forty years. What a dame!"

"Please excuse my sullen mood, I really haven't mourned yet. I guess I've been so wound up." She hugged him fiercely. "Thanks. I needed that."

Bones suddenly made a beeline for the curie and pulled out a medallion. He flinched, sensing its purities. It was the one and the same. Even in human form, the touch of silver felt like a mild irritant. He spotted a tissue and used it to pick up the necklace. He insisted, "Wear this!

She put her hands to her hips. "Why?"

"It will protect you from me."

Doc demanded, "How did you know it would be there?"

He answered, "Not to include money, Rosa normally locked anything she treasured inside of it, especially, iconic things."

She sneered, "You mean her collection of crosses."

He replied in a patient tone, "Rosa had rituals like inspecting the grounds, growing garlic around the château's openings and sipping her morning black-pekoe tea."

Maria smiled. She felt a special bond between Nige. Not many people had gotten to know her mother who was a pleasant lady, but viciously private.

“I remember Rosa telling me she wasn’t always a woman of faith. She was raised in a liberal Jewish family. Dracula, my curse, and her dealings with the damn Nazis made her realize evil existed.”

“That’s pretty much Aunt Gwenn recently told me.” It also reconfirmed to Maria that her mother was telling her the truth.

“Rosa did her best to protect this place and, obviously, you from both the supernatural and twisted people.”

“Mom always shot her pistol and bow every week.”

“Silver bullets and wooden arrows?”

“No, but she had them at the ready.” Maria added, “Mother only used normal ammunition on the targets.”

“I can’t blame her… silver isn’t cheap.”

"Mom also hosted several pastors, priests and nuns over here for tea and prayer on Thursday evenings." The physician paused before saying, “Some of them even exorcised our home.”

“Smart lady.”

“Yeah, but the woman even made me go to Sunday school."

Nige shrugged. "Was that so bad?"

"No," Maria giggled, "just wished I could have slept in."

"Most kids are that way," Rathbone said with a smile. “I think we all could use some more faith and values."

"Your no-nonsense approach reminds me of my mom."

“Rosa and I are old school.”

Maria appreciated her mother as a strong disciplinarian and consistent parent. They later became good friends as she grew into a mature young lady. She never resented her mom, even when she was a moody teenager with raging hormones. She wished her sweet mama was here right now, so she could hug and speak with her.

He handed her the amulet saying, “This can save your life.”

“This stilly idol will save my life?” Maria asked shaking her head. “I’m a physician not a witch doctor.”

He said matter of fact, “It’s mostly made of silver mixed with traces of wolfsbane and other plants.”

“You’re kidding.”

“Believe me, that thing makes me cringe. I trust my Aunt Francesca, who used to be a missionary in Africa and Europe. She was one of my mom’s few relatives that were kind to me. The mild scents, prayers and metal is what truly wards off lycanthropes.”

Dr. Wilder frowned. "Lycan what?"

Bones shook his head. "Don't medical doctors, study ancient Latin or Greek these days? Lycanthrope comes from the Greek word, *Lukanthrōpos*. Combine the Greek words, *Lukos* for wolf with *Anthrōpos* for man and it means wolf-man or werewolf, a person afflicted with lycanthropy."

"Come on Nige," she said with a *get real* look in her eyes.

He pointed at Maria and stated, "You saw me become one!"

She hesitated before saying, "I guess… I did." She then grasped the medallion from his hand, mostly to comfort him.

Nigel recollected, "My sweetheart, Shelly, had it returned to my Aunt Francesca after they buried me in our family's crypt."

"So, how did you become a lycan?"

He sighed. "A werewolf killed my cousin, Holly, while we were walking west of Slains Castle. I slashed the beast in the throat with my silver-lined knife and it changed back to one of the Earl's family members."

"And it bit you?"

He pulled down his collared-shirt to reveal the scar, "That bloody werewolf got me here, millimeters from my jugular vein."

"You're lucky to live."

"Unlucky!" Bones growled, "It happened before I had a chance to save my cousin."

"Sorry to hear about that."

He clenched his fists. "That poor girl was right as rain. Holly didn't deserve to die that way."

She tenderly said, "You were just trying to defend her."

He scowled, "It should have been me, not sweet Holly."

"Oh, poor Nige… you can't go back."

"I wasn't innocent like her. I struggled with anger and disrespected too many elders."

"You were young."

"We reap what we sow, "he said sullenly. "My poor mom stabbed me with the same knife when I was lurking near our home one full moon." Doc shuddered at the thought. "My Aunt Francesca warned her of the werewolf's curse and the mark I freshly bore upon my neck." Nigel bitterly smiled. "My sweet mum's last words to me were: *It is all well my son – you will rest in peace.*"

"So sad."

He nodded. "Years later, I was informed my mom and dad hunted down two more werewolves with silver-tipped arrows. I also discovered I slew Sir Flynn who had served as a distinguished ambassador in Her Majesty's Diplomatic Corps for twenty years. The poor soul brought back lycanthropy when he retired."

"You mentioned silver twice. What is so special about it?"

"There is an old Gypsy proverb: *Always carry a silver-edged blade in case you run into a werewolf or vampire.* It is considered a pure metal to combat the undead, especially, werewolves."

"How?"

"Stab, shoot or beat down a werewolf with silver to destroy one. Just like a human, sometimes it takes one or more fatal blows."

"And vampires?"

"Silver must remain lodged in their hearts just like a piece of wood," he said matter of fact, "or maybe used to cut their throat."

"Then, why are you here now?" demanded the physician.

"I rested in peace for many years until grave robbers broke into our family crypt."

"Ghastly!"

"They opened my grave," he graveled, "during a full moon."

"And you slaughtered them?"

"Yes. Killing hard-core criminals, rapists and child molesters never bothered me," he said, "but the innocent haunts me."

Doc looked down at the metallic object. "Absurd."

"This amulet will protect you." He demanded, "You must wear it!" She enjoyed feeling him clasp the medallion around her neck. "Reluctant werewolves usually attack those they are closest."

"What do you mean reluctant werewolves?"

"They are the rarest type that take on more of a human form. Such two-legged wolfans are the hardest to destroy and will arise the night before or after a full moon if they don't feed. Most lycanthropes resemble a larger, four or two-legged wolf."

Her heart yearned for him. "Nige, please stay here with me," Maria sweetly said, "I enjoy your company." He was bothered she wasn't taking him serious enough, but her almond-shaped, bluesy looking brown eyes melted his ability to resist her.

48 - MURPHY'S LAW

November 20, 2005

It was just past noon on at a private airfield outside of town. Petty Officer Ross yelled, "Chief Jaworsk, the helo is loaded up with wooden arrows and garlic powder. We're just waiting on that Nun friend of yours so we can fill up the super soakers."

The Navy Chief corrected Petty Officer Ross by saying, "Her name is Sister Tréson!" Jaws looked at his watch and bit his lip. "Crap, another minute and you boys would have owed me a nice bottle of some of my favorite liquid."

Ross's eyes lit up. "Chief, I reckon ya owe us some brewskis!"

Jaws smiled as he saw his favorite Nun, affectionately known as Sister T-Tee, walk into the smaller hangar bay. "Sorry about my cussing. Could you please give a benison over the water and our mission?"

Sister Tréson nodded with a smile. "Heads bowed! Father God, may these men do your work and kick those vermin back to Hell in the name of your only and Holy Son, Jesus Christ."

Everyone exclaimed, "Amen," even Odin.

Chief Jaworsk nodded in respect to his beloved Nun. "Thanks Sister T-Tee."

Sister Tré gently touched Jaws's right shoulder. "Chief Jaworsk, don't you hesitate to call me if you need prayers or more Holy Water." She shook her head and muttered, "What you men are up against is a large reason I retired from the Coast Guard and became a Sister of the Cloth."

Jaws looked at her surprised, not knowing what to say.

The Nun bit her bottom lip before stating, "You're lucky. Not many in my line of work are privy to such information." Sister Teresa Tréson grinned mischievously as she departed. "And in spite of your terrible potty-mouth, Chief Jaworsk, you are still one of the most honest men I know."

The special operators were surprised to see Chuck Shotzski walk up wearing a dark brown hunting vest, an olive-green shirt and pants, and brown hiking boots. They were accustomed to him sporting a stylish old-fashioned suit and straw golf hat that didn't flow with a loose tie and dark sneakers.

Ross chuckled, "Shotz, your duds finally match."

Chuck Shotzski graveled, "Don't lecture me on style. Most of you fellows only wear short sleeve shirts, shorts and sandals."

They all laughed together for a moment before heading to Rav's private helicopter to stow their field packs inside.

Michael Raven stroked his helo. "My baby is fast, holds close to a dozen men and maneuvers great. I even welded in a body mount on each side, so a gunner can safely lean outside and pop off some accurate shots."

Fin inquired, "How could you afford this?"

Rav bore a wide grin on his face. "Lucky in the stock market before *Sam's Club* and computers really caught on. I probably could earn a lot of money with my Doctorate's in Economics." The warrant then crossed his slim arms over his sinewy chest and frowned. "But who in their right mind wants to read twenty newspapers a day?"

Senior Chief Samson shook his head. "Not me!"

Chief Warrant Officer Raven's eyelids slightly narrowed. "Most of the investors I know have their asses glued to a chair and eyes tattooed to a computer screen every day. That is definitely not my cup of tea. Nah, that would be boring. I love the military life."

Senior nodded. "Amen to that brother!"

The men rehashed their attack plans several times. They then rechecked their weapons, synchronized their watches and departed at 1330 hours sharp.

CWO5 Raven touched his helicopter down on the eastern dock of Gemela at 1430 hours. He instantly noticed many of Gemela's trees were ravaged by Hurricane Katrina.

Commander Lawlur pointed out, "We should search the resort area first. Barnum and I never encountered any vampires resting inside the water plane's warehouse."

Raven signaled with his hands to head out on a foot patrol in a wedged formation toward the resort.

Four figures approached the special operators within three-hundred meters of the hacienda.

Sergeant Kramer yelled when they got twenty-five meters away, "Ya fellas better stop or I'll plug ya."

The four appeared to be in a slight daze and each one bore a queer smile. One uttered, "We mean you no harm."

Kram didn't buy it. He tapped a double-count to the speakers' shoulders. Its body barely jerked back from the bullets impact but the thing kept charging.

Chuck Shotzski shakily instructed the group, "Damn, I knew it. These creeps are known as vombies. Either severe their spinal columns, stake their hearts with a piece of wood, or destroy their brains."

Ross and Jaworsk cut down two heads with their machetes.

Odin easily tapped another two between the eyes and smiled. "I bought me the regular lead just in case." He frowned, murmuring, "Hope we didn't wake the dead."

Shotzski continued, "Dr. Van Helsing revealed some crafty vampires have been known to bite their victims once and use some kind of a voodoo-zombie ritual to make them into a vombie. They are vampire-zombie hybrids that are hard to kill, very obedient to their masters, appear normal to most humans, and can venture in sunlight."

The gunner sighed. "At least, they're easier to destroy."

Chuck nodded. "The wise professor noted vombies almost make the perfect vampire guardian. However, they have a nasty habit of feasting on the blood of insects and rodents, are ashen in complexion and demonstrate an uncanny grin on their faces when on the attack."

Jaws shook his head. "That's weird."

Fitz nodded and continued, "That Van Helsing book pointed out vampires are normally in a comatose state until several minutes before dusk."

Odin swung his index finger sideways and said, "Normally? Hey bro, that is too much of Murphy's law!"

The team had swept most of the rooms inside the main structure, club house, and pump room. So far, nothing had been encountered except cob webs.

Rav spoke into his encrypted headset, "Teams. Status!"

Petty Officers Odin and Griffin cleared their last room on the west wing. Odin replied, "Coming down now. Only had to pick two doors on the second floor. Each one was updated with queen beds and bathrooms."

Grif added, "Both rooms had reinforced doors and windows."

Odin stated, "Rest of the place looks like Bubba's room."

Kram bellowed, "You never complained before."

Petty Officer Hugsby quipped, "You walked into that one Nipsey."

CWO5 Raven interjected, "Stop the BS!"

Petty Officers Fitz and Ross finished their rounds in the east wing. Fitz spoke into his mouthpiece, "We also discovered two rooms in decent shape, also on the second floor. Otherwise, the place seems unoccupied."

Rav said flatly, "Looks like a pattern."

Ross stated, "The doors I picked were sealed and fortified."

Odin replied, "Same here. More like to protect someone from the inside."

Petty Officer Rockford interjected, "Nothing found in the servants' quarters. A pair of new washers and dryers were in the laundry room. We're heading to the barn."

The officer clicked his toggle twice in acknowledgment.

Chief Jaworsk said, "The kitchen and family room are in decent shape. Spotted food in the refrigerator. Not just vamps live here."

"Probably human guards that also can take care of official business during the day." Shotzski muttered, "This is a very clever game plan."

Petty Officer Griffin leaned against a wooden panel between the kitchen and grand foyer. It swung open to the inside. "Crap," he hissed almost falling, "Got stairs to a basement."

A handful of the operators quickly followed Grif down the wide steps.

Senior Chief Samson added, "Just walked by the pool. Looks like it was maintained until recently. Also, spotted a satellite dish and generator."

Hugs lost his patience and grumbled, "I haven't seen crap, besides a worn-down resort." The cellar appeared empty except for wine vats and shelves. He noticed the time. "Only forty minutes til dusk and no vamps."

Odin kicked at the basement's floor. "We've searched all the structures around this resort and found next to nothing."

Staff Sergeant Kramer rinsed his mouth with water after spitting out his dip on the wine cellar floor. Kram noticed something peculiar. The water and saliva disappeared under the wall.

Odin's eyes opened wide. "Look at that Bubba."

Kram bent down with his hands to the floor and said, "Check this out, I feel a draft." The sergeant pushed and then pulled open a wine shelf. "Hot damn... it's a secret door."

Ross and Rav were the first of the group to turn on the lamps affixed to the top of their mini-Kevlar helmets. The rest followed suit as they made their way through the opening. The illumination provided enough light for the operators to realize they were in a very long and open space.

Kram whispered, "This place is huge."

Rav added in a low tone, "Probably the foundation to one of the wings."

After several paces, Petty Officer Hugsby tripped.

A hand grabbed Hugs by the collar that kept him from falling. "Watch it!" Grif warned the others, "A pile of dirt to the left."

"Thanks, Grif," Hugsby whispered into his mouthpiece, "Moving on." The men then followed their point man down the corridor in a staggered formation.

Shotzski and Rockford descended the hacienda's back steps. They walked across two fairways and a grove of citrus trees.

Chuck looked up at a large wooden structure nestled near the ridge. "The barn looks to be in decent shape." He sniffed the air, "Kind of musty."

"Hey Shotz, what's that huge hole over there?"

"Ah yes," he chuckled, "That's the smell. It appears to be a humus pit that farmers would use as natural fertilizers on crops."

"My Grandpa Rockford always said animal dung is healthier than chemicals and just as effective as pesticides."

"You're correct, sir, but many people can't handle the smell of manure," Chuck said with a smile, "no matter how green they claim to be."

49 - DESPAIR

Gemela, November 20, 2005

Boatswain Mate Hugsby moved down the dark corridor feeling spooked. He joked to take off the edge, "Why don't we head back. We're just chasing ghosts."

Sergeant Kramer said, "Hugs. You were just bitching it was too slow and now you're acting chicken shit."

Chief Jaworsk whispered, "Focus guys!"

The special operators probed their mini-head lamps through the darkness. "Looks like rectangular-shaped boxes on the far end," said Odin.

"Those aren't boxes dipshit," Kram graveled shaking his head, "They're caskets."

The operators gazed upon three scantily dressed beauties in coffins resting peacefully. Fitz drooled. "Aye, caramba!"

Rav blurted, "Cut the crap and finish the deed."

Fitz pleaded, "Come on. They're so voluptuous, innocent looking and skin a shade lighter than pale."

"So, you clowns are into necrophilia," sneered CWO5 Raven. "That's morbid." He made a gesture with his head. "Your six o'clock." They wheeled around and stared in awe.

Three females floated inches above the cellars floor. They caressed their faces and swayed their hips seductively.

Brides from the Crypt

The men saw dessert but it reminded Raven of how a cobra entranced its prey before attacking. The vampire brides kissed Kram, Fitz and Hugs. The guys dropped their weaponry.

Gunners Mate Odin protested, "Training time out, not fair." Yellow eyes and red pupils appeared with sharp fangs. The three vampires clamped down on their victims' jugulars. Odin backed up and screeched, "Yikes."

Rav pulled up his bow. "Get down!" The men struggled to break free as their bodies convulsed wildly. The undead we're too strong and kept feeding past the norm of a single bite.

Grif, Odin, Ross and Jaworsk tackled their bitten comrades to the ground. Rav and Lawlur shot wooden arrows into two of the vampires' bosoms. Jaws flung around, plunging a stake into the third vamp's heart.

Shotz and Thor heard the commotion on their headsets. They bolted toward the main structure to help their teammates. Chuck growled, "I don't see a way leading downstairs."

Rockford spoke into his mouthpiece, "ALCON. Where's the way to the cellar?"

Rav replied, "You should see a wooden panel opened between the kitchen and foyer."

"No joy," graveled Thor.

"Look behind the grand staircase."

"Got it!"

Ross stuffed garlic in the vamps' mouths. He whacked off their heads with a small silver-edged machete. In fact, the entire crew had recently acquired some sort of silver-edged blades.

Fitz bellowed, "I don't feel so good."

Hugs moaned, "I think I just pooped my pants."

Bubba-Kram put in a dip of Copenhagen and said, "I feel fine you ball-bagging wimps." He then fainted and crashed to the cellar's floor.

CWO5 Raven's beeper chimed. "Drop dead time, fifteen mikes til dusk." He barked, "Grab the fallen!" Grif, Jaws, Odin, Ross, Shotz and Thor took turns carrying the wounded and guarding their perimeter. The pilot high-tailed it to his helo. The guys made their way up the hidden staircase and into the open foyer.

Samson discovered his men carrying downed teammates and exclaimed, "Good God, no!" Dracula's bloodshot eyes snapped open. He bore his fangs and noticed the solar rays from his open coffin still barely seeping into the small slit in his hidden chamber.

Rav landed his helicopter near the front of the hacienda's lawn. The shadow of Gemela's western mound had not overtaken the setting sun deep in the northern valley. The men jumped inside the helo and it lifted off seconds after dusk. A pair of vixens darted inside as Grif and Jaws pumped Holy Water into snarling faces. Their skin melted away and they dropped hundreds of feet into the water. Chief Jaworsk yelled over the sound of the helicopter's rotors, "So far, Professor Van Helsing's instructions are spot-on."

1900 hours: A shapely gypsy woman outfitted in tight leather neared Gemela's northern jetty. She maneuvered the smaller vessel along the dock before the men jumped out and secured the lines. Hours earlier, Daciana had been on business with her fellow gypsies when the master summoned them. The vampire lord met his servants inside the foyer. They approached him with caution. Dracula's eyes burned with a vengeful rage they did not wish to engage. Swallowing her fear, Daciana reminded her master of their fealty by saying, "We refueled the boats and the smaller one got a tune-up."

His countenance remained fierce but his malice was not for them. Dracula hissed, "Gemela has been hit for a second time and several of my brides were destroyed." He knew it was time to fade for a while but was bent on revenge. The three servants rose from their knees after he waved them away. Their master suddenly uttered, "Prepare to leave!" He then informed Daciana where he wanted to go before, she returned to plug in the boat's waypoints.

Two burly men struggled to carry a pair of crates as a team. The nosferatu carried off two medium-sized crates and two coffins in a couple of trips like they were suit cases full of clothes. Both gypsies feared the undead prince and were especially amazed at his strength. They immediately departed. The craft zigzagged through the bayou before the compass pointed north by northeast.

2200 hours: Gunners Mate Odin shook his head in despair sitting at the hospital's waiting room. "Communist vampires!" He sneered. "If those evil suckers exist, then there has to be good too."

Petty Officer Ross patted Odin on the back. "Most people I know, associate goodness with God."

"Then, why is there so much evil in the world?"

"I believe we bring it on ourselves with our disobedience."

Odin growled, "So, it's our fault and not the Big Guy's?"

The Frogman said, “Is that too tough to stomach?”

“Yes, it is!” the boat guy replied bitterly. “I’ve read a lot on history and science. I don’t buy all that pious crap!”

Ross shot back, “Many so-called enlightened institutions and media are twisted with agendas… Just remember those blood thirsty vampires didn't like those horizontal and perpendicular objects.”

Odin struggled between his mind and heart. “Guess I am not an atheist anymore,” he admitted reluctantly, “but still an agnostic."

The SEAL grinned. "You're coming around brother."

It was one-minute past midnight when Count Dracula unloaded his coffin in a marsh, north of Leprechaun’s Links. It was centrally located and isolated. If he wanted to venture north toward Château Wilder, there were no fresh waterways to slow down his progress, compared to Shaded Grove. Vlad then praised his Szgany servants by stating, "Daciana, you and your people have served me faithfully for five-hundred years."

She said with a nod, "It's a privilege." Her fellow gypsies nodded as well.

Dracula continued, "Before I am welcomed into Dr. Wilder's château, you must hide my crates in her dungeon. Ensure your men update the equipment to revive the monster. Afterward, return to my homeland and restore my secret mountain top lair. Make it suitable for the living.” He gave her the proper directions and papers to fulfill her chores. “Grab more soil and return here for my necessities. I need as many safe havens as possible.”

Daciana bowed and kissed his ring, "Yes my lord."

Nurse Isabela Fernandez walked into the waiting room. She frowned sympathetically. “Your friends lost too much blood. Sorry gentlemen, but Mr. Hugsby, Fitz and Kramer expired at 4:45 a.m. We tried resuscitating them for the past half-hour.

Shotzski suddenly looked at Rockford. "Thor," he whispered, "the faster they die, the faster they rise."

Thor Rockford bolted toward the stairs while Chuck took the elevator down to the morgue. He quickly returned to the waiting room. “Hey Grif, can I borrow your crucifix?”

“Not a problem.” The Special Warfare Combatant Craft Crewmen (SWCC) operator removed his mother’s family keepsake from his neck. "Don't break it, brother. It is old and from Spain." Griffin then kissed the image of Cristo Jesus and handed it to Thor.

A female doctor spotted Nurse Fernandez walking into the room containing the bodies of the special operators. She arrived to confer about the men's loss of blood. "That's strange they all had bite marks on…" Three figures arose beneath the sheets. The physician trembled murmuring, "It's too soon for rigor mortis."

The linen slid off their undead bodies. The men bore evil red eyes. "Hello ladies," they giggled with deep demonic like tones.

The women jumped back, screaming in terror. The fanged trio enjoyed the chaos and said in unison, "Scared little ones?" Rockford darted into the room as the undead we're about to feast. The nurse kicked Hugs in the balls and jumped behind Thor.

Hugs groaned, "For that my little Latina you will be dessert. I will drink your blood ever so slowly."

Rockford thrust the small crucifix toward them. The undead gasped, falling back. Kram hissed, "Crush him with the bed. We'll make him one of us." They slid the heavy metal bed into Thor. It smashed him into the wall.

Shotzski skidded into the room as the crucifix flew out of Rockford's hand and slid under the curtain. Chuck rolled, dove for the window curtain, and ripped it open. The rising sun disintegrated Kram and Hugs. Seconds later, bones crackled to the floor.

The tall surgeon passed out on the floor. Fitz stumbled back into a shaded corner of the room and his fangs retracted. The vampire's face suddenly appeared like a frightened child. His voice inflection changed to a sweet tone, "Please don't hurt me."

Isabela seethed, "You're not innocent," tearing open the other curtain. Fitz's skin quickly peeled away layer by layer.

Thor grabbed Chuck's arm and said almost out of breath, "Thanks Shotz." The SWCC operator then nodded at the pretty nurse. "Bien hecho Señorita Fernandez."

Nurse Isabela nodded. "Thank you for saving us." She then bent down to pick up the crucifix. "You forgot something."

Thor noted it was still in one piece and let out a sigh of relief, "Muchas gracias." Isabela smiled and then pulled up her coworker.

Shotzski turned toward the perplexed doctor and sighed. "Have fun filing this on your report." He felt disgusted, but knew it was better that Rockford's friends were the undead no more.

50 - PARTY CRASHING

November 21, 2005

Long marble colored fingers opened a coffin at dusk and a slim figure in a dark suit rose. Dracula closed his eyes to concentrate. He was determined to find his ultimate bodyguard after evading those deadly mortals that attacked his remote residence on Gemela. He had heard rumors of a giant saving a boy from the jaws of an alligator. He knew that account had to be true.

Transforming into a wolf, it didn't take the vampire long to track his servant's scent to a makeshift shack in a forested area outside of town. Too impatient to wait, Vlad began to follow the enormous footprints. He smiled, knowing how the brute often used the shadows to nab backyard fruit and vegetables, unattended barbeque, or thrown away food from a store.

Frankenstein's Monster crept close to Le Grande's private golf club. He spotted two teenagers smoking around the outdoor pool. He emerged from the shadows of a large magnolia tree and waved his hands in an open gesture. "Cigar?"

"Nope," the young man said, "but do you want a hit?"

Franki smelled it and said with a sour face, "What is this?"

The young man replied, "It's some fine weed man."

The dirty-blonde laughed, "Doobage dude."

He eyed the pair disagreeably and stated, "Doobage bad!"

She looked at her beau confused. "Does marijuana make people look big and bluish-green?"

The teen rolled laughing on the concrete slab, "Uh, I don't know babe? I think we just met the not so jolly green giant."

The titan stomped toward the clubhouse. He smelled a pleasant aroma and followed the scent to the putting green. The course's assistant greens keeper looked up. "Shur would ju mind?" He looked up another two feet and said, "I must be seeing things. Just like Ozzy, too much drugs and booze, not enough hugs."

The goliath excitedly grabbed the stogie from the greens keeper's mouth. He took a puff and exclaimed, "Cigar, um - good!" The worker tripped backward. The creature prevented the frightened man from falling and gently set him down.

The maintenance man shook his head. "Whoa, my drug and alcohol counselor said I might have flashbacks."

"Thank you," Franki said, contently exhaling the pure tobacco smoke. He then headed toward the clubhouse.

An athletic doorman stepped in front of him and said, "Sorry sir, no smoking inside this charity event." The giant bent down, snarled and flicked his pinky into the jock's chest. The blow knocked the doorman ten feet back into a parked car.

The creature forcefully swung the massive double oak doors open and grunted, "Ruh." The hinges loosened. He noticed a sign promoting San Pedros Catholic Church and Reggie's Charity Drive. He then muttered, "Oops," casting his head down in shame.

Mouths dropped open at the gigantic stranger. He spotted a tray full of appetizers and beverages. The brute forgot what little manners he had and grabbed some food. He eyed the tall, burly bartender sporting a motorcycle mustache and demanded, "Give me a drink now!"

The barkeeper who many patrons swore was the spitting image of Sam the bartender played by Glenn Strange on the *Gunsmoke* television series, couldn't believe the thing towering in front of him. The creature stood at least two heads taller than his six-foot five-inch frame and carried the girth of at least a pair of NFL linemen but in one body. He finally asked, "What kind?"

"Brandy!" Ironically, Looking Glass' popular hit *Brandy you're a Fine Girl* was playing over the speakers.

Even as an amateur bodybuilder, the barkeeper nicknamed 'Tiny' knew not to mess with this straggler and respectfully said, "Your drink, sir."

A wolf ran near the pool sniffing. It transformed into Count Dracula. He stared into the green eyes of the pretty young blond and commanded, "Come to me!"

A teen tried to defend his girlfriend but she lazily pushed him away. She embraced the Count like he was a love magnet. The young man weakly mustered some courage by murmuring, "Bud, I am the only one that can kiss her."

Dracula replied with his mouth full of blood, "A little too late for that." He snapped the young woman's neck sideways and let her lifeless body splash into the pool.

The kid began to sob and tripped back into a large water fountain. The vampire lord hissed at the running water, "Pathetic little boy," and jetted toward the clubhouse.

The greens keeper wet his pants behind the tree's shadows and whispered to himself, "The gophers can mock me all they want. Mommy, I need more rehab." He then dialed 911 on his cell phone.

Vlad politely greeted the doorman, "May I come inside and make a donation?"

The young man obliged, "Please do, sir."

Count Dracula entered through the broken doors donning his natty black and white dinner attire. He pranced into the charity event with his usual panache. A priest turned around with a visible aluminum cross dangling from his neck. The vampire lord instinctively whirled around and shielded his face with his cape. He spotted the monster and gasped, "C-come here."

The priest piously advanced toward Vlad. "Party crashing is forbidden. You and your big, rude friend must leave!"

This time, the crucifix didn't faze Dracula. He crumpled the aluminum piece taunting, "Father, you have to have faith for that to work against me." The clergyman did not understand. The prince of darkness locked eyes with the priest uttering some ancient Latin words. He then pointed his long index finger toward the man's chest and made a fist. Like voodoo or a black spell, the cleric instantly suffered a massive heart attack.

Pastor Reggie didn't know what to do. He just witnessed this foreigner kill the Catholic priest with some evil beckoning in a language he only studied at seminary but never spoke. His self-defenses instinctively overtook his gentle giant like manner and smashed a chair into the intruder.

Vlad instinctively moved to the side. One of the chair legs plunged into his back. He began to weakly pull it out. The retired football player tried slamming the leg deeper into the stranger's back but the vampire backhanded Reggie. The blow sent the former NFL star sprawling to the floor. "My lucky night," said Count Dracula, "a faithless priest and now fake vwood."

51 - BULLIES

Sister Tréson downed her cognac and retrieved two items from her backpack. She calmly walked over to her fallen friend, whispering, "Give him a sprinkle." She then tossed a flask of Holy Water behind her back. Pastor Reggie caught it in mid-air. The nun spun around and, then, thrust a communion wafer in front of Count Dracula. "I believe!" she said forcefully.

Reggie immediately flicked the special water at the stranger. "So, do I, you lap dog of Satan."

Dracula shrieked, "No!" The Holy substance burned through his clothing and into parts of his skin. He also sensed the blessed wafer. It repelled him backward off his feet. His hands and legs flailed about before he smashed into the stucco wall. He made eye contact with the monster and pleaded, "Help me, friend."

Frankenstein's Monster stopped munching on food, stunned by the commotion and someone he knew. "Master?"

The vampire lord hissed, "Take them down!"

The creature nodded and grabbed the NFL player like a doll, bowling Reggie into the bar. The bartender was afraid the titan was going to harm the nun and came from behind, slamming a putter head with full force into the stranger's skull. The metal broke into two pieces. The brute turned around with amazing speed, grabbing Tiny by the front of his shirt and said disappointedly, "I wouldn't hurt a woman of the Cloth."

Tiny put up his hands and pleaded, "Sorry bud." The giant shook his head, barely thrusting his palm forward. The two-hundred and sixty-pound bodybuilder was propelled rearward, hitting the top of the bar and flipping back into the wall. The mirror and liquor bottles shattered down on the unconscious barkeeper.

The feisty Sister lectured, "You're a bunch of evil bullies." The monster growled at the Fraulein and walked away.

Vlad heard sirens in the distance and ordered, "We must go!" As the two fiends reached the valet's registrar, the Count stumbled. "That's strange - I am buzzed and feel the need to feed. Ah yes, that blond girl's blood has been tainted with some kind of impurity. The islanders call it hemp."

Normally, a vampire's typical feeding was an equivalent to slightly less than a third of a human's blood supply every third night. However, the young girl's drugged blood and Dracula's burned flesh increased his metabolism which gave him an unquenchable thirst.

The valet felt like prey and retreated. Vlad felt the lad's pulse and fear quicken. The young man fell backward as he saw outstretched arms coming at him. The vampire lord quaffed some of the mortal's life force before breaking his spine asunder. The Count's scorched skin and clothing became whole again.

Chuck and Thor heard about the ordeal on Shotz's police scanner. The reporter phoned Susi Ann at the Snowbirds' office. "Ms. Chang, have you been sleeping on your watch tonight?"

"No!"

"You just missed a big scoop over the police frequency."

Susi Ann said with a sigh, "No lectures Chuck!"

"I got one word for you - amateur!" Shotzski shook his head, hearing the Snowbird's phone line go dead.

Chuck and Thor quickly drove to the scene of the crime. They saw an ambulance drive off. The pair snooped around the pool and inside the country club's banquet hall, questioning witnesses.

The retired cop sighted a stocky nun pacing around the clubhouse's entrance. He walked over to her and smiled. "Evening Sister, my name is Chuck Shotzski."

"Sister Tréson."

"I am a reporter with Snowbirds. No one has said much except that there was a big guy throwing people around. Two people lost lots of blood but there is little of it on the ground or around the victim's bodies. Did you see anything beyond normal that could explain this conundrum?"

The spunky nun folded her brawny arms across her chest and looked Chuck straight in the eyes. "The Church has no problem discussing an exorcism but not vampirism. Well, we were up against one of them tonight."

He snorted, "I believe you. Did you tell that to the police?"

She laughed shaking her head, "I tried."

"Typical." Chuck tipped his hat out of respect to the Nun. "Thank you for your time Sister Tréson."

Ricardo Lombardi Jr. spotted Shotzski. He immediately put his head down and walked the other way.

Chuck caught the sudden movement out of the corner of his eye. He trotted over to Ricardo and said, "Uh hum, Sheriff Dick."

Lombardi spun around and jabbed his right index finger into Shotzski's chest. "You call me D like in defense, Rico, or Sheriff

Lombardi." His jaws tightened. "Don't you sass me with Dick or Ricky again, that's reserved for my Papá! Capiche?"

"Take a chill pill Sheriff D."

Sheriff Lombardi scowled and turned around to walk away. The reporter tapped the back of Rico's shoulder. He raised his arms in frustration. "What now Chuck?" Shotzski adjusted his shades. "You got to be kidding me. It's dark outside and you're wearing those silly sunglasses."

"What's the big deal?" the reporter said nonchalantly.

"Shotz, you're as seedy as they come, so if you want to talk to me, take off those damn shades." The lawman glared at him. "I want to be able to read your eyes!"

He shot a big plastic grin at the sheriff as he quickly tucked his shades inside his left breast pocket. His smile was so artificial, it would have caused career politicians to cringe. "Rico, did you check out those two perforations on the valet's neck?"

"Come on, Chuck, they are mosquito bites."

They walked over to the pool as two cops dragged the blond from the water. "Sheriff, look, she has the same marks. Are you going to tell me those are mosquito bites also? Both of them lost a lot of blood. What, by insects?" He then pointed. "That little hippie over there is so scared that he's in shock."

He stomped his feet, snatched the reporter's straw golfing hat and slapped him with it. "Fade, Shotzski, just fade!"

He lectured, "D, you need wooden stakes and garlic, not batons or regular bullets."

The lawman barked, "Get out you schmuck."

"Wait a minute sheriff."

Rico Lombardi Jr. rolled his eyes. "No buts. I do not give a hoot if my dad still vouches that you are his best reporter."

He grinned. "Your pops should tell me that more often. By the way, this is Jerry Rockford's son and my friend, Thor."

"My pa, your editor, has also told me many times that you have the most outlandish stories. He isn't sure if you are all there," Rico said pointing to his noggin. He then nodded at Rockford.

The Sailor said, "Nice to meet your sheriff."

"Likewise, kid." The lawman added, "Wait a minute. Thor can't be your friend, Chuck. You have less than a handful and I know them all."

He smiled half-heartedly. "Very funny sheriff."

"Vampires, come on Shotz. What kind of story are you trying to scam? You know Le Grande can't stomach any more superstitious crap."

"Junior," the reporter said with a frown, "you better heed or your posse will be the undead."

He lunged forward. "You two clowns want to visit the boys in jail?" They both shook their heads, trying to stop grinning as Sheriff Lombardi's face became florid.

"Rico, you are so damn sexy when you're angry."

"Shotzski…zip the lip and scoot!"

He kicked at the grass. "Stubborn goat. You can just fade."

Sheriff Lombardi Jr. reached for his handcuffs. Shotz and Thor bolted toward the private golf course's parking lot. They both laughed so hard they could barely breathe.

"Sheriff D seems to not like us."

"He does. Junior is like his pa, Rico Senior. They both struggle facing the facts, especially, when it deals with the bizarre."

Rockford said, "Kind of like my dad?"

"Yep, but one's my boss and the other can lock us up."

Thor and Shotz

52 - PROFESSOR DALB AL-UKHARD

November 21, 2005

An antique grandfather clock chimed nine times inside Château Wilder. A large bat slowly hovered above a towering figure making huge strides as they near the estate. Leathery wings and a body quickly transformed into Count Dracula. Moments later, he tapped one of the metal knockers against the sturdy door.

Dr. Wilder answered and tiredly smiled. "What may I help you with sir?"

Dracula held both hands to his blazer and slightly bowed. "Good evening, my name is Professor Dalb Al-Ukhard. I'm an old acquaintance of your family."

She welcomed the tall and athletic looking professor into her abode, "I'm Dr. Maria Wilder." She suddenly felt a chill as he entered the threshold.

"I know you are one of the best neurosurgeons in the world coming from a family of geniuses," Dalb complimented her.

She shrugged. "I'm over-rated."

"Humility is such a lost art," he said snapping his fingers.

The Frankenstein Monster bowed down to get his enormity under the eight-foot, double doors. "He's got to be the biggest man in the world," Maria noted.

"Rightly so, he was amalgamated by the largest and choicest body parts the good doctor could muster." Al-Ukhard chuckled, "Though not the prettiest operation."

She stepped back in wonderment. "He's not real but fake."

He raised an eyebrow. "Such an astute physician and this is all you can say." She frowned at his braggadocio inflections. The prof said placing his hand on the giant's arm. "Using the freshest, biggest and most genetically sound corpses simplified the procedure and guaranteed a successful one for young Frankenstein."

"That is just a myth. I studied premed with a relative of the Frankenstein's. He balked at such rumors." Maria was not sure of her words. She studied his skin tone and scars. She then rubbed at his yellowish-green skin and tugged at the scars around his wrists. No make-up rubbed off and the keloid tissue was real.

The prof expatiated, "Probably because your friend was too ashamed of the consequences wielded by his late ancestors or he knew nobody would believe such hearsay." Doc laughed, shaking her head. "What the unofficial doctor didn't count on was that the creature only wanted love and friendship. Instead, Victor Frankenstein abandoned the monster, horrified at the wretch he stitched together and brought to life. His lack of compassion for his creation ignited an unpredictable titan full of vengeance."

The physician sassed, "Stitched up body parts?"

"To make matters worse, Dr. Frankenstein had only a few brains with high IQs at his disposal. The first was from a farmer but it had not been preserved properly. The second brain came from a philosophy professor and the third - a man said to be violent.

Maria said, "You're putting me on."

"Not at all. Interestingly, Frankenstein's records do not indicate which one he used." He raised an eyebrow. "Some theorized the latter brain was abnormal, but records indicate he was likely a master criminal prone to violence to achieve his objectives."

Frankenstein's Monster appeared ambivalent to the discussion, revealing nothing but a stone-cold poker face.

Dalb stated, "From his matrix, this great specimen stood eight-feet tall. Originally, he had the strength of over a dozen men weighing a gauntly two hundred and eighty pounds. Amazingly, his cells battle each other for supremacy and his freakish immune system makes him almost immortal. The creature's different-sized body parts are enlarging to become one unified body."

She stared at the brute. "He appears to be between eight and eight and a half feet tall, weighing around six-hundred pounds"

Al-Ukhard grinned with pride at his day guardian. "Close Dr. Wilder and if you factor in his height, weight and girth, he is almost five times bigger than the average male." Maria stood in awe. The professor said with a smirk, "His strength is almost like a superman when he's healthy but this one cannot fly."

She whispered under her breath, "Somebody had to make him." Her logical side wrestled with such a kind, this modern-day Goliath. She pulled at his scar tissue another time, just to make sure this was not a sick hoax. She gasped, realizing how dense and tough his outer skin really was. It felt like treated layers of hardened leather but animate skin.

"Dr. Victor Frankenstein meant for him to be bigger, stronger and superior," Al-Ukhard explained. "The genius was so precise in assembling this fantastic specimen that the stitches showed no outer signs of blood or decay." Maria eyed the giant, intrigued but still doubtful. "Dr. Frankenstein later realized he used the most powerful rays of lightening to bring him to life. Such fabrication guaranteed the creature ultimate power and a cell structure that gives him a healthy longevity beyond reason."

Doc retorted, "This defies the Second Law of Thermodynamics - entropy. Everything goes from complex to simple - decay."

He gibed her, "Only because he was artificially made, my friend can defy your science. Because of this, he has adapted over the years, growing incredibly. Now that he is even bigger, this fantastic specimen will probably have the strength of over one hundred and twenty-five healthy men when restored to his maximum." She paced nervously, fidgeting her hands. He patted the monster's chest. He then escorted her around the foyer and whispered in her ear, "The creature's so obdurate and needs a new brain, eager to please his master."

Dr. Wilder rolled her eyes. "Brain transplants and resurrecting a man from dead bodies, rubbish, it contradicts science."

He glared at her repugnantly. "I have studied your science."

She raised an eyebrow. "What… on cartoon network?"

Dalb sneered, "Reputable sources point out that a few dinosaurs still walked the earth when Prince Vlad Tepes Dracula of Wallachia protected his people from the perverted Ottomans."

Doc said testily, "Come on professor, dinosaurs died out millions of years ago!"

He chuckled, "If that is what you want to believe."

She countered, "That's what I know."

He insinuated, "Besides instructing my younger brother and I in advanced sciences and mathematics, most of the ancient Turks were refined. A few corrupt Ottoman officials molested my weak sibling, Radu, and continually beat me when we were children. For that I despised them. I hated the aristocrats from my homeland even more. They betrayed my father and brother." She did not yet understand who Dalb really was or his winded gibberish. "My father was scalped, removing the skin from his face while he still lived. At the same time, they gouged out my older brother's eyes and buried him alive." His face longed for the past saying, "So, I learned how to fight like a Berserker. Oh, how those molesters and traitors paid dearly for their treachery after my resurrection."

"Resurrection… You're talking fables, sir."

He turned to face the doctor. "Do you think George and the Dragon is simply a fable? Every legend is based on a kernel of truth. Scientists have discovered many species that they once thought were extinct, including the Coelacanth which is supposed to be a prehistoric fish."

Doc taunted, "Oh, now you're trying to talk science again?"

He snorted, "Tell me this Dr. Wilder: How can modern scientists date the earth and the universe if it all was created at a young, fully developed state? It would be like trying to gauge a man who was cloned or created in a day, but appeared to be physically twenty-one years of age."

Her eyes widened. "True… that would be impossible."

The professor winked at her. "Exactly, whether the universe dates back between thousands to billions of years, it's hard to verify. However, I have noticed too many western scientists are on a witch hunt for those who stimulate any talk of microevolution."

She sneered, "You mean adaptation."

He grinned. "Those in your field would be surprised how fast species can adapt to all kinds of variables. It is well-documented there are no true missing links, yet such hearsay continues to be printed in textbooks and taught in many science classes."

Maria folded her arms across her breasts. "Excuse me professor, but what is your expertise?"

He put his hand to his chin and thought for a moment. "I am a master of several subjects: alchemy, ancient warfare, geo-politics, history, and the dark arts."

She said sarcastically, "So, you are not a real professor?

He sighed. "I am, but my point is the necessity for your community to concentrate on the research of gene therapy, DNA alteration, organ transplants, and so on."

"Definitely."

"Who cares about your religion of Darwin or God? It is a sad fact that too many scientific geniuses who embrace views other than evolution are outcast by your close-minded peers." Maria frowned as Dalb continued, "Such a lack of Socratic debate only cheats the advancement of mathematics and science."

The man was getting under her skin, revealing some painful truths. She lost it saying, "Don't lecture me on science or should I say weird science."

The prof cackled, "And that is hardly the democratic way of your fellow cadre who are liberally stacked in most universities."

Doc waved her finger as if to stop him and he retorted, "You should respect your elders!"

She rolled her eyes. "Please… you look my age."

He snarled, barely revealing his upper incisors, "You have no idea… I am Vlad Drakhol!"

"Come on."

He stomped his foot amok and bore his fangs. His strong native accent came through as he testily stated, "I vwas VWallachia's Voivode, Prince Vlad Tepes III, son of Vlad II Drăculea, and grandson of Mircea the Elder." He showed his gold ring, bearing Dracula's crest.

Maria put one hand to her mouth. "Wasn't Vlad Dracula that cruel, oppressive leader who staked people to death?"

"I only staked enemies, cowardly soldiers and those who raped, murdered or stole. I did so to keep law and order." Vlad paused before he continued, "Most of my people respected me, like you Americans admire George Washington."

"You?" she chuckled.

"Yes… the Pope used me as Europe's first defense against the Ottoman invaders. My soldiers impaled our enemies along the roads. That drove a dreaded fear into their hearts."

"That sounds way too severe."

Vlad made a fist as he growled, "Many historians comfortably critique my methods as barbaric, but they didn't have to live on the front lines or deal with the carnage. My homeland was always on the brink of extinction. I did what I had to do, unlike many of your sissy politicians, today, who prefer protecting terrorists' and child molesters' rights."

She said, "Your political discourse is giving me a headache." Dracula moved up the grand staircase to the second floor and back to the foyer in a blur, no more than a few seconds. She was dumbfounded. Her hands began to slightly shake as she thought: *No human can move that fast.* Maria put the back of her hand to her mouth and, yet, she still yearned for his alluring dark presence.

Prince Vlad Tepes III snapped his fingers back and stated, "I call such psychological and guerrilla warfare that I waged centuries ago truly efficient."

Her forehead crinkled. "So, you're six-hundred years old?" He nodded. Maria added, "And some stories say Vlad became the undead?"

He winced before acknowledging, "I am Count Dracula."

The physician shook her head in disbelief. “Whoever you are - you don’t look a day over forty-five years old.”

Dracula sighed before removing a steak knife from the buffet. He slit his wrist and the wounds instantly disappeared. "The creature and I should be proof enough but you still deny us." She turned away and he lectured, "Yet you have no qualms believing that a man can transform into a werewolf during a full moon."

She eyed him angrily. "You've been spying on me."

"I have my ways and you should heed or suffer. Careful woman, love is blind and it will betray you. My cowardly brother, Radu cel Frumos, and the Turks were on their way to sack my mountaintop lair. My first wife was distraught and *fell* off Castle Poinenari’s terrace. She refused to be taken their prisoner.” For the first time, Dracula seemed to show an iota of human emotion. “My beloved’s body was discovered in the Arges River below.”

Maria was fighting the feelings of compassion she felt toward Vlad as he expressed his sincere love for his first wife.

He bitterly smiled. “We were deeply in love despite years of marriage. She was so youthful and full of life." The dark prince suddenly shook his fists at Heaven and yelled, "How could a loving God let such a sweet woman take her life?”

The physician jumped up in fright. She began to back up like a cornered animal, gasping for air. She pivoted to get away from her guest.

He quickly moved with her. His sudden outburst made him appear like he was possessed.

She could have sworn he had bushy eyebrows and fangs.

53 - SPELLBOUND

Vlad Drakhol dropped his head to his chest and lamented, "Love is such an ephemeral emotion." Maria bumped into the corner mirror and froze. She slowly looked at the professor and then at the mirror a couple of times. He cackled, "Is anything wrong?"

She gulped, "You have no reflection."

"As I have told you, I am Dracula."

She thought his healing from a bloody wound was just a parlor trick. His ability to move up and down the foyer so quickly had gotten her attention, but no reflection removed all doubts. Dr. Wilder quivered saying, "You defy science."

"Science you know." He soothingly held her arm. "Relax and join me, with your gifted skills, we can defy the laws of nature."

She recoiled. "Never, your plans are of a raving madman."

He exploded with anger but quickly regained his composure. He waved his index finger. "Never is such a poor choice of words. How can such an enlightened lady be so obstinate? I am giving you a choice and you can learn from Frankenstein's genius."

"Not this woman!" The Count rolled his fingers to entrance her. She stated, "Don't try that spellbound chicanery on me."

"Look into my eyes… You will obey me or perish."

"Whatever!"

He twirled his hands staring at her. It took all her willpower to keep her head down. He repeated, "Look into my eyes." Maria couldn't pull away from his hypnotic gaze. The vampire lord put his arms around her slender waist and bent her to his side. She gladly embraced him, moaning as he sucked just a smidgen of blood from her inviting neck. He swirled his tongue around the bite marks, mixing his saliva with her blood. "From now on, you will know me as Professor Dalb Al-Ukhard."

"Yes, Professor Dalb Al-Ukhard."

"You will obey my every command. You are to seek out the perfect brain for the monster. I will know the second you find such a donor. Then, the creature and I will return for the operation." She nodded. Her countenance resembled a zombie without its free will.

The creature, Vlad and Maria exited the library's French door. They walked down the cavernous dock's steps. Dracula motioned with his hands toward the water. "Come here!"

A john boat pulled up to the concrete pier. Two gypsies jumped out. They pushed against the dock's side wall, five feet above the pier. It revealed a four by seven-foot secret limestone door. The stockier Szgany grabbed a two-foot wide plank and braced it against the lower ramp. They then began hauling electrical equipment through another secret door leading into a labyrinth.

Doc stood silent under the Count's power. He smiled at her unspoken curiosity. "Daciana and her spies are very resourceful." He took Maria's hand and escorted her up the plank.

The creature followed but his heavy girth split the sturdy wood in twain. "Argh!" he grunted annoyingly. He got back up on his feet and jumped into the opening.

Maria noticed a hidden smaller cave inside. She would have normally squirmed, seeing various chains and shackles attached to the walls but she couldn't.

The trio then ascended through the winding passage. They reached a large secret door leading to the spacious former lab up in the exercise room. The two gypsies came and went via the hidden hinged wall as they continued to haul old and new equipment.

This secret labyrinth stirred her memory. It reminded Maria of Nigel being interred in that secret nook behind the garage. She read in her mom's journal that Rathbone had never felt an afterlife during his previous deaths. They only seemed like deep, dreamless sleeps. Sometimes, he questioned the existence of God until meeting such evil as Dracula or being reminded of his bestial side. She recalled Nige yearning, *I long for the time when I stop hibernating, each time I'm destroyed, and would actually feel the first sting of death.* She rubbed her neck and asked, "Where did you get these electrical machines?"

The Count snickered, "I see that some of your memory is coming back." He raised an eyebrow. "Good, you will learn these parameters and be of some use. Much of them have been stowed here for forty years. We also updated some of the equipment based off of Victor Frankenstein's notes to revive his creation."

"You have Victor Frankenstein's notes?"

"Of course." Vlad presented her an updated copy of the great scientist's secret booklet, *The Amalgamation of Life*. He began pointing out the functions of the electronics. The gypsies hooked up wires to the giant's electrodes which had been grafted into his skin. Dracula ensured that the monster would be charged correctly in order to strengthen him. He let out a wicked smile as he zapped the monster. Electricity sparked and scattered over the tiled floor. "The creature still has his ill-temperament. He is a free thinker, strong-willed, very smart, and my hypnosis over him doesn't last long."

"Do you think Dr. Frankenstein used a violent brain?"

He smirked. "Do you mean the brain from a mastermind?"

Maria admitted reluctantly, "Yes."

"Not sure. From what I've learned from the notes on this amazing creature, his brain seems to have forgotten its previous life and history. He has lashed out violently, but that was more indicative of being lonely and treated very badly."

She nodded. "Can't say I blame him."

Dracula sighed. "He's just too cunning and calculating." The giant seemed to eye the Count wearily from across the room. Even with his super-sensitive ears, the hulk could not hear their conversation over the loud electrical equipment. Vlad whispered, "His brain is too intelligent to be a tractable servant. Otherwise, he's more virile than any other creature that has walked among us. It's all recorded here, his genesis and history are in this revised journal."

Doc saw an instrument oscillate while volts of electricity flowed through the bolts and into the monster. "Incredible, it's as if his skin is glowing bluish-gray. He seems more robust?" The giant's chest and body contracted and broke from the leather straps. He jumped off the huge metal table and stepped toward them.

"Usually, he's sustained by a normal diet. Though, he has endured long periods of being encased inside ice or under a brackish lakebed. His body slowed down to preserve itself until he could be artificially reenergized. Thanks to today's technology, this modern-day goliath can naturally draw in an abundant amount of electrical energy bouncing around his immediate surroundings."

Dr. Wilder read the diagnostics hooked up a computer, "The creature is now at one-hundred percent power."

Vlad patted the Frankenstein Monster's chest. "You will be my perfect guardian, my friend, and live almost indefinitely."

"Yes master," the giant said in a deep monotone voice.

Dracula said enviously, "You can walk by day and take in the sun. What a wonderful thing that must be!"

54 - CLOUDS IN MY COFFEE

November 22, 2005

Nigel Rathbone brewed a pot of coffee just after daybreak. He read the label out loud, “Vanilla Nut, froufrou if you ask me.” He sipped the hot beverage and exclaimed, “Hey, this hoodoo jag has a pretty good kick and tastes good.”

Maria Wilder smelled the wonderful aroma of brewed coffee and freshly grounded beans. She walked into the kitchen laggardly. Doc poured the hot beverage into her San Diego Zoo mug. "I thought all you Scots and Brits prefer tea?"

Bones noticed that the doctor lacked her typical perkiness. "Most of us do,” he replied. “I prefer coffee like my dad. We used to travel in the summers as professional knife throwers."

"That sounds like fun."

"The best."

"All that travelling, is that why you don't have much of a Scottish accent?"

"Suppose so. I also lived much of my life in the States with my dad's relatives.” He shook his head. “I miss the old man. We were quite the father and son team. Pa even taught my mom to be deadly at wielding a blade.”

Maria smiled. Nigel then stared at the kitchen’s tile floor in anguish. Doc was so tired that she rested her chin on the table. She saw the torment in his face and asked, “What’s wrong Nige?”

“I guess I was angry that my mother’s relatives ostracized my father. The stiff lips did not approve of their marriage. My parents never divorced and were happily married. However, mother’s side always loathed my father’s mixed heritage. His dad was an American of Scottish and English descent, hence the last name of Rathbone. It didn’t matter that gramps was wealthy or one of the best engineers of his time. He wasn't a blue blood.

"Huh?"

"Born into wealth."

She sassed, "No official title? "

Bones raised an eyebrow, "You could say that."

Maria's smile turned into laughter, "If it makes you feel any better, many of us on this side of the pond make fun of those 'respectful' stuffy types."

Rathbone grinned. "I hear ya. As a kid, I took every chance to escape, whether it was assisting our blacksmith or fishing in the woods. I especially enjoyed accompanying my Grandma Isa to visit some of the family in the states." He stared at the floor. "But after she passed, that's when things got really ugly."

"I would have thought the loss would have brought your family together?"

"My mother's relatives discovered my dad was part gypsy," Nigel scowled, "or a Pikie, as the haughty types would call them. An article from the Peterhead newspaper reported my Grandma Isa was one of the best Gypsy knife throwers in circus history before gramps caught her eye. It was a great tribute and romance write-up about them, but it embarrassed the hell out of my well-to-do maternal side."

Her head tilted to one side. "Pikie. What does that word mean?"

"It is a derogatory word for gypsy. My paternal grandmother was born in Scotland. Her family was travelling gypsies who took their shows throughout Great Britain and Europe. It was during one of their summer trips, she found my American grandfather collapsed near their camp. Grandma nursed him back to health from influenza."

"Was your grandfather travelling alone?"

"Partly. His cousin accompanied him but took the train between major towns. My grandpa liked to hike and breathe the air as he would tell me."

Dr. Wilder's eyes sparkled. "A true adventurer!"

"You got that right. Gramps wanted to get away from the posh lifestyle of home and see parts of Europe." Nigel shrugged. "My grandfather made a deal with his dad. If he graduated from college with a 3.0 grade average or above, he could then travel Europe for the summer and work for the family afterward. Always thought my great grandpa was wise in giving my grandpa such incentive."

Maria nodded. "It kept him focused."

Nigel chuckled, "Gramps told me numerous times how the olive-skinned beauty took in a stranger and he quickly fell in love with her. It was also endearing to him that my grandma wasn't aware that he was from a rich family and loved him for who he was."

She beamed. "That's so romantic."

He smiled reminiscing of better times. "Definitely. My grandfather asked her family's approval to marry her soon thereafter. They went back to the US to live."

Doc appeared nervous before asking, "Did your American family mind that your grandmother was a gypsy?"

"Heavens no!" Nigel grinned and continued, "How could they? Isa saved my grandfather's life. They gladly welcomed her into their home. If anything, my grandpa's dad understood her predicament, coming from a poor family himself. He worked hard as a builder and then an engineer. He didn't become wealthy until the middle of his life."

"Did your grandmother ever go back to see her family?"

"Every few years or so. Grandma Isa was busy raising her three children in the states. However, as a teenager my dad would visit my grandma's family. He worked throwing knives from late June to early August."

Maria asked, "Is that how your parents met?"

Nigel nodded. "My mom resisted dating him at first. She said dad was full of himself. But the ole man was persistent with the red-headed gem every season he visited. After a few years, she succumbed to his charm and good manners."

She laughed, "Now I know why you are such a charmer."

"Perhaps. Unfortunately, the happy tale ends there." He frowned. "As I mentioned before, my grandmother's gypsy background came out after she passed away. My mother didn't reveal that part to her family. She just spoke of my dad' wealthy American roots. Shortly after her funeral, one of my cousins called my Grandma Isa a 'no good, dark-skinned Pikie' to my face."

Doc gasped, "That's terrible."

Rathbone's nostrils flared. "I was only a kid at that time. However, I thrashed my cousin so badly that he was in the hospital for a month with broken ribs and almost lost his left eye."

"Is that why you went to live your family stateside?"

"Partly. I didn't feel comfortable around my mother's relatives or many of the villagers. I stood out inheriting much of my father's olive-skin and darker hair."

"Did your brother look like you?"

"Yes and no. We shared the same face and larger stature. But my brother was lighter like our mom." He bit his lip. "I just wanted to get away from the cold stares, so I asked to go live in America."

Maria softly said, "I wouldn't blame you."

Rathbone paused before confessing, "The circumstances made it an easy choice for me to leave since my brother was several years older and would be the heir to the estate."

"Didn't your parents love you?" the words shot out of Doc’s mouth before she could stop.

Nigel blew off her mortification with a wave of his hand.

"I apologize. I could have chosen my words better."

"It's okay." He paused before saying, "They loved me very much. However, things over in Britain can be very proper. My mom was next in line to the estate."

"So, she couldn't just leave and go with your father's family in the states?"

"They could have and it would have been much more peaceful. However, my grandpa only trusted my mom."

Dr. Wilder noted, "Quite the responsibility."

"Not for my mom. She loved the grounds and its history. She, especially, cared for the workers." Nigel crinkled his nose. "Her other relatives next in line, didn't give a damn about anything but themselves."

"Wished I could have met her. Sounds like quite a lady."

"She was," a tear trickled down his cheek, “my dad enjoyed working the circus in the summers. Mom's side could never understand a man of wealth working in such squalid conditions."

Maria raised an eyebrow. "Glad I never met her relatives."

Bones nodded. "That is why my parents thought it would be best for me to go to boarding school in Britain - proper etiquette." He looked out the window. "I refused, hiding out in the woods and living off the land."

"You were just a boy."

"Yes, but a stubborn, resourceful one. A search party found me weeks later. My parents' hands were tied. By that time, my mother's family put in a court order for me to get some counseling in order to respect authority and deal with my anger."

"Did it help?"

Rathbone's demeanor grew dark and he shouted, "No!" He looked at the ground and wiped his mouth as if to gather himself. "That doctor was cold and cruel in his methods, but I didn't allow him to break my spirit. After a short time, I escaped and contacted my relatives in America. Fortunately, they took me in. It was my grandpa who taught me how to forgive and move on, not some quack from an institution."

Doc sighed. "I thought I had a complicated childhood."

"My grandpa also got that court order dismissed. The stipulation was I couldn't return home until I was eighteen or older."

"Your parents never came to see you?"

"No. We corresponded by mail."

Maria frowned.

Bones read her eyes. "It was different back then. No jet airplanes, just ships… It took over a week to cross the Atlantic."

"Oh, I forgot… that was an entirely different era."

He nodded. "When my brother was killed in a boat crash, I returned home to pay my respects. It had been years since I saw my parents. They were the same fun-loving couple. We jested about silly traditions before my mother insisted that my father and I to go on a circus act to avoid her cold-hearted family.

Dr. Wilder replied, "I can understand that."

Nigel's eyes lit up for a moment. "My mom did make it perfectly clear that she wanted me home, study law and be the next heir to the estate."

Maria smiled. "That probably meant a lot to you?"

"The closeness yes, but not the title. Besides some painful memories, it was nice to be back..." he groused, "until that bloody werewolf bit me."

Doc nodded in sympathy. Nige normally was a quiet man. She knew it did him some good to open up a bit. Maria wanted to lift his mood, so she changed subjects. "Hey. You never answered why you like coffee over tea."

Bones replied, "Sorry. I can be temperamental at times. Due to our circus tour, I traveled much of Europe with Pa and that is when I caught the coffee bug. Italy, France, Lebanon and Turkey brewed some of the best grounds."

"And tea?"

"Tea is fine in the afternoon, but nothing beats the smell and texture of a good coffee bean. If given a choice, I'll take a cup of java.

The doctor grinned. "Kind of like good pipe tobacco."

Nigel exclaimed, "With a pint of course!" His smile quickly faded. "I wished my sweet cousin, Holly, wasn't killed by that beast!" He cast his head down and muttered, "Something I'm cursed with... and so sick of spilling blood."

Maria squeezed his hand to comfort him. Rathbone looked at her beautiful face and temporarily forgot his torrid past. She raised her mug and stated, "To the Scots and the USA."

Doc took a sip after Nigel toasted her in return. She suddenly staggered back to the edge of the breakfast nook. He grasped her slender frame from wobbling to the side. “Easy there, woman.”

“Oh Nige, I'm terribly thirsty and have a headache."

"What's wrong?"

"Nothing much, just tired,” Doc replied. “I need to get some electrolytes into my system. I had a late chat with my mother’s old colleague.”

Nigel became edgy and asked, “Who was it?”

“A middle-eastern man named Dalb Al-Ukhard and his big friend," Maria responded dreamily.

Bones tilted his head. "I dreamt of electrical storms last night." His face appeared puzzled and scratched his head. He scrambled the name Dalb Al-Ukhard around. He finally penned down Blad Drakhula and groused, "No, it cannot be. The Dracula’s have used other names such as Count de Ville, Baron Romaine, and Dr. Vlasko. That scheming son of the devil is up to his old chicanery.”

She looked at him confused.

He grabbed Maria’s shoulders staring into her eyes. “Did his big friend stand over the door frame and have a scar all around his upper forehead? Was his complexion an ashen yellow?”

She stared into her ceramic cup. “I’m not sure. It is all like clouds in my coffee. I have little memory except that we spoke."

Nigel looked at her quizzically before asking, “Those electrical storms, you didn't energize that titan, did you?"

Doc stretched her head to one side, yawned and rubbed below her jaw. "What?”

Rathbone noted two small punctures on the left side of her neck. Maria fainted in his arms. He forcefully said, "I must destroy Dracula to break the spell he has you under!"

55 - LADIES LEAGUE

November 22, 2005

The group met at Leprechaun Links' before their 1:00 p.m. tee time. Thor Rockford made the proper introductions with a proud smile. "Chuck, Kati and Jack, this is my lovely lady, Lise Alegría."

Shotzski shook his head in disgust at Rockford's Green Bay golf bag. He griped, "Oh wonderful, a die-hard Packers fan."

Thor stated, "Shotz, don't step on the Pack!"

"Whatever!" Chuck's eyes beamed at Lise and he shook her hand. "Well, at least, you have a pretty girlfriend."

Kati hugged her. "I know Thor's dad will love to meet you."

"I hope so." Lise then greeted Jack Grumblier. She glanced sideways at Thor and her eyes narrowed like a wild cat.

"Lisers. Why are you giving me that look?"

She pushed her knuckles into Thor's chest and whispered, "Honey, you never told me you had close friends of the family living nearby. We should have visited them earlier."

Jack Grumblier laughed hearing their little squabble. "Perhaps you need advice from moi, *Miss Judy-Judy*."

Lise exclaimed, "No way. You're my favorite columnist."

Jack nodded approvingly. "Thanks honey. I took over her column before she passed."

"I would have never guessed *Miss Judy-Judy* would live in little ole Le Grande."

Grumblier replied, "Lise, I prefer a town big enough where everybody doesn't know your business but small enough you can travel from one end to another in less than ten minutes."

Shotz waggled his driver. "Lise, don't sweat not visiting us. Kati and I didn't know Thor was stationed down here until recently."

Rockford shrugged. "You had been at that nursing conference. I figured you'd prefer meeting everyone in person."

Since the course was empty and the ladies' league already teed off, the starter allowed them to golf as a five-some. Lise spanked her *Cleveland Launcher* driver two-hundred yards down the center pike with a bit of a draw.

Shotzski's voice wavered, "Great, she hits the ball like me. If I could only go back a few seasons, I'd show you all up."

"Dear, you have used that excuse for years," Mrs. Shotzski said sarcastically.

"Well, at least I still can hit it farther than Grumpy."

Jack's anger got the best of him and he sliced his drive one-hundred and eighty-five yards into a bunker.

Near the end of their round, Thor noted the pretty scenery of the small lake with its water fountain behind the fifteenth green. He winked at the Shotzskis. Chuck dialed Jerry Rockford on his cell phone and began videoing.

Thor knelt down and said, "Sweet pea, your shoe is untied." He unfolded his palm, bearing a golden diamond ring, and affixed it to her shoestring. The sunshine hit Lise's eyes, something shiny reflected back at her from the turf. She began trembling. Her eyes began to well up in tears. He offered the token of love to his beauty queen. "Will you take this ring to marry me in sickness and health, in both good and bad times? Mi chocolate y miel, will you take this as a symbol of love in a binding, nurturing marriage, as long as we both shall live?"

An ashen-green leviathan walked past the five golfers. The thing headed toward the nearby restrooms and soda machine. All their mouths dropped open in disbelief, especially, Rockford's. The Giant looked exactly like he was when he rescued Thor as a kid.

The phone flew out of Chuck's hand. It popped shut as it hit the turf. He scowled, realizing he missed photographing the giant.

The man-made monster disappeared inside the gazebo surrounded by large manicured bushes. He began to shake a pop machine when a well-built greens keeper whistled, "Wait one big man. I'll treat you." Franki waved him off. "Well, probably not you. You'll need at least two," the young man said, finally noticing the brute was quite large.

The monster enjoyed the moment. That the fellow talked to him and did not run in fright was refreshing. The pony-tailed greens keeper inserted six quarters. Three Dr Peppers shot out from the machine and he threw two at the creature. The giant drank one instantly. He belched loudly, "Sowwee, excuse me." He downed the other pop and said to the assistant greens-keeper, "Danke!" He then disappeared into the swamp.

Shotzski remained mesmerized. "I've seen vampires, a werewolf, a swamp beast and a headless phantom but this tops the pudding. That thing had to be close to nine-feet tall, built like the Incredible Hulk and scarier looking."

Young Rockford still was in a daze, knelt on one knee in front of Lise.

Grumblier stood behind a bush quaking in fear. Chuck grabbed Jack's upper torso before his coworker fainted. He then mashed in Jer's number, before videoing Lise and Thor for a second time. He whispered, "Jer, we're back."

Lise jumped Thor and straddled his body. She laughed and cried with joy, "I do. I will marry you, mi corazón."

Kati's faced filled up with joyful tears. Jerry Rockford blared through Shotz's cell phone, "Congratulations to my son and future daughter-in-law."

Lise looked up at the cell phone surprised the ordeal was being photographed. Thor hugged his fiancé and smiled at the lens. "Thanks pops."

Shotzski nodded with approval. "Rock, I figured you'd want to see this."

"Thanks, Shotz," Jerry said over the phone to his best friend.

Chuck hung up and dialed another buddy. "Deputy Ron, you might want to check out a very large man in the swamp and park area northeast of Leprechaun's Links. He seems quite abnormal."

Deputy Ron barked, "What do mean abnormally large?"

"I mean the thing looks like an eight-foot or taller beast of a man with an olive-green, yellowish complexion."

"So, what?" stated Deputy Ron.

Shotzski replied in an authoritative manner, "Because he fits the description to a *T* of the huge man that trashed San Pedro's and Reggie's Charity Drive yesterday."

The deputy growled into the phone, "You better not be joshing me, Shotzski!"

"Deputy Ron when I report, I do not joke."

Susi Ann Chang was on the ball, listening to the scanner. She called Shotz, "Chuck, get over to the park ASAP. The cops are mobilizing like never before, especially for this lil place."

"Good ears Susi Ann, but I'm the one who tipped them off."

"Shotzski, could you ever learn to give me some credit?"

"Chang, you've been sucking a lemon all week."

Kati saw her husband's look and stated, "We're celebrating an engagement tonight. You can get the scoop later!" Chuck knew better and grudgingly obliged.

56 - REINFORCEMENTS

November 23, 2005

The police harried the biggest man they ever had encountered at a park north of Leprechaun Links late in the day. After asking to speak with him, the lawmen attempted to apprehend the giant. As they began to cuff him, he threw them around like dolls.

One of the deputies drew his weapon and stated, "Buddy, come with us!" The goliath shook his head. He then tore a sixteen feet tall tree from its roots. The lawman froze in disbelief at such strength. He finally popped off three shots before the towering figure easily heaved the tree at him and four Le Grande deputies.

Deputy Ron, a retired Explosive Ordinance Diver (EOD) of thirty years, knew his men needed backup. He immediately called in for a helicopter and patrol boat crew.

About a mile away, a coffin rose from the swamp. A violet-grey fog slowly escaped from the edges of the sealed lid. The smoky substance began to hover above the black casket. Motes of bluish looking dust danced in the moonlight. More and more the particles gathered until they appeared to take on a phantom shape. Blazing red eyes suddenly shot open from the figure floating above the unclean aquatic sepulcher.

Count Dracula sensed Frankenstein's Creature was struggling nearby. He concentrated for a second. His tall, sleek muscular frame instantly transformed into a large, dark bat. The nocturnal flying mammal darted toward the commotion.

The police shot at the giant from various positions. Most of the bullets bounced off him.

The vampire lord quickly joined in the battle. Both creatures thrashed dozens of gung-ho lawmen and a bunch of camping vigilantes.

A few men from the helicopter began pumping gunfire at the monster.

The giant made a clothesline with his left arm, knocking a hefty bearded man off a street bike. He picked up the man's motorcycle and hurled it into the hovering helo. The aircraft crashed to the marshy floor, spitting out orange flames.

The speed boat arrived and extracted a few deputies that had been called in from off duty. They shot semi-automatic bursts of fire in an effort to get around the monstrous duo.

Bullets passed through Dracula and one nicked the boat's steering chord attached to the back motor.

The fiendish pair despoiled the rest of their antagonists. Some men lay dead and others sprawled on the ground, seriously injured.

Deputy Ron knew there was no hope in defeating this grisly pair. The spry, elderly deputy placed his index finger to his mouth and signaled to his crew to remain quiet and play dead, despite their seething pain.

The Count began to feast on a pretty biker chic. The feisty blonde fought back, slapping him in the face and kneeing his mid-section.

Dracula moaned, holding his private area. He then jumped the voluptuous woman and snapped her neck. "That's for resisting me," he hissed. He momentarily gazed upon her corpse and said with a hint of remorse, "Too bad, you would have made a pretty bride and hell to reckon with."

The behemoth ambushed the boat on the marsh's bank. He held it from reversing with his left arm and his right was grounded to a massive tree root protruding from the red clay.

The vampire lord glided into the boat and taunted the coxswain by stating, "Head southwest toward the eastern bayou of St. Bernard Parrish if you want to live." He then put the boat's pilot under a trance.

The Frankenstein Monster pushed the boat from the bank and jumped inside. His enormous weight lowered the draft so much the boat dropped several inches into the water.

The speedboat skimmed over the calm waves at fifty miles per hour following the coastline. It then veered southwest across the Mississippi Sound.

November 23, 2005 - 9:30 p.m.

The boat arrived to the foggy, outer edges of Gemela with the fuel tank at almost empty. The steering chord suddenly snapped and the speedboat spun out of control. The coxswain lost his grip on the wheel, and was thrown forward into the water. He tumbled wildly over the current like a skipping stone until he hit the sand hard.

The vessel exploded into the rocky shore. Pain surged through the coxswain's ribs and extremities. He was certain several of his bones were broken. He caught movement out of the corner of his eye. The man grunted as he moved to one side to get a better view. Some sort of dark mass was falling from the sky.

Dracula landed on the bank, next to the human.

The man groaned in pain lying on his back. "What the...?"

The Count smirked.

"Who the hell are you?"

He stared at the mortal.

The lawman screamed, “What in God’s name are you?”

Vlad took a step back, hissing at the man.

The injured coxswain slowly reached for his knife. He was relieved it had not been lost in the water. He unclipped it from his belt.

The vampire lord sensed one of his kind nearby. He quickly scanned inland. He spotted one of his brides standing on top of an old tee box, overlooking Gemela's northern shore.

The voluptuous vampire wetted her lips. The Count could see she was hungry and nodded.

Something moved amongst the rubble and the boat seemed to levitate. Dracula headed toward the wrecked vessel.

The female vampire darted in for the kill.

The downed lawman saw the woman rushing toward him, moving faster than any NFL player he’d seen on television. He slowly opened the blade and slashed at her as she approached.

The vamp’s flesh split open below her knee. She snarled. Her emerald eyes turned red.

The mortal screamed trying to move back, but he was too injured. He looked at her leg and it healed within seconds. He held up his knife, making small swipes as she inched closer.

The curvy bride leaned her head toward the man and said in a sweet tone, “I was going to take it easy on you, mister.” She gripped the blade with her hands and yanked it from him.

Fear welled up within him as he stared up at her.

Her blood dripped on him. The vamp tossed the blade to the side and licked her palm. “Can you kiss it for me?”

The lawman tried to scream but was too terrified.

The vamp mockingly laughed at the mortal. Pearly white fangs emerged as her nice smile turned into a wicked one. “Sir, didn’t anyone tell you it’s not nice to stab a lady.”

The coxswain screamed as she tore him apart.

Two giant hands appeared gripping the wreckage. He threw the charred boat fifty feet into the inlet.

He smiled at his superhuman servant. The creature's lacerations and burns faded within seconds. The only scars he still bore were the ones prior or during his making when Doctor Frankenstein compiled a *Prometheus Unbound*. "Come my friend," Dracula said, beckoning to follow him to the mansion nestled upon a low hummock.

November 24, 2005

Dr. Maria Wilder parked her 2004 Toyota Tacoma PreRunner. She grabbed her coffee and headed for the hospital. She stopped in her tracks, shaking her head. "What the hell's wrong with me? I've been so forgetful." She then returned to her quad-cab truck and retrieved her duffel bag.

Nurse Lise Alegría spotted her coworker across the parking lot and waved. "Yoohoo, Dr. Wilder!"

Maria stared ahead before slinging the bag over her shoulder.

She didn't think much of it. Lise figured her friend did not see her and walked into the hospital.

The physician unclipped the medallion Nige gave her as a gift to ward off the werewolf's imprecation. She washed up and lethargically changed into her surgical garments. The amulet slipped from her blouse's pocket and lay at the bottom of the locker.

The nurse greeted the doctor enthusiastically. She wiggled her hands in the air and hummed, "Doo-dee-doo," proudly displaying her brand, new engagement ring.

"Am I missing something?" Maria said to herself.

"Aren't you going to congratulate me chic?" Lise rolled her eyes. "Hello!" Her reproof didn't even faze her friend.

She looked past the nurse like she didn't know her.

"What's wrong with you, Doc?" One tear rolled down her high cheekbones. Nurse Alegría did not know what to make of her dear associate's rude indifference.

57 - STALKER

Thanksgiving

Nigel Rathbone overheard two gentlemen quietly remark about a mighty giant and cunning vampire. The only other thing he could make out was that the monstrous duo literally annihilated part of the town's police force, the previous night.

The pair secured eight Kwik Star coffee lids before departing. Thor Rockford slowly drove off, careful that none spilled.

The fugitive tracked the men in Maria's 2004 Toyota Tacoma. Bones tried not to follow too close. He was relieved to see the 1967 Ford Mustang finally pull into a driveway.

Chuck Shotzski was about to step into his home when he noticed they were being stalked. He looked at Ross and pointed back. "Who is the mug tailing us?"

The SEAL eagerly kept the door open for the coffee couriers and replied, "Not sure. We figured he was with you two clowns." Ross then grabbed one of the flavored roasts.

The man walked up to the door and extended his hand. "Pardon me, my name is Nigel Rathbone. Your strange conversation at the convenience store pricked my attention."

Shotzski's gut told him this guy had the goods. "Get inside!"

"Thank you."

Chuck heard the accent and asked, "Are you British?"

Nigel grinned. "No. I am an American-Scottish hybrid."

The men laughed at his dry humor. Rathbone then began to explain, "The reason I followed you here is because I've had my run-ins with that giant and vampire you were discussing. But it has been a bloody while, over forty years ago."

Griffin laughed, "You can't be older than forty."

Rathbone ignored Grif and stared the group down with a steely look of determination. "We must destroy Dracula."

Chuck's voice squealed a little, "You mean we are dealing with *The* Count Dracula?"

Nigel responded, "Unfortunately, yes!"

After a long pause, JT Rockford said, "Leave the Giant alone. He's kind-hearted," he looked at his teammates, "but like anyone of us, if provoked, he'll lash out."

Chief Jaworsk looked at Petty Officer Rockford strangely. "And how would you know this, Thor?"

The boat guy said tentatively, “The Giant saved me when I was a kid.” He didn’t have the nerve to tell his buddies anything else. The men stared at Rockford blankly for several seconds and then burst out laughing.

Bones stated, “What Thor just told you about the creature’s persona is the truth!” The group’s laughter simmered down and they began to huddle their chairs around Nigel.

Shotzski smirked at his best friend’s son. Jerry Rockford grumbled about his kid’s supernatural encounters.

“Gents, there are few vampire lords in the world and Dracula is the most potent. Every time a master is destroyed, the eldest becomes the strongest. To make matters worse, he has my friend, a neurosurgeon, under his spell." Nigel shook his head. "She has a private practice at her Château many miles to the northwest.”

"Not Doc!” Thor exclaimed. “She works with my fiancé at Le Grande’s hospital and is one of her best friends. Lise’s half-brother is the caretaker of the château."

Rathbone nodded. “Sadly so.”

Rockford couldn’t believe how bad it had become. The remaining team’s damp mood improved briefly when they realized Thor was going to tie the knot. Some of the guys joshed him by saying his freedoms would soon end. The group then quickly switched gears to prep more anti-vampire weaponry.

Sister Teresa Tréson rang the doorbell. Chuck Shotzski peered out his storm door. The nun puffed at her Cubano and exclaimed, “Howdy y’all.”

“Come in.” He smiled. “Never seen a nun smoke a cigar.”

Sister Tré blushed and admitted, “It is my only weakness.”

A six and a half feet tall bruiser hobbled next to Sister Tréson on crutches. "I would like to help you fight those monsters, but the big bloke broke my left arm and leg," graveled Pastor Reggie.

Ross looked the man of God in his eyes. “No worries but we do need your prayers... Holy Water to be specific.”

The nun and minister went into the dining room and began their benisons over the water. Minutes later, she walked back into the family room. Something nagged at her heart. Sister Tré whistled for the guys to gather around. "Let’s pray!"

They began to hold hands in a circle before bowing their heads. She spotted one of the guys with a hat on and uttered, "Pss."

Jaws slapped the back of his pal's head to get his attention. Ross slightly jumped before removing his ball cap. "Pardon me."

Sister Tré nodded at the Frogman and smiled. She spoke in an authoritative but humble voice, "Dear Lord. We praise your Holy Name. We pray this future mission be a success. Give to all involved courage and swiftness to vanquish this evil. May we remember to rely on your strength and wisdom, and not ours."

"Amen," all said as one. The group then went back to prepping weaponry to combat the undead.

Mid-afternoon, Kati Shotzski popped her head out of the kitchen and exclaimed, "The bird will be ready in twenty minutes!"

The entire group helped set the table with Thanksgiving themed place settings, side dishes and beverages.

Pastor Reggie said a quick prayer, giving thanks for the meal and the families who lost loved ones.

Sister Tréson lifted her glass full of cognac. "To freedom, liberty and our fallen friends." The clink of glass upon glass could be heard before everyone began to enjoy their turkey dinner.

After finishing off the meal with some pumpkin pie and coffee, everyone helped the Shotzskis cleanup.

Kati excused herself for a long walk. Football was on the tube but the group was too focused to enjoy the game.

A tall, burly figure approached the Shotzski's front porch, minutes after Pastor Reggie and Sister T-Tee departed.

The man squinted through the screen door as he knocked. "Hello, anyone home?" The group only saw a blur of a silhouette, but that voice...

"Anyone here?" the man repeated as he pressed against the storm door's screen. The crew looked up as if they saw a ghost. Hans received a barrage of bear hugs as he walked inside.

Ross hooted, "What a wonderful Thanksgiving treat! Steve. Where have you been these past months?"

Staff Sergeant Hansen shrugged. "Dr. Wilder found traces of an unexplained virus in my system after the ambush. That very next day, men in black suits arrived and rushed me to Washington DC."

Odin grinned. "Did the men in black wear dark shades?"

"No but the scientists at John Hopkins discovered my viral infection was the same found in our fallen comrades." He shook his head. "Only I had not lost as much blood and my spine was intact." Hans rubbed the back of his neck and said, "My system returned to normal except for a lingering concussion and some mild aches."

Odin's brown eyes grew big. "You should a seen Dr. Wilder come charging into the base without a pass. She made quite a scene, demanding what happened to her missing client. I had never seen base security get so spun up. Hell. We didn't even know where you were? Boy, was Doc pissed, thinking you went AWOL."

The staff sergeant grinned mischievously. "Yeah. Nastea snuck into Hopkins and told me." He looked surprised seeing the commander and happily yelled, "Hey Lawdog. You're alive."

He chuckled, "Yep."

Hans hesitated, almost afraid to ask, "Where's Barnum?"

Lawlur said, "Bar-none is still up at John Hopkins."

The staff sergeant appeared perplexed. "Really?"

Commander Lawlur nodded. Those men in black suits are pretty wily. I was up there until recently."

"Like I would have known, they had me locked-up in the psych ward." Steve put his head down and admitted, "No matter how much hockey or ice cream that place was depressing."

CWO5 Raven looked at Hans with a hint of concern.

"Don't worry Rav. The shrinks grilled me but I never told them or investigators the truth." He chuckled, "The scientists kept badgering me why their blood specimens were destroyed. I didn't mention to them their vials were stored near a window during the day." He scanned the room and said, "Where is Kram?"

Raven placed his right hand on the soldier's shoulder. "Steve. I am truly sorry to have to tell you, but Hugs, Fitz and Kram died after we conducted a raid on Gemela four days ago."

He fought back tears and sadly said, "I thought Kram was too damn ornery to die." Hans shook his head. "Hugs, such a joker, just like Broadstein who could get under your skin, but you loved those clowns. And Fitz was that cool quiet man."

58 - PROFESSOR SIODMAK

Nigel Rathbone threw a bag on the table and stated, "You may want to melt these silver coins into bullets."

Odin's eyebrow rose. "Can silver destroy vampires?"

"Sometimes, but definitely against lycanthropes."

Shotzski eyed Bones suspiciously. "Who's the damn lycan?"

He breathed deep and muttered, "I become one at full moon."

Griff sighed. "What the hell, vampires and now a wolfman."

Nigel said, "It's best if the slugs will penetrate the heart, but not pass through it. That will definitely stop me in my tracks."

Rav folded his arms across his chest. "Anything else you need to tell us, Mr. Rathbone?"

He nodded. "Wolfmen can't stand the touch of silver. Being shot or beaten down with the pure metal will destroy them, unless it's removed from their body and then exposed to another full moon.

Fin asked, "And nosferatu?"

"What I know about vampires, they don't like touching silver, but it's only deadly if lodged directly into their heart cavity."

The reporter added, "Or cut off their head with a silver blade." The Scott nodded."

Hans growled, "What is this, a monster convention?"

Odin, their ablest weapons expert, began preparing the correct parameters of silver bullets per Bones' instructions. "Nah. It's more like a Monster Mash," replied the gunner nonchalantly.

The men listened to Nigel's exploits with the infamous duo. They were mesmerized by such outlandish tales. Rathbone saw the wonder in their eyes. He could also see they wished it were not so and explained, "Against Count Dracula - you have a bit of a chance that some of you will walk out alive, especially, if you can find that bloody nosferatu's resting place during the day."

Jaws demanded, "What about the Frankenstein Monster?"

Nigel shook his head. "The creature is like fighting a mythological titan. He's total raw energy and nearly indestructible."

Grif asked, "What can we do about this goliath then?"

"Not much… I am your best chance against him. Lycanthropes can jump very far and move like a cheetah.

Michael Raven said, "How strong is a werewolf?"

"Its normal strength ranges between two to eight humans, but that doesn't factor in their claws, fangs, and speed."

"Petty Officer Ross inquired, "Why such a large range?"

"Different type of lycans," Rathbone explained, "and much depends on how strong you were before you were bitten."

Odin shook his head. "Same damn concept as vampires but werewolves are slightly more powerful."

"What the hell," Chief Jaworsk griped, "did someone document all this wolfenlology shit?"

"Yes," Nigel replied, "a Professor Curt Siodmak was the expert on lycanthropy for much of the twentieth century."

Shotzski interjected, "Did this professor compare the strength of lycanthropes to vampires?"

"Quite thoroughly!"

"Can I get a copy?" asked Shotz.

"Professor Siodmak's books are quite rare." Bones shrugged. "It may take some time."

"Reliable sources are worth the wait and money."

Rathbone put up a hand. "I almost forgot to mention. A werewolf's claws and fangs can destroy the living dead."

Rav's eyes lit up. "That's kind of refreshing."

Fin said, "Anything else we need to know?"

Nigel sullenly replied, "Less hairy human looking werewolves are the weakest, but the craftiest, almost double their human strength. Large four-legged ones are about twice as strong as well. Those with wolf heads but a man's body are three times stronger."

Ross stared into the newcomer's eyes. "What is your type?"

Bones growled, "The strongest – a wolfman or wolfan. We exhibit more of a man's head and body, and heavily covered with short wolf-like hair." He shook his head. "Our claws and fangs can tear a man apart in seconds."

The Frogman shook his head. "Damn dude."

"The good news is Wolfmen rarely kill more than one victim each full moon, unless provoked." Nigel sighed. "The bad news, if you're my target, God help you."

Petty Officer Ross inquired, "What about your strength?"

Rathbone reluctantly admitted, "Wolfans are four times stronger than their normal selves."

"So, you're stronger than Dracula?"

"Yes… Being a tall stocky working man, I've been twice as strong as most guys." Bones pursed his lips. "As a lycanthrope, I am eight times more powerful than your average bloke."

The SEAL gasped, "Bloody hell, ole man."

Nigel placed his hands to his face and said, “The problem is werewolves crave human flesh. They must kill every time the moon is full. It is better that you die by their bite than endure the curse of the beast. If not, you may live in agony for ages."

Petty Officer Odin tried to lighten up the mood by saying, "Wolf-dog has the moves and Franki wields the power."

Nigel grabbed Odin’s throat and shouted, “Don’t say that! It’s not funny." His eyes appeared to peer in the past and continued, "I live with thc guilt of savagely shredding innocent people to pieces as one of the damned.” He then let go, apologizing profusely.

Jaws shoved a silver-tipped arrow at Nigel and firmly said, “Take your own life, now, while you’re in a mortal state.”

Rathbone let it drop to the floor and growled, “You fool! Do you want to be my next victim and, possibly, survive as one of the children of the night? I only appear mortal but as long as I bear this mark,” he revealed the lycan scar below his left neck, “I will always be a malefactor during luminous moons.”

Jaworsk said, “My apologies Nigel.”

He griped, “I’ve tried taking my life. Instead, I instantly turn into a wolfan, whenever, I or someone else tries to destroy me with silver. Then, I just kill someone even when the moon is not full.”

The whole band of men breathed deep. They were relieved nothing transpired.

Nigel looked up and sadly admitted, “I was once Dracula’s day guardian for thirteen years. We met in London, around 1950. He tracked me down one full moon when I was a werewolf. The next night, Vlad took me in and helped me cope with my curse. He encouraged me to follow thieves and known thugs on the evenings before a full moon, so I would kill what I thought were expendable elements of society. At first, we were friends, but I became stricken with guilt year after year, realizing the monster that he truly is. That bloated tick used me to help him track down men in London for one year he said were murderers. I later found out we wiped out most of Van Helsing’s secret Vampire Hunter Team.”

Shotzski eyed Rathbone and asked, “What happened to Professor Van Helsing?”

“Dr. Van Helsing died of old age shortly after I naively aided the Count hunt down men that were actually fighting for good.” Bones sneered, “I finally had my falling out with Vlad late in 1964, when I discovered he was going to transplant some poor medical assistant’s brain into the monster. He wanted a loyal and more lethal day guardian. And I wasn't going to let him murder another human being so he could have the perfect brain for his superhuman servant. It was then, I knew Dracula had to be destroyed."

Chief Jaworsk's eyes focused before stating, "Bones. We got your back." He then smiled at him. "Just don't bite us."

Nigel nervously grinned. "Thanks for that pun. I guess you could probably give me some peace and shoot me up with silver." His face grimaced in agony. "No. I would probably kill a few of you before it's all said and done."

Raven stated, "I think we need you."

He scowled, "You need me against those two fiends."

Joe Samson stared at Rathbone for a few seconds before asking, "What guarantees us that you will not turn on us first?"

"Nothing but sometimes you need badness to fight hell itself." Nigel sighed, "What I do know is that will attack the Count and the monster when I'm that noisome beast. We have too much bad blood between us. That may give you time to finish off Dracula and don't underestimate him, he has many backups."

Fin noted, "We can use this to our tactical advantage."

He stated, "If you destroy Vlad, then please finish me off."

The Shadow Hunter smiled. "Not a problem."

Rathbone grinned. "As morbid as that sounds, that would be appreciated." His face grew serious. "If you break the spell Dracula has on the Frankenstein Monster, he may leave you alone. As Master Thor pointed out earlier, the giant is normally ambivalent unless he's provoked."

They chuckled hearing the Scot use the words, *Master Thor*.

Bones continued, "The only problem is the Count hypnotizes Frankenstein's Monster for dastardly deeds. He also protects those who are kind to him. The creature does not speak much but is very intelligent."

Odin placed the silver bullets on the tray. "If this creature is so smart, then why can't we reason with him?"

"Imagine every normal person has shot, beat, or scowled at you spanning almost three-hundred years. Then, there is one man with a shady past that treats you well and talks with you every day." Rathbone shrugged. "Who would you trust?

"Point taken Nigel."

"The giant and I were friends for over ten years but he wouldn't think twice to destroy me in order to protect Dracula. Besides, I never had another chance to reason with him. He stormed out of Château Wilder chasing after Stan Keaton. I believe Frankenstein's Monster lay dormant somewhere until recently. And I am very sure the Count never told him he was going to replace his brain with another." The Scott shook his head and said, "The creature wouldn't believe it unless he heard it straight from Vlad's lips."

Kati returned from an hour walk after burning off her turkey hangover. Mr. Whiskers hissed at Rathbone and skirted around him. Mrs. Shotzski picked up her big pussy cat and inquired, "Chuck. Now what's going on?"

Nigel interjected by saying, "You probably were busy in the kitchen preparing the bird while we talked business this afternoon."

Kati looked at her husband suspiciously and demanded, "What kind of business?"

Chuck Shotzski folded his arms over his chest and replied, "Baby. You do not want to know."

Kati Shotzski revealed a hawkish smile. "Oh, yes I do!"

Chuck sighed, "Why don't we sit down and have a chat over some tea, if that is okay with you, dear?"

Kati's eyes narrowed. "Sure."

Chuck looked over at the Scottish bloke and grinned. "I am sure Mr. Rathbone wouldn't mind."

Nigel graciously admitted, "I would like that very much."

Mrs. Shotzski looked up and down at the man's pleated wool pants and V-neck sweater. "You don't dress like the rest of the military guys."

Rathbone nodded. "Forgive me. You had several guests today and I forgot to introduce myself." The Scot extended his hand to the lady of the house. "My name is Nigel Rathbone."

She was pleasantly surprised by his manners. "Call me Kati please."

Nigel chuckled, "By the way, thank you so much for the splendid food this afternoon. I haven't had a turkey meal in ages."

Kati nodded. "It was a pleasure." Bones then began to recount to Mrs. Shotzski his long and sordid past.

59 - SNOWBIRDS

The buck stops here!
President Harry S. Truman

December 15, 2005

The Snowbird's office had been abuzz for the past half hour after its editor and partial owner, Ricardo Lombardi Sr., unlocked the doors at precisely 9:00 a.m. The majority owner, Kati Black Shotzski, completed one of the most important chores of the day, brewing a pot of coffee.

Susi Ann Chang and Jack Grumblier began piecing together stories, coupons, advertisements and editorials for the Sunday and Monday editions. Tuesday and Friday were the only other days the paper was circulated.

Shotzski had a smirk on his face as he left Lombardi's office. He had wanted to say, *the buck stops here*, but held his tongue. Rico stuck his head out the door and yelled, "Shotz. You already went to that damn bayou."

Chuck Shotzski curtly replied, "Come on Dick. It is not like we are running a big newspaper here. Besides, I've covered all of the sports until we get the college scores later tonight."

Rico Lombardi blasted his best and feisty reporter, "I've had enough with the supernatural adventures of Shady Shotzski!"

Chuck almost pointed his index finger up his editor's nose. "Ricky. I never liked the silly nickname," he scowled, "but if you want to be correct, then it's the *Shadow Hunter*."

"Nah, nah, if Kid Coroner had known you like I do, his hospital staff would have tagged you, *Shady Shotzski*," Lombardi retorted. "Why don't you report on something real for a change?

Chuck walked away from his boss and waved him off.

Rico's nostrils flared. "Shotzski. If you don't work today, then you can forget about golfing or fishing next Thursday! Capiche?"

Shotz whispered under his breath, "If you ever see me again."

Lombardi slightly cocked his head. "Shotzski. What did you just say?"

Jack Grumblier laughed at their squabble. Shotzski snarled, "Grumbles. If you have any kind of balls, then tag along." Jack immediately stopped grinning.

Kati sobbed in her husband's chest. She looked up at him and firmly said, "I'll cover the college scores, but you better come back in one piece and alive!"

Chuck rubbed off some of her smeared mascara and said with a smile, "Yes, dear."

Ricardo Lombardi Sr. put his hands up in the air. "What the hell is going on here?"

Kati grabbed a tissue and muttered, "Rico. You wouldn't believe it."

Shotzski opened his desk drawer and grabbed his silver crucifix. He stashed it alongside a mallet and wooden stakes inside his backpack. He kissed his wife. "Heading to Château Wilder to grab Nigel."

Rico said, "You better not doing anything you'll regret!"

He winked. "A good reporter has to snoop around."

He eyed him warily. "What your packing says otherwise."

Shotz looked at his watch. "Running late… Ciao Rico!"

Susi Ann answered the phone and whistled, "Ricardo. Your son wants to talk with you."

Snowbirds' Staff

Lombardi shut his glass door. “Hey Junior. What do you need?” he asked covering his lips.

“Dad. Chuck Shotzski has been telling me some crazy stuff but nothing else makes sense. A handful of the county's deputies were recently killed and one patrol boat went missing.”

“That bad?”

“Yep. Our budget, the Sheriff Department’s only helicopter and, most importantly, my men have been decimated,” Ricardo Lombardi Jr. put up his hands in frustration, “by a giant and some phantom.”

Rico Sr. looked around and whispered, “Son. Don’t tell anyone that I told you this but you better listen to Shotz on this one.”

Rico Jr. grumped, “Dad. I wished the Shotzskis, Grumblier, Chang, and you never teamed up on Snowbirds.”

“Junior. It was your idea that Le Grande needed to revamp its newspaper.”

“No dad. It was my idea that you, Grumblier, and Shotzski come here to retire.” The sheriff sighed. “That was not a problem until you guys got bored.”

The remaining Special Operators had prepared methodically the past two weeks for this day.

The holiday season wasn't laid back for them this year. They broke bread together, gave thanks and toasted their fallen friends. But their focus never wavered - to destroy Dracula's vampire haven NO MATTER WHAT!

It was 1100 hours. They were about to depart when Murphy threw in a wrench: The helicopter had a mechanical issue to resolve. Petty Officer Griffin was sent to obtain the replacement part.

CWO5 Raven spotted Hans sitting in the back of the helo. “Get out!” he ordered. “You’re not going.”

“Warrant. Have you heard of strength in numbers?”

“Hans. Your body is still dealing with balance and equilibrium issues,” Rav replied in a calm and steady voice. “You’re more of a liability than help. Besides, we would not want to contend with you, if one of those bloodsuckers instantly turned you into a healthy vampire. You’re a big boy!”

Staff Sergeant Hansen folded his arms over his chest and pouted, “My place is with you guys.”

"I had a feeling it would come to this. We don't have time for this crap." Rav plunged a needle, containing a fast acting but mild sedative into the side of Steve's leg.

The staff sergeant was surprised and weakly smiled. "Warrant, y-you got me."

Rav held his neck from crashing into anything. "Hans. I admire your spirit." He whistled, "Guys. I need some strong hands." Ross, Odin and Samson came over to carry off their drugged comrade.

Senior Chief Samson noticed a small leg under the canvas seat. "What is that?"

Michael Raven recognized the tennis shoes. "Brett. Get out of there!"

The ten-year old crawled out and gave the pilot a big hug. "Daddy. I don't want you to go," he pleaded. "It is dangerous."

Raven bent down and calmly said, "Son, worrying does us no good." He diverted his kid's attention. "Can you do us a favor?"

Brett smiled at his dad and answered, "Uh huh."

Rav pointed to the phone on the wall. "Call your mother after we leave. Make sure she picks you up and drops that sleepy guy lying over there at his home." Mike looked around mystified and asked, "Hey. How did you get here?"

"I rode my bike." Brett shrugged. "It's only five miles. Please do not be angry, Pappi."

Raven grinned. "Tiger. I like your courage but you need to think about mom." He kissed his son on the cheek. "You are the man of the house while I'm away. Okay?"

"Okay," said the kid begrudgingly.

"I love you."

The lad looked up and smiled. "I love you too, daddy."

Grif and Ross finished fixing the minor glitch. The group boarded the helicopter after rechecking their gear.

Brett rendered a salute to his father from the side of the hangar bay. CWO5 Raven proudly returned a salute to his young son as he lifted off at 1315 hours.

60 - OPERATION ROGUE

December 15, 2005

Less than ten of the forty-four special operators were alive from the ambush in February and op in November. The survivors had made a pact to destroy the undead, even if it cost their lives. Jaws had labeled their government-free mission, *Operation Rogue.*

CWO5 Raven's helicopter reached the rocky northern banks of Gemela at 1430 hours. It touched down on one of the fairways to the northwest side of the hacienda. He knew it was in a spot where the eastern mound's shadow would not impede the next sunrise. The pilot silently prayed the mission would not last that long.

Within two hours, the crew discovered more vampire vixens resting behind another wine vat. They dragged the corpses out of the old resort and flung them under the solar rays. The undead beauties withered into ashes. Grif couldn't believe things so beautiful could be so deadly and remarked, "All those ladies are so fit, so fine. I'd guess the Count has his choice of prey between foreigners vacationing in nearby shores and the Big Easy to the north."

Chuck Shotzski nodded before eyeing his watch. "It's almost 1700 hours and we've searched the entire hacienda."

Bones nervously squeezed his hands. "I know that walking corpse. I bet he's holed up like a rat where no man can touch him."

Chuck spit at the ground. "Yeah but that would take days to tear through every room, attic and hidden door." He hit one of the front porch's pillars and leaned on a wicker chair, shaped like a throne. "Crap, that's time we do not have."

Thor graveled, "We'd be better off burning this place down."

Shotzski pursed his lips. "The fiend would only escape. It is too close to dusk before a fire could overtake this gigantic structure. Besides, your men's leave is almost up. This is our last chance to give them hellions a good fight."

A large crew cab pickup came to an abrupt halt. Mrs. Raven said, "Wakey-wakey Stevie! It is just shy of 5:00 p.m."

"Oh, Okay, thanks," He said with a slight lisp, not recalling how he got into her truck. He stumbled into his condominium and quickly grabbed a few necessities before turning off the lights. Minutes later, he exited through his back-patio's gate and headed downtown a few blocks away. The special forces warrior sat down on a sidewalk bench kitty-corner to Snowbirds' office. He knew of Shotzski's fellow reporter, a timid guy by the name of Jack Grumblier. Hans had to somehow convince Jack to help him. He decided to scope out the place instead of barging in.

Susi Ann Chang winked at her colleague. "Hey Jack, how does a few Café Lattes grab you?"

"That sounds great."

"I buy you fly?"

Jack Grumblicr gladly accepted her money and headed for Ma and Pa's Café. Hans began to tail Jack. He pulled out his cell phone and dialed one of his faithful fishing buddies.

"Hello?"

"Sister Tré. This is Steve."

"I heard you're back in town. How are you?"

"Fine," he replied. "I don't mean to be short but could you meet me down at the sheriff's office ASAP?"

"What's this about?"

"Jaws and the guys headed for Gemela. I know you and some pastor have been helping them out."

Sister Tréson replied, "Are you referring to Pastor Reggie?"

"Yeah, that's him. I really believe the guys could use some back-up," Steve said. "However, I need to get some help from a few operators I know but without the sheriff onboard, it's probably a no go. Sheriff Lombardi doesn't know me very well but seems to respect you and a fellow by the name of Jack Grumblier."

"The sheriff better because I know too much of his dirty laundry." Sister Tré giggled, "That Jack, well, he always rats out Shotzski, so Sheriff Lombardi loves the prissy lad."

Staff Sergeant Hansen chuckled, "So are you in?"

"I'm in. What about transportation, coordinates, and gear?"

Her grasp of mission readiness surprised the Green Beret. "Oh yeah, weren't you in the Coast Guard?"

"You betcha."

"You still got your rotors?"

"One never gets rid of a helicopter after obtaining it so inexpensively." Sister Tréson added, "God bless Coasties who caught the drug runners."

Hans was relieved. "Great! I got coordinates, some garlic wreaths, and several silver bullets left over from the guy's mission preps. We can hash out the rest at the sheriff's office."

"See ya soon."

"Rog." He hung up and quickly called his Army National Guard neighbor, Major Goodew. He flipped his cell phone shut and spotted Sheriff Lombardi's favorite Shotzski informant struggling to open the door with two cups of java in his hands. Grumblier seemed to skip out of Ma and Pa's Café. He was in the white zone, not paying attention to his surroundings. A tall, burly figure put his arms around his shoulder. "Thanks for the coffee, Jack."

The Judy-Judy columnist said shaking, "Who are you?"

"Let's just say I believe you, Sister Tréson, and my neighbor, Major Goodew, can add some persuasion for some needed backup." Hans said forcefully, "Now, if you value your well-being, then let's walk peacefully toward the sheriff's office."

The Special Warfare Combatant Craft Crewmen (SWCC) operator didn't see the legless vombie crawl underneath him until he felt the tug on his boot. Chief Jaworsk shrieked, "Sweet Jesus!"

Dracula hissed as his piercing red eyes suddenly shot open.

Jaws then bashed the vombie's skull with his rifle stock.

The Count groggily peered toward the silver dollar-sized peephole. The sun was close to setting. After several minutes, his body levitated from a horizontal to vertical position. He yawned and grabbed a shiny apple from the dumbwaiter, eating it in three bites.

Petty Officer Ross snuck up on a vombie. It turned, sensing a human. The frogman swiped the abomination's head off. He whispered into his headset, "I just whacked one too."

Chief Jaworsk replied in a hushed tone, "Whack 'em all."

The vampire lord paused inside his door less, attic chamber, fortified with cement and steel, and within seconds, bat wings were flapping. The large chiroptera flew toward the fireplace, accelerated up the chimney, and darted for an apple tree.

The Frankenstein Monster was sleeping in the maintenance barn. He lay suspended on a reinforced hammock, a dozen feet above ground. His huge carcass was camouflaged under a pile of mosquito nets. The Count said in a rhythmic tone, "Awaken my friend."

The hulking figure stirred. The vampire lord handed his servant an apple and the creature began to munch on the fruit.

Vlad twirled his hands and said, "Armed men are here to do us harm. We must annihilate them."

The giant stood over the loft's edge and said, "Yes master."

The Count & Creature

The titan yawned, stretched and jumped ten feet to the floor. The ground quaked from the impact of his ginormous weight.

The full moon beamed. Rathbone instinctively tore off his shoes before the painful change set in.

Ross noticed a look of anguish on the Scot's face. The SEAL said, "You okay, Nige?"

No response came, except for painful grunts. Bones tried to calm down, taking in deep breaths to slow down the process.

Raven and Ross didn't understand until Nigel began to appear less human as joints popped and his body convulsed. They slowly backed away. He grew more muscular and nails turned into claws. Halfway through his transformation, he garbled, "Get away, now!"

The frogman jumped back in fright and said in a low voice, "Rathbone, remember to attack the monster or the Count."

"I will," Bones' reply switched from his normal voice to a creepy growl, "t-tryyy!" Both operators quickly disappeared into a grove of citrus trees. A thick body of fur began to cover his skin. An under bite and four sharp canines replaced his teeth. The wolfman crouched down, ready to prowl. It howled at the moon, "Awgh, awgh," sniffing the early evening air.

Dracula scowled, hearing that all too familiar howl.

Gunners Mate Odin kept his scope on the target, whispering into his mouthpiece, "I got Franki at the entrance of the barn."

Senior Chief Joe Samson swung the muzzle of his weapon toward the large opening. He said under his breath, "Remember what Bones and Thor said, leave the big guy alone."

"Yeah but we got him in our sights. Let's put the creature out of his misery."

"Only if he gets closer."

"We need to distract the giant, otherwise, he'll help Drac."

"Monsters and vampires," Joe groused, "it pisses me off."

Gunner Odin sighed. "It's been a hellacious fight."

Senior Chief Samson spat, "It's going to get uglier."

The goliath pivoted, walking toward their general direction. The gunner nodded at his SWCC mate. The pair clicked their switches from safety to semi-automatic. The metallic clicking got the creature's attention. The boat guys quietly stepped back into the shadows. The giant looked around for a moment. Not noticing anything unusual, he picked a piece of fruit from a tree.

They slowly took a few steps. The Frankenstein Monster leaned against the barn, enjoying his juicy meal. The duo nodded at each other. Both Samson and Odin pulled their triggers. The M-4 rifles burst open with well hit rounds into the giant's upper torso.

The rounds stung. The brute grunted, "Aah," as the fruit fell out of his hands. He tumbled behind a 1945 Farmall B tractor for cover.

The men moved forward. Samson ordered, "Let's keep it continuous, sawing away at his legs and arms." Three-round bursts of well-aimed shots hit the creature's massive calves and forearms. He growled, crouching behind solid objects, but still on his feet.

"I don't know?" Odin gasped. "Maybe Thor was right."

Joe ordered, "Target his softer areas." They flanked, hitting the brute with twelve more rounds to the sides and belly.

The gunner fumed, "I don't think he has any weaknesses. His skin seems to be like triple Kevlar.

Senior Samson hit the hulk with three perfect shots to the chest, barely piecing his skin. He scowled, "Hell. I am not even sure a 240 machine-gun would take him down?"

Gunners Mate Odin released another burst, hitting his lower neck. He graveled. “Look at those flesh wounds heal.”

“No shit,” Joe said mystified. “His body seems to regenerate in seconds.”

“Shoot and cover,” Odin said. “Let’s move east.”

Joe nodded. They heard metallic clicks as they began to shoot and move. The men quickly switched out their magazines and continued to sweep the large barn.

The creature surprised them, jumping from a loft. The two SWCC operators pivoted and fired at their target, but the hulking figure became more enraged, rushing forward.

The gunner calmly moved back and hit his objective. The titan picked up a loose twelve-foot long six by six-inch plank and batted Odin. The cracking of ribs could be heard as his back hit the barn’s wall. His frame hung impaled to a rusty tool rack several feet above the ground.

Senior Chief Samson shouted, "No!”

The young man coughed up blood and painfully chuckled, "Joe, I'd always mock foxhole believers." Senior Chief Samson held up his teammate’s body to lessen the pain. Odin looked up and prayed out loud, "Please forgive me for all the wrong I've done, dear Lord." His head slumped down and he exhaled his last breath.

The giant shook his head despondently and walked away.

Rage consumed the SWCC operator at the man-made abomination that just took his Sailor's life. Joe twirled around and raised his weapon. Frankenstein’s creation grunted, feeling the well-aimed shots pellet his back. The titan turned, provoked once again. Joe’s rifle blazed more lead into the brute after he quickly replaced another mag. The goliath bent down with many rounds stuck an eighth of an inch into his massive body. He flexed his muscles and the bullets popped from his skin.

Samson dove for Odin's downed weapon and yelled, "Die you bastard," spraying the thing with more volleys. The bullets only annoyed the monster. He roared and tipped the old red tractor over. It crushed the SWCC operator before he could get off a burst of rounds to the hulk’s face.

61 - MONSTER MELEE

Gemela

The wolfman fought its libidinous desire to hunt for a mortal. It jumped to the barn's roof. The beast's snout flared as it entered through the ventilator shaft. It smelled the stench of the undead.

The vampire lord quickly transformed. The werewolf leaped at the dodging bat, lacerating a forelimb. The creatures of the night plummeted to the barn's floor.

The large vampire bat transformed back into Dracula. He winced, setting his left shoulder into its socket.

The lycan shook off the dizziness and charged his nemesis. Both of the creatures of the night clawed each other. Their blood sprayed across the barn's interior.

Chief Warrant Officer Raven and Petty Officer Ross swept the barn's side door. The helicopter pilot gasped at the scene before them, "Damn… That's one hell of a battle."

The frogman said, "It's more like a monstrous melee."

The vampire and werewolf tore, bit and darted from the floor to the wall and into the rafters. Chunks of their immortal flesh flung into the air. They landed on separate lofts, glaring at each other, too exhausted from their wounds to make a move.

Dracula opened up his cape, revealing his silver-headed scepter. The Wolfman snarled, sensing the metal's purity even from eighty feet away. It slowly squatted back. They clashed in mid-air, cutting each other to shreds as they hit the floor.

The Count swiped his nemesis off its feet and vaulted to a loft. The beast rolled on its hind legs, springing upward.

The living dead hissed, feeling the deep sting of the razor-like claws into his back. He grasped inside his cloak and juked around, trying to avoid the beast's ferocious swipes.

Canines snapped at his wrist. Dracula flicked the end of the silver scepter into its fury jaw. The werewolf let out a wail before crashing on its back twelve feet below.

The lycanthrope was too much for the master vampire. He peered forty-foot above at the vaulted ceiling and soared toward a ventilator shaft. A claw dug into his calf before he could make his escape, pulling Vlad down.

Both creatures of the night crashed on top of a stunned Frankenstein Monster. The werewolf held Dracula's hand from bludgeoning him to death as they wrestled on the ground.

The titan instinctively pummeled the pair. One of the blows knocked the scepter from his master's grasp. Dust flew from the dirt floor and the lycan rolled away to the stable area.

The hulking figure roared, looking for his nemesis through the dusty haze. He thought he spotted a dark head of fur standout above a pile of seedling bags. Frustrated, he rushed his objective, fists high - ready to smash.

The beast jumped into the air, flipped around and slashed the creature's rib cage. It lunged for the giant, honing in on his jugular.

The monster of Frankenstein grabbed the werewolf's arms and slammed it to the ground. He grasped the furry throat and flung the beast underhanded. It crashed upward through the barn's tattered roof and landed into an orange tree.

Dracula fumed with hatred, ignoring pain and weakness. He realigned his broken frame, bones and joints popping back into place.

The beast weakly pulled its impaled flesh from two tree limbs and fell to the ground.

The vampire lord grabbed his silver-headed dragon cane by its wooden shaft, ready to hunt down his nemesis. The lycan was nowhere in sight. Commander Lawlur jumped the Count as he begun to glide in the air. They both fell to the floor and Dracula feasted on Frodo's quivering body.

The Frankenstein Monster spotted Rav nearby. He grabbed a rusty, long scythe and was ready to dice the pilot, as if he were the Grim Reaper.

The wolfman sprung over a hundred feet back into the barn. Its paws kicked into the monster's chest. It sent the titan crashing through timber.

Raven sprinkled gasoline in a circle around the undead prince and Ross squirted him with holy water as he dove on top of Chuck, Grif, Jaws, and Thor. The vampire shrieked in pain.

The lycan stirred from the ground and bayed at the moon. It sniffed around and crouched low, heading toward Dracula. Vlad snapped his head to the side, snarling at his lethal adversary.

The pilot and Frogman quickly spiked three crosses laced with silver to repel the wolfman and trap the Carpathian. The beast yelped and backed off.

Dracula shielded his face from the holy symbols. The distractions gave Chuck time to grab a piece of wood.

The top layer of silt flew as the metal clanged into the clay. The pair lit the gas circle and threw crushed garlic on the Count.

Shotzski the Shadow Hunter stabbed the vampire lord with a stake. He missed his undead heart by centimeters. The dark prince gasped and removed the wooden piece. He reeled back in pain, trying to shake off the garlic powder.

All the men pounced on him, wrestling him down. He crouched down, and, then, thrust up, throwing the squad in different directions. He bore his fangs. "Garlic," Vlad coughed, "your choice of weaponry is most impressive. You still dare to challenge me, one who has commanded armies?"

JT Rockford shook his fist. "We do and take these stakes in Holy matrimony to impale your evil soul back to hell."

Chuck patted Thor's shoulder. "Take it easy with the charm. This ain't over yet."

The Count jeered, "My lord Lucifer's greatest trick was to convince others that he does not exist. Now you shall see just a shadow of his vast powers."

Jaws flung more garlic on Dracula and said, "You talk too much." The nosferatu ingested some of it and gagged, blindly circling around like a wounded animal.

The Frankenstein Monster stirred underneath the broken timber. He benched a large cross-section of a wooden frame to his right.

The Wolfan heard the creature's movements. It quietly shifted to an open area for the best lane of attack. It let out a low growl and leaped for its target as the giant stood up.

The monster caught the sudden movement from the corner of his eye. He thrust his left arm out just in time to grab the werewolf by the neck. The hulk's right arm simultaneously clenched the beast's left forearm. He immediately side-slammed his nemesis into the ground before it could swipe him with its sharp claws.

The wolfman whimpered from the heavy impact before passing out. The Frankenstein Monster kicked the beast in the ribs. He saw no movement and heard no animalistic sounds. Satisfied, he turned to defend his master.

Moments later, a deep howl echoed throughout the night's air. The werewolf ran on all fours and speared its right shoulder into the giant's mid-section.

This time, the brute let out a painful moan and collapsed to his knees. The lycanthrope locked arms with the kneeling monster. Frankenstein's Creation squatted upward. His massive hands began to pulverize the wolfan's wrists.

The men heard the beast's gurgles and brute's grunts nearby, but they ignored being drawn into the monstrous melee.

The wolfman head-butted the creature. The blow stunned the giant for a few milliseconds, allowing it to break loose from the juggernaut's overpowering grip.

The monster overpowered the beast by at least fifteen times over. However, the lycan's speed and agility kept the behemoth on his toes. It circled the creature several times, swiping at him and throwing the hulk off balance. The werewolf finally jumped to the side and disappeared into the barn's rafters.

The monster of Frankenstein grew dizzy as he pivoted to one side and scanned the upper darkness for any movement. Seconds later, the wolfman dove for the brute. The heavy blow to the chest, sent the titan crashing hard on his back.

The creature laid stunned on the dirt floor for a few seconds before rolling on all fours, gasping for air. The lycanthrope leaped over the monster, clawing at his left torso. The behemoth grunted annoyingly at the mild swipe.

The wolfan jumped the brute a second time. The hulking figure surprised it by quickly jumping to his feet and side-stepping to his left. He immediately caught the lycan in mid-air.

The Frankenstein Monster spun his nemesis around. He momentarily held the furry beast upside down and crashed backward. The impact was felt by the men over sixty feet away.

The monstrous duo rolled into the kindling fire that had spread to a few wooden planks stashed to the side of the barn. The Wolfan yelped as its fur singed. It rushed outside, rolling in the dew. The giant smiled briefly, seeing that furry little fiend, flee in discomfort. His burning skin began to quickly repair itself to a yellowish-green tone.

Grif shot two wooden arrows into the living dead, piercing a lung and abdomen. Dracula yanked out the arrows, moaned and shielded his face with his cape, "Fools, you'll soon be my slaves." He latched onto the living dead's leg before the vampire could spring into the rafters and escape. The nosferatu grabbed Griffin by the neck. He barely sunk his teeth into his skin when part of the roof cracked. It crashed on top of them and the Frankenstein Monster. The timber crushed the SWCC operator's lower extremities. Grif tried to crawl under the heavy frame but passed out.

The monster arose and instinctively punched the Count Dracula back into the tipped tractor. He confused his master for an intruder in the dusty haze.

Lightning crackled and thunder boomed. Rain poured down through parts of the roofless barn and slowly quenched the fire.

The undead prince was enraged. He flipped over Frankenstein's Creation and slashed his neck with steel like claws. He suddenly raised his palms in front of the monster to calm him down. The giant growled. "No, I didn't mean to do that my friend," petitioned the vampire lord.

The wounds from Frankenstein's nightmare disappeared but the hypnotic spell had been broken. He lifted Count Dracula up to eye level, staring at him angrily. The vampire felt his torso and windpipe being crushed by the huge hands. The monster snapped the living dead's arm. He then passed his former master into the rushing wolfman as if he were a javelin. Their skulls exploded into each other.

The werewolf was the first to recover. Its bestial instincts slowly guided it outside. It could faintly hear the sound of rotors in the distance.

Dracula arose broken. He wheezed, scowled and uttered a command in Latin. He ended his words by pointing toward the giant. His jet-black hair turned white at the temples and widow's peak. Hands stiffly began to crawl out of the ground. Thirty-three vombies and sixty-six vampire brides arose from graves encircling the barn.

Many of the vamps appeared undernourished with crackled skin. Both the vombies and vampires swarmed the Frankenstein Monster. The creature now was fighting foes that rivaled his strength. He wasn't aware of the statistics nor did he care.

The more nourished female vampires had speed and agility but they all had numbers and fangs to tear at the monster's almost impregnable flesh. Many minutes passed with a gruesome battle ensuing. The goliath smashed or tore off all of the vombies' heads, but the decimation of the day walkers had provided the vamps valuable time to attack him. He knew enough to pierce the undead with scattered pieces of barn wood.

62 - DEMISE OF THE UNDEAD

Late evening, December 15, 2005

Sister Tréson touched down her helicopter on Gemela next to Raven's. She made a silent prayer it wasn't too late. The retired Coast Guard pilot then shouted at the passengers, "This is it. Take no prisoners."

Sheriff Lombardi and six National Guardsmen exited. Hans then pushed Jack Grumblier out of the metal bird.

Sister Tréson smacked Maria across the face. "That was from Lise." Doc sat there unfazed. "Get up!" the pilot barked. She lost her patience and slapped harder.

The physician stared blankly ahead. The spell she was under had gotten stronger the closer she was to the master vampire.

"What's with you?" the stocky nun said, splashing a dash of Holy Water across her face.

Dr. Wilder hissed.

"Snap out of it, woman!" She then whisked her with more of the holy substance.

"Stop that… it stings.

"About time you wake up," she griped. "Here's the gun loaded with silver bullets."

"Huh?" Maria said, sluggishly grabbing the weapon.

"Stop goofing off, Doc," Sister Tré said, "We got vampires to destroy!"

The children of the night just kept coming. They eventually began to shred parts of the creature's skin before he destroyed half of them. By the time the vamps realized they could not take the titan force on force, he had destroyed a dozen more of them.

The Frankenstein Monster noticed his wounds were so numerous that he wasn't healing as rapidly. He even began to grow tired. He was furious at Dracula's betrayal and determined to destroy the last of his brides. He crouched low, eyed one of the most defiant vamps and roared defiantly.

The vampiress let out a high-pitched hiss and, then, gestured with two hand signals to her remaining kind.

The goliath staked many more circling him when a handful of the vamps began to transform into a pair of large bats and over a hundred rats. The crawling rodents and pair of bats encompassed his entire body. Their razor-sharp teeth fixated around his eyes, ears and mouth. The giant let out an unnerving wail. He kept his eyes closed and tried to protect them with his hands. All he could do was chomp at anything that got close to his mouth. He blindly tried to shake them off but could not.

The remaining she-vamps grabbed the brute's massive torso and extremities. They were able to slowly lift him into the atmosphere. He continuously thrashed about during the ascent and the rats eventually began to lose traction. He was finally able to free his hands and open his eyes. He swept the vixens into a bear hug. They plummeted toward the earth four-hundred meters below. The vampires tried to use their powers to slow down the rapid descent but the giant's mighty grip was too overpowering.

During the downward spiral, Frankenstein's Creation smiled, embracing the fact this may be the final moments of his lonely and tortured existence.

Panic stricken and unable to concentrate with their upper extremities bound, Dracula's brides were barely able to lessen the fall from reaching the speed of terminal velocity. The bundle hit the tattered barn's roof. The undead took the brunt but the giant's mass was the main cause for the ground to quake. Two of the vampires were impaled by broken lumber as they impacted the ground.

It had been a long time since the monster felt such searing pain. Parts of his extremities seemed to be out of joint and bones fractured. He lay motionless but his incredible immune system and antipathy for these unholy creatures overcame his sapped strength. The macabre form painfully stood up for one last fray.

The flattened she-vamps slowly rose, circling him. The brute was barely able to quash their depleted forms. His body needed more time recover. The scattered vampire rats were too weak from the fall to completely merge back into their vampire shells.

A pair of vampire bats swooped down. Two shapely vixens suddenly emerged. They were magnificent looking until they snapped at the giant.

He recognized the raven-haired beauty as the lead female vamp. He held a small piece of timber hidden behind his enormous frame. The creature desired to be left alone but knew he had to take care of the remaining duo.

Both she-vamps moved slower from the long battle and being undernourished.

The behemoth noticed their sluggishness. One of the things he learned from the craftiest of their kind was to never underestimate them. He realized he had the advantage but kept a stoic poker face. Though exhausted and injured, he hunched to one side for added affect. He looked past the corner of the raven-haired vampire's back shoulder and scowled as if more were about to attack him.

The lead vampire bought the bait and slightly turned her head. She hissed just as the creature thrust the pointy wooden piece in an under-handed motion into her chest. Blood oozed out before her body turned into a skeleton and then dust.

The last of the she-vamps froze for several moments. He smirked at her. She snarled, revealing her long fangs. Enraged, the vampire then attacked the titan with outstretched arms.

He moved to the side, knowing the last vamp to attack him would be anti-climactic. The goliath accidentally tripped over a wooden cart. His strong leg caused the old farm wagon to flip in the air. He tackled the female vampire before the heavy cart pinned them down into the bowels of the pit.

Lightning instantly hit a nearby orange tree and caused the roots to spring up. The soil loosened as the tree trunk was jolted out of place. Several tons of heavy, wet soil covered the vampiress and exhausted Frankenstein Monster into a deep muddy grave.

Dracula tried to locate his treasured scepter trapped under the smoldering rubble. It was nowhere to be found.

The wolfman barely smelled a familiar scent in the rain. He spun around, facing the northern bank.

Lawlur began forming fangs with yellowish-red eyes.

The Count was down but not out. He needed nourishment after expelling so much energy. His pride craved revenge instead of safely retreating to recover. He snuck up on Thor's back.

A hissing Lawlur crept toward Shotzski. Rav's ribs were bruised and his skin singed, but he had plenty in him to aim a silver-tipped wooden arrow at Lawdog. He whispered, "Sorry bud."

Jaws plunged a piece of the Count's broken cane into the back of his cape. It pierced the Carpathian's heart before he could pounce on Thor. The vampire lord thrashed about, trying in vain to remove the wood from his left shoulder blade.

Rav's arrow penetrated Elsworth's left lung. He shot a second into his heart. Chuck's mouth opened in terror, realizing the SEAL almost bit him. Lawlur let out a weak hiss. Blood trickled from his mouth and chest, saturating his field cammies.

Unable to dislodge the broken wooden cane from his back, Dracula fell to his knees in agony. Ross pumped his chest cavity and face with Holy Water. Parts of his undead skin began to burn.

Sister Tréson walked up, puffing her Honduran stogie. She threw a garlic stringed necklace over Vlad's neck and rebuked him, "You shouldn't have switched to the dark side. You guys seem like you're winning with your power and riches, but you will lose."

Gasping, Dracula weakly demanded, "How could you, mere mortals rival me?"

JT Rockford stated, "Faith, sweat, blood and tears." He glared at the master vampire. "Your arrogance helped."

Chuck Shotzski said, "Less conversation kid. Finish him off!" Too weak to do anything else, the vampire lord snarled at him.

Thor hammered the shovel's metal backing into the wooden cane as if he were the Norse god himself. The ancient gopher wood plunged all the way through the vampire's heart.

Blood splattered outward as the end of the wooden cane protruded through the living dead's upper left chest. The crimson color soaked his white-collared shirt. Blood oozed from his mouth and he collapsed to the ground. The vampire lord weakly uttered in Latin, "Daciana come for me!"

The group of mortals looked at each other perplexed.

Dracula's rattled frame lay sprawled on the ground destroyed. The rest of his thick hair turned white while his eyes and skin began to decay. His corpse disintegrated into a mixture of bone and mummified flesh.

Lawlur groaned, the fangs retracted and his eyes returned to their baby blues. The SEAL was a vampire no more but the arrows had done their damage. Another friend lay dead.

The vampire lord's soul descended past the wailing shrieks in Hell. Count Dracula's remaining victims ceased to be under his spell, of which there were only two alive on Gemela, Petty Officer Griffin and Dr. Wilder.

Grif awoke, moaning in pain. His left leg was broken and the smoldering timber kept him pinned down. He screamed terribly as the embers burnt into his thighs.

Hansen and Grumblier smelled smoke. They headed toward the haze. The Green Beret recognized the face and immediately lifted up the burning frame. "Grab Grif!" Hans' neck ached from the heavy weight and his lingering concussion began to make him feel dizzy. He groaned as burning embers melted into his palms. Jack grunted pulling Grif by the armpits.

Half-way between the northern bank and hacienda, the wolfman was lurking closer to Maria. She felt its bestial presence. She turned around and paused. The werewolf pored over her in confusion from forty feet away.

Ricardo Lombardi blasted the back of the werewolf with his shotgun. The lycanthrope fell to the ground and, then, slowly rose. It pivoted around, ready to strike down the sheriff.

Dr. Wilder yelled, “It’s me you want!” Tears fell from her cheeks. "I love you Nigel Rathbone."

The lycan glanced back and forth. It seemed funereal and whimpered. The beast soared for its prey.

Maria triple-tapped the wolfman in its left chest. The lycanthropic heart beat slowed. The hoary figure collapsed to the earth, falling motionless within inches of her.

The sheriff witnessed the wolfman molt back into Rathbone. "Oh, him again," he said nonchalantly. He covered his mouth with his hand, realizing how cold his answer had been. Tears streamed down her cheeks. He said, "Please forgive me, Doc.”

Sister Tréson wiped a tear from Maria’s face. At the same time, the nun grabbed the revolver from her trembling hand.

Rico hugged her. He then compassionately looked her in the eyes and said, "Maria. You had to do what you had to do."

Dr. Wilder collapsed to her knees and cried as she cradled Nige's face in her bosom.

The lawman gently said, "Doc. We still need your help."

Maria softly replied, "Give me a moment." She pulled out her handwritten copy of Francesca’s verse that Nigel had recited to her. She began to tearfully read it out loud, *“You traversed the earth in rocky places. May you find God's grace and rest in peace until Judgment Day.”*

Sister Tréson squeezed Maria’s shoulder to comfort her. After a few moments, Doc gently placed Nigel’s head on the ground.

63 - THE UGLY TRUTH

December 16, 2005

It was just past midnight after the remaining group huddled together. Reality was beginning to set in and it was ugly. Chief Warrant Officer Michael 5 (CWO5) Raven whistled to muster most of the survivors, "This is the part no one likes to do. Split up and sweep the area for the fallen and hopefully some survivors!"

The group immediately dispersed and began the search. Rav, Ross and Thor headed toward the barn's interior.

The SEAL cursed, discovering Odin's lifeless body impaled to the wall. Ross' teammates helped him gently lay Petty Officer Odin's remains on the ground.

From the corner of Mike's eyes, he saw a pair of boots underneath the tipped over tractor. "Oh, dear Lord," he whispered, scrambling around the other side. He immediately spotted Samson pinned under the tractor and groaned, "Fin. Why did you have to get yourself killed, ya jackass?"

Eyelids suddenly fluttered. CWO5 Raven knelt to his knees and admonished his friend by saying, "Hercules. You've bench pressed so damn much that you couldn't escape."

Senior Chief Joe Samson struggled to take in shallow, painful breaths. He barely had enough energy to mouth, *Get this tractor off me, dumbass.*

Rav realized the front end of the tractor landed on two worn-out tires, pinning Samson down and crushing his upper chest. "You're one lucky Sailor."

Thor and Ross came running back with Dr. Wilder and several men. They barely were able to nudge the small tractor off Fin and carefully pull him to safety.

Maria opened her first aid kit. "His lungs seems to be okay but the upper chest is severely bruised." She issued instructions to the Army National Guard Medics and said, "Put him on the stretcher and let's get him to the helicopter."

One of the medics said to the senior chief, "Stay calm and don't talk." Fin barely nodded as the medics began to stabilize him.

Jack Grumblier yelled from the darkness as Dr. Wilder and the group passed by with Senior Chief Samson on the stretcher, "I've got two men down. They need medical attention!"

The doctor forcefully replied, "We'll be back!"

A few minutes later, the doctor and an army medic ran up to Jack Grumblier with two other National Guardsmen carrying stretchers.

Raven, Ross and Thor returned after securing Fin inside the helicopter.

Dr. Wilder was seething when she recognized her lost patient. "Staff Sergeant Hansen, you're as bull-headed as they come," she hissed with her hands on her hips.

The clod didn't hear Maria. Thor laughed at his unconscious friend and then looked at Doc, "Hans may be stubborn but he means well."

Dr. Wilder scowled before she realized Grif had a compound fracture on his left leg. She spotted CWO5 Raven nearby and yelled, "I need more supplies. Grab me a first aid kit from your helicopter!"

Rav quickly returned, handing the physician his medical bag. Maria and one of the Army National Guard medics began tending to Han's and Grif's 2nd degree burns. They also stuck them with IVs. Raven remembered Van Helsing's instructions and immediately poured Holy Water over the vampire bites on Griffin's neck.

Grif grunted as the Holy substance purified the vampire marks. He murmured, "I always thought my father was full of beans when he told me my great-great uncle, Dr. Jack Griffin, was the Invisible Man."

He shook his head hearing another strange tale and calmly said, "You're going to be alright buddy. Just try and relax."

Petty Officer Griffin weakly smiled at his Task Unit Commander and passed out.

Michael was reminded again that his grandmother Raven's eastern European wives' tales were more than met the eye. The helo pilot shuddered as he thought; *Not just seeing it first-hand but encountering what is not supposed to be.*

The medic mustered help from Thor, Ross and three of his fellow National Guardsmen to help secure Grif and Hans on stretchers. They carefully loaded the pair into Rav's helicopter along with Senior Chief Samson.

The chief warrant officer was healthy enough to fly the wounded and Dr. Wilder to Le Grande. Mike quietly prayed as he lifted the helicopter into the air, "Almighty God, please help the rest of us get to safety and no more monsters. Amen."

Sheriff Lombardi Jr. was tired of looking for the scab. The reporter said surprised, “Dick?” Rico turned around and Shotz asked, “What’s with all the people?”

The lawman sighed. “Seventy percent of my men are either hospitalized or dead. So, I enlisted the help of Chaplain Goodew with a handful of his National Guard troops."

“Good call sheriff,” Chuck said with a shrug.

Jack Grumblier waved his finger and exclaimed, “Rico. It was actually Staff Sergeant Hansen’s suggestion.”

Shotzski gave Lombardi an ‘Aha look.’

“Just stifle, Chuck!”

"Zany or not, your lawmen better stake any people who were killed by Dracula and his vampire brides.”

“How the hell are we supposed to do that in Le Grande?”

“Incognito.” The reporter sighed. “Think outside the box for once.”

"You know Shotz, you're the best golfing buddy a friend could ever have but when you speak, you lose all credibility.”

Chuck stood up in righteous anger. "Sheriff. We lost the majority of Thor’s comrades and many of yours. Plus, a few civilians were killed due to these ghastly creatures.”

Ricardo’s face began to turn purple.

The Shadow Hunter pointed at the lawman. “We were the only ones who were able to defeat these dreadful things.”

“You’re lucky I don't write you up for murder."

The reporter growled, “Don't let people’s deaths be in vain! Besides, how can you kill the dead, isn't that an oxymoron?"

Lombardi barked, "Shotzski, don't push it!"

"You encountered a werewolf, a strongman almost nine-feet tall that was nearly indestructible and several vampires." Shotz roared, "Come on!”

Rico’s veins from his neck and forehead bulged.

“Just like your old man, you have the truth staring in your face. So, you do the sensible thing and not the right one.” He pointed toward Count Dracula’s corpse. “Why don’t you remove that broken wooden cane?"

Sheriff Lombardi began trotting over to the vampire lord’s emaciated corpse.

“Rico,” Chuck griped, “what in the dickens are you doing?”

Thor ran toward the shouting pair. He made a knife cutting motion with one hand across his neck to settle down and calmly insisted, "Shotz, be nice to the sheriff."

The reporter put his palms in front of Rico and admitted, "Okay, I got a bit reckless with my words. Please, please… Just keep the stake in this one and the silver in Rathbone."

Rico Lombardi breathed in and out to calm himself down.

He eyed his friend and gently patted the lawman's shoulder. "D, I am getting too old for this crap."

Sheriff Ricardo Lombardi yelled, pointing at the bodies of Count Dracula and Nigel Rathbone, "Medics, body bag these two and zip-tie the bags securely. No one touches them except for the coroner and only under my direct orders."

The medics froze.

The sheriff barked, "Just do it!"

Shotzski chuckled, "What's that dangling?" He gestured to the cross necklace around Rico's thick neck.

He rolled his eyes and replied, "You see… I was going to Mass when Pastor Reggie told me about your exploits."

The portly nun looked at Rico like she had slapped him across the face.

"Well…"

Tré scolded him by saying, "I should whack your buns Sheriff Lombardi. Reggie did call to warn you, after I left our group's weekly Bible study, not Mass! I know you haven't been to our Parrish. The only times I've seen you, was at Christmas and Easter."

"But…"

The nun continued, "Most importantly, your wife, bless her soul, is a regular and you should have the decency to go with her."

"Yes ma'am."

Sister Tré pointed toward the Heavens and then eyed-balled the lawman. "He's watching you, sonny."

Rico nodded meekly and Shotz roared with laughter.

64 - COVER-UP

Early morning December 16, 2005

Lombardi jabbed his index finger into Shotzski's chest. "If you print any of this in Snowbirds, you'll be sorry!"

"Your family has a tradition of covering up the truth."

"No kidding Sherlock… The real story would make Le Grande a ghost town."

He gritted his teeth. "Of course, your Pops won't print it. To quote Dick Senior: *This would send the populace into a panic*."

Rico roared, "Nice to see you have some common sense."

"Veritas et Fortitudo!" The Snowbirds' reporter muttered under his breath, "But I will log it into my personal notes."

"What Chuck?"

"I didn't say one word, Junior."

"That's right," the lawman seethed, "sometimes I wish you never came to Le Grande."

Shotz smirked as he pointed toward the Count and Nigel. "Make sure you bury those two in unmarked graves. Stuff garlic in that vampire's mouth, cut off his head and burn his undead body without removing the stake."

"You know Chuck, Le Grande was a peaceful place until my dad's dysfunctional entourage, mostly you, began snooping around."

"That buried story from the 1960s says otherwise."

Captain Meling reported, "Sheriff, we've tended to the downed men. The area is clear."

The lawman stated, "Have your men body bag those marked with an OK on their chests."

"Yes sir!"

Lombardi added, "Captain, remember we already got your men's signature never to disclose any of this!"

Captain Meling nodded and Major Goodew said, "Sheriff, little of what we just saw, my men and I have no qualms keeping quiet." The guardsmen then walked off to finish their duties.

Chuck tipped his trademark straw golf hat.

Rico grumped, "You better stifle Shotz."

The Shadow Hunter bore a wry smile. "I didn't say a thing."

Chief Jaworsk finished leveling the decomposition pit and sighed. "Hopefully, this will be the last we see of the giant."

Petty Officer Ross exclaimed, "Oh yeah!" He picked up a large piece of rusted metal, resembling a cross. "This should work."

Jaws noticed Chuck and Thor walking up. “Thank God, for a moment, I thought we were all goners.”

Ross scratched his head. “Well, I am just glad that Drac didn't sick those vombies and vampire babes on us."

Shotzski groaned, rubbing his aching hips. "Young men, maybe he was too preoccupied with Franki and the wolfman?”

Thor said, “I’d theorize Dracula’s pride was his own downfall.”

Ross nodded. “The Count could've escaped a few times."

Chief Jaworsk limped over. “Sheriff Lombardi, I am supposed to retire in six months. A lot of my friends and your men are dead. If you need another deputy that will keep his mouth shut but knows what to look for - I’m your man.”

He felt relieved hearing that. “Chief, you would be gladly welcomed.” Rico Jr. added, “Just come on down and apply.”

Chief Jaworsk replied smartly, “Aye-aye sheriff!”

Ross pierced the metal icon over the creatures' muddy grave. Jack Grumblier let out a high-pitched scream after hearing the first metallic clang. Normally, that would have made people laugh but not under the present circumstances. They were relieved that was all it was, a piercing metallic sound and Jack’s screeching voice. Instead, the group hugged and mourned over their lost friends.

Captain Meling whispered something into Rico's ear. Sheriff Lombardi then stated, "Jack, Shotz and Thor, gather wood to make a fire. The rest of you pile those damn things on the funeral pyre before we light it up."

Shotzski replied, "You mean the undead."

The sheriff hissed, "Yes Chuck."

CWO5 Michael Raven landed his privately-owned bird down at Le Grande's helicopter port.

Nurse Lise Alegría came running out from the hospital to help the US Navy officer and physician with the wounded.

Maria quickly hugged her associate and explained, “Lise. Your beau is okay."

"Thank God!"

Michael said, "They should be back later this morning."

Doc shed a tear. "Too many good men are gone, including my Nige." Nurse Alegría gave her coworker a tender hug. Maria tearfully added, "For Nigel, it was the best."

CWO5 Raven paced the rooms to ensure his men were all stabilized. He caught Lise's attention in the hallway. "Not to be rude, but I got to refuel and help with the crew back at Gemela."

She smiled. "Do you need anything from us?"

He reluctantly said, “Probably not, just cuts and bruises.”

Her eyes grew wide. "That can lead to infections." He then winced several times as the nurse cleaned his wounds. After treating him, Lise forcefully said, "I know you need to go but those wounds will probably have to be looked at again."

"Roger that."

Nurse Alegría said in a cautious tone, "The antibiotics we gave you won't make you groggy but be careful!" She eyed the cabinet for a moment and grabbed a plastic bottle. She put two pills in a zip lock bag. "If you need to, take one of these. I gave you a second one, in case you lose one."

"What are they for?"

"Keep you awake."

Rav chuckled, "All of us have probably broke every SOP in the book dealing with this crap!"

"No kidding!" she said with a raised eyebrow. "It’s not every day, one battles monsters." He looked at her surprised. "Sir. That giant of a thing strolled past our group on the golf course when my sweetie asked me to marry him."

"Well, I'll be..."

"And Sister Tréson and Pastor Reggie stashed Holy Water here." She added, "That nun schooled us quick. She even provided us with some unique weaponry in case things turned south fast."

He chuckled, "You're tougher than you look. Gracias, Lise!"

The nurse nodded. "De nada."

As Raven neared his helo, someone tapped his shoulder. He turned around to see his boss carrying two cases of water.

"Get in the other seat!" ordered Colonel Perry Thomas. "My flight hours are up to date."

He wanted to protest but was too tired to argue. "Roger that sir." The helicopter pilot then asked Compound X's Commanding Officer, "How'd you know I was here?"

The Special Forces officer chuckled, "Your son was my eyes and I had your helo tagged."

Rav shook his head. “Damn surveillance guys!” He quickly showed the colonel the chart and GPS coordinates to Gemela. A few minutes later, Perry lifted the helo in the air and Rav nodded off.

After the bird departed, Dr. Wilder called Nurse Alegría into her office. She confessed, "I haven't been much of a friend lately."

"No need to apologize." Lise reminded Maria by saying, “You weren't your normal self.”

"Everything has been so blurry but that is no excuse."

"I have seen some of this crazy stuff too." The nurse smiled at her coworker. "And I know you went through much more, so don't give it a second thought."

Doc got teary eyed. "Well, I forgot to tell you something."

"What's that?"

She smiled. "Congrats on your engagement, Chic!”

Lise giggled. She was happy that one of her best friends had truly returned to the land of the living.

"Mike. Time to wake up!" yelled Colonel Thomas over the *thwump-thwop* of the chopper blades. Moments later, the Green Beret touched down the helo on Gemela. Both men made their way toward the living. The surviving operators were surprised to see their boss handing out water.

Shotzski grabbed a bottle from the short, muscular stranger. Both men did a double-take and pivoted around. "Shotz?" asked Colonel Thomas.

Chuck nodded and cocked his head before saying, "Perry?"

"Damn Skippy!"

"That's Colonel Thomas to you!" stated CWO5 Raven.

"Oh no!" protested Shotz. "I'm a civilian."

Colonel Thomas shook his head. "Still the sassy son of a..."

He cut him off saying, "Don't talk bad about your mama."

“Look here, dumbass.”

The reporter smirked. "Still the same foul-mouthed, glorified grunt."

Compound X's Commanding Officer shook his head. “You're one Army Ranger that never gave me any respect."

"Why should I?" Shotzski shrugged. "Did you forget who saved your hide?"

"Wait one. That was a combined effort." Perry momentarily smiled at Chuck and asked, "What's it been?"

"About thirty-four years."

The colonel graveled, “It seemed like yesterday.”

Raven gasped, "Shotz was the guy that saved you?"

"No… I was on a rescue mission to save his dumbass."

Chuck added, "And we were seconds from being goners."

The colonel nodded. "That damn shape-shifter almost had us." Shotz couldn't believe Perry said *shape-shifter* out loud, after their superiors had ordered them to shut their sucks.

CWO5 Raven shook his head. "A giant, werewolf, vampires and, now, a damn shape-shifter."

"It's not something I advertise," Perry stated looking at Shotz," but we saw what we saw."

"You did provide us time to destroy that imitator thing. So, thank you, sir."

Perry nodded. "Nice to see you're not as cocky as I remember you."

"May be a bit less." Shotzski grinned and put his palm to his hear. "But you still haven't mentioned that Vietnamese fellow."

"You, pompous little shit..."

"I got at least five inches on you. So, who is the twerp?"

"Screw you, Shotz!"

"Ah, the gratitude," Chuck sarcastically said as he limped toward Grumblier, "And such language from an officer!" Jack helped his aching coworker walk over to the large fire. Shotzski grinned. "You got here late Grumbles but you came. Thanks!"

"As I said, Hans forced me on this venture."

Chuck then said, "Thor. Your dad may think you're a kook sometimes but you're alright in my book."

"You're not so bad yourself, even if you're a bit of a loon."

Jack threw garlic on the fire. A legless zombie escaped the flames. He screamed as it crawled toward him. Shotz kicked the day walker in its temple and Rockford tossed it back into the bonfire. Grumblier fainted smelling the undead flesh burn to a crisp. Chuck broke his coworker's fall. A marker fell out of Jack's pocket. Shotz smirked and inked *Wimpy* on his forehead.

Sheriff Lombardi walked up chuckling, "That's cold."

"We've seen too much death. Some comic relief is needed."

He laughed, "Can't believe Jack was a cop."

"Sheriff," Shotz advised, "I really don't want to, but we should stick around past daylight and do another sweep." The lawman reluctantly nodded in agreement.

65 - REFLECTION

Kati said, "You grilled some delicious bratwurst, honey."

Chuck Shotzski took a sip of his unsweetened iced-tea before replying, "Thanks. Your potato salad, as always, scrumptious!"

"How's your audio log on Gemela?" He headed to the patio to clean the grill, pretending not to hear her. She said through the kitchen's screen, "Stop with your selective schnauzer hearing."

Shotz said under his breath, "Busted."

"Sweetie, you should begin your notes this instance."

"I've been clobbered covering the Super Bowl."

She crossed her arms. "That game's history."

He graveled, "Those refs gave the game away. Not the Steelers fault - great team. Just hate seeing such one-sided calls."

"You wrote a great Seahawks-Steelers article but stop stalling! Get started before March Madness begins." The reporter knew she was right. He had been delaying it for too long. Kati added, "Don't worry, hon, I got the dishes."

He disliked elaborating on recent memories where people he knew were killed, but the details were important, especially, in case others ever needed it. After three hours of journaling, Shotz turned off his computer and grabbed two waters. He walked into the family room and heard that familiar voice on Turner Classic Movies, "Hi. I'm Robert Osbourne and I will be your host for tonight." He handed his wife a bottle. "Gotta love TCM!"

Kati jumped from the sofa recliner. "You scared me!"

"Honestly, I didn't mean to."

She made a fist. "One of these days."

"Gonna get popcorn." When he returned, he saw Jimmy Stewart and Margaret Sullavan bickering. "What's on TCM, babe?"

"One of my favorites, *The Shop Around the Corner*."

He sat next to his wife. "Ah yes, great story and cast."

"Quiet and watch the film!"

The man of the house said shaking his head, "No respect!"

Mid-February 2006

The Shotzskis had just returned from a swim and then eaten a light supper. Kati said, "Appreciate you doing dishes."

"The least I could do for that wonderful Ahi tuna salad.

"Almost done with your audio journal?"

"This should be it," he said before kissing her. The reporter then grumped, "Several weeks of elaborating on Frankenstein's Creature and the undead. Enough with monsters!"

"I don't blame you, honey, but it needed to be done."

Moments later, Shotz grabbed the computer's microphone and said, "Item: Rathbone and Dracula were buried in two remote cemeteries under false tombstones." He chuckled, "My other golfing buddy, Deputy Ron, let me know that the entire department was ordered by Sheriff Lombardi to stake all the dead victims who mysteriously lost any blood in or outside of Le Grande. All the bodies were cremated and, then, mixed with crushed garlic."

Chuck sighed. "I was there when the sheriff began to recount the story to his dad. Of course, Ricardo Lombardi Sr. kicked Jack and I out. He did not want to discuss the facts with me. However, we quickly made amends and took our wives for a jaunt to fish and golf before the spring break rush began." Shotz squeezed an exercise gripper and continued. "Item: A morgue tech disregarded Sheriff Lombardi's orders and removed the silver bullet from Nigel Rathbone's chest. No one knew about it until after he was buried in an undisclosed grave. Oddly, it was my defunct newspaper colleague, Susi Ann Chang, who got the scoop. I guess she is not totally worthless? By that time, no one wanted to tamper with Bone's remains." He shook his head in disgust. "Oddly, of all the vampires, they did not burn the Count's body or cut off his head. At least, Doc got her wish and Sheriff Lombardi ensured that Rathbone was buried with wolfs bane. I later read in Van Helsing's book that wolfmen decay at a much slower rate, if the traces of silver are removed from their heart or bodies. Instead, such two-legged werewolves remain dormant unless exposed to moonlight."

An hour later, Kati hugged her husband and said in a sweet tone, "Hi honey. Do you want some wine?"

"Please babe." Shotzski continued speaking into the microphone, "Lise and Thor wed shortly after the fiasco on Gemela in December 2005. They are on a late honeymoon in Italy and we just found out Jerry Rockford is going to be a proud grandpa." Kati glowed, knowing she would be a surrogate grandma, holding an adorable baby in her arms. He continued. "Item: The mysterious deaths from Gemela and Le Grande were brushed aside. The authorities didn't have the stomach to handle the truth, so they deemed them as operational fatalities or accidental deaths. My editor, Rico Lombardi Senior, had no qualms printing such a cover-up."

The lady of the house entered the kitchen and opened a new bottle of wine. He heard the faint *pop* of the cork from the other end of the house. He exclaimed, "What a sweet sound indeed." She grabbed two wine glasses. Shotz playfully roared toward the hallway, "Now no surprises!"

She heard her husband's last words not as an admonition but as a challenge. She was light on her feet. Kati knew the fact she could sneak up on Chuck frustrated him to no end. This aversion, largely stemmed from his tour in Vietnam. Both were retired cops and knew the importance of stealth. It was ingrained in them to take every precaution to minimize being surprised. Even at restaurants, the couple good-naturedly bickered over which seats to take in order to cover their sixes.

She often thought about the times he had encountered the bizarre. His resilience amazed her. He got frightened like anyone but he adapted when most would have turned to jello. He fought the Vietcong, criminals and things that went bump in the night and for all his quirks, she was grateful for her ole man's true grit.

He thought of that wine his wife promised minutes ago. He yelled over his shoulder, "My fair lady, where's my drink?"

Mrs. Shotzski heard his plea. She whispered to herself, "I'll get ya two in a row!" She snickered before slowly departing the kitchen with the vino. She never tired of their cat and mouse games.

He spotted his wife's fit frame appear through several mirrors strategically placed between the den and hall. He spun his chair around as she stepped into the room. She jumped, almost spilling the pinot noir. "Ah, it is so nice to see a real reflection for a change," Shotz beamed, "and a pretty one at that."

"Oh darn," she grumbled, "I wanted to scare you."

He rolled his eyes. "I think your damn posse kidnapping me on New Year's Day was scary enough!"

She giggled handing him his wine, "That was wicked funny!"

"You could make up for that. How about some kissy-kissy?"

She eyed him seductively. "Finish your task and romance will come." He playfully smacked her rear as she departed. Kati said over her shoulder, "Better not spill, or I'll give you a spanking!" He almost coughed up his drink as her last words registered.

The reflection of her slinking feline exit, really caught his eye. He whistled, "Aye Chihuahua! I believe my work is done."

Her voice reverberated through the hall, "Focus Chuck!"

The Snowbirds' reporter sighed and got back to the business at hand. He grabbed the microphone and spoke, "Item: This should be the last time I expound on this surreal theme, unless my reporting colleague, Archer Pike, finds out about this and writes another book. Mr. Pike elaborated about my run-in with the vampire, Baroness Angelique Hemos, in the Dubuque area years ago. Of course, the Iowa authorities did their best to buy and/or destroy all of Archer's copies. Most people do not want to hear that zombies, mummies and spooks on the loose truly exist."

The house lights flickered. A strange shriek echoed from outside. The two schnauzers, the Shotzskis were dog sitting, paced nervously about the hallways, howling. Their feline hissed and arched its back. He quickly motioned Mr. Whiskers to jump up on his lap. The cat's purring relieved him a bit but he still bobbled with the microphone before speaking, "If you are ever in these parts, especially, at night and with a full moon, then, respect the dead. Leave them be, undisturbed. Whatever you do, do not welcome any strangers into your house from dusk until dawn. So, think about it and try to tell yourself, whoever you may be. In the quiet of your safe little haven, try to tell yourself it couldn't happen to you." Chuck sipped at the pinot noir to calm his nerves. He shook his head in disbelief and said, "Nah. No one would ever believe it."

A sound like a fingernail scraping along glass could be heard. The dark hairs on his upper neck rose. The miniature schnauzers rushed the window, growling as if there were vermin outside. He slowly cocked his head toward the open blinds, looking up in fright. The image moved too fast to make it out. The reporter began to tremble. The glass of wine slipped out of his fingers and shattered on the floor.

THAT same evening, an electrical storm hovered over Gemela. A bolt of lightning struck the metal cross and it glowed a metallic blue. Currents of electricity shot deep into the soil. Something stirred besides worms before a downpour of rain purged the tainted ground.

FOREIGN VOCABULARY

Aconitum Vulparia – Eurasian herb, commonly known as Wolfs Bane (Latin)

Allium Sativum – European bulbous herb, commonly known as Garlic (Latin)

Cosa Nostra – Our thing, aka the Sicilian Mafia (Italian)

Dem kathir – Lots of blood (Arabic)

Drăculea – Son of the dragon (Romanian)

Drakhol – Dragon or devil (Romanian)

Falutin' – An air of aristocracy or upper-class stuffiness (North American colloquialism)

Kazikli Bey – Impaler Prince (Turkish)

Lukanthrōpos – Werewolf, wolf-man; a person afflicted with lycanthropy (Greek)

Pikie – Derogatory for Gypsy (Scottish term)

Progne Subis – Purple Martin bird, swallow (Latin)

Radu cel Frumos – Radu the handsome (Romanian)

Saimiri Boliviensis – Squirrel monkey (Latin)

Sturmabteilung – Nazi stormtroopers (German)

Székely – Finest warriors of medieval Transylvania; frontier guards (Romanian)

Vlad "Tepes" – Vlad the "Impaler" (Romanian)

GLOSSARY

Aft – Back or rear (part of a boat or ship)

Fore – Forward or front (part of a boat or ship)

Lycan – Lycanthrope, werewolf, "wolfman," wolfan

NAVSPECWAR – Naval Special Warfare; short name SPECWAR

Port – Left (side of a boat, helicopter, ship, etc.)

RIB – Rigid Inflatable Boat; aka - Rigid-Hulled Inflatable Boat

SEAL – Sea, Air, Land (USN); aka frogman or commando

SBT – Special Boat Team

SF – Special Forces Commando (USA), aka Green Beret; A-Team; or Operational Detachment Alpha

SOF – Special Operating Forces, i.e. US Green Berets, SpecOps helo crews, SEALs, EOD and SWCC operators

Starboard – Right (side of a boat, helicopter, ship, etc.)

SWCC – Special Warfare Combatant Craft Crewmen (USN), aka Special Warfare Combatant-Craft Crewmember, Boat Guy, River Rat or Dirty Boat Guy

USSOCOM – United States Special Operations Command

Vamp – Short for vampire, aka bloodsucker, living dead, nosferatu, undead or vampyre

Vombie – A hybrid vampire-zombie

Wolfan – A rare type of lycanthrope that takes on more of a human form, aka wolfman.

ACKNOWLEDGMENTS

This book is based upon Bram Stoker's *Dracula* and Mary Shelley's *Frankenstein* & inspired from novels by Tom Clancy, Vince Flynn, Stephen King, Anne Rice and Jeff Rovin's *Return of the Wolf Man.* The classic spoof, *Abbott and Costello Meet Frankenstein* (one of Jerry Garcia's and Elvis Presley's favorite films) & 1970s *Kolchak the Night Stalker* TV series were also sparks of inspiration.

JP Thorson (written author) renders a genuine thank you to Acri Creature Feature, Julie Adams, Robert Aragon, Stephen J. Cannell, Ron Chaney, reel gill man Ben Chapman, Robert Conrad, Mary Davanzo, Todd Elliott, Famous Monsters of Filmland, Jeff Ferguson, Jack Grinnage, Cortlandt Hull, Moonshine Jones, mijo Justice, the lovely Sara Karloff, Jim Lammers, Jeff Lindaman, Béla Lugosi Junior, Anne Rice, Ray Santoleri, Elias Savada, John Sullivan, Robert Taylor, Linda Touby, Doug Trueg, Rob Tullo, Holly Zobeck, and several others who must remain anonymous.

The written author also extends much appreciation to his loving and patient wife, Lise; sister Mitch's and friend Bill Diamond's superb illustrations; buddy Steve Hansen's story editing; cousin Cory Thorson's and pal Mark Jacobson's artistic editing, friend Randy Majerus' architectural advice on Château Wilder; Hansen Elementary teachers - Rosemary Anderson and Nona Smith who helped him combat dyslexia; Cedar Falls High School teachers - Diane Engel, Susan Kimball and Erik Melberg; and history Professors Foote and Konigsmark of North Iowa Area Community College (NIACC).

JP and his sister, Mitch, are very grateful to their mum Frankie's free-spiritedness, dad Jer's advice, *if you don't know how to spell a word, then look it up*; sister Tré's inspiration & story review; grandparents' love; and most importantly, they are eternally grateful to the good Lord above for his guidance and mercy.

AUTHOR, ARTISTS & TALENT

JP Thorson (written author) History, sports and thriller aficionado who first penned this story in 1996 while at NSW training. Hooked on Acri Creature Feature, Aurora models and Famous Monsters by age four. His lovely wife is a Creature from the Black Lagoon and Boris Karloff fan who acted as a crucial advisor in this tale.

Interesting trivia: General Zebulon Pike (of Pike's Peak fame), and Almanzo and Laura (Ingalls) Wilder are distant cousins to JP Thorson and his sisters, Mitch and Teresa.

Mitch Sears (B&W and ink sketches) Wife, mom, and part-time artist. She's grateful for her husband Mike's and kid's encouragement, brother JP's nudging to include her artwork in his story, Norman Rockwell's inspiration, and Mr. John Ryder's artful tutorials at Hawkeye Tech many moons ago.

Bill Diamond (color drawings) Renowned puppeteer who has won two Emmy awards for television production. His artistic endeavors include working for Jim Henson, Broadway's *Little Shops of Horrors* and *Phantom of the Opera*, *Fraggle Rock* and Monster TV Network. Bill thanks his wife, Ruth, family and friends.

Steve Hansen (story editor) Proud papa, US Navy veteran, stage actor, musician & writer. Hans is a professional book reviewer.

Mark Jacobson (illustrations editor) Family man, Iowa Hawkeyes' fan & bike/traveling enthusiast. Jake is a graphic artist.

Cory Thorson (illustrations editor) All about family and coaching baseball & basketball. Cor's a teacher, graphic artist & Twins' fan.

Made in the USA
Middletown, DE
09 December 2019

80368251R00172